A Very Fake Boyfriend

Scarlett Avery

Edited by John Hudspith

Proofread by Jamie Betts, Melody Fuhrman, Angela Tyler, Lisa Fearday, and Jacqueline (Jacks) Larson.

Portuguese Consultant: Luisa Tremeschin Uezono

ISBN 978-1-77498-118-4

No part of this book used automated software or AI in its creation. The content was written by a human (Scarlett Avery, the author). The cover was professionally designed and the interior was professionally formatted.

Dedication

For my readers who are unapologetic about their addiction to smut, but also need all the feels.

Get the A VERY FAKE BOYFRIEND
Secret Chapter

Join my mailing list and grab the Exclusive Secret Chapter or Storyboard for this romance.

Great extra goodies. Hot deals. Zero spam.
www.MyRomanceAddiction.com

Chapter 1

Zane

I enter the Evangelista Lounge.

No surprise, there's a queue to get seated.

Three groups of people stand in front of me—a couple embracing, three women decked up to the nines, and five men in sharp suits, sporting pricey watches. As I wait, my weary eyes sweep around the space for potential threats.

The coast is clear.

Reassured I won't have to deal with the embarrassing drama I had to endure the last time I was here, I relax.

I scan the room once more to determine if I should consider another one of the lounges in the hotel. I spot a few tables that seem to be ready to clear.

Good.

I pull out my phone and shoot Carl Tucci a quick text to let him know I'm early.

My phone rings.

"Hey, buddy," I say, answering the call. "No need to rush. I'm twenty minutes early. Monday was wearing me down, so I bailed early from work."

"I'm sorry, Zane. I don't think I can make it."

Carl is a friend and MBA alumni from Columbia University who moved to Arizona four years ago. Distance and hectic lives aren't the best to maintain a close friendship even with technology, but I keep in touch with Carl more than I do with other grads who still live in New York. He's in town for business with his wife in tow.

"What happened?"

"I had to cut my meeting short. Debra texted me between bouts of puking sessions to let me know the baby was having a field day today."

"Poor Debra." My eyes bounce around the lounge. "Give me a sec. I'm going to step outside so as not to disturb other patrons." It's only good manners not to force people to listen to your conversation.

"Okay."

With a few long strides, I'm standing outside the lounge.

"Not that I have first-hand experience, but a number of women from work have complained about the whole 'morning sickness' thing." I pace back and forth. "Apparently, it can last all day and it's pretty rough sailing."

"It is," he says. "And you're right, 'morning sickness' isn't a lie. Unlike cappuccino, which goes out of favor by lunchtime, morning sickness can occur morning, day, and night. That's why my beautiful wife is barfing her brains out at seven p.m."

I cringe at the imagery.

"Priorities first, my friend. Take care of Debra. I know your schedule is jam packed while you're here, but maybe we can do lunch tomorrow if Debra is feeling better?"

"I was going to suggest an early morning breakfast before my meeting. Debra can stay in bed while we meet. I don't want to put any pressure on her."

"Understandable."

"I'll be back in New York in March, and I'll make sure to bring her with me. You can meet her then."

"Sounds good," I say. "Let's meet here. There are few top-notch restaurants that serve the best continental breakfast options in town."

"Done! Meet you at the Bymark Hotel bright and early tomorrow. I'm sorry again for the inconvenience."

"Please. I hear the baby dictates, not the parents, so stop apologizing."

We chuckle.

"See you tomorrow, Zane."

"Catch you tomorrow, Carl."

I end the call, tuck my phone in the inside of my suit pocket, and head back to the lounge as a wave of patrons leave. When I enter, the maître d' waves me over.

I've never seen him before, and I breathe a sigh of relief.

Chances are he doesn't know what cluster fuck of a mess transpired the last time I was here.

After the niceties, I speak. "I reserved a table for three, but my friend just called to let me know that his wife is ill and he can't make it. That said, I'd still like to have a drink."

I'm here and I'm not leaving without injecting booze in my veins. It was that kind of a day.

"I see." He lowers his brown eyes to the iPad screen. "Would you consider a seat at the bar?" he asks, meeting my gaze.

"That works!"

"Excellent!" He extends a hand, inviting me in.

"Thank you," I say with a nod.

As I strut toward the bar, a tall blond man waves me over before pointing to a seat at the bar.

I tilt my chin in recognition, a smile creeping on my lips.

"Rick," I say, taking a seat on a high stool next to a black balding man. The guy is engaged in an animated conversation with a black woman clad in an eye-catching purple blouse with an elaborate over-sized bow, sitting next to him.

"Mr. Keller. I thought you had moved out of state." Rick chuckles. "It's been a while."

"I've been laying low."

"I hear you." His green eyes shift left, then right before settling on me. "Man, your ex knows how to leave a lasting impression—and not a good one at that."

I grumble. "Don't remind me. Let's not talk about her."

"Your wish is my command." Rick responds with a salute. "What's your poison for tonight?"

"A vodka tonic, please."

"Do I open a tab?"

"Yes, I'll need more than one drink to ease this day."

"I'll be right back with your drink," Rick says, turning towards a row of top-shelf bottles.

The last time Carl was in town, I suggested the Bymark Hotel. He loved it so much, he wanted us to meet here because he wanted his wife to experience the opulence the Bymark has to offer. Without his insistence, I would still be MIA. I wasn't sure what to expect showing my face here again after my certifiably mental short-lived-ex-girlfriend fucked things up for me.

I clench my teeth as images from the cringe-worthy confrontation come flashing back.

So much fucking drama.

What a nut case.

Good riddance.

The movement of a hand appearing seemingly out of nowhere jerks me back to the present.

Rick sets my drink in front of me.

My eyes zoom in on the tumbler before meeting his green eyes.

"Thanks."

"It's behind you, man," he says with a wink, as if he's able to read my mind.

I nod.

I take a long sip of the vodka tonic, my thoughts still racing.

It's been two months and my ex should be a distant memory, but I look over my shoulder one more time.

I don't recognize any familiar faces.

Satisfied, I return my attention to my drink.

Not only have I been avoiding the Bymark like the hotel was contaminated, I've also been avoiding women. I needed to purge my system for a while. As a result, I eliminated unwanted drama in my life. Alas, I also eliminated the pleasure of losing myself between the plush thighs of a sexy lover.

I need to get laid.

Now!

Fuck jerking off.

I'm desperate for a warm and inviting pussy.

It's been too long. I'm done.

I drain my drink in a few gulps, a sudden urgent need coursing through my veins. I slam the tumbler on the bar a little more forceful than intended, the sound catching Rick's attention.

He motions to my empty glass. "Another one?"

"Not yet."

"Flag me when you're ready."

I nod. "I will."

He shifts his focus to a newcomer who sits next to the woman wearing the purple blouse.

I stand up, intending to give myself a little privacy as I consider the list of past hookups that speak my language—a drama-free, illicit night of raunchy sex with no strings attached.

I'm about to shoot off a few texts when I lift my eyes.

A jaw-dropping sight stops the rhythmic beating of my heart.

Holy fuck.

A striking redhead stands in front of the maître d's stand. They're engaged in a back-and-forth conversation for a few long seconds. When the maître d' extends a hand, the woman's eyes lift up, looking past me.

The beauty nods and sashays in my direction, swinging her hips left to right, strutting across the lounge like she owns the damn place.

My gaze follows the sensual sway of her wide hips, hypnotized.

Her luscious curves threaten to give me a heart attack.

She's wearing heels, but she's much taller than the average woman.

I'm guessing five-feet-ten or five-feet-eleven, barefoot. Still short compared to my six-feet-six frame.

With each step, I take her in.

Her sexy-as-fuck body is clad in a mouth-watering outfit.

Jesus.

I do a quick mental inventory, going through the catalogue of our collections to find out if the bombshell is wearing Curves Envy Fashion.

I give up the search.

One, we have way too many items. Two, this woman is doing things to me and preventing me from thinking straight.

She's the kind of voluptuous temptation capable of making a grown man drop to his knees and thank God for his beneficence.

Patrons stop mid-conversation to admire her.

I don't blame them.

I'm as riveted, shamelessly staring. I couldn't look away even if you paid me a cool billion.

For a long beat, I stand stock-still, staring at the gorgeous woman, my cock twitching in my pants, my heart pumping blood at a maddening speed, my head filled with naughty visions of me fucking the hell out of this woman from behind, so my body can slap against her full ass with every hard thrust.

My mouth waters.

The redhead glances left to right, as she captures every straight man with a pulse and functioning dick's attention with her self-assured stride.

With each elegant step in my direction, my heartbeat spikes.

Wow!

As Smoking Hot Redhead waltzes by, her cascade of long, straight hair swinging with each step, her gaze drifts toward me.

Hello, beautiful.

She flashes me a smile.

There's a touch of shyness in her smile that hits me straight in the heart.

I approve.

Her hips keep in rhythm with an upbeat song I don't recognize as she sashays through the lounge like she owns the damn place.

My cock salutes her, and I respond with a cocky, lopsided smile.

Fuck that beautiful hair.

Fuck those wide hips.

Fuck that radiant smile.

Hot damn, woman!

I only snap out of my trance when she heads towards the empty stool next to mine.

As if pulled by a powerful magnetic force, I rush back to my seat as I shove my phone into my pocket.

Come to Daddy, sweet thing.

Chapter 2

Shay

As I enter the Bymark Hotel, my phone rings.

I park myself to the side and fish for it inside my handbag.

"Hey, Jana," I say, accepting the call.

Behind every boss lady there's a formidable executive assistant. Jana Dalton is my secret weapon.

"Hey, Shay," she says. "I just heard from Alice Laurent—"

"She's running late due to the storm raging in Chicago?"

"She's *still* in Chicago."

Alice Laurent is a representative for Tullier in the US to meet with luxury retail stores and beauty vloggers like myself. Tullier is a seven-generation manufacturer of high-end makeup brushes located in Saint-Brieuc in Brittany in northwestern France. They recently reached out to me for a co-branded line of brushes. I'm not going to lie, even though I'm blessed with a formidable online following, this kind of stuff never gets old. Since starting my Beauty with Shay channel I've been blessed beyond belief.

"What happened?" I ask.

"All planes are grounded until further notice," Jana says.

"Yikes."

Snowflakes are fluttering in the sky and it's a little colder than yesterday, but thank God we don't have to deal with the kind of storm that shuts down a city. Heck, we can barely manage a few inches of snow without New Yorkers going bonkers.

"Alice couldn't call to warn you because her phone dropped in the toilet at the airport as she was flushing—"

"Gross!"

"I know, right?" Jana says. "She bought a replacement phone, but she's starting from scratch. Since she doesn't have your number memorized, she sent a private message on social media. I checked our accounts a few minutes ago and saw it."

"I just stepped into the Bymark—"

"Crap! Sorry, Shay. I checked our social media accounts earlier. I answered all queries and made sure to interact with our followers. Alice must've contacted us soon after I was done."

"Don't apologize," I say. "Since I'm here, I might stick around for a bit."

"Cool!"

"All right, I'm heading to the lounge. See you tomorrow!"

"See you!"

I end the call.

I'm just about to tuck my phone into my handbag, when an incoming text flashes on my screen. I shake my head after reading my little sister's message.

Briar: Ma just texted, guilt tripping me about 'you know who's' impending wedding. Fair warning, you're next.

Right on cue, my phone rings.

Mom doesn't bother texting. Instead, she's pulling out the big artillery—she's going to guilt trip me in real time.

I grumble.

I have zero desire to deal with this right now.

I debate whether to let it go to voice mail, but I know it's only delaying the inevitable.

Pulling my big girl panties up, I accept the call.

"Hey, Ma," I say. "Sorry I didn't get back to you." I jabber on. "My weekend was jam-packed with store appearances for my new makeup line, and you know Mondays... so unpredictable."

"Shay O'Hara, you must think I'm daft."

It's going to be one of those conversations.

I stroll further into the hotel, searching for a more secluded spot for this conversation. When my eyes land on a coat check sign, I head towards it. I turn a corner, and I'm relieved to discover an empty corridor.

"Absolutely not," I say.

"Stop lyin' to your ma." She only uses that pronounced accent when she's pissed.

I respond in kind with an exaggerated Boston accent. "I'm not lyin'. My weekend was as busy as the President's—"

"Enough with the fake excuse! I'm calling to address a serious issue—"

"I've told you time and time again, Ma. I'm. Not. Going. End of story."

"You *will* attend this wedding." She ignores my protest. "The same applies to Briar. Mark my words, you two *will* show up."

"Ma, I don't need to witness my stepsister marrying the boyfriend she stole from me. It's a reminder she wormed her way into his bed, like she'd done many times before with my former boyfriends. That's who she is—a two-faced backstabber. She seduced Briar's last boyfriend in your own home—"

"What?" Ma's piercing voice spills from the phone.

"Briar caught Imogen with her lips wrapped around her boyfriend's manhood after the Sunday dinner you prepared the weekend of Thanksgiving last year."

"Good God."

"Yup!" I say. "A few weeks before Imogen sunk her claws into my boyfriend, she had her go with Briar's—"

"Your sister never mentioned that."

"It's a little embarrassing. Not to mention, it's classic Imogen. Briar was too happy to kick the spineless boyfriend to the curb. Better to find out sooner rather than later that he's a cheater. He was only nineteen years old—so, eight years younger than Imogen!" My hand flies in the air before landing on my thigh. "Showing my face at that wedding would only further my embarrassment. I'm not going to give Imogen the satisfaction."

Apparently, refusing to show up at your bitch of a stepsister's wedding is poor form. Go figure.

My mom lets out a long sigh. "I get it, Shay. To this day, Imogen is unpleasant to me"—she means, a raving, ungrateful bitch—"but Alan is *still* your stepfather." There she goes, hitting me in the jugular. "And Imogen is his daughter. You and Briar *have* to be present. Even if it kills me, I'm putting water in my wine and intend on showing up with a smile."

"Imogen has an extra reason for wanting to get married sooner rather than later..." Ma's words trail.

"Other than the fact she can't wait to become Mrs. Fitzsimmons and rub it in my face?" I sneer.

"Aunt Eileen overheard a conversation..."

"What did Aunt Eileen overhear?"

"Well..." *Well...?* "This is unexpected..." More hesitation.

"What aren't you telling me?"

"Imogen is pregnant."

"What?!" I shriek, then remember where I am. With a more controlled voice, I say through gritted teeth, "You can't be serious."

"You know how Aunt Eileen no longer trusts Imogen since the incident—"

"*No* one trusts Imogen, Mom," I say. "Alan is her father, so he's blind to the kind of conniving woman she is." They say the apple doesn't fall far from the tree. Imogen is a carbon copy of her mom—inside and out. My stepsister's mother spewed so much bullshit about my mom after she married Alan. It was all lies, but nonetheless humiliating and hurtful for Ma.

"When Aunt Eileen let the cat out of the bag over dinner a few days ago, Alan refused to believe her—"

"Is Imogen pregnant or not?"

Silence.

"Ma?"

"Alan confronted her this morning."

"And..." I do a hand gesture hurrying her up, even though she can't see me.

"It's confirmed." I intake a sharp breath. "She's two months pregnant."

I pinch the bridge of my nose. "Freaking. Fantastic."

No matter how much I try to eradicate my bitch of a stepsister and my cheating ex-boyfriend from my life, they find a twisted way of pulling me into their drama. I want no part of it. First, the wedding, and now, the baby news. It's like being sucked into the Bermuda Triangle's vortex of death.

"She wouldn't be caught dead walking down the aisle with a baby bump." Ma continues sharing upsetting details. "Maternity wedding fashion isn't what she wants reflected in her wedding photos."

I shake my head in disbelief.

"Of course, she would want to snare Elias— I mean, entrap the sucker. No, no, no." I shake my head, knowing full well Ma can't see me. If you're going to do sarcasm, might as well go all the way. "What I'm trying to say is, Imogen wants to make sure Elias is under her thumb— There I go again. Sorry." *Not sorry.* "They're in love, and this baby is an extension of their love." *Right.* "It has nothing to do with my stepsister manipulating everyone around her to get what she wants." Bitterness rolls off in waves.

"Shay!"

"What?"

"Let Imogen have Elias Fitzsimmons. I told you this before, he doesn't deserve you. You don't need a weak man that can be so easily distracted by a skirt. I don't care if Imogen cast a voodoo spell over your ex's head. There's no excuse for cheating. None."

"Imogen has exceptional sorcery powers because it keeps happening over and over again." A sudden burst of rage billows inside me. I'm so done with this conversation. "Ma, I have to go."

"Shay, there's a man out there with balls of steel who's impervious to Imogen's snake oil salesman charm." This is a rare dig from Ma who's careful not to show how she feels about her stepdaughter. "That unicorn is waiting for you to bump into him, sweet child."

My anger dissipates, and I dissolve into a fit of laughter.

Ma joins me.

"What about the wedding?" Ma asks when she regains her composure.

I let out an audible sigh, as I ponder her question for a long beat.

"I'll let you know my decision when I make it."

"Shay—"

"I heard you, Ma." I interject before she launches in to lecturing mode again. "I get it." I'm caught between a rock and a hard place." I have to think of Alan." I exhale. "Give me a day." I love my stepdad, even though I loathe my stepsister. "I'll be in touch."

"Fair enough."

With that, I end the call.

My fingers fly on the screen as I type my best friend, Keeley, a text to let her know of this latest zinger.

You're a fucking bitch, Imogen.

When I'm done, I stare at my phone with gritted teeth for a long while.

A text message flashing on my screen catches my attention.

Briar: If you show your face at the wedding, don't come alone. Hire an escort or something. I'm on a site right now, making my selection. Some of these guys are kind of hot. Contrary to my preconceived notions, they don't all look sleazy.

Shay: Did the hospital drop you on your head when you were a baby?

Briar: Har. Har. Don't knock it 'till you try it. I'm telling you, the selection is far better than I expected. Bonus, each candidate has a pose in a suit and tuxedo. Very apropos.

Shay: Why not enlist the help of one of your guy friends from college?

Briar: If I pay for my male companion, he's contractually obligated to ignore Imogen.

Shay: Funny.

Briar: Do you want me to text a few profiles? Some of these guys are right up your alley?

Shay: I'm good.

Briar: You're sure?

Shay: Positive.

Briar: Okay. Your call. If you decide to come, don't give Witch Imogen the satisfaction of showing up unaccompanied. If you do, she wins.

Shay: Copy that.

Briar: Okay, got to go. I'm going to send Ludwig—with the ten-pack abs—a message to see if he's available. His name matches his blond Viking good looks. Could be **very** promising.

She's crazy.

~

After that conversation with my mom and my baby sister revealing she's on the hunt for a male escort, I'm in desperate need of booze. Since I was a skip away from the coat check, I drop off my winter coat, and head to the upper level. Even though Alice is a no show, I still have my reservation, and I intend on putting it to good use.

I enter the Evangelista Lounge.

After a brief explanation of my situation, the maître d' asks if I'd consider a seat at the bar, given it's just little ol' me. A quick sweep of my gaze around the lounge tells me everything I need to know—it's a full house. I'd be willing to sit in the bathroom if it meant I can get a drink.

"The bar is fine," I say.

He extends a hand to the back of the room, and I thank him.

I smooth down my skirt and take a confident step forward as a song kicks in. The catchy beat pulls something inside me, transporting me back to my heydays.

Even though I no longer work the catwalk, I sometimes slip back into the role of model and strut my stuff. Why walk when you can sashay?

A few patrons stare at my skirt.

I opted for an emerald sequin skirt that hits me at the knee, which I paired with a high neck black blouse with sheer sleeves. I completed the look with metallic heels. Since I took a taxi from the office, I figured I was safe. The outfit is flirty and calls attention to me. I'm okay with that.

As I stride towards the bar, my eyes shift from one side of the lounge to the other. There're a lot of gorgeous men here tonight.

Instead of an escort service, maybe I might be able to bribe one of them into accompanying me to the wedding from hell.

I chuckle at the absurdity of this ridiculous idea.

As I approach the bar, a tall, blond bartender points an animated finger to an empty stool.

"Thank you." I mouth my appreciation.

I stride past a man, who's height suggests he might be a basketballer, cradling a phone in his hands, and I can't help but do a double take.

Holy mother Mary, he's hot! Hawt, hot!

I chance a second glance in his direction, this time checking him out with purpose. The navy-blue pinstripe suit paired with a navy tie with white circles, white shirt, and white pocket handkerchief looks killer on him. The man has impeccable taste. As my eyes travel to his face, I catch him staring straight at me.

Dear God, he's handsome.

A swarm of butterflies flap their wings around in my stomach.

Placing a hand on my tummy, I compose myself, and I flash him a smile.

Mr. Tall and Handsome responds in kind.

Whoa, buddy! Dial down the hotness factor, would you?

With my heart raging in my chest, I slide onto the stool and drop my handbag on the countertop. I glance over my shoulder and catch a glimpse of Mr. Tall and Handsome as he sits on the stool next to mine.

Chapter 3

Zane

As I slide into my seat, I lock eyes with Rick.

He cocks a knowing eyebrow.

I respond by pursing my lips and nodding slightly.

Yes, she's fine.

The bartender shifts his attention to Smoking Hot Redhead, and flashes her a flirty smile.

Don't ask me why, but a wave of possessiveness washes over me.

"That was a hell of an entrance," Rick tells the beauty sitting next to me.

I chime in. "I second that. All eyes were on you."

She lets out a throaty little laugh before her gaze meets mine. "Blame the song."

Even under the low lights, it's impossible not to get lost in the ocean blue of her eyes.

Then she smiles.

Dear God.

When she flicks her head back, sending a cascade of locks

flying behind her shoulders, I'm consumed by a burning thought.

Is she a natural redhead?

The urgency to solve the enigma with my tongue lapping at her pussy tightens my balls. I'm assaulted by imagery of fisting her long, gorgeous, thick, hair while I'm fucking the hell out of her from behind, and my cock is on alert.

I shake my head, breaking the trance.

I adjust myself on the seat, doing my best not to look obvious.

"I reckon the sexy woman is to blame," I say.

"You're a smooth talker, mister."

"Once again, the sexy woman is to blame." I wink.

She bites on her lower lip and drops her gaze to the bar, her cheeks blazing.

Confident with a touch of shyness.

I like it. I like it a lot.

"What can I get you?" Rick asks the striking redhead.

"I'll have rum and cream of coconut on ice served in a martini glass, please. Oh, shaken, not stirred."

"You mean, a Sex on a Snowbank cocktail."

"Yes," the beauty says with a sheepish cringe. "I love the drink, but the name is a bit out there. It can easily be misinterpreted as an invitation."

One I'd accept.

"Good one," Rick says. "Another vodka tonic for you?" he asks me.

I lift my tumbler. "Yes, please."

"I'll be right back," he says.

"Thank you," the redhead says. "Whomever came up with that drink name must've been three sheets to the wind."

"'Three sheets to the wind' is a British expression."

"It is. My mom is Irish."

"I gather you're a natural redhead?"

Her cheeks burst into flames. She brings a hand to her face and pats the back of it against her cheek.

"You're reading a lot into my question."

"Your tone was suggestive."

I lean into her slightly. Our bodies aren't touching, but there can't be more than an inch between us. "It wasn't. When I intend for my tone to be suggestive, you'll know, beautiful."

She lets out a little laugh—the mixture of shock, disbelief, and amusement. "I've been told."

"It's gentlemanly of me to warn you."

"You're way out of my league, mister."

"You're selling yourself short."

She opens her mouth to respond, but nothing comes out.

I give her a onceover, taking my fill of her.

Stunning doesn't encapsulate her ravishing beauty, but that's the only word I have right now.

"As of tomorrow, I'm petitioning the Bymark Hotel to name one of the lounges after you," I say, changing the subject.

"Isn't that going to be hard to do if you don't even know my name?"

I nod. "You're right."

"Is that your not-so-subtle way of asking for my name?"

"You're right again," I say. "You're acing this game."

"You're good with words."

It's on the tip of my tongue to tell her that's not the only thing I'm good with, but I refrain.

"I'm Shay."

"Well, Shay, in order for me to get a lounge named after you, I'm going to need your last name."

"I'm Shay O'Hara."

I extend a hand. "I'm Zane Keller."

"It's a pleasure," she says, slipping her hand into mine.

Heat floods my body at the contact and my pulse pounds in my ears.

Goddammit.

When our gazes meet, it's as if I can see my future in her blue eyes, as if I were peering into a crystal ball—her, me, us—

Whoa!

Where the fuck did that come from?

A few minutes ago, I was about to reach out to a woman for a booty call, and now I'm seeing forever with a stranger?

I need to get my cock wet.

I snap out of it.

"At the fault of sounding cliché, the pleasure is all mine," I say.

I'm still holding onto her hand, and she doesn't make an attempt to break the contact. We stare at each other for a long beat.

Rick chooses this moment to return with our drinks.

"Here you go, boys and girls." He sets down a martini glass with the rim decorated with coconut flakes, containing a white liquid in front of Shay.

"Thank you," she says.

He nods at her before setting my drink in front of me.

"Thanks," I say. "Her drink is on me."

Shay's eyes snap up to mine. "Oh, no, you don't have to."

"I know I don't, but I want to."

"I appreciate it."

With that, Rick moves his attention to another couple.

I lift my glass. "*Sláinte!*"

Surprised eyes squint at me. "You speak Irish?"

"I know the essentials. My cousin got married to an Irish American in June. I got more than three sheets to the wind at her wedding, and again at Thanksgiving last month. Man, those Irish..."

"We can hold our liquor."

"Not that I want to go down my drunken lane of shame, but I agree. *Sláinte!*"

"*Sláinte!*"

We clink glasses—and, as we do, we hold each other's gaze. We don't break eye contact as we each take a long swig of our drinks. In a slow, deliberate movement, I drop my glass on the counter, my eyes still boring into hers.

Shay mimics my move.

Damn.

I swear the electric current between us is set at ten thousand watts.

"Out of all the lounges in the hotel, how did you wind up at the Evangelista Lounge?" I ask, forcing her attention back on me.

"My business meeting is stuck in Chicago."

"They're having a doozie of a storm."

"All the planes are grounded."

"Chicago is a great city, but the storms are brutal," I say. "I've been stuck there during the winter months a few times myself."

"Thank God we rarely have to deal with severe storms like that in New York City."

"I agree."

We take another long swig of our drinks, eyes locked.

She breaks the connection, averting her eyes.

Damn.

She looks around the lounge before fixing her gaze on me again. It's as if she needed a reprieve. *I get it.* "Most people are here in couples or groups. What's your story, Zane Keller?"

I give her a brief explanation about Carl's pregnant wife's condition.

The edges of her mouth turn down. "Poor thing."

“Much respect to pregnant women,” I say. “I can’t imagine what it’s like to have a life growing inside you.”

“Yeah, neither can I.” There’s a tinge of sarcasm to her words, but I don’t press.

My phone vibrates, and I hastily reach into my suit jacket pocket to retrieve it. I read the text message.

My brother can wait.

I meet Shay’s gaze. “I apologize. Let me turn it off so we’re not interrupted again.”

“No problem. Actually, I should do the same,” she says, reaching for her designer bag.

Satisfaction rushes through me at her words.

I don’t even bother hiding the cocky grin stretching across my lips as I tuck my phone into my pocket.

She’s into me as much as I’m into her.

“Other than your secret love for dirty sounding drinks, what else is there to know about, Shay O’Hara?”

“That’s a loaded question, Zane Keller.” Her tone is playful.

“You don’t have to hit me with the hard stuff. Ease me into it, nice and slow.”

“Even though I’m too young to have been part of the illustrious group of 90s super models the lounges in this hotel are named after, I used to work the catwalk professionally here in the States and in Europe.”

“You were a model?”

I’m not surprised.

She nods. “I was.”

My eyes rake over her body. “Why the use of the past tense?”

“I used to be *skinny*,” she says in air quotes. “Now, I’m not.”

“Plus size models are in demand.” I should know.

“They are.” She nods. “I could’ve made the transition

from a size-two model to a plus size model, but once I made the decision to step off the catwalk, there was no going back. The reason I stepped away is one of those life altering moments that prompts you to reconsider everything in your life."

Sounds like there's a layered story behind her words, but I don't push.

"That sounds heavy," I say.

"I'm sure there's tremendous pressure for plus size models. That said, the modeling industry is cutthroat for *skinny* models. The constant focus on your weight and the number flashing on the scale is exhausting."

"How did you reinvent yourself?"

"These days, I'm known as Beauty by Shay."

I frown.

"You're not my demographic."

I study her for a beat. "With your striking features and your flawless complexion—"

"With the right foundation and makeup brush, you can hide a constellation of freckles."

I continue, undeterred. "With your striking features, your flawless complexion, *and your constellation of freckles*, I'm willing to bet every dollar to my name, you're a beauty vlogger."

"You're good at this game." She borrows my words from earlier.

"Beautiful *and* witty. You're winning me over."

"And to think, I wasn't even trying."

I shake my head. *Oh, she's good.* "So, I guessed correctly?"

"You did." She nods. "Beauty by Shay started off as a beauty vlog. And before I could blink"—she snaps her fingers together—"my following grew from my mom, stepdad, half-sister, great aunt, best friend, and a few models I still kept in touch with, to an eye-popping number of loyal followers."

I reach for my phone in the inside pocket of my jacket, pull it out, power it up, and do a quick search.

Whoa! She's right. These are serious numbers. "You have over fifteen million followers on YouTube. And your other social media platforms show formidable numbers. You've been busy since you stepped off the catwalk."

"It's wild," she says. She's humble about her success. That's refreshing. My brother Xavier, the COO of our fashion company, deals with temperamental influencers. Some of them have egos bigger than the state of Texas. "I try not to look at the number too often or else I get performance anxiety." There's a boatload of vulnerability in her statement.

I scroll through one of the social media platforms, my head spinning with possibilities. Her high video views are testament to a strong connection with her audience. She's a hell of a marketer on top of her other attributes.

I lock eyes with her. "You have your own makeup line?"

"That's another blessing," she says. "A few years ago, MAC cosmetics approached me for a co-branded line. My obsession with eye shadow palettes was paying off. I never suspected it would catch on like wildfire. One makeup line turned into several others," she says. "Three months after my co-branded makeup line hit the market, Anastasia Beverly Hills reached out, wanting to create a line of co-branded eyebrow kits—another one of my obsessions. And the blessings keep pouring in. The woman stranded in Chicago I was supposed to meet with represents high-end makeup brushes manufactured in France—"

"Another lucrative partnership in the making."

"Fingers crossed," she says. "We're still in preliminary talks, but they've made it clear from the beginning, they're interested in making it worthwhile for both parties. I never take anything for granted, so I'm cautiously optimistic."

This woman isn't dicking around.

"There are a lot of beauty vloggers out there, it can't be easy to stand out."

"It's not." She shakes her head. "To the uneducated eye, it looks like we're playing with makeup all day, but there's a lot that goes into the conceptualization, production, editing, planning, and the list goes on."

"What's your claim to fame?"

Her lips part into a smile. "No one's ever asked me that question before," she says. "You're paying attention."

Damn right I am. "Sweetheart, I'm taking copious notes."

"You're a good student."

"I'm more of a *Master* than a student, but I get the gist."

Blotches of rosiness color her cheeks.

"Maybe that was a little much."

"Give a girl a warning next time," she says.

I wink.

She takes a long swig of her drink.

"To answer your question," she says, dropping her glass on the black marble countertop. "I took the classic 'before and after' shot to the next level by only applying makeup to one side of my face. The side-by-side comparison was striking and something no one else was doing at the time. The video went viral in a New York minute. Now, there's a slew of copycats, but I started the movement."

"Smart." I'm thoroughly impressed by this woman's ingenuity. I pull my gaze away from hers and keep scrolling. My eyes widen in surprise when I land on a photo of her wearing a familiar dress. "You've included fashion segments to the mix."

"Yes."

"What prompted the addition?"

"During several of my makeup sessions, I've shared highlights of my past as a model. My followers loved the insider scoops so much they insisted I branch out into fashion. I hesitated. When I do makeup tutorials, people only see me from the chest up"—she gestures. "If I'm flaunting clothes, I can't hide."

I'm dumbfounded. "Why would you want to hide?"

My cousin Max insists it's in our DNA. Keller men are wired to be attracted to plus size women. The gorgeous women with plenty of curves my brother, cousins, and uncles love, are testament to my cousin's statement. Mom and Dad are no longer together, but my father was forthcoming about the reason he was head over heels for my mom at first sight.

Shay holds my gaze. "Throughout my modeling career, I was a size two—"

"What are you? Five-ten? Five-eleven?"

"Five-ten."

"Five-ten and a size two?"

"Yes."

"Did you ever eat?"

"Enough not to pass out."

I shake my head.

"Only in the 90s supermodels were allowed to have slender curves," she says. "Back then, a size six wasn't considered plus size. Muscles, boobs, and butts... were healthy and normal."

"I see."

She continues. "My mom sided with my followers. She suggested fashion segments would be a great opportunity for me to have a better relationship with my body. I struggled when I stepped off the catwalk. My weight yo-yoed a lot..." Her words trail. "It took me several weeks to come around to the idea. When I mustered up the courage to do my first fashion video, although I was fully clothed, I felt naked in front of the camera. I was petrified. In fact, I expected an avalanche of body-shaming comments—"

"I'm guessing that didn't happen."

She flashes me a beaming smile. "So many plus size women left comments or sent private messages thanking me for showing off my curves. Their reaction gave me wings. Little by little, a video at a time, I started accepting my body." I have to speak to Xavier about sending her items of our next collection. This knockout represents our brand to perfection. "It's been a long road, pegged with ups and downs, but I'm proud to be the face of women who don't have a thigh gap."

I lean into her. "Let it be known, I *love* women who don't have a thigh gap."

She pulls away from me. Her long, dark eyelashes flutter like crazy. "You, mister, need to come with a warning."

You have no idea, love. "Back to this dress..." I say, changing the subject. Using my free hand, I scoot my stool closer to hers, my body ignites at the proximity. *Down, boy.* I angle my phone so she can see the screen. "It's a Curves Envy Fashion creation."

Shock flashes in her eyes. "How did you know?"

"I'm the CFO. I co-own the company with my cousins and my brother."

She slaps her forehead with her palm. "Zane Keller, as in Xavier Keller's brother?"

"The one and only."

She shakes her head. "What a small world."

"Indeed."

"I love your clothing and I love what you're doing for plus size women," she says. "The photos of your brother and his fiancée in *Sassy* magazine this month are incredible." She places both hands against her chest. "How romantic!"

Movement in my peripheral vision diverts my attention away from the gorgeous former model turned beauty vlogger. Tables are clearing.

Perfect.

I turn around and lift a hand up, calling Rick over.

"Don't tell me. You want me to mix you a Sex on a Snowbank."

I chuckle. "Not yet."

"I'm disappointed. How can I help you?"

"It seems a wave of people are leaving. I'd like to add my name to the wait list for a table for two."

"Let me see what I can do," he says, before walking away.

"We're moving the party to another location?" Shay asks, amusement coloring her tone. She blatantly looks me up and down as if unsure what to make of me. "A little presumptuous, don't you think?"

"To fully take in your beauty, I have to turn my head or angle my body. It's uncomfortable. I'd rather stare at your gorgeous face as I get to know you better."

Shay blushes. "Even by New York standards, you're forward, Zane Keller."

"The chemistry between us is through the roof since you sashayed into this lounge, channeling your supermodel badass self. You know it. I know it. Let's stop wasting time."

She doesn't have a comeback.

"You're in or you're out, beautiful?"

She considers me for a long, heated beat behind a curtain of dark lashes.

She bites her lower lip.

I know her answer before the words pass her tempting lips.

"I'm in."

Thank the fuck, God.

"You're in luck, Zane," Rick says, approaching us. "Three tables for two cleared in different spots. I put your name down for one. There's a party of six and another one of eight waiting to be seated, so you're in luck."

"Excellent!"

"I have a waiter waiting to show you to your table. You can't miss him," Rick says. "Once you're seated, he'll fetch your drinks and bring them to your table."

"Thanks!"

"It's a pleasure."

I stand up and extend Shay a hand. "Shall we?"

Chapter 4

Shay

I came to the Evangelista lounge because I needed a drink—or two—to anesthetize the jackhammering in my head after Ma shared the unpleasant news about my stepsister's pregnancy. It's not like I'm in love with Elias. I don't think I ever was. I'm pissed off a humiliating episode in my life seems to follow me around like a dark shadow.

The tide is turning for me.

I should send Imogen a thank you card and flowers. Getting entangled with the likes of Zane Keller is thrilling and exciting. Intoxicating, even.

Be still my beating heart.

For the first time in what feels like an eternity, a man holds my attention.

Scratch that.

A *real* man holds my attention.

I don't even mind his cocky side.

In fact, his self-assuredness is a major turn on. Unlike Elias, there's nothing wishy-washy about this man.

Since post my-stepsister-stole-my-boyfriend slump a year

ago, I've been out on a few dates. Getting back on the horse and all. I even agreed to go out on a date Ma organized a few months ago.

The guy is the twenty-nine-year-old brother of one of my stepfather's patients who works for the mayor's office. We're both Bostonians, living in New York, so why not, right?

There was zero chemistry between us.

In fact, he struggled to make conversation during dinner that wasn't centered around politics. Since we sat on opposite sides of the political table, most topics were like landmines. I'm all for a good debate. He was more into indoctrination.

After dessert, he suggested we continue the date at his place or mine. I was taken aback. I shared more of a connection with my plate of creamy mushroom gnocchi than I did with him. Unwilling to waste another minute of my time, I told him point-blank, it was a bad idea. His pride took a hit, but I wasn't in the mood to bullshit anyone, let alone myself.

The chemistry between Zane Keller and me is explosive. It also helps the hunk is one of the hottest and most charming men I've ever met. He's all swagger, style, and smoldering sexiness.

As if his list of attributes isn't long enough, the man is gorgeous. Really, really good looking. Seriously, what man needs cheekbones, or lips, or eyelashes like that? His sexy smile lines are five-alarm hot and that five o'clock shadow I want to run my tongue over drives me crazy. The man's sex appeal is lethal.

Zane Keller is the equivalent of a charcuterie board—too many tempting options in one serving.

I hope the other shoe doesn't drop.

In my experience, devastatingly handsome men, wearing expensive, bespoke suits are narcissistic assholes.

My eyes bounce from his outstretched hand and his cocked eyebrow.

I'm not usually a shameless flirt and I never reveal that much about myself to a complete stranger, but something about this guy makes me open up and be a lot more reckless than usual.

Don't overthink it.

I place my hand into his. "We shall."

He shoots me a dazzling smile and winks, his charm blinding me like high beams. "Good answer, beautiful."

My stomach clenches.

Like the first time we touched, the zing of electricity is unmistakable, causing my lady parts to sing '*Hallelujah*' Pentatonix-style.

Zane searches the space and spots our waiter, standing dutifully near a table. He places a gentle hand against the small of my back, surprising me, but I don't flinch and I don't pull away from him. Nothing makes my skin crawl more than a man touching me without my permission. Zane's hand on my body doesn't make me uncomfortable. On the contrary, every cell in my body comes alive.

This close, the man smells like do-me-now-please pheromones.

As he guides me towards our table, an iconic oldies song blares through the speakers.

I do a double take.

He can sing?!

Even though the volume is high, I can still make out his incredible voice. He knows the lyrics by heart, and puts on a show singing them.

He keeps singing as he helps me to my seat.

A gentleman with a good singing voice.

Can I please keep him, God?

He doesn't stop singing until he rounds the table and takes a seat across from me.

He lets the singer do the rest.

We're not seated at a booth, but our table is in the corner, giving us a bit of privacy.

I lean into the table. "You have a great singing voice."

"I can hold my own."

The waiter is back with our drinks.

From the look of it, Rick refreshed mine.

Bless him.

After thanking our waiter, he scurries off.

"Are you telling me you're an executive who moonlights as a lounge singer?"

"Nah. Nothing that glamourous."

"What's the story, then?"

"The song is one of Dad's all-time favorites," he says. "He's played it so many times, Xavier and I know the lyrics by heart."

"Does your brother sing as well as you do?"

"Xavier is the athlete in the family. He can't hold a tune to save his life."

"You have different sets of talents."

"You could say that."

Striking hazel green eyes stare back at me.

I was so swept away earlier, it's only now I notice the color.

Locking eyes with Zane Keller is like forging through a lush, Amazonian forest. Sitting across from him, I might have to reassess my earlier verdict.

This man is going straight to my head like a pricey bottle of champagne.

Guys like him fall into a category Aunt Eileen dubbed, the mold-breaker. Translation, God was in such a delightful mood when he created certain specimens, he had to break the mold to prevent chaos or else women would be in heat twenty-four-seven. I've never met a man who exemplifies my great aunt's hilarious observation… until now.

Zane lifts his highball. "Here's to us sticking around and being willing to drink solo even though the people we were supposed to meet couldn't make it!"

I lift my glass. "I'll drink to that!"

I dip my lips into my drink and take a long sip.

He does the same.

"I admire you. Like your brother, I can't sing to save my life. I'm tone deaf." I drop my glass on the table. "In fact, singing in public is one of the things I dread the most. Kudos to you for going for it."

"As a nerd—"

"You, a nerd?" I scoff. "Right."

"I am."

I purse my lips, still not believing him.

"I'm six-six. With my height, I could've been a professional basketball player, but I've preferred books to sports. Music videos were my outlet to be as badass as I wanted behind the safety of the four walls of my bedroom."

"So instead of playing video games, you were playing air guitar and lip-syncing?"

He points a finger at me. "I was!"

A visual of a young Zane head banging, strumming a fictitious guitar flash in front of my eyes.

"I graduated from lip-syncing to singing. I'll never get a record deal, but I'm okay with that."

"I never would've pegged you as a nerd."

His hazel green eyes burn into my gaze. "And I would've never have pegged you as someone who shies away from being center stage."

"It would be boring if I were perfect," I say with an exaggerated eye roll.

"I have a sneaky suspicion you don't know how to spell boring." He flashes me perfect white teeth.

"Flattery will get you everywhere."

"In other words, if I keep this up, I'll end up in your bed? Or you'll end up in mine?"

I'm stupefied by his bold comment, but by now I've come to know Zane Keller is all about pushing buttons. So, I take a page from his book.

"We're inside a hotel, I'm sure you can charm your way into getting a room for the night."

He cocks an eyebrow and considers me for a long beat.

"Be careful what you wish for, love," he says in a gravelly voice.

I selected this blouse because it's sophisticated and chic. Now that Zane turned up the heat to scorching levels, it feels like a straitjacket.

I pinch the front of the blouse with two fingers and fan myself. It's a futile exercise to cool down, but it's the only one in my arsenal.

I change the subject before I melt into a pool of lust. "Tell me more about yourself."

"Do you want the full novel or should I give you the cliff notes?"

His sharp wit is another feather in his cap.

"The cliff notes, please!"

"You already know what I do for a living," he says. "It's only me and my brother. I'm thirty-seven. He's younger. I was born and raised in the Big Apple. I'm half Brazilian and half British—"

"What a wicked mix."

"Good wicked or bad wicked?"

Fucking amazing wicked. "Not bad wicked." My tone is flirty, and he picks up on that.

"I can live with that."

"Do you still have family in Brazil?"

He nods. "I have close family in Brazil and the UK, as well as here in New York. Mom used to send my brother and I during summers so we could learn the language."

"You speak Portuguese?"

"*Eu faço, baby.*"

"What does that mean?"

"I do, baby."

Lord.

"What about you?" He turns the tables on me. "Do you speak any other languages?"

"I'm pretty good at mimicking my great aunt's brogue when she intermingles English words and Irish words when she's ticked off, but I wouldn't be able to hold a conversation."

"*Então só fale inglês.*"

Damn, that's hot.

"My Spanish leaves much to be desired, but I did pick up on *inglês*—English, I assume. I didn't get the rest, though."

"You only speak English." He translates.

With his rich voice, I bet I could come from him whispering something dirty in my ear in Portuguese. The naughty thought causes a ripple of thrill to run up my spine.

Keep it together, Shay.

Just because it's been a long time, doesn't mean you need to fixate on this gorgeous man who is a stranger.

Best to move on before I drool all over myself. "What else do I need to know about Zane Keller?"

"I hate cats, because one attacked me when I was at an aunt's house in London as a kid. I was so petrified, I wet myself. I cried for an hour, afterward." *Poor kid.*

"Cats scare me, too."

We exchange a complicit smile.

He continues. "I'm a Capricorn—which I only know because my mom and my aunts are into astrology. I was born on January first, which means the whole planet celebrates my birthday at the stroke of midnight in their time zone—"

"Good one!"

He winks at me and keeps talking. "I don't have to know how to cook because I share a chef with my brother and my cousins, but I make a mean steak frites."

"You do?" I ask, skepticism coloring my voice.

He nods. "One taste of my meat and it'll ruin it for all others."

I shake my head.

He flashes me a sorry-not-sorry grin.

His perfect white teeth contrast against his olive skin.

Lord, the man is a masterful dirty talker and cocky as hell. I wish I found that to be anything but a major turn on.

"Seriously, after visiting Paris for the first time many years ago, I was hooked. Such a simple combination, yet, so incredibly delicious. You can take it up by several notches with truffles, fancy mushrooms, or you can keep it to the basics. Add to that, deep-fried thinly sliced potatoes instead of chunky fries? What's there not to love?"

"When I was modeling in Paris, I kept it to salads and the occasional *spaghetti à l'huile et à l'ail*—"

"What's that?" he asks.

"Spaghetti, a bit of olive oil, garlic, and herbs. I skipped the parmesan cheese and I would never have a full portion. That said, it was my little treat."

"Holy shit!"

"When I went back a few years ago, I went crazy. I literally ate my way through Paris. Steak frites was high on my list. So were French desserts."

"I agree on both accounts."

"What else do I need to know about you?" I'm utterly fascinated by him.

"Even though my housekeeper deals with changing, washing and folding my sheets, I still think fitted sheets are the devil's creation."

"I agree!"

"How the hell do you fold those things?"

"There aren't enough YouTube videos to help you get it right."

"Thank you!"

We laugh.

"Other than singing"—*and charming the panties off unsuspecting souls*—"what's your superpower?" I ask.

I brace myself for a dirty comeback, but he surprises me.

"PowerPoint and Excel. I thrive on slide shows and spread sheets."

"Isn't that a given for any self-respecting CFO?"

"I was crushing complicated spreadsheets as a teenager. A lot of my professors at Columbia University commented on how my proficiency surpassed theirs." He points over his head. "Self-confessed nerd."

I refuse to believe this man was ever a nerd.

"I took my skill set to the next level by approaching small to medium-size finance and accounting firms and offering my services. I even started tutoring other students. Being a nerd paid off. I was so proficient, I used PowerPoint presentations to sway my parents whenever I wanted to dip into the money I was saving for college to buy an expensive electric gadget or software. It was my money, but it's not like they wouldn't notice."

"Did it work?"

"Like a charm." He flashes me his high beams again.

"Every. Single. Time. It's all about having a disproportioned pros column."

"You're speaking Greek right now. PowerPoint and Excel are two things I suck at. Without my formidable executive assistant, I'd be useless with either software. Numbers and graphs aren't my superpower."

"What is your superpower?" he asks. "I want to hear *your* cliff notes, Shay."

Chapter 5

Zane

The beautiful redhead sitting across from me takes a long sip of her drink, as if needing liquid courage. She drops her glass on the table and lasers those pools of oceans on me. She sits a little straighter in her chair and brushes strands of her long hair behind her ear.

I'm entranced.

Damn, I want—no, I need*—to fuck this woman.*

She holds my gaze. "Here we go."

"Hit me."

"I'm twenty-six. A Gemini. My great aunt Eileen—everyone calls her Aunt Eileen—reads her horoscope every single day. Then, she reads my mom's, my twenty-year-old half-sister's, my stepfather's, and mine before sending us a daily text *with* commentary."

"That's hilarious."

"That's typical Aunt Eileen for you." Her lips curve up. "In case the name wasn't a dead giveaway, I'm of Irish descent. Very Catholic. Ma is a first-generation Irish American. Dad was Irish American."

I pick up on the past tense, but let it slide.

"My grandfather on my dad's side was an Irish immigrant who married an American. Dad used to claim his mother had some Irish, British and German in her. I went to an all-girls Catholic school with uniforms and nuns. I never attended college because a modeling scout agent discovered me when I was seventeen. It was an opportunity I couldn't walk away from––"

"Good on you for not letting the opportunity slip between your fingers."

"It's one thing to approach an agency, it's a whole other to be discovered."

"I agree." I nod. "Where are you from?"

"North End—a suburb outside of *Bawstin*." I don't miss the upward inflection.

I mimic her. "*Bawstin, eh?*"

"Yup! I'm a natural redhead from *Bawstin*. You can't get more Catholic Irish American than that," she says with an exaggerated accent.

"You're pretty good at concealing the accent," I say. "It's only now I pick up on it."

"My modeling career uprooted me from Boston, transplanting me to New York and then Europe. During that time, I worked on softening my accent. When I'm pissed off, the *Bawstin* in me comes out loud and clear."

"Note to self. Don't piss off the redhead from *Bawstin*."

She waves a motherly finger. "You've been warned."

"I have." My voice is far deeper than intended.

We grin at each other for a long beat.

"You still haven't revealed your superpower," I say, breaking the trance.

She worries her lower lip. "I'm not sure I have one."

"We all have one."

She ponders on my words for a few short seconds. "Helping women accept their beauty regardless of their dress size," she says with the utmost confidence.

"That's a damn good superpower!"

Over a few too many drinks, I tell her more about Curves Envy Fashion, our family business. I briefly share the origins of the company my cousin Max inherited from our Brazilian uncle Arturo Barros.

I give Shay a bird's eye view of the structure—Max is the CEO. Xavier is the COO. Deidra Summers is our VP, Candice (Candy) Westerman, aka Max's fiancée, works on the lingerie and swimsuit lines, and the latest addition is an executive assistant Deidra and Xavier share. I don't bother telling her about my cousins, Gabriel and Lucas. Max's older and younger brothers are silent partners who focus on their successful businesses.

We also have a separate—and massively lucrative—division geared towards investments and acquisitions, but I bypass that detail.

She gives me an in-depth overview of a day in the life of a beauty vlogger. No wonder she has such a massive following. That said, it's not as easy as it looks.

Throughout the light banter and the drinks, the sexual tension between us grows with every sip. I'd venture to say she's nicely buzzing, but not shit-faced. It's the same for me.

My desire for her licks at me like the flames dancing in the lounge's fireplace.

My eyes zoom in on her beautiful mouth, and I'm overcome with an overwhelming urge to kiss her until we both run out of air.

She giggles.

Not the reaction I was hoping for.

My eyes shoot up to hers. "What's so funny?"

More laughter bubbles out of her.

She covers her face with one hand, placing the other on my forearm, and my cock jolts at the unexpected touch.

"Aunt Eileen takes cosmic compatibility very seriously."

I frown my confusion. "Are we talking about astrology here?"

She nods.

I watch intently as she scrolls through her phone, a huge smile plastered on her beautiful face.

"Oh! This is one of Aunt Eileen's favorite sites!"

More scrolling.

Her eyes meet mine. "You're a Capricorn, right?"

"I am."

She gives me a satisfied nod. "According to this, Capricorns are experimental lovers," she says in a tone that would make a professor proud. "You're an eager advocate of a healthy sex life—translation, the more sex the better. Because you have a goal orientated mindset, giving your partner multiple orgasms is top of mind."

"Jesus, whoever wrote that had a lot of time on their hands."

She forges ahead. "Your stamina is unparalleled, which means, you can last a long, long time—"

"Tell me something I don't already know."

Wide eyes stare at me.

She started this game. I'm playing along.

It takes her a few beats before she regains her composure.

"Ah! Here's something you might not know. Reading through our list of cosmic comparability, Geminis and Capricorns aren't a match."

It was all fun and games until that last part.

"I cry foul play!" I extend a hand. "Give me your phone."

She drops the device into my open palm.

I scroll until I find what I'm looking for.

I peruse for sexual astrology, and choose to focus on the essentials.

I lock eyes with her. "Three things jump out at me."

"Oh, yeah, what?"

"According to what I'm certain is scientifically verified information"—the sarcasm is thick—"you're a high energy lover. I approve. You're eager to try out new positions—with the lights on. I'm all for a woman willing to let me take in her curves in all their glory. Ah!" I lift my eyes from the screen and lock them with hers. "Here's something I didn't expect."

Her eyebrows knit together. "What?"

"You're a top-notch dirty talker."

Her head jerks back. "That's not what it says."

I angle my screen.

"Holy shit!"

"Holy shit, that's true. Or holy shit, that's a lie."

She blushes from ear to ear.

I keep reading. "It also says it's easy to turn on a Gemini. Let's put that theory to the test."

Her eyes grow wide, threatening to take over her face.

"What are you going to do?" The nervous tremor in her voice is audible.

"Nothing X-rated."

"Okay." She nods, but her gaze remains skeptical. "You're not going to do anything that'll get us kicked out for indecency?"

I ease her worries. "I won't," I say. "Extend your arm on the table."

She obeys my command.

With my gaze boring into hers, I run a finger up her arm. The movement is gentle, a languorous caress. Her lips part into an O before she folds her bottom lip between her teeth.

Fuck, that's hot.

As an encore, I trace my finger down her arm.

When her blue eyes meet mine, they're veiled with lust.

I pull my hand away. "Too bad on the cosmic level, we're incompatible."

She squints at me. "You're an evil man."

"You can't believe everything you read online, love..." I bore my eyes into hers. "As far as I'm concerned, *we are* compatible, regardless of what that silly website proclaims." My lips curve up. "The question is, do we want to do something about it?"

Several heartbeats thump against my chest as we stare at each other.

The heat wafting between us, burning hotter than lava.

Her chest rises and falls, forcing attention to her spectacular breasts.

"My evil stepsister and my ex-boyfriend are getting married. I-need-you-to-be-my-fake-boyfriend-at-the-upcoming-wedding." She blurts the words out in one go.

My eyebrows shoot to my forehead.

"What?"

She hesitates a little before speaking. "You'd make the perfect fake wedding boyfriend."

I heard it correctly the first time around.

I expected a yes or no to my question.

This wasn't even on the radar.

Chapter 6

Shay

My heart is beating so hard against my chest it's like it's going to explode.

I'm still in shock by my boldness. Or is it foolishness?

In all fairness, the words left my lips like a projectile, gushing out of my mouth, my brain taking a leave of absence.

I blame the booze and this man's intoxicating presence.

Both went straight to my head.

I also blame Zane's sharp wit and easy-going personality.

Briar is right.

Showing up alone at Imogen and Elias's wedding reeks of I-got-dumped-and-a-year-later-I'm-still-single. I won't allow my stepsister to lick her fangs at my expense. It doesn't matter if I scream it from the rooftops, I'm not heartbroken over their deception—which I'm not, I'm pissed off—nothing says I've moved on like an illegally hot wedding date. Fake or not.

Sure, I could show up with an escort, but my stepsister is like a scavenger. She smells blood ten thousand miles away. If she ever found out I resorted to paying for an escort, I'd never be able to play it down. She'd ridicule me for the rest of my life.

I wouldn't be surprised if escorts have some acting training. After all, they play a different role with each date. That doesn't mean I'd be able to pull it off. How comfortable can you be with a man who sleeps with women for a living? Would I let him touch me? Nope. No way. Not happening.

Zane Keller is different.

I'd let that man touch me all over.

Speaking of the hot as fuck executive, he's still staring at me, eyes full of disbelief, his long, dark lashes, fluttering like crazy.

He's dumbfounded.

I don't blame him.

I came here for a drink. Not to wrangle a wedding date.

I open my mouth to plead my case, but he speaks first.

"We need to switch from drinks to coffee for this conversation."

Excitement and trepidation hit at the same time.

He didn't shoot down my preposterous idea.

He signals to the waiter, who rushes over. "Is espresso okay with you?" he asks me.

I nod.

"Please bring us two espressos." His gaze shifts from the waiter's and locks onto mine. "This gorgeous redhead has some explaining to do."

Oh, boy.

Chapter 7

Shay

My phone rings, waking me up.

I extend my hand and tap around the surface of my nightstand until my fingers clench around my phone. I bring the device close to my face. I have to coax myself to peer open one eye, then the other.

Keeley.

I sit up in bed and accept the call.

"Hey," I say in a groggy voice. "You're back." I brush my mass of hair away from my forehead before pulling the covers up to my neck. Since I prefer to sleep with the heat set on low, it's a little cold in the morning.

"I just landed. I'm still at JFK."

New Yorker Keeley Corbin and I met when we became roommates in Milan. There were six models living in a house, but Keeley and I became fast friends.

She also transitioned into a new career after stepping off the catwalk. While I'm still in front of the camera, she's behind the scenes as a TV show wardrobe stylist. Her latest gig is working for a popular morning show. They were filming a one-week special in Australia.

She was hoping and praying to find her Chris Hemsworth and never come back to Manhattan. She had a lot of smutty sex with a few devastatingly handsome Aussie hunks, but no marriage proposals.

"You missed me so much, you decided to wake me up?"

"I pretty much slept the whole way from Hong Kong to New York. It's only now I checked my text messages." *That explains it.* "What in the actual fuck?" Keeley barks on the other end. "The cunt is pregnant?"

"Apparently so." I sneer. "She got my boyfriend, she's using pictures from *my* Pinterest board as inspiration for her fairytale winter wedding, she bought her wedding dress at the same boutique I intended on buying mine from, and now she's pregnant. I wouldn't be surprised if she stole my baby names."

Given the animosity between us, I didn't expect my stepsister to follow me on social media. When Mom shared details of Imogen's wedding, she was describing many items on my wish list. I blocked the stealing witch's ass.

Elias never popped the question, so it's not like those boards were about my pending wedding or anything like that. If I'm perfectly honest, I never envisioned walking down the aisle with him. The Pinterest board wasn't my Shay + Elias forever story. It was more along the lines of... *someday*.

By passing my ideas as her own, the incident was a reminder Imogen has to steal from others to make up for her lack of creativity. She's been trying—and succeeding far too many times for my liking—to usurp my life. This whole wedding farce is further proof she's a leech.

"Her usual MO is to copycat my life, but in this case, she one-upped me," I say.

"Puh-leeze." I can just see Keeley rolling her eyes. "I pity that poor child. He or she will have two cheaters as parents."

"True."

"The woman has no shame." Keeley does little to hide her disgust.

"None whatsoever."

"She's a jealous, manipulative bitch," Keeley says.

"One I'm related to."

"Even though your mom insists you show your face, you're not going to attend that wedding, right? You're standing firm in your decision, right?"

"I wasn't planning on changing my mind, but Briar brings forth a good point—"

"Which one?" Keeley's tone stings like an elastic band snapping against skin.

I share everything that transpired from the moment I stepped through the doors of the Bymark Hotel, up to my texting session with my sister.

Keeley shakes her head. "That girl is a hoot. Let's see if she has the lady balls to go through with that ludicrous idea."

"I'm pretty sure it's all talk," I say. "I filed it as preposterous, but it got me thinking—"

"Please tell me you don't intend on hiring an escort as your date for Imogen's wedding?!" I pull the phone away from my ear.

"Great, not only have I lost my hearing, but everyone at JFK knows my business."

"Sorry, I didn't mean to broadcast it like that. Seriously, Shay, don't go there. That shit only works in the movies."

"Not that I want to be judgmental, but I know myself. I wouldn't be able to play the part. I get that women in a city like New York hire escorts as platonic companions to accompany them at galas and such, but let's be honest, most times, it's for sex."

"Exactly! Do you want to play lovey-dovey with a guy who's had his tongue up God knows how many va-jay-jays and assholes?"

I didn't see that coming.

I lose it.

"Thanks so much for the visual," I say in between bouts of laughter.

"A girl has to think of these things," she says. "Heck, I can't even read romance books where the hot guy is an escort, even knowing he'll give up all the others for the heroine, and there's a guaranteed happy ever after. It doesn't change the facts. The guy's been around the block a few *thousand* times."

I double up in laughter.

"None of those things were a factor in my decision, but thanks so much for highlighting them."

"What are best friends for?"

"All that to say, Briar planted the seed in my head and I might've found a workaround."

"This is New York. An actor is a much safer bet."

"I'm not talking about an actor." I set her straight.

"Who do you have in mind?"

"Needing a drink after that conversation with my mom, I headed to the Evangelista Lounge. After giving up my table, the maître d' suggested the bar." I sigh. "Keeley, last night was my night."

"What does that mean? And how does that relate to the escort?"

I tell her all about Zane Keller.

"Ooph..." She exhales into the phone. "Baby it might be cold outside, but it's hot in here. You can't see me, but after that story, I'm fanning myself. The man sounds like sex on legs."

"The man *is* sex on legs." I correct her. "He says he's a nerd, but Zane Keller is male model material."

"How tall?"

"Six feet six inches of man candy deliciousness."

"No way!"

"Way!"

Keeley is an inch taller than I am, and the woman loves her high heels. Height is an aphrodisiac for her. I'm not gonna lie, it gets my engines revving.

"Was he wearing a suit?" she asks.

"I'm willing to bet everything to my name he only wears bespoke."

"You bitch!"

"Thank you!"

She grumbles on the other end.

"I lucked out," I say.

"At six-six, you know the man has a huge ass cock."

I choke out a laugh.

Leave it to Keeley for having her mind in the gutter this early in the morning.

"So, did he agree to be your plus one to what will undoubtedly turn out to be the wedding disaster of the year?"

"He didn't say yes and he didn't say no."

"Huh?"

"I laid my cards on the table, and he listened."

"And..."

"He asked me if he could sleep on it."

"When is he going to give you an answer?"

"We're meeting tonight at the hotel. We exchanged phone numbers. He'll text me later with details."

"This is promising, Shay."

"Fingers crossed." I intertwine my fingers together and say

a little prayer, hoping God is listening. "He would be perfect for the job."

"More than perfect," she says. "He's going to tower over your ex."

"The thought has crossed my mind," I say, my tone giddy.

Barefoot, Elias and I are the same height, something that bothered him throughout our relationship.

"If Zane says yes, I'd try to make it a fake boyfriend *with benefits* deal."

I shake my head, even though she can't see me. "Why am I not surprised you'd say that?"

"There's nothing wrong with a little—or a lot of—mattress tango. After all, your hot CFO is half Brazilian."

"Newsflash, the tango is from Argentina. Lambada is Brazilian."

"Look at you, Miss Dancing with The Stars." She snickers. "Don't think I don't see right through you. You're avoiding what's important here, i.e., the opportunity to get his cock inside your vagina."

"Keeley, it's too early for this kind of talk. You need to set your energy volume to low."

"That'll never happen, and we both know it. Besides, I can't help it. This guy sounds scrumptious."

"That. He. Is."

"At least you're willing to fess up to that much."

I shake my head.

"You've been experiencing a severe drought for a year and a half—since you found out your stepsister and boyfriend were fucking behind your back for four months before you caught them." I couldn't understand why Elias was all of a sudden too tired for sex. "Let Zane Keller punch your ticket. Even Aunt Eileen's cosmic compatibility website says the man is up for the job."

"You're crazy."

"When was the last time you went on a date that resulted in a second one?" She doesn't give me time to answer. "Every single guy you've been out with, you cite the same excuse—zero chemistry. From the sound of it, Zane and you are combustive together. He even said so himself."

"We were both a little tipsy last night. The flirtatious banter might have been a side-effect." I caution her.

"Or the flirtatious banter was a precursor to something more."

I bite the inside of my cheek, pondering on her words.

"In my experience, men who talk dirty, fuck dirty."

Images of Zane fucking me silly against a wall, flash in front of my eyes. When you're a tall, curvy girl, it's a fantasy few men can make happen. It requires height, strength, and stamina. Three qualities the smoking hot CFO possesses.

Get your mind out of the gutter.

Focus on priorities.

"I just want to get through the wedding from hell," I say. "Let's see what happens after three days of fake dating."

No way am I allowing my evil stepsister to have the last laugh. The mission is to checkmate Imogen Manning by showing up at her wedding with a tall, dashing, drop-dead gorgeous date. Not to get thoroughly fucked by said drop-dead gorgeous date. Zane Keller can make a girl lose her head. If I don't keep my wits about me, I'll never be able to pull this off.

Chapter 8

Zane

I was the only one in the office when I got here this morning at six-thirty. Without any interruptions, I was able to knock off a lot from my list. I was even able to squeeze in a thirty-minute conference call with a group of directors at our manufacturing plant in Brazil.

Now, the office is buzzing with activity.

I stroll across the floor, dropping morning greetings here and there as employees smile and wave, as I head to my brother's office, located at the opposite end of the building from mine.

Even though his door is open, I knock with my free hand.

Xavier pulls his gaze away from his iMac, swinging his hazel brown eyes my way. "Morning!" He greets me with a warm smile.

"Morning!" I stride towards his desk, carrying breakfast. "Seems like the snow is coming down harder than it was a minute ago." I shift my gaze towards the floor-to-ceiling window. The sprinkle of flurries dancing in the sky resembles a snow globe after someone shook the hell out of it. "Mother Nature is on point. It's winter white outside."

"As long as we don't get hit with a severe storm like the one they're battling in Chicago, I can live with a little snow," Xavier says. "No one needs the kind of storm that would shut down the city. New Yorkers would never survive."

"Ain't that the truth."

I set the cardboard container and the craft paper bag on his desk before pulling out the treats I bought. "Along with coffee from your favorite coffee shop, I also got you some cranberry-almond pound cake. Perfect for the holiday season."

I sound off even to my own ear.

Xavier cocks an eyebrow. "What's up with you today?"

I feign ignorance. "What's wrong with breakfast?"

After three hours of focused work, I needed a break. I figured, might as well kill *three* birds with one stone, so I walked up to our favorite coffee and pastry shops, which happened to be next door to each other. Although I had to brave the morning madness, the short distance from the office allowed me to clear my head.

Xavier points at his screen. "From the time stamps of the first email you sent today, it looks like you got here before the morning newspapers were delivered. Then, you text me wanting to know if I wanted breakfast. Now, you're trying to butter me up with pound cake and coffee from my favorite shops. Do I look like a bloody fool to you?"

Our father arrived here when he was twenty. Even though his British accent is still strong, my brother's posh accent is courtesy of years living in London, pursuing his dream to make it big as a football player.

"You're making too much out of it." I downplay it.

He shoots me a dubious side gaze. "Okay, if you say so."

He remains unconvinced.

I unbutton my suit jacket and take a seat in one of the guest chairs.

My baby brother goes straight for the treat, taking a huge bite out of it. He chews, pointing an animated finger at the cake before giving me a thumbs-up.

"Why do people put disgusting frosting on cakes? Naked cakes, pound cakes, and coffee cakes are the way to go."

"You say that every time you eat naked cake."

"Because it's true."

I shake my head.

Over coffee and cake, we make small talk.

"I need to bounce something off you," I say, dropping my empty cup on the desk.

"So, this was more than breakfast."

"It was."

He discards his empty cup. With his eyes locked onto mine, he plants his elbows on his desk and splays his fingers together. "I'm all ears."

I launch into story mode, telling him about meeting the redhead bombshell that preoccupied my dreams last night, and her surprise proposal.

Thinking of her has my cock hard.

I shift in my seat, readjusting myself.

Even after jerking off while imagining all the dirty, filthy things I wanted to do to that woman's heavenly body, my cock remains unsatisfied.

I don't blame the fucker.

When I finish my tale, Xavier is staring at me, his eyebrows knitted together in confusion.

"Why are we having this conversation?" Annoyance is audible in his tone.

"Two words." I drop an elbow on his desk and flash him my digits. "Ember Dankworth."

Getting an early start to my day wasn't so much about eagerness, it was because memory of the amazing night with Shay were marred with unpleasant flashbacks, filtering into my naughty dreams of the buxom redhead. I needed a distraction.

"Ah." The word drops from Xavier's lips as his back hits his seat. "The conniving woman, so desperate to hold on to you, she'd be willing to lie as her last attempt to sink her evil claws into you."

"We're not having this conversation because I don't have game."

"You had me worried there."

"It'll be a cold day in hell before I ask my baby brother for advice about women."

He chuckles.

"I know what to do with a delicious, curvy woman like Shay." I jab a hand in my hair. "After Ember..."

"You're cautious." He finishes for me as if reading my thoughts.

"I am." I nod. "Ember's accusations of me wanting to 'stick my dick' into any woman that so much as walked by me, was grating at my last nerve, but I never suspected she was borderline psycho." My jaw twitches. "I never gave that woman cause to be jealous, yet she had too many jealous bones in her body to count. And to think, when we first started seeing each other, she proclaimed she wasn't the jealous type. My ass." I sneer. "That should've sounded an alarm bell in my head. In all fairness, the first few days of us seeing each other, she came across as the ideal partner. Then, her crazy came out all at once. I don't want to step on another landmine. I was commitment phobic before Ember, but now..."

Xavier considers me for a long beat before speaking. "Ember is a bitch for having pulled the *I'm pregnant card* when she wasn't."

I bring my fingers to the bridge of my nose. "That would've been the equivalent of buying myself a lifetime sentence of misery." I shiver at the thought.

"If she were pregnant, we would've *all* suffered," Xavier says. "Ember is like getting an intravenous poison injected into your veins. Soon, every organ shuts down. Being forced to deal with that woman because she was the mother of your child would've been our demise—not only yours."

Thank God we all dodged that bullet.

My two-week fling with Ember was a train wreck from the beginning. We were fundamentally incompatible. When I broke things off, she resorted to stalking me. As I was putting the move on a sexy lawyer, visiting the city on business, Ember burst into the Evangelista Lounge, spewing lies that could've changed my life for the worse, causing a scene to end all scenes.

It took her a week to fess up to the fabricated bullshit stories she spun that would've had me tied to her for the next eighteen years. Had I not demanded we go to the doctor together and start working on legal papers, she'd still be stringing me along.

Lying, conniving bitch.

After two months, it's still a struggle for me to shake off the events of that day. The whole thing was unsettling. That's why I hadn't set foot anywhere near the Bymark Hotel, fearful the drama had stained my good name.

"Ember is a certifiable nut case," Xavier says. "You said it yourself, her jealousy is a pathology." I consider him. "Ember is fifty shades of crazy, that's for sure. And a world-class liar. That said, not every woman in New York City is unstable, high maintenance, and incapable of moving on after you repeatedly tell her it's over."

I had to get a restraining order on Ember's ass to keep her away.

"Worst case scenario, accompany the sexy redhead to the wedding, but keep it in your pants," Xavier says. "If the arrangement remains platonic, you'll avoid any confusion... therefore, avoiding drama."

Yeah, and I'll also avoid devouring a woman I fucking want with every fiber of my being.

Chapter 9

Shay

As I make my way through the lobby of the Bymark Hotel, it's clear New Yorkers aren't willing to let a little snow blanketing the street put a damper on things. The high-end hotel is bursting at the seams, buzzing with activity.

I usually look forward to the last two weeks of December—so many parties, so little time. It pisses me off my stepsister's wedding will soon become a dark spot at an otherwise enchanting time of the year.

Thanks for nothing, Imogen.

When I step out of the elevator on the forty-first floor, Zane greets me.

The man is sex on legs.

My heart beats a little faster.

"Good evening," he says, leaning into me before dropping a soft kiss on my cheek.

I'm surrounded by his expensive, masculine scent.

His *Eau de Pheromone* is working double time already.

A whoosh of heat travels from the tip of my toes to the root of my hair at lightning speed, causing my lady parts to flutter in excitement.

I'm so taken aback, I'm rendered speechless for a beat.

He takes a step back, his eyes brushing up and down the length of my body. Although he doesn't touch me, the sweep of his gaze is like a caress against my skin.

The man has superpowers he isn't even aware of.

"You look incredible, beautiful."

My throbbing cheeks warm up like a hot oven. "Thank you," I say. "It's one of your designs."

Of course he knows it's one of his designs.

Stop babbling.

"It looks far more arresting on you than it ever did on the model."

I'm giddy.

"You dress like a woman who doesn't mind attention." His stare caresses every one of my curves. "I like that about you." His voice is a low rasp.

Lord, it's getting hot in here.

It would've been foolish of me to select another designer to wear for tonight. I own a few Divine Curves Couture designs, so I was going to wear one of their designs. I couldn't choose which one from Curves Envy Fashion's high-end clothing line to select.

Keeley set her alarm so she could drag herself to my place to help me with my wardrobe. Even jetlagged, you can't snuff the stylist out of her.

With her help, I selected a 50's inspired vintage cobalt blue dress. The design is reminiscent of the kind of showstopper an old Hollywood actress like Ava Gardner would wear for a cocktail party. The bright color makes my hair and eyes pop, and the clingy fabric flatters my curves.

I arrived here with a cashmere cardigan but left it at the

coat check. I'm wearing the dress sleeveless. I've long come to accept my curvy body, but knowing Zane has a thing for women who aren't stick figures heightens his attractiveness.

"Another stylish suit." My eyes rake up and down his tall frame. "You dress well." Like a man in charge of an empire.

My heart is beating double time at the sight of this gorgeous man.

He adjusts his jacket. "Unlike your dress, this suit won't stop traffic."

Every straight woman in this city would argue with that statement. A three-piece suit can look too conservative and even stodgy on certain men. And it would dwarf shorter men. A tall, Adonis like Zane Keller looks like suit porn perfection in it.

I've dated wealthy men before, but never felt like I was out of their league. I do with this man.

I tear my eyes away from his and scan my surroundings.

"This is my first time up here," I say, meeting his gaze. "I thought this floor was more hotel rooms."

"No, this floor is the VIP Den—a private members only club where a selected group of executives meet to learn from each other and strike a deal or two."

"So, this is where all the serious wheeling and dealing is done in New York City."

"Something like that." He chuckles. "As of mid-December, it's ghost town up here. There aren't any meetings scheduled until the new year. Other than the concierge"—he points a thumb over his shoulder—"it's just the two of us tonight. Given your request, I figured it was best to meet in a more private setting. That's why I reserved a fully catered meeting room. Even though the lounges are packed, and music is playing in the background, the proximity of the tables makes it easy for anyone to eavesdrop. It doesn't mean anyone down there knows your stepsister, but why take a chance?"

I'm touched he'd go to this length to help me pull off this subterfuge.

I bite on my lower lip. "Does it mean you agree?"

"A beautiful woman needs my help. Who am I to say no?"

I flash him a beaming smile.

He responds with a cocky wink.

"The meeting room nestled on top of a luxury hotel is a great idea," I say.

"We have to forgo the lounge's cool ambience and chill-out vibe, but we're guaranteed privacy."

"I'm okay with that." I nod. "So far, only my best friend Keeley knows that in a moment of insanity, I asked you to be my fake boyfriend."

He closes the gap between us. "Are you having second thoughts?"

In the deserted space, his voice comes out deep, rich, chocolatey.

"No," I say with upmost certainty, "I had a freak-out moment last night when I got home, but I figured the worse that could happen is you saying no."

His eyes bore into mine. "I wouldn't be able to say no even if I wanted to, Shay."

"We only just met, and this may come across as ludicrous, but I don't think I'd be able to pull this off with anyone else but you."

"I'm glad you trust me."

I nod. "I do."

"Full disclosure, my brother knows."

"I can deal with two people knowing."

"Good," he says. "Let me give you the tour and we'll head to our room."

He extends a hand.

I stare at it for a few long breaths, anticipating the charge of electric current that coursed through my veins when his lips touched my cheek.

My gaze flickers up to his.

The intensity emanating from his hazel green eyes would have me agreeing to pretty much anything.

Holy hotness.

When I muster up the courage to slip my hand into his large one, I bite down against a moan.

Chapter 10

Zane

I swear Shay O'Hara is the sexiest woman alive.

The sight of her in that bright blue dress took my breath away. And then, there's the knockout body and tempting curves that get my blood pumping at a frenetic rate. I want my hands on every inch of this goddess's skin.

I have to sit down with Max and Xavier, and discuss how this bombshell should be rewarded with our spring and summer collections. I'm willing to bet my fortune our sales would triple because every plus size woman in America would want to look as good as she does.

Shay leans into the table.

My eyes drop to her cleavage.

The swell of her breasts spilling above the garment makes my mouth water. And the peek of her lacy bra in the same shade... I'm this close to shooting my load into my pants.

"This meal was out of this world." Her eyes lift up to meet mine. "I expected finger food, canapés, and dips. The roast beef tenderloin with mushrooms and white wine cream sauce served with cheesy sweet potato gratin was not only unexpected, it was extraordinary."

"One of the perks of being a VIP Den member is having access to the Bymark Hotel's irreproachable chefs. The food here never disappoints."

"No kidding."

The conversation has been flowing over a meal fit for a king. We haven't delved into the heavy-duty stuff yet, but that's about to change. As much as I'd be content to sit here all night, admiring her gorgeous face and enjoy her infectious laugh, there's a lot for us to discuss.

I point to the tart. "Another slice?"

"I wouldn't say no," she says. "This tart is a homerun."

"One slice isn't enough."

"I agree."

"Why don't we move to the sofa. It'll be more comfortable than sitting on these chairs."

"Great idea!"

She's already on her feet.

My eyes are glued to her ass as she sashays away from me in those sexy as fuck high heels. The way she undulates those wide hips with each step makes me want to drop to my knees and worship the ground she walks on.

Goddammit, that fine ass.

I drag in a sharp breath. She stokes a primal urge in me.

I want to rip that dress off her body and lick and suck every curvy inch of her, and then fuck her senseless until she begs for mercy—

Get a grip, Keller.

A platonic arrangement means a drama-free arrangement.

I avert my gaze as she's about to sit down.

I serve us both another slice of the rich and creamy white chocolate cranberry tart. When I'm done, I grab the bottle of white wine sitting in a bucket of ice and top up our glasses. A couple of trips is all it takes for me to set everything on the coffee table.

Her eyes find mine. "Thank you."

"It's my pleasure." I sit next to her on the sofa.

Big mistake.

When she was sitting across from me at the table, the temptation was at arm's length. Now, the temptation is within reach.

Not good.

I take a long sip of my wine and drop the glass on the coffee table.

Time to get down to business before I do something stupid.

I clear my throat. "Neither of us are professional actors, so the more I know, the easier it will be for me to step up to the plate."

She frowns. "I told you a lot yesterday."

"True, but let's make sure we have all the basic facts covered."

She drops her dessert plate on the coffee table and angles her body. "Okay, what else do you want to know?"

"You told me your stepsister is getting married this coming Saturday and you'd prefer not to show up unaccompanied. Is there more to it?"

The question has been nagging at the back of my brain.

Her proposal was more than the need for a date. It was more like a crusade.

Something she hasn't revealed yet fuels her quest. I need to know what I'm getting into.

Her big eyes stare at me as her teeth work her lower lip.

"To pull this off successfully, you're not only going to have to trust me, you're going to have to be transparent, Shay. What I don't know, may explode in my face."

She lets out a suffering sigh.

"For whatever reason, my stepsister Imogen decided she would become the thorn in my side from the moment my mom and I moved into my stepfather's house."

"She didn't approve of the marriage?"

"At first, I thought it was because she resented having a stepmom. Ma said some time little girls have to adjust, so I had to be patient like I have to be patient and wait for summer to come around before putting on my pretty dresses. Summer never came around when it came to Imogen. She was a frosted princess who grew up to become a frosted queen. After years of trying to win her over, I had to accept the facts. Imogen thrives most when she makes other people around her miserable. She excels at stirring shit."

"Sounds like it."

"So, your stepdad had full custody?"

"No. He had joint custody with his wife. Imogen lived with her mom and came over during holidays and a month during summer vacation. Seven years into the marriage, Imogen came to live with us while his ex-wife was pursuing an international political career at the US Embassy in Belgium before becoming a news anchor in New York."

"Got it," I say. "Are you and your stepsister the same age?"

"No. We're two years apart," she says. "When Ma got married, I was elated to gain an older sister. Over the years, the elation turned into regret the more I got to know my stepsister."

"You and Imogen have been locking horns for a long time."

"Yup!" She pops the P. "Before I left Boston, she made it her mission to sabotage every single one of my relationships by sleeping with my boyfriends. Becoming a model allowed me to get the hell away from her. Once I decided modeling was no longer for me, I could've moved back to Boston. Imogen was one of the reasons why I stayed put here in New York. Then, she decided to move here."

"Why New York?"

"She professed that she was destined to become famous."

"Did her dreams come true?"

"It was a rude awakening. The entertainment business isn't for the weak. They don't call it *cutthroat business* for no reason. Since she didn't have the fortitude to stick it out, she gave up. Three months after I started my Beauty by Shay channel, Imogen copycatted me. She bailed out in a New York minute. It's deceiving, but being a vlogger is hard work. The only reason she never tried her hand at becoming a runway model is because she's vertically challenged."

"She's jealous of you."

"I don't think it has anything to do with me. She's a despicable human being with everybody. She treats her father like an ATM machine."

"And the award for Miss Congeniality goes to... *NOT* Imogen."

"Oh my God, that's funny. You nailed it."

"Since she failed at her mission to become famous, what does Imogen do for a living?"

"After countless short-lived positions, her mother rescued her ass by finding her a position at the television station where she works. She's the assistant to an asshole newscaster."

"Karma is a bitch."

"Speaking of biatches, I forgot to mention when Imogen moved here, she had the gall to suggest she move in with my best friend Keeley and me when we were roommates."

"No shit."

"Once I made it clear, I preferred to dive out of an airplane without a parachute than to live with her, she moved in with one of her cousins on her mom's side. Her mother was blissfully enjoying husband number two. Hence, making her daughter an unwanted third wheel."

"Maybe her contentious relation with her mom explains her… attitude."

"It doesn't help the overall nasty vibe she gives off. That's for sure. But it certainly fuels her Wicked Witch of the West act."

I frown. "You lost me."

"Imogen's cousin lives in Fort Greene, Brooklyn. On the same street as Elias, my boyfriend at the time."

"What a bad coincidence."

"More like an omen. The irony wasn't lost on me. I did my best to put distance between my stepsister and I, just for her to end up being my boyfriend's neighbor. From there, your guess is as good as mine as to how Imogen snaked her way into his bed. Six months ago, she moved in with Elias, and now plays house with my ex."

Everything makes sense now.

"How long had you and your boyfriend been dating?"

"Shy of a year."

"How did you find out he was cheating on you?"

"Elias Fitzsimmons is a radiologist. He has a thriving medical practice with his older brother. All of a sudden, he started using work as an excuse to cancel our dates. Around the same time, he had to attend a one-week conference in Denver. Things were busy for me, so my days were interminable. For a two-week window, we only communicated via phone and text—and I don't mean sexting."

"The flame was snuffed out between you."

"Our exchanges were drifting into the friend zone at an alarming rate. After two weeks of not seeing my boyfriend, I decided to set our relationship back on track. Wanting to surprise him, I showed up at his door—"

"The joke was on you?"

Her lips twist. "You can say that again."

"Sorry, I interrupted you."

She brushes it off. "I used the key he had given me to let myself in. He must have forgotten he had given me one."

"He wasn't alone?"

Her gaze fixes onto mine.

The big, beautiful blue eyes that usually radiate heat, are ice cold.

"It was a Saturday morning, and I figured, I'd slip into his bed and we could spend a weekend together. My world came crashing around me when I tiptoed into his house. As I approached his bedroom, I could make out groans and grunts. I thought maybe he fell asleep with the TV on. Boy, was I ever wrong. When I came to stand in front of the ajar door to his bedroom, I was treated to a show I can never unsee, no matter how many times I wash my eyes with bleach."

That doesn't sound good.

"My stepsister was riding my boyfriend's cock reverse cowgirl style, her small breasts bouncing up and down, her hair flying wildly, her moans rivaling that of a porn star."

"Jesus."

"I wish I could bleach my eyes to unsee it, but I'm stuck with the visual for the rest of my life."

"How did your stepsister react when she saw you standing there?"

"She smirked and doubled her efforts."

"Didn't your cheating ex clue in he had an audience?"

"It took him a minute. When he did, he freaked the hell out and begged my stepsister to stop riding him, but she was determined to go for the grand finale. Since his hands were in handcuffs, his fingers interlaced around one of the posts in the spindle headboard, and his feet were shackled, she had all the control. She started riding him so hard, he had no other choice but to take it. Frozen in stupor, I watched my boyfriend explode inside my stepsister's pussy." She keeps talking without taking a breath. "Elias is a screamer when he comes. He's so loud, you can hear him in Alaska. In his confusion, he couldn't figure out who he was fucking—my stepsister or me."

More like who was fucking him.

"So, he screamed *Imo-Shay* over and over again, furthering my mortification. When Imogen got off him, I got another doozie of a surprise. They didn't use a condom. Like a coward without *cojones*, Elias had the gall to pull the *it's not what you think* card. I would've had more respect for him had he owned up to his sins since I caught him red-handed. I pinned the scumbag with a glare of contempt and told him to fuck off. I didn't bother acknowledging my stepsister. Then, I ran out of there like I was being chased by a pack of wolves. The next thing I knew, they were announcing their wedding. Yesterday, my mom informed me Imogen was two months pregnant."

"Your ex was into handcuffs?"

"Apparently."

"And you?"

Her face puckers like a toddler sucking on a lemon. "It's not my thing," she says. "Elias was pressuring me to take on a more dominant role in bed"—she forms quotation marks with her fingers. "He also wanted us to visit a bondage/dominance club. I refused both suggestions. He accused me of being sheltered and unwilling to explore all the aspects of my sexuality—"

"Being an asshole is a sure way to get you to change your mind."

"It only made me more resolved in my decision."

"Good for you."

"My refusal was the perfect window of opportunity for my scheming stepsister. Imogen made sure to let me know that, unlike me, she was more than willing to fulfill Elias's filthiest fantasies."

I shake my head. Her stepsister is a conniving bitch, but I refrain from sharing my opinion. As for Elias, he should lose his balls.

"Imogen sounds like she's a gem." My tone drips with sarcasm.

"Right. I'd sooner trust the devil."

"That's one dickless, loser of a boyfriend, and one shameless stepsister."

She snorts with an eye roll. "You can say that again."

"Were you in love with Elias?"

She regards me for a long breath.

If she's using me to let those two idiots know she's moved on, that's one thing. But if she still has feelings for Elias, that's another. I'd rather know what I'm getting into.

"I didn't have visions of us tying the knot, but Elias knew of my long-standing feud with my stepsister." Her lips curl up in a snarl. "He should've never cheated on me to start off with, but Imogen? What an asshole. He betrayed everything I ever shared with him. So, to answer your question, I wasn't in love with him, but I would've appreciated it if he had manned up and broke things off instead of going behind my back, and then lying about it."

"Like I said, your ex is a dickless loser."

"The signs were there, but it took me too long to clue in."

"Can I ask a personal question?"

"Sure."

"Correct me if I'm wrong, but yesterday, it sounded like you referred to your father in the past tense."

Her eyes shut for a beat and she lets out an audible sigh. "I was three years old when my dad passed away, so I don't remember him. That said, the way he died was so tragic. He was an emergency nurse and had worked a series of brutal shifts." She lowers her eyes for a beat. "His supervisor sent him home for two days of rest. By then, the hours had already accumulated in his system." Her eyes lower to her hands, fidgeting in her lap. "Daddy fell asleep at the wheel on the drive home. His car veered into oncoming traffic and he came nose-to-nose with a semi-tractor trailer."

Oh, shit.

I place a hand over hers, and squeeze. "I'm sorry if my question brought back bad memories."

Her blue eyes meet mine. "You didn't know," she says in a small voice. "If we were dating, that's something you'd know about me. If Daddy were still alive, Imogen wouldn't be in my life."

"Your mom and stepdad have been married a long time."

"Yes. Ma married Dr. Alan Manning two years after Dad died. Twenty-one years later, and they're still in love."

"What's your stepdad's specialty?"

"He's a dermatologist."

I nod.

We sit in silence for a long stretch.

"Since I didn't bother doing a Google search on you, I assume you're single?" she asks. "Not that you can believe everything you read online."

I'm not as photographed as my cousin Max or my brother Xavier. I might be dubbed a playboy, but you'll be pressed to find me in any compromising or embarrassing situation—Ember being the exception. Still, I like that Shay didn't Google me, preferring to hear it from me.

"I'm single."

"Good. There's going to be enough drama at the wedding, I don't need to add to it."

"I'm not big on drama myself."

She offers a genuine smile. "That's something we share in common."

I wink. "Let's see if we can find a few other things."

As we finish our dessert and wine, we exchange a string of facts—family history, growing up in Boston versus New York, where we went to school, favorite color, food, hobbies, likes, dislikes, and traveling destinations on our bucket list. Our backgrounds are different, but that's to be expected. Nothing she shares surprises me much until we get to the allergies.

"You're allergic to strawberries?" I ask, shocked.

"It's an unusual allergy, but yes, strawberries don't like me very much."

"Is it a severe allergy?"

"It is." She nods. "I carry an EpiPen everywhere I go."

All of a sudden, panic grips my chest, my eyes dropping to the empty dessert plates.

"I'm not allergic to cranberries," she says, putting my mind at ease.

Thank God.

"I'm not sure if I would react to raspberries or blackberries because Ma never wanted to take a chance. That said, strawberries are my nemesis."

"Note to self. No strawberries for Shay."

"Now you know everything about me."

"I don't believe that lie for a second. I'm sure there's a lot more to know about you, but at least I know the most important things."

I tell her about my brother's previous illustrious career as a professional soccer player in Europe. I also tell her about our humble beginnings. Both my parents were immigrants. Mom was a housekeeper. Dad had a landscaping business with two of his brothers. Until I started putting my PowerPoint and Excel superpowers to good use, there was just enough money for the basics. I share how a high school teacher who believed in my potential, helped me secure a scholarship. Thanks to her, I ended up with a bachelor's in finance and an MBA from Columbia University. I finish by telling Shay about my parents' hat-trick marriage and divorce.

Her beautiful face registers shock. Not surprising. "Your parents married *and* divorced three times?"

"Alexander James Keller and Bárbara Barros Keller prefer to repeat their mistakes in threes. It's not something I usually broadcast. It might never come up when we meet your family, but in case it does, you know. It's not the kind of fact you should find out about at the same time as the rest of your family."

"You're right. I doubt I would've been able to school my expression." She shakes her head. "I can't believe what that must've been like."

"Chaos, confusion, and fear." I don't bother sugarcoating it. "My brother and I lived in a constant state of limbo. One minute our parents were fighting, the next they were making up."

"At least they didn't go for a fourth run?"

My lips curve up in a small sneer.

Shay's eyes widen. "No way?"

"There was talk of them trying again at a family member's wedding four years after divorce number three. My brother and I told them if they walked down the aisle one more time, *we'd* be the ones divorcing them."

"Wow."

"I know."

"Are they single or did they find their perfect match?"

"Both have had a solid relationship, but that's in the past."

She shakes her head.

"I feel confident we know enough about each other's background to fool everybody," I say, moving the focus away from my parents and their relationship fuckups.

She worries her bottom lip. "You think?"

"Had it been a one-week destination wedding, it would've been a lot more challenging. We only have to remain in character for three days. From what you've described, your stepsister is so self-centered, it's unlikely we'll be center stage. We got this."

"She'll do everything to keep the spotlight on her, but she won't miss the opportunity to rub her good fortune in my face."

"And you won't give a flying fuck because your incredible boyfriend will consume all your attention. You won't have time to pay that devious witch any mind." I punctuate my ceremonious tone with a cocked eyebrow.

Shay loses it.

"Come on, I want to hear it. Repeat the affirmation."

With a swing of her long mane, her shiny red hair catches the light, then falls behind her shoulders. There's nothing sexual about the movement, yet the grace with which it's executed is so seductive.

She shimmies on the seat and her blue eyes meet mine.

Pressing a hand to her chest, she says, "I won't have time to pay that devious bitch any mind."

"Oh, you're a dangerous one."

She rewards me with a wicked smile.

"There's one more thing."

She frowns. "I thought we had it in the bag."

"We do," I say, "But there's something important we haven't addressed yet."

Her eyes shift left, then right before fixing onto mine. "What?"

"The kiss."

Twin blotches of color appear high on her cheeks.

She opens her mouth to speak, but nothing comes out.

I soldier on. "If we don't kiss during the three-day affair, it's going to blow our cover."

She shoots me a suspicious side gaze.

"Are you blowing smoke up my ass?"

Darling, there are a lot of things I wanna do to your fine ass. That's not one of them.

I set her straight. "My cousin Luisa got married six months ago and there was a lot of kissing going on—and not just from the happy couple. Weddings bring that out in guests."

She nods. "Okay, you bring forth a good point."

"Kissing for the first time in front of your family will end up being awkward. I suggest we practice so we don't come across looking like amateurs."

She motions a finger between us. "You mean us kissing? Now?"

"That's what I mean."

I can't stop staring at her gorgeous mouth, the desire to kiss her to validate the insane chemistry between us is a newfound obsession.

"Oh."

"Don't look so disappointed."

"That's not what I meant." The words come tumbling from her lips in a rush. "In my haphazard plan, I hadn't accounted for that."

"The devil is in the details," I say. "If we don't act like a *real* couple, Imogen will sniff us out like a hunting dog."

"You're right."

"It's the same for public displays of affection." Her eyes bounce up to mine. I reach out and stroke my thumb along her arm. She shudders. "Couples are comfortable touching."

She nods as if in a trance.

"I suggest we spend the next little while kissing, touching, and getting to know each other *a lot* better."

"So we're able to fool everybody," she says in a near murmur.

I match her hushed tone. "Believability is key."

"What if you don't like kissing me?" The feeling she breathes into that false statement is reminiscent of a Shakespearean tragedy.

My eyes fall to her lips. "What if I like kissing you too much?"

We exchange a complicit smile.

Something flashes in her eyes, transforming the blue hue into a vibrant, electric shade. "That could be a problem."

"A *good* problem."

She bites against her lower lip, and I stifle a groan.

Damn, that mouth. Those plush, pale pink lips I'm dying to taste.

"Can we fake a convincing kiss?" she asks, blinking up at me with big blue eyes.

"Just because the relationship is fake doesn't mean the kiss can't be real."

"Oh."

Color splashes across her chest and creeps up her neck to stain her cheeks in an arousing rosy shade, pulling my eyes to her ample chest once more. I'm dying to know what her phenomenal tits look like. I want to take her nipples in my mouth, roll each one on my tongue, suck on them like it's a matter of life or death. Alas, you don't always get what you want. If we go down that road, there's no way I'll be able to put on the brakes. It'll be pedal to the metal until I come gushing inside her.

It's best to take it nice and slow.

I place a hand behind her head and pull her closer to me.

The many layers of her lovely perfume wafts between us.

Bold and sophisticated. Just like her.

With my free hand, I caress her face. I'm startled by how soft she feels.

"The more we practice, the more you'll be accustomed to feeling my lips against yours."

I don't give her time to answer.

I crush my lips against hers.

She moans into my mouth.

I taste the white wine on her breath as I take her tongue.

Her hands run through my dark blond hair, and I deepen the kiss.

"Fuck, Shay."

She lets out a little mewling sound that tugs at my balls.

I growl against her mouth as our kiss intensifies.

Even with a gun pointed at my temple, I wouldn't be able to deny my attraction for this woman.

My senses are reeling.

My pressing need for her consumes me.

Her beauty ensnares me.

I'm enchanted by her.

If I had any chance at self-restraint, it slipped from my fingers the moment our lips touched.

I got it bad for this woman.

It's because she embodies the fine balance between a strong woman who has her shit together and the vulnerable soul—a combination that flares the protective alpha in me.

Fuck.

I was a fool to think I could kiss her and not be caught in her web. Good God, I'm having a chemical reaction to this woman.

Fuck platonic.

There's no going back now. I'm barreling down a one-way street with no exit.

There's an urgency to consume all of her all at once. It's

unlike me to fall in lust, but damn if I'm going to waste time explaining my attraction to this woman. I'm willing to shred to pieces the pages of my own damn rule book for Shay O'Hara.

I give everything to this kiss, and she takes it all like a good girl.

I alternate between fucking her mouth with my tongue and kissing her passionately.

Her hands rake through my hair, holding my head to hers as her body responds to my touch. Her sexy little moans are more potent than an aphrodisiac.

My blood turns hot, my desire for her ratcheting to another level.

With this kiss, I become a hunter, and Shay O'Hara is my prey of choice. I need to fully sate my hunger.

Fuck, yeah.

It's with herculean effort I don't rip the dress off her and brand every inch of her skin with my tongue. I abstain. After all, there's a fine line between being an alpha and a backwards thinking caveman.

"You taste so sweet. I bet every part of you is as sweet."

She groans at my words as my lips brush against hers. I drop a flurry of kisses along her neck. More groaning and panting that travel straight to my cock. My lips move along each collarbone and over each shoulder, tasting and nibbling every inch of exposed skin.

"Oh, God, Zane."

"Fuck, Shay."

I bring a finger to the trim of her dress, resting at the highest swell of her tits. With a languorous touch, I follow the scalloped pattern until I'm cupping her breast. I grope and squeeze, relishing how she's more than a handful.

She hitches in a breath.

From the way her body trembles, I'm willing to bet her arousal is spiking as fast as mine.

Good.

It's a tug of war, but after a few long pleasurable seconds, I abandon her breasts. My hand glides down her body, caressing her soft stomach, imprinting her luscious curves into my memory. She's so soft all over, and that makes me growl like an animal. I continue my trajectory until my fingers flirt with the hem of her dress, my already fraying resolve dwindling a little more.

I have to put my stamp on her...

Chapter 11

Shay

Sweet baby Jesus, the man can kiss.

White chocolate still coats his tongue, making this kiss even sweeter.

The way his mouth expertly explores mine causes a pull to build in my core. It's a surprise, given my lady parts have been on strike for a long time.

It's like I've never been kissed before. Now I know what it feels like to kiss a scorching hot, formidable, sexy alpha of a man.

This kiss forces me to recalibrate everything I knew about kissing.

I moan into Zane's hungry mouth.

I swear, I could come from his tongue dancing with mine.

This kiss sets the bar for all future kisses. I feel bad for the guys who will follow this masterful kisser.

Heck, I'm not sure I want anyone to come after him.

Everything about this man is overwhelming in the best possible way.

The nickname he has for me...

Love?

Totally swoony.

Someone needs to slap me awake, because surely, I'm dreaming.

Zane pushes up the hem of my dress, higher and higher.

I can hardly breathe.

When he brushes his long fingers between my thighs, my pulse jackhammers in my throat.

My whole body is ablaze.

As I succumb to the pleasure, a frightening thought reminds me of our location.

"Zane." I squirm. "Wh—what if someone catches us?"

His hazel green eyes meet mine. "Unless you scream, the concierge won't bother us."

"I'm not going to scream."

"You will, when I make you come."

"I— I thought we were practicing kissing?" I'm out of breath because this man is blowing my mind.

"We are, love." He cocks an eyebrow. "I can't ignore your other set of lips."

I'm speechless.

Holy. Hell.

I stare at him, my lashes fluttering.

"You— You're— I mean—"

My delivery is as jumbled as my brain.

His heated gaze burns into me. "Yes, that's what I mean. Let's make this a quid pro quo—"

"What does that mean?"

He slides off the sofa and kneels in front of me.

"You need a fake boyfriend, and I'm dying to devour your pussy until I'm fucking drunk."

Oh.

My.

Fucking.

God.

His promise sends a chill up my spine. My clit tingles in anticipation.

I'm not sure when things started sliding into an abyss of pleasure, but I'd be a fool to put an end to it.

Thank you, God, for the snowstorm that kept Alice Laurent grounded in Chicago, and thank you, Imogen for pushing me to drink.

Without yesterday's encounter, Zane Keller would never have happened.

"So, Miss O'Hara, do you want to be on Santa's good girl list or his naughty girl one?"

"Naughty. Definitely naughty." The words rush out of my mouth.

He flashes me a wolfish smile. "Good answer, love."

Zane's hands hike up my dress as his caress trails up my thighs.

His fingers freeze. "Thigh highs?"

"Yes."

He growls. "This is like a fucking invitation. One I intend on accepting."

This is the best gift ever.

My best friend balked when I told her it was too cold to expose the upper part of my thighs. Thank God she insisted I jack up the sexy factor even if I'd be the only one to know. Hosiery would've been a deterrent.

"Not that it would've mattered," Zane says. "I'm so desperate for your pussy, I would've ripped your hosiery apart to get to your sweet spot."

No barriers for this guy.

I shouldn't be turned on by his caveman statement, but God it's so fucking sexy.

With his eyes boring into mine, his finger slides along the waistline of my panties, his touch, caressing my belly.

My breath hitches.

"You're such a responsive little one." His eyes—a hypnotic kaleidoscope of green shades dotted with gold—stare at me from behind hooded eyelids. "And this is merely a warm up."

I'm not sure if I can survive what he has in store for me, but what a way to go.

I'm woefully unprepared for what happens next.

In one swift movement, Zane rips the panties right off me.

My wide eyes shift to the torn lingerie he's holding up like a prize.

Blink!

Blink!

Blink!

Holy shit!

Who does that?

I'm so shocked, words fail me.

"Were those Sexy Curves?"

I shake my head, because I can't think fast enough to respond.

"They weren't one of ours?"

I shake my head again.

"If they weren't from Curves Envy Fashion, they had to go, then." A smile edges his lips. "I did you a favor, love. That fine ass of yours should only be clad in the best."

The panties he tore to pieces were expensive, but now might not be the time to point that out.

"I'll have a truckload of sexy panties and bras delivered to your door."

I can live with that.

He tosses the ripped panties over his shoulder, his attention never wavering from me. Slowly, ever so slowly, his gaze travels down the length of my body until it lands between my parted legs.

Feeling a little exposed, I bring my legs together.

He tsks. "Did I tell you to do that?"

I shake my head.

He places a hand near his ear and leans in slightly. "What was that?"

I find my voice. "No, you didn't."

"In that case, I expect you to give me what I asked for."

I hesitate at first, but obey.

"Better." His eyes lift up to mine. "Why are you so fucking beautiful, Shay?" His tone is solemn.

How in the world am I supposed to answer that question? "Your words..." That's the best I can come up with.

"Every part of you is perfect." This man holds a PhD in seduction. His hazel green eyes glide over my skin like a caress. "Such silky-smooth alabaster skin. Lush thighs. And an enticing landing strip." A cocky grin tugs at his lips. "You *are* a natural redhead. You said so yesterday, but I've been dying to find out for myself. What a difference a day makes. I get to confirm you weren't fibbing."

I giggle like a silly girl.

"I can't wait to get my mouth on that beautiful pussy, love."

Pure, unadulterated lust whooshes through me with the same intensity as a tornado, and my body shivers.

"You eager little one," he says.

I don't even have a comeback.

I'm no match for this man.

He outmaneuvers me and there's no chance in hell I'll ever be able to spar at his level when it comes to the dirty talk.

He trails a languorous finger from my belly button to my pussy.

I bite against my lip to curtail the pleasure, but it's in vain.

His touch is heaven.

I intake a sharp breath when his fingers slide between my pussy lips, skirting around my clit, scooping my juices.

"You're nice and wet for me."

I have an out of body experience when he brings his soaked fingers to his mouth and lick greedily.

The desire I read in his eyes is unsettling.

I've never had a man look at me with such hunger.

I've never felt this beautiful in my life—not even when I was strutting the catwalk in outfits that cost as much as a corporate salary.

"I want the whole nine yards with you, but if I'm too greedy, I won't be able to put the brakes on. We can get away with a little naughty, but not with full-on fucking." It's a good thing I don't have anything to add to that because he keeps talking. "Tonight, is all about pleasuring you—"

"That's not fair!"

"We'll spend three days together. There's plenty of time for you to make it up to me." He taps the inside of my thighs. "Open wide for me, love."

I obey his command, spreading my thighs, giving him the access to my body.

He slides two long fingers inside me. The motion is so slow, it makes me moan.

He begins stroking my needy clit with his thumb while simultaneously, pumping in and out of me with his other hand.

With an animalistic growl, he leans down and tucks his head between my thighs.

I jerk back, but his strong hands keep me in place.

Mother Mary.

He drops a soft kiss against my pussy, and it takes my breath away.

Determined to make me lose my bearings, he slides his tongue between my pussy lips, gliding it every which way.

Teasing.

Sucking.

Licking.

"Oh, oh, oh, yesssss!"

He devours me. All the while, he continues to finger-fuck me with zealous mastery.

The sensation is indescribable.

My eyes roll back into my head as I cry out with pure pleasure. The sound is foreign. One that's never escaped my lips before. A sound that could be misleading. It's uncertain if I'm coming or dying.

Zane's wicked tongue flickers against my clit at a velocity that threatens to push me off the cliff.

My insides clench.

Needing more, I lift a leg and place it over his shoulder, letting it dangle along his back.

He growls against my pussy, causing me to gasp.

"God, Zane..." I'm swept away by all the dirty things he's doing to me.

His tongue picks up the pace.

Oh, fuck.

I place my other leg over his shoulder, holding his head in a vice-like grip between my thighs.

"That's it, choke me between your luscious thighs," he says in a murmur against my pussy. "Force me to make you come."

I glance down between my legs.

The sight of this powerful executive on his knees in front of me with his head tucked between my legs is so heady.

I'm so turned on, my legs tremble.

What am I talking about?

I'm quivering from head to toe.

"You're going to come hard for me?"

I nod.

"Say it. I want to hear the words, Shay."

"Yes, I'm going to come harder than I ever have in my life."

His beautiful lips curve into a satisfied grin against my pussy lips. "It's fucking hot to know I'll be the one to take you there."

Maybe that was a bit of an overshare.

Oh well, it's too late now.

He resumes his mission.

He's unrelenting in his pursuit to make me lose my mind.

"Don't stop, Zane. Please, don't stop."

He doesn't disappoint.

His masterful tongue sweeps around my dripping pussy and skates around my clit once, twice, three times before catching the engorged bud between his lips. He sucks hard, and my pussy throbs in staccato pulses. The muscles of my core begin to clench, robbing me of the last vestige of control I pretend to hold onto.

Who am I kidding?

He's been in control of me since he kissed me.

My labored breaths take over the space as my vision goes blurry.

And then... I'm done.

My body heaves and bucks against him and I shoot off like a rocket into space.

"Oh, God—"

With an outreached hand, Zane muffles my cry as it crescendos.

I'm enveloped in a blissful sensation I've never experienced before as I come, and come, and come. Unable to contain this orgasmic tsunami, I let it all escape in Zane's palm. Even with his hand pressed over my mouth, I'm loud.

With my eyes closed tight, I ride one climatic wave after the other, panting for air.

Dear God.

Little white stars dance behind my closed eyelids. To say this is the most mind-blowing orgasm of my life would be an understatement.

With past boyfriends, oral sex was an insurance I'd reciprocate.

I'm not going to lie and say I've never had an orgasm before, but not one that's made my toes curl. No one has performed oral sex like that. Zane was feasting on my pussy. He wasn't slobbering around my pussy, with fingers crossed, hoping to hit the jackpot. He knew where to find the bull's-eye.

He was eating me out with purpose.

With confidence.

With passion.

It was all about *my* pussy.

A first for me.

I'm still floating when he speaks. "Your body is mine, until the end of this fake arrangement." My eyes pop open. "This is just the beginning for us. I want *benefits* with our arrangement."

My jaw drops.

Chapter 12

Shay

I'm standing at the arrival gate at Boston Logan International Airport, surrounded by a swarm of people waiting for their loved ones.

This is a first for me.

I've never waited for a guy at the airport before.

Elias has been to numerous medical conferences and trainings, but I've never been compelled to make the trip to the airport to wait for him. Glad I never bothered.

Sure, Zane and I could've met at the hotel, but I couldn't wait to see his handsome face, especially after finding out he went above and beyond. He was initially supposed to land at Hanscom Field—a smaller airport designated for private jets outside of Boston in Bedford. Instead, he asked his pilot to reserve a landing slot at Boston Logan.

I pull out my phone from my handbag, giddiness making me bounce like a jumping bean. My fingers fly across the screen to confirm my location.

I lift my eyes, anticipating the moment he sees me.

Oh, there he is!

Spotting him through the crowd of people spilling from the open doors is as easy as spotting a five-hundred-euro note tucked in a stack of dollar bills. There's no lack of tall men exiting alongside Zane, but the sexy executive stands out.

My nerves hit me in one hard rush. I want to run to him and jump in his arms, but I refrain. First, I'm not one to make a big scene. Imogen is the drama queen in the family. Second, that kind of over-the-top reaction would freak him the hell out considering we've only known each other for less than seventy-two hours. Third, it's best to redirect my giddy energy to putting my plan into action.

I regroup.

I tuck my phone into my handbag and grab the large sign nestled tight between my legs. I hold it up over my head and wait.

When Zane spots me, his gorgeous face breaks into a huge grin.

He shakes his head.

I flash him a beaming smile.

As he strides towards me, each confident step eating the floor beneath his expensive looking boots, and his eyes glued on mine as everyone watches him, I notice a few curious onlookers ping-ponging their gaze between the man who could double as a model and the person he's walking towards. Me!

"Hey, you." He chuckles as he stops in front of me.

"Hey, you."

"You didn't want me to get lost?" He nods to the sign where I scripted his name in big block letters.

"I know this isn't your first time in Boston, but since this is more personal than business, I wanted to make it memorable," I say. "Welcome to the City of Champions, slugger!"

"I thought New York was the city of champions."

I shake my head. "Nope. Boston's history of dominance in

sport is well documented," I say in my best sports broadcaster's voice.

"Is that so?" His tone is skeptical.

I came prepared. "The Boston Red Sox, Boston Celtics, Boston Bruins, *and* New England Patriots have each won multiple national championships. NYC can't claim those accomplishments."

"You might reside in New York, but your heart will always belong to *Bawstin*."

His exaggerated accent is comical.

I lower the sign. "Always, slugger."

"How was your flight?" he asks, changing the subject.

The bulging sales of my co-branded makeup line prompted MAC Cosmetics to fly me to Miami for a series of store appearances to meet fans face-to-face. I visited three stores in one day. I couldn't get over the screaming fans. You'd think I was a rock star and not a makeup and beauty vlogger. I was beside myself when the director for the region divulged sales quintupled during the time I was down there. I was scheduled to fly to Boston earlier today, but it so happened the French representative I was supposed to meet in New York on Monday was also in Miami. The timing worked out well because I arrived an hour before Zane landed.

"Business class is sweet, but I'm guessing not as sweet as flying in your own jet."

"It's a *company* jet."

"Semantics." I scoff on the heel of an exaggerated eye roll. "A private plane offers privileges the rest of us can only dream of."

"If that's your plea to be part of the mile-high club, just come out and say it, love," he says, low and throaty.

My breath hitches, a slight gasp leaves my lips, and my cheeks burst into flames at his suggestion.

I wasn't alluding to that, but now that he's planted the bawdy seed in my head, visions of him fucking me thirty-seven thousand feet in the air cloud my mind. I wonder if Keeley is right about the size of his—

"You naughty girl." I'm caught red-handed. "You're itching for an introduction." He allows for a pregnant pause. "I'm. Your. Man."

Blink.

Blink.

Oh.

My.

God.

I don't answer.

I can't.

That would put me in a compromising situation.

We stare at each other, seemingly frozen in time as the rest of the world busies around us.

I can't help but take him in.

He's wearing an expensive looking black coat, perfectly tailored to his tall frame, a burgundy scarf wrapped around his neck. His dark blond hair has a sexy little tousled look to it. Even the man's travel hair looks hot. His eyes are piercing into mine, the green hue more prominent thanks to the contrasting color of his scarf.

It's unlike me to gush over a man, but Zane Keller makes it easy.

He returns the favor by raking his gaze down my body before he flicks his heated stare back up to meet mine.

He speaks, putting an end to our eye-fucking session. "I look forward to spending the next few days with you, love," he says, leaning into me before dropping a kiss against my cheek. He snakes a hand around my waist, pulling me closer to him. His masculine scent envelopes me. "It's only been two days, but it feels like I haven't seen your gorgeous face in far too long." He murmurs the incendiary words into my ear.

A blush rushes from the tips of my toes throughout my body, hitting my cheeks full force. Truth be told, my body is still humming from the illicit episode on the forty-first floor of the Bymark Hotel. Those words spoken low transport me back to our naughty evening. Every cell of my body is still branded by his touch.

I pull away from him before I melt into a pool of lust. "We were at opposite ends of the country."

"We have three days to make up for it." He leans into me again. "I'm all too happy to bypass our paltry attempt at sexting. Instead of me telling you what I'll do to you, I'll just do it."

His promise jolts my senses.

We exchanged a flurry of text messages during our time apart, but unless you're in the same time zone, sexting isn't as sexy when there's a delay.

"We have a wedding to attend." *Alas.* "Along with all of the super fun pre-wedding festivities." I don't even try to conceal the sarcasm in my voice.

Imogen insisted on a big family dinner a day before the rehearsal dinner. She wanted something more informal for tonight. I had no compunction to make my terms clear with Ma. I'm determined to minimize my time spent around my ex and my backstabbing step sister by skipping dinner at Elias's parents' place. I wouldn't be able to sustain the humiliation. Zane and I will meet everybody at the bar for drinks.

My war tactic is simple.

I stay out of Imogen's way and she stays out of mine. That's why when Ma suggested I stay in my old room and Zane stays in one of the guest rooms, I shut down that preposterous talk by reminding her redheads should never wear orange under any circumstance. Prison wear would look garish on me. I just have to survive the next three days without killing the bride-to-be.

Like me, Cheater Elias Fitzsimmons is an Irish American from Boston. To keep with tradition, he'll stay at his parents' house until the wedding while my no-good stepsister stays at my parents'. Staying under the same roof as her was out of the question.

As a stubborn Irish mom determined to keep her family together, it wasn't an easy pill for Ma to swallow, but in the end, she relented.

"True," Zane says, "but when we don't have to put on a show, your fine ass is mine."

I swallow hard.

"You're ready for this?" he asks, changing the subject.

"I oscillate between 'we got this' and 'this lie is going to explode in my face', arming Imogen with more ammunition to ridicule me."

He considers me.

His hand comes up and he pushes my hair behind my ear, his thumb lingering on my cheek before stroking it gently. I lean into his touch.

"Since we've been apart, let's make sure we nail the kiss."

I don't have time to respond when his mouth crushes mine.

I drown in the passionate kiss.

Breathing is so overrated...

Chapter 13

Zane

The flight from San Francisco to Boston was all business. I wanted to wrap up as many loose ends as possible before devoting myself to the role of fake boyfriend.

I was in San Francisco, meeting with different tech companies for a custom program to boost the efficiency of the operations in the Brazil manufacturing plant all day yesterday and this morning.

The short business trip was intense, packed with back-to-back meetings throughout the city. You'd think that would be enough to preoccupy my mind.

Not in a million years.

I placed a losing bet on a tried and tested concept. Turns out, in my case, out of sight *isn't* out of mind.

I couldn't stop thinking of Shay.

Over and over, I relived our sexy encounter. Deep-diving between that woman's legs on Tuesday night on the forty-first floor of the Bymark Hotel was so fucking hot. The slightest flashback and I was hard as steel. You have no idea how difficult it is to concentrate, when your other head is doing all the thinking. I blame the beautiful redhead who was waiting at the airport with a goofy sign held over her head. No other woman has ever given me a reason to miss her... until Shay O'Hara.

During the limo ride from the airport, Shay and I update each other on our time away from New York. It's the little things that will poke holes in our well-crafted fake relationship story.

The town car comes to a stop in front of the hotel.

The chauffeur gets out, circles the front of the vehicle, and opens Shay's door.

She steps out, and I do the same.

I pull up the collar of my coat to ward off a gust of cold wind.

Shay rubs her gloved hands together before clasping her fingers in prayer.

It's so cold, I bet there are dogs stuck to fire hydrants all over Boston after taking a leak.

Our attentive driver heads to the trunk of the car to pull out our luggage.

After tipping him, I lace my gloved fingers with Shay's, and trail towards the hotel's entrance. We're staying at the Mandarin Oriental—my *pied-à-terre* when I'm in the city.

When we step into the lobby, Shay pulls against my hand, forcing me to slow my stride to a halt.

"Wait!" I cock an eyebrow. "As a Bostonian, I've never set foot in this hotel before. I've never had to. I need a minute to soak in this magical Christmas décor—" Shay stops midsentence. Then, her jaw drops.

Why does she look so freaked out?

"What is it?" I ask.

"Oh no."

She's dumbfounded.

My eyes dart around the lobby.

I spot three women walking our way, waving with both hands, huge grins stretched across their lips.

She squints. "What are they doing here?"

It's clear she knows the trio, bundled up in dark-colored coats and wrapped in colorful scarves, marching decisively in our direction.

It takes me a minute to clue in.

The tall redhead approaching us is a mirror image of the redhead standing next to me with her mouth agape. The woman who I'm guessing is Shay's mom is flanked by a shorter older blonde woman and a young woman with dark auburn hair.

"The welcoming committee?" I chance a guess.

"I didn't expect them to be here," she says in a stage-whisper. "That's my mom, leading the pack. My sister is to her right. Aunt Eileen to her left."

I do a double take. "Aunt Eileen doesn't look old enough to be a great aunt."

"I'll fill you in later," she rushes to say. "For now, it's show-time!" The nervous tremble in her voice is audible.

"Relax, Shay. I've got you."

She responds with a nod before swinging her gaze away from mine.

The young woman leaves the pack, picking up her step, launching into a light jog. "You're here!" She slams her body against Shay's, wrapping my fake girlfriend into a warm embrace.

"Briar!"

The women sway side to side like an old school metronome.

"Shay-bear! My baby is here!" Shay's older-self rushes towards the duo, circling her arms around her daughters.

Aunt Eileen lags behind, but soon joins the trio.

A group hug ensues, followed by a lot of squealing, and some jumping around.

"You guys are going to choke me," Shay says.

"Oh, stop with your complaining, lass."

I'm not sure who spoke because they're still huddled together. That said the Irish brogue is unmistakable.

"It's so good to see your beautiful face," Shay's older-self says, coming up for air. "It's been so long." She caresses Shay's cheek before clasping both cheeks in her hands. She then showers her daughter's face with kisses.

"Stop it, Ma." Shay objects like a preteen incensed by PDA.

"Shay Briony O'Hara." Shay's older-self adopts a distinctively motherly voice. "You were doing your swanky makeup thing in Australia—big tour Down Under and all—so you weren't here for Thanksgiving. I haven't seen you since the summer. You know how proud I am of you and your skyrocketing success, but I'm allowed to miss my first born."

I glance around, searching for annoyed faces, but no one seems to care we're using the lobby as a living room. Guests and hotel staff are going about their business, paying us no mind.

"If this were a covert operation, you three just blew my cover," Shay says.

"Oh, Shay-bear, tall redheads like us make terrible spies." Shay's mom removes her light blue wool hat and flicks her long hair behind her shoulders. "It's not like we can enter a room undetected."

I cut in. "I concur!"

Surprised eyes shift in my direction, as if it's only now they notice me standing there. For the first time since the three women burst onto the scene, they're quiet.

Shay's gaze meets mine, a sheepish smile curving her lips. "Zane, I'd like you to meet my crazy family," she says, her tone laced with amusement. "This is my mom, Kathleen Doherty O'Hara Manning, aka Katie. My sister, Briar Manning, and the sassy blonde is Eileen Doherty, aka Aunt Eileen." She points to each woman. "Crazy family, this is Zane Keller."

"Ladies," I say with a ceremonial head bow. "It's a pleasure."

Katie approaches me. "*A thiarcais...*" *Well, that sounded Irish to me.* "Oh my..." she brings a hand to her chest. "That's *your* Zane, Shay?" The question is intended for my fake girlfriend, but Katie doesn't shift her gaze away from mine. Her blue eyes, the color of aquamarine stones, take me in from head to toe. "*Is fear an-dathúil é.*"

"*Aontaím.*" Aunt Eileen nods.

"Ma thinks you're hot and Aunt Eileen agrees." Briar translates for me.

Shay hides her face behind her hands.

Ignoring her daughter's comment, Katie gives me another onceover. "And he's so tall." A delightful grin spreads across her face. "That's important for tall girls like us." She nods a few times. "*Your* Zane is a serious upgrade from Elias."

I bite off a smile.

Shay shakes her head.

"*That's* Zane Keller, Ma." *For the next three days, I'm technically yours, sweetheart.* "You're treating him like he's a thoroughbred you're evaluating before dropping a couple of million on it."

Katie glares at her daughter. It's the same glare my mom uses when she wants me to know she's disappointed in me without saying the words. And yes, I've been on the receiving end of that glare more times than I can count.

"Shame on you, Shay, for keeping this fine specimen a secret? From me? I'm your mother. You should've told me earlier. Is this what our relationship has come to?"

"You can stop with the guilt trip, Ma."

"Ignore our Ma's theatrics Zane. Shay and I are convinced Ma was an actress in a past life."

Touché, little sis!

Katie's lips press in a thin line.

Briar steps forward, thrusting a hand out. "It's a pleasure to meet you."

I shake her hand. "The pleasure is mine."

Her eyes rake the length of my body.

Briar is also tall, although she's a solid inch shorter than her mom and Shay. My fake girlfriend is a full-figured curvy girl, whereas her sister and mom aren't as curvy.

She studies my face. "This close, I understand Ma's reaction. Where did my sister find you?" Her green eyes sparkle with mirth. "Is there a website where I can find your kind? You know like, www.NYCHotStuff.com?"

"Briar!" Shay scolds her sister.

"I want to know as well," Aunt Eileen comes and stands in front of me, closing our little circle. She's about Briar's height, so much shorter than I am. She tilts her head way back until her gray eyes meet mine. "You give a whole new meaning to man candy, lad."

"Well, thank you," I say on the heel of a chuckle.

"I'm going to have to demand a refund," Aunt Eileen says.

I frown my confusion.

My eyes lift to meet Shay's.

She's as puzzled as I am.

Readjusting her glasses, the blonde with slender curves who can't possibly be old enough to be called great aunt gives me another thorough onceover. "I haven't seen anyone as delicious-looking as you as part of my Tinder lineup."

All eyes are on Shay's great aunt.

"You have a Tinder account?" Katie asks, widening her eyes in shock.

"Aunt Eileen, how dare you keep that from me?" Briar asks.

Aunt Eileen shrugs. "How else am I supposed to meet husband number two?" she asks matter-of-factly.

Briar focuses on me again. "Seriously, where did my sister find you? You're too good to be true."

She's in the know, so she's playing devil's advocate. Warning me her mom is a little theatrical is like the pot calling the kettle black.

Bring it on.

I motion a finger between Shay and me. "Our story is as New York as can be. The people we were supposed to meet had to bail out at the last minute. We both had survived a long and grueling day. We were already at the lounge, so we decided to forge ahead. Translation, drinks—even solo—were mandatory that night. Since we had to give up our tables, we ended up sitting next to each other at the bar. The rest is history, as they say. Isn't that right, love?"

"Love?" Briar's green eyes widen so much, they threaten to take over her face. Her head whips in her sister's direction. "He calls you, love?" She points at me. "That's his nickname for you?" Her eyes seem even wider now. "I want one of him for Christmas, too." She pouts like a toddler.

I suppress a chuckle.

The act is believable.

"I know, I know. He's a keeper." Shay plays along. "I knew at first blush, he was special."

I flash Shay a complicit smile.

I up the ante. "When my eyes locked into her ocean blue ones. I fell so hard, I'm still sporting bruises on my behind."

With a cocked eyebrow, Briar nods, seemingly impressed by my own acting abilities.

Katie is none the wiser. She clamps both hands over her heart and tilts her head to the side, her eyebrows knitted together. "Awww." She tilts her head to the side. "That is so incredibly romantic." The emotion in her voice comes out loud and clear.

"Do you have a brother?" Aunt Eileen asks me.

I chuckle. "My younger brother Xavier is off the market."

"Blimey!" She snaps her fingers. "The best ones are always taken. Cousins? Uncles? Distant cousins? Distant uncles?"

The woman is on a mission.

I rip the Band-Aid off. "The ones in America are married or in a relationship—"

"If any of your male relatives living abroad look as good as you, I'm *very* open to a long-distance relationship."

"You're impossible, Aunt Eileen," Shay says.

Her gray eyes beam up at me. "Don't I know it."

"Ma," Shay says, "when you texted me to find out if I was on my way to the hotel, I thought it was general curiosity. I didn't expect you to show up. Aren't you supposed to be at the Fitzsimmons's place?" Shay asks, shifting the topic of conversation away from me.

"Alan is already there with his parents, siblings, nieces, and nephews. He's representing the family while I welcome my baby and her new boyfriend home," Katie says.

"Thanks for giving Imogen another reason to hate me." Shay twists her lips. "She's going to be pissed off you chose me over her."

"That's because you're *the better* half-sister," Briar says.

"I love you too, kid, but I doubt Imogen will appreciate being upstaged over the next three days by *the better* half-sister."

"I'm happy to delay the time we're going to spend sitting down at a table across from your ex-boyfriend and his family, pretending we're all happy douchebag Elias is marrying my devious half-sister," Briar says.

"Briar! Language!" Katie's tone is scolding.

Briar's retort is quick. "I agreed to attend the farce of a wedding and witness two cheaters tying the knot, it doesn't mean I have to stick my head into the sand like an ostrich, Ma."

Sounds like Imogen is a gem.

"Speaking of dinner..." Aunt Eileen places a hand over her tummy. "If I'm feeling poorly. It must be indigestion. I should stay home."

Katie shoots her a pointed stare. "Don't you dare pull the upset stomach card on me, Aunt Eileen. We both know you *aren't* feeling poorly. You were jumping up and down at the idea of seeing Shay again."

Aunt Eileen rolls her eyes. "Imogen is bloody insufferable and Elias Fitzsimmons lacks balls."

Much respect to Aunt Eileen for not diluting her frank talk and disdain for the couple on my account.

"This isn't about..." —Katie stops, her eyes scouring around us. I'm not sure if she's looking for the right words or if she's keeping a vigilant eye out for eavesdroppers— "my ungrateful stepdaughter. This is about my husband. We need to show Alan our solidarity."

"Fine," Aunt Eileen crosses her arms over her chest. "I don't care if the Archangel Gabriel comes down from heaven, knocks on my door, and offers to make me immortal, I'm not showing that little witch with the serpent tongue an ounce of kindness—even on her wedding day. And, I can't guarantee I'll smile on the bloody family photos."

Katie turns her attention to me. "I apologize for the family drama, Zane."

I lift my hands in truce. "I'm no stranger to family drama.

Things can get heated pretty fast when people disagree, especially at weddings."

"Half Brazilian?" Katie asks.

"Yes. And half British."

"Do you have any Irish in you?" Katie's question takes me by surprise.

"I'm not certain..." I hesitate. "Maybe on my dad's side?!"

Did I need an ancestry.com search to pull this charade off?

"But you celebrate Christmas?" Katie asks.

"Yes, I do. Both my parents are Catholics. Mom, being Brazilian, is devout."

Katie claps, glee shimmering in her eyes. "That means you and Shay will give me beautiful Catholic grandbabies!"

Whoa, lady! That goes above and beyond the arrangement I have with your daughter.

"*Ma!*"

Shay looks mortified.

"What?" Katie shrugs. "How much longer do I have to wait to become a grandmother?"

Knowing what it's like to have a pushy mom, desperate for grandbabies, I bet my fortune this conversation is torture and punishment for my fake girlfriend.

"Beauty may be in the eye of the beholder, but you weren't guaranteed beautiful—or tall—babies with Elias," she says. "Zane is the definition of when one door closes, another one opens..."

Briar chimes in. "My sister stepped up her game with you. You're everything Elias Fitzsimmons will never be. I can't wait to get to know you better."

"I'm honored."

Aunt Eileen isn't done sharing her two cents. "That still doesn't mean Shay shouldn't kick Elias in the junk at the church when the priest asks if anyone objects to the union." Her evil grin is both hilarious and frightening.

You don't want to be on Aunt Eileen's bad side.

I'm not sure what beef she has with Imogen, but they have history.

Katie gives her aunt a warning stare. "Aunt Eileen! Shay will not harm another human being—even a despicable one. There will be no violence. I raised her better than that." Her features morph into the wicked expression her aunt was sporting a minute ago. "My daughter will take the highroad." A devilish gleam shines bright in her eyes. "She'll *upstage* the bride."

And here I thought Brazilians had cornered the market when it comes to dramatic and unpredictable weddings...

Chapter 14

Zane

The apple doesn't fall far from the tree.

After meeting Shay's mom, sister, and great aunt, it's no wonder she's a feisty little one. Katie, Briar, and Aunt Eileen, entertained us until they had no other choice but to head to the dinner at the Fitzsimmons's house. Alan had to call his wife five times, before she budged. All three women kept looping from one animated story to the next. Shay gave me a crash course on the dynamics between her and her stepsister. The three women who just decamped from here were the equivalent of a PhD.

My fake girlfriend apologized profusely for the unexpected greeting committee, but I brushed it off. My family is as exuberant... if not more.

"Knock, knock, knock," I rap my knuckles against the door of our adjacent hotel rooms. "Are you decent?"

"I am!" Shay shouts, amusement in her voice.

Beggars can't be choosers.

Given this is a last-minute trip right before the holidays, the picking was slim. Thanks to my VIP status, I was first on the wait list for a cancellation. Since we're still virtually strangers, the connecting rooms I scored offer the best of both worlds. After checking in and a shower to wash off the grime from traveling, it's time to hit the town.

"Can I come in?" I double check.

"Yes!"

I let myself into her room and freeze.

Holy shit.

"Your mom suggested you upstage the bride at the wedding, not at tonight's casual event." I wink.

"Flattery will get you everywhere."

I stalk towards her.

That. Fucking. Dress.

Those. Fucking. Boots.

Shay selected a little black number with a sexy neckline that accentuates her phenomenal cleavage. The dress hits her below the knee and flatters her curves to perfection. Her high heel red boots should be certified as objects of scintillating seduction.

Goddamn, the woman is a bombshell.

Unable to resist, I reach out to stroke a rounded breast.

She places her hand on my forearm, but I'm not sure if it's to stop me or urge me on.

I vote for the latter.

I take my time feeling her heavy breast in my palm.

She moans with pleasure.

I can't wait to have these in my mouth.

"If I wasn't already your fake boyfriend, I'd be campaigning like a politician with a one-track mind for the position because you look so fucking hot in that dress." Her cheeks turn a bewitching shade of pink. Damn, I love it when I do that to her. "Is it one of ours?"

"It's not."

"That's a *bloody* shame."

"Please don't tell me Aunt Eileen rubbed off on you."

"My dad is British and my younger brother has a strong British accent."

"You two didn't grow up in the same country?" Surprise is audible in her voice.

"Once the seed was planted in his head, Xavier's desire to become a professional soccer player became an obsession. He moved to London when he was a teenager and lived with family as he pursued his dream. So, the accent rubbed off on him."

"I see."

"Speaking of your family," I say, "there's no way Aunt Eileen is a great aunt."

"She is."

"She was either blessed with great genes or she has a highly-skilled plastic surgeon."

"Good one." She chuckles. "Aunt Eileen was a surprise baby. My great-grandmother had a hard time conceiving. After many miscarriages, she had my grandma. My grandparents were hoping for a second child, but no matter how much they tried, it never happened. Then one day, Aunt Eileen happened. There's a twenty-year difference between my grandma and my great aunt."

"That's a significant age difference," I say. "When you gave me the cliff notes of your life on Tuesday, you didn't mention your grandparents."

"Mom was thirteen when her parents died. My grandfather had a conference in Des Moines, Iowa. At the time he was the chief accountant for a state grocery market chain that had been bought out by a bigger fish. His new boss had sent him for further training. Since Ma was at summer camp for two weeks, my grandparents decided to drive and make it a road trip. They died in a car accident on the way back home. Aunt Eileen was twenty-three when she became my mom's legal guardian. She was recently widowed, too. She was born in Ireland, but came to America when she was eighteen to live with her older sister —my grandmother—who had moved here years prior. Eventually, she fell head over heels for the all-American boy next door—a soldier to boot. A new family had moved into the neighborhood. When the son came home on a leave of duty, he caught Aunt Eileen's eye. They started dating and it didn't take long for them to marry. Two months after her husband was deployed on another tour, she found out she was pregnant. Three months later, her husband was killed in the line of duty. They were married less than eight months. The news devastated her, causing her to lose the baby. Five months later, her parents died. Then, her sister and brother-in-law die. Poor Aunt Eileen was grieving her husband, unborn child, parents, and sister when she took on the responsibility of her teenage niece. There's only a decade difference between Ma and Aunt Eileen. That's why calling her 'great aunt' doesn't suit her."

Good God.

"I understand why Aunt Eileen gives off the vibe of a strong woman."

"You summed it up perfectly," Shay says. "Aunt Eileen sacrificed a lot to make sure Ma had a good life despite the fact she had lost both parents. She made sure Ma didn't lose her Irish heritage and roots. None of us speaks Irish as well as my great aunt, but she made sure Ma spoke it. The same applies to Briar and me."

"I like Aunt Eileen."

"It's mutual."

"I hope it's not only because of my *good looks*." I wink.

"It runs deeper than that," she says. "Aunt Eileen's bullshit detector is set to high. She doesn't sugarcoat things, she's allergic to political correctness, and if she doesn't like you, she does little to hide it."

"I'm on her approved list."

"Unlike my ex."

"What did he do to get on her shit list?"

She snorts. "He was on it from day one."

I like Aunt Eileen even more.

"The first time I came home with Elias for Thanksgiving, Aunt Eileen barely acknowledged him, stating he came across as wishy-washy. Untrustworthy, even. The second Thanksgiving and Christmas were pretty much the same. Aunt Eileen never warmed up to him. We all thought she was being unreasonable—"

"Her gut instinct was right."

Shay nods. "You get high marks for winning her over so early in the game."

Too bad our relationship has an expiration date—

What the hell?

Where did that come from?

I veer the conversation to safer ground. "Back to this dress..."

"You're obsessed with this dress."

"I am."

"Is it because it's not one of yours?"

"It's because it looks fucking good on you, love," I set her straight. "What about the lingerie?" I ask.

She bites against her lower lip, her big blue eyes shining bright with mischief.

"Answer me."

"Maybe."

"I want to know which one of our collection you shimmied your sexy ass into. And I want to see it."

"What if I told you instead of showing you?"

"Not good enough."

She shakes her head. "You have a serious lingerie fetish."

"It's a professional hazard, but when it comes to you, you're right, it's a fetish. Sue me. The glimpse I caught on Tuesday was a mere tease."

She places a hand on her waist and juts a curvy hip out. "A mere tease?" Her tone is indignant. "You ripped my new panties to shreds and you made empty promises—"

"I didn't give you a timeline as to when I'd replace them. I haven't wavered on my promise. I intend on making sure you have a lifetime supply of Sexy Curves Lingerie."

That seals the deal.

Her expression softens.

I soldier on. "Now do I get what I want? Give me a peek?"

"Why do I get this nagging feeling you're playing me?"

She's onto me.

"I'm not playing you. That said, I'd love to play *with* you before we leave."

"I'm going to look like a hot mess if I lie down."

I study her gorgeous face.

Her perfectly applied makeup is flawless and her hair is pulled back tight in a low bun, betraying her preposterous suggestion. I'm willing to bet good money that, after multiple orgasms, she'd still be the portrayal of perfection.

"Who said anything about lying down?"

She blinks up at me, stupefied.

Her eyebrows draw down. "If I don't lie down on a sofa or bed, how is it going to work?"

Such innocence.

"So, you're in for a little dirty fun?"

"I'm curious about the logistics."

Bullshit.

"Step back."

She doesn't move.

"You said you were curious about the logistics."

"I am."

"It'll make more sense if I show you instead of telling you."

"Okay."

"You trust me, Shay?"

She nods.

"I want to hear it."

"Yes, I trust you." The words come out breathy.

"In that case, I expect you to do as you're told."

Like a good little girl, she obeys.

"Again."

She takes another small step back.

"One more."

She doesn't argue.

I hold an index finger in the air for emphasis. "One more step."

She looks over her shoulder. When her eyes meet mine, the lust I read in them makes my cock jolt.

She just clued in.

"We're pushing the envelope." *Damn right we are.* Her futile argument is a contrast to the heated gaze she's leveling me with. "Zane, when you're done with me—"

"You'll come hard with my name on your lips."

Step.

"And you'll look like a woman whose fake boyfriend is obsessed with pleasuring her."

Step.

"Because I am, Shay."

Step.

"For the past two days, I've been consumed with fantasies of you coming all over my face like you did so beautifully at the Bymark Hotel."

Step.

I'm standing right in front of her.

I place one hand on her cheek, another on her hip, and push her back against the wall and hold her in place.

"That was the hottest encounter of my life," she admits. "I swear I was floating."

With a growl, I crash my lips against hers, devouring her mouth in a possessive kiss.

We're all lips and tongues.

I slide my fingers down her face until they reach her chin. I tip her head back so I can kiss her harder.

She moans.

The delightful sound sends a jolt to my hard cock.

I deepen the kiss, owning her delicious mouth.

When I break our embrace, we're both panting, chests heaving, lips trembling.

This woman must've put a spell on me. I've never been this turned on from a kiss.

Through half-lidded eyes, we stare at each other.

"I've never been kissed like that," she admits between heavy breaths.

"Good thing I agreed to be your fake boyfriend, so I could show you how you deserve to be kissed."

"Lucky me."

"And you're about to get luckier."

Her eyes drop to the bulge between my legs, and she swallows hard.

"When is it *your* turn to get lucky?" she asks.

I bring my hand to my cock, stroking the outline of my erection.

"You want me to fuck your face?" My voice is rough and husky.

She stares up at me, eyelashes fluttering a mile a minute.

When she remains speechless, I reach for her hand and bring it to my crotch.

She cups my cock, squeezing hard.

A low groan—a mix of pleasure and pain as my balls tingle inside my boxer briefs—drops from my lips.

Tilting my hips forward as I keep the pressure of her hand against my cock, I grind against her palm.

"God, you're hard. And huge." She whispers her astonishment like we're in church.

"It's all for you."

She strokes my cock with more vigor.

"Such an eager little girl. You want my cock?"

A sly smile splits her face.

"I don't want the first time I fuck you to be a quickie," I say. "I want to take my time with you, so I can draw as many orgasms from you as I can."

"I've said it before. Your mouth needs to come with a warning."

"Funny, you don't complain about my mouth when I'm kissing you or devouring your pussy."

She blushes. "You're doing it again."

"Is that your way of saying you don't want me to do the filthy things I did to you in New York? Message received."

I make to leave, but she clamps a hand on my wrist, stopping me.

"I never said that."

I hold her gaze for several breaths.

"You want me to do filthy things to you or not?"

She nods.

I open my mouth to demand words, but she precedes me.

"Yes, yes I want that. For the past two days, imagery of your head between my legs was my go-to as I made myself come."

My cock twitches.

"You touched your pussy, thinking of me?"

"Yes."

"With your fingers or your toys?"

"Both."

She upped the ante with that perfect answer.

"I've been rock hard for the past two days, since the last time I had my mouth on your pussy." I kick the inside of her ankle. "Spread them wide for me."

She parts her legs, assuming the position.

With my eyes locked onto hers, I undo the buttons of my black shirt before rolling up the sleeves to the elbows.

I drop to my knees in front of her.

She gasps.

Urgency courses through me as I slide my hands under her skirt, caressing my way up her thighs. I expect to discover the lacey edge of her stay-up stockings, but I'm dead wrong.

My eyes fly up to hers.

"You're wearing a garter belt?"

"I didn't expect for anyone to see them."

"We both know that's a blatant lie."

She giggles.

My hands celebrate this woman's body as they slide her skirt up until she's fully exposed to me.

"Holy fuck!"

Lust tears through me like a bushfire.

Her curvy body is clad in our Savage Heart collection. The red satin trio of bra, panties, and garter belt against her pale creamy skin is sinful. The nude stockings accentuate the milkiness of her skin.

I shake my head in admiration

"You're not going to rip my panties this time?" she asks, worried.

"No. These look too perfect on you to rip to shreds."

"Are you saying the other pair didn't look good on me?"

Sassy little thing.

"Everything was rushed on Tuesday when we were on the forty-first floor of the Bymark Hotel. I wanted to taste you so badly..." I let my words trail as my eyes feast on her heavenly body. "Now, I can take my time and admire every glorious inch of you." I'm in awe. "And, Goddammit, Shay, you're my wet fantasy come true."

"Zane, you don't have to—"

"I mean every word I said, Shay."

She responds with a shy smile. "How did you know what I was going to say?"

"It's written all over your beautiful face, love."

"Oh."

"Do you think I'd lie to you?"

She responds with a one-shoulder shrug. "No one's ever wanted me this much."

"Even though I was laying it on thick for your mom's and aunt's benefit, what I told your sister earlier was the truth. You knocked me to my ass when I first laid eyes on you. I thought the distance might dampen whatever it is we have going on between us, but it didn't. I couldn't stop thinking of you. You were constantly on my mind, and I was consumed with the idea of having you melting all over my tongue again."

She doesn't have a comeback.

"I need you to pull those panties aside for me."

With tentative fingers, she obeys, exposing her beautiful pussy.

"Your job is to make sure they're out of the way. Mine is to take care of your pussy."

Her big blue eyes bloom with desire.

I lean in close and fill my nostrils with the scent of her arousal.

Salty, sexy, and ready.

"Fuck, I love you like this—exposed, wet, and needy," I say and slide a finger between her luscious pussy lips. She moans softly as I scoop up her juices before bringing my finger to my mouth, tasting her sweetness on my tongue.

"You taste divine, love." I slide that finger deep.

She gasps, then presses her lips together, as if she's biting off a moan.

"Unlike the VIP Den, you can be as loud as you want here," I say. "Give me all your moans, grunts, groans, sobs, and cries. I want it all. Got it?"

She nods.

I cut her some slack and don't demand words.

I resume my mission, stroking back and forth between her clit and puckered hole.

"Oh, God."

I tease her like that until her body trembles.

"You're going to kill me." Her voice is shaky.

"Not before I make you come."

I part her lips with my fingers and bury my face between her legs, flick the tip of her clit with my impatient tongue, and toy with her hard nub.

A growl rumbles up my chest.

I plunge two fingers deep inside her, pumping in and out, beckoning her orgasm.

"Zane!"

My tongue skates every which way between her pussy lips, languishing in her juices.

She whines and thrusts her hips forward. "Sweet Mother of God."

Greedy girl.

My hungry mouth devours her dripping pussy with gusto.

She grips my hair and babbles incoherently, as she rides my face.

Thud.

Thud.

Thud.

My eyes dart up as she throws her head back against the wall.

A groan works its way up my chest.

"Dear God, yes! This is so fucking good. Don't stop."

I show her no mercy.

My fingers slide in and out of her in a ruthless cadence until her pussy clenches tight around my sweet intrusion.

"Yes, oh God, yes. Make me come. Please make me come. Zane, please. I'm begging you."

Jesus Christ.

Giving her permission to be as loud as she needs to, is like breaking the dam of a raging river.

The more I lick, the more her voice crescendos.

Her grunts, sighs, and gasps echo in the room like the chorus of a porn video clip.

My impatient cock responds to her throaty pleads, desperate to give her another reason to call out my name.

I glance up again.

The expression on her face is so hedonistic, it causes my balls to tighten.

Now I'm starting to think I was a fool to delay fucking her.

Her shaky breaths let me know she's close.

Use my tongue.

Give me what I want.

Come hard for me.

A wicked thought crosses my mind.

I pull my mouth away from her pussy, keeping my fingers lodged deep inside her.

She doesn't have time to protest.

I crook my long digits, searching and finding her sweet spot, putting an end to her groan of protest.

I rub her there, determined to pull an epic orgasm from her.

Her shallow breathing becomes more and more ragged with each stroke of my fingers.

Her body goes rigid and she lets out a choking sound.

She glides against the wall, sitting on my hand, fucking my fingers.

Bullseye!

I thrust in and out of her.

We're perfectly in sync as I stroke her clit with one hand, twisting my fingers in and out of her with the other.

"I— I— Oh— Fuck— Zane—"

My fingers skate across her clit with more velocity.

She tenses up, then like a mantra, she chants my name over and over and over again.

And then it happens.

Her juices gush from her pussy like a fucking geyser.

I drink it all up like a man who hasn't had a drop of water in weeks. No way am I letting any of this sweetness go to waste.

Her cries of ecstasy as her abundant juices keep flowing into my mouth make me feel like a fucking king.

That was hot.

Her limp body slides down the wall.

Fuck.

In a blink of an eye, I'm on my feet, pulling her spent body into my arms, holding her close.

"I got you, love."

Her curvy body trembles in my arms.

I don't rush her.

With lidded eyes, she glances up at me.

"This doesn't make any sense," she says in a faint voice.

"What doesn't make sense?"

"What you do to my body." She shakes her head as if she's having a conversation with herself. "I didn't even know my body could do that."

"From the way you've responded to me since our first encounter, I'd say you've been waiting for me your entire life, Shay." My lips curve. "And to think, I haven't even fucked you yet..."

Chapter 15

Shay

There's fashionably late and there's late, thanks to Zane's wicked fingers and skillful tongue. We fell into the latter category as we rushed to Slaney's—the Irish pub where Imogen and Elias's friends and family post-dinner gathering is taking place. I'm more of a *foe*, but tonight, I'm willing to put water in my wine. After all, I'm still levitating. I suspect I'll be in a state of bliss for hours to come.

To be perfectly honest, I feel like someone new. Someone who knows things few women ever will. My fake boyfriend didn't administer my first O. BOB holds that title. Heck, until Tuesday, BOB was my guaranteed go-to boyfriend for a good time. Zane Keller dethroned BOB. My fake boyfriend sent me flying off a cliff in a spectacular way. The heady experience was so transcending, so core-shaking, so all-encompassing, it's like I grew wings to fly closer to the sun.

In one crazy, reckless moment, I made a decision that could've backfired.

It was the only way I knew how to save face.

I lucked out. I scored the perfect wedding date *and* the

perfect lover. This is an instance where getting more than you bargained for is a darn good thing.

After making me come so hard, I thought I was going to lose my mind, Zane wanted an encore. I thought he was a little ambitious and a lot delusional. No way was my body going to be able to perform that kind of prowess twice in a row.

Heck, it was a first for me.

I thought that sort of craziness only happened on Pornhub.

He proved me wrong.

Things got a little wet after my first orgasm, but after the second climax, it's like the hotel room was flooded. We had to jump into the shower and change clothes. My cocky seducer tried to trick me, suggesting taking a shower together would save time. I was having none of that. I had to lock the door to the adjacent room to keep him out. For extra precautionary measures, I requested he wait for me in the lobby. Zane Keller is too dangerous... and too irresistible.

Had I not put my foot down, we'd be more than an hour late.

We were cutting it so short, we had to give up our reservation at a chic French bistro not far from the hotel.

It's pub food for us tonight!

As I wait for Zane to return from the coat check, I pull out my phone and text my sister to let her know we arrived.

"You clean up nicely, love," Zane says, returning by my side.

"Right back at ya!"

"You were born to wear dresses," he says, brushing his hazel green eyes up and down the length of my body.

"I like my jeans and comfy outfits, but during this time of the year, I feel it's important to up my fashion game."

"Mission accomplished."

We had to send everything we were wearing to the hotel's

dry-cleaning service... epic orgasm and all. Even my beloved red boots were casualties. The hotel employee assured me they'll be as good as new by the time they're done with them. All in all, it was a bit of a mess, but God, was it ever worth it. Lucky for me, my makeup and hair survived my multiple orgasms. I was careful under the shower with my face and I used a shower cap to prevent my hair from getting wet. Once I was done, it was a question of a quick touch up, and slipping into fresh underwear and clothes. The navy-blue dress with a seductive V-neckline I selected for tonight, fits the bill perfectly. The same goes for the burgundy high heel boots.

Zane looks dashing in head to toe black. Very New York.

He slides a possessive arm around my waist, pulling me closer to his body. "You look all put together," he says, his lips flirting with my earlobe. "No one would ever know half an hour ago, you were riding my tongue like the dirty little slut you are."

Before I can respond, he takes my mouth hard.

My mind is reeling from the passionate kiss, him calling me a slut, and me not objecting.

A wave of pleasure crashes over me, and my pussy flutters with excitement, as if the greedy bitch hasn't already had way more fun than should be permitted.

What is this man doing to me?

After a long beat, his lips part from mine, leaving my knees wobbling underneath me.

How the hell does he keep doing that to me?

I expected us to put on a show when we were in public for the benefit of an audience. Not when it was the two of us.

This moment is so intimate, too intimate for a fake couple.

My heart skitters, thundering against my chest. It's more than arousal. It's like my insides jiggle like Jell-O.

I curse the short-lived nature of our relationship.

Silly Shay, you're getting things confused in your head.

I'm about to open my mouth to deflect the situation before I lose sight of the arrangement we have, when Briar speaks.

"You're here!"

I pull from Zane's embrace, cursing the distance, and turn around to face my sister.

She pulls me into her arms and hugs me.

After a long moment of us rocking side to side, I break our embrace.

She treats Zane to the same warm welcome.

Not to be forgotten, Aunt Eileen demands hugs from me and my fake boyfriend.

We're happy to oblige.

"Imogen is going to hate you for looking this good," my sister says, taking in my outfit.

"Haters will be haters." Aunt Eileen scoffs. "And that woman has a lot of hating in her."

Yes, she does.

My sister studies me, eyes squinted.

It's so intense, it's as if she's memorizing every one of my freckles.

"Nice makeup." She's studying my face with the laser focus attention of a plastic surgeon assessing a patient. "Is that a new blush? It seems a lot rosier than usual. I want that glow." Briar says that like a kid who wants another piece of birthday cake.

"It's a special edition. Isn't that right, love?" Zane reminds us of his presence.

I squint my eyes at him in a menacing way.

He cocks his head to the side, his gaze full of mirth.

"Hmmm..." Briar's green eyes ping-pong from mine to Zane's. "There seems to be a little conspiracy going on here." She motions a finger between my fake boyfriend and me.

Aunt Eileen offers her perspective. "That's because they're perfectly in tune with each other. I bet they're cosmically aligned." *Oh, no.* My great aunt opens her mouth to add something—no doubt requesting Zane's astrology sign—but my sister soldiers on in her crusade.

"Can I borrow the new blush? I promise *to never* give it back."

"I applied a little more than usual. That's all," I deflate the situation. Time to veer the conversation. "You didn't have to come out here to greet us—"

"Yes, we did," Aunt Eileen pipes up. "Had you not texted to let us know you were running late, I was going to pull an excuse from my arse and get the hell out of here."

I furrow my eyebrows. "Aren't Ma and Alan in there?"

Briar and Aunt Eileen shake their heads.

"How come?" I ask.

"The Fitzsimmons suggested the *adults*," Aunt Eileen makes air quotes, "stay behind to enjoy spiked eggnog, classic Christmas music, and conversation, instead of heading to a bar," Aunt Eileen says with an exaggerated eye roll. "I bailed out. I can't stomach eggnog. Spiked or not." With a grimace contorting her features, she shudders in revulsion.

"Oh," I say. My eyes shift left to right as I consider if we shouldn't make a run for it since Ma and my stepdad won't be here to act as buffers.

"Katie wanted to slip away, but she's putting Alan first," Aunt Eileen says.

"Ma is in a tough situation."

Briar's head whips in my direction. "One your stepsister *and* ex-boyfriend put her in."

"I haven't forgotten!" I snap at my sister. "It's just that it must be difficult for Ma. Same for Alan."

"It's way worse for Alan," Aunt Eileen says. "Through no fault of his own, the poor lad helped in the conception of a whore's knickers"—I'm sure you guessed that's not a term of endearment—"which is how he finds himself caught in the middle of an unpleasant stepsister versus stepsister war. Since Imogen has always been a *raicleach* to Katie—"

I meet Zane's gaze. "That means, bitch." I keep my response low enough so my voice doesn't carry.

He nods. "Got it."

"I'll need to give you a crash course on Irish swear words so you can keep up, lad," Aunt Eileen says.

"I'm game."

"You're a keeper." Although the compliment is addressed to my fake boyfriend, my great aunt's gaze is trained on me.

Zane has her wrapped around his little finger.

She loops back to her explanation. "As I was saying, your ma doesn't feel as torn as your stepdad does. A year later, and the man is still self-flagellating for his daughter's *striapach* ways." She shifts her attention to Zane. "That means, slutty ways."

"Copy that," he says.

My stepdad took the highroad as we all navigated this prickly road Imogen and Elias paved for us. I had to beg him to stop apologizing for his daughter's behavior. I didn't realize the guilt by association was still a burden.

Aunt Eileen keeps talking. "I like Elias's parents as much as I like the bloody wanker. I held up my part of the bargain and showed up. I had enough of pretending the Fitzsimmons's spawn wasn't a cheater and this upcoming wedding didn't stink to high heaven. The only reason I'm willing to breathe the same air as Imogen and Elias is because I'm dying to see their reaction when they meet Shay's man candy. Ha!" Aunt Eileen claps her hands before rubbing them together as if she was trying to start a fire like they did in the prehistoric days. "That's going to be priceless." More hand rubbing. "The other reason I'm here is because I wanted to spend more time with Zane." She cozies up next to my fake boyfriend and interlaces her arms around his, looking up at him with fondness. "You're good people." She beams up at him. "I can sense it."

He winks. "Right back at ya."

Aunt Eileen's gray eyes find mine. "He's *perfect* Shaybear." She stage-whispers her approval in a pronounced Irish lilt, as if said perfection wasn't standing right next to her.

I shake my head.

She doesn't even know him.

Then again, she's such a good judge of character.

"How many people showed up?" I ask, pointing a finger over my sister's head.

She's about to answer when a man's voice booms from the speakers.

"Unleash your inner superstar! Karaoke kicks off in an hour, boys and girls. Brave souls can now come up and add their names to the list."

My eyes widen. "This is a karaoke bar?"

"Yes." My sister scrunches her nose. "Didn't you Google the place before coming?"

No. I was too busy coming my head off.

"It's in line with the *Hollywood theme wedding*." Briar adopts an affected tone that would make a soap opera star green with envy. "Imogen stole the idea from the movie *My Best Friend's Wedding*."

I scoff. "She's taking this way too far."

As a failed actress, it's no surprise Imogen would want her Oscar night. Her theme wedding is the closest she'll ever get to walking the red carpet.

"You should've seen what was on the menu for dinner." Briar rolls her eyes. "We were treated to an Academy Oscar menu—aka, fancy finger food and itsy-bitsy pieces of cake.

Everything was skewered with toothpicks, so we didn't end up smearing our lipstick."

"Finger food? That's it?" I ask.

"*Fancy* finger food, lass," Aunt Eileen says. "No deviled eggs, or pigs in blankets, or celery sticks stuffed with cream cheese, or pizza bites. Audible gasp!" Sarcasm drips off her.

"Those options are far too low brow," Briar says. "Commoners serve those at their pre-wedding receptions. Not the future wife of a prominent doctor."

"Everything was tiny, tedious and pretentious. Like the bride-to-be herself," Aunt Eileen says.

It takes everything in me not to crack up at the exaggerated Irish brogue.

"Spending more time with 'Imogen + Elias Forever' wasn't high up on my list, but like Aunt Eileen, I'm up for a little drama," Briar says. "Since you weren't aware Ma and Alan were staying behind, I figured I'd show up. I didn't want you to hate me until the end of time for not giving you the heads up or acting as a buffer."

"Thanks for having my back, kid."

"What are baby sisters for?" She responds with an exaggerated wink. "The pub's highly-rated classic Irish menu was also a big selling point. Aunt Eileen and I are debating between the shepherd's pie and the roast beef dip sandwich—the dipping *jus* is made with Guinness. We were waiting for you guys to arrive before ordering."

Zane chimes in. "Both options are right up my alley. I'm famished after that *vigorous* workout."

Thanks for throwing me under the bus, buddy.

I give him a *Are you fucking kidding me* look.

He responds with a *What?* look.

To his credit, the man is a trooper for patiently standing

there like a Roman statue while the three of us jabber on, so I cut him some slack.

"You're so dedicated." Briar's green eyes roam up and down Zane's tall frame. "No wonder you're in such great shape—"

"Why am I not surprised Shay O'Hara would try to make this weekend about her?" A voice that grates at my nerves with the same annoyance as nails scraping down a blackboard, chirps, letting her know of her presence.

I turn around to face my nemesis.

A five-feet tall bundle of pure venom stilted on super high heel designer black boots stares up at me, light brown eyes narrowed with menacing determination.

Imogen Manning, aka my despicable stepsister.

As usual, the twenty-eight-year-old blonde is dressed to kill, the chip on her shoulder as present as always.

Shouldn't all brides-to-be have a sunny disposition two days before their wedding?

"Imogen," I say, my lips frozen in a half smile. My eyes shift to the lap dog—aka, my thirty-three-year-old cheating asshole ex—standing by her side. "Elias."

"Hey, Shay!" he says, as if we're long-lost friends. "Glad you could make it. After all, we're gonna be family," Elias says with a forced Boston accent.

In New York he adopts a more neutral accent, but the moment he crosses state lines, he's all Southie and shit. *Make up your mind, douchebag.*

I roll my eyes in response.

"It's true," he says. "You're going to be my sis-in-law."

Quit while you're ahead, jerk.

I dig my fingernails into the palms of my hands, so I don't reflexively punch my ex's lights out.

Aunt Eileen mutters a curse under her breath.

Elias's hazel brown eyes shift away from mine. "Hey, Aunt

Eileen, you have to be nice to me. I'm your soon-to-be great-nephew," Elias says. The pitiful expression on his face is as lame as his comment.

"It's *Eileen* to you." My great aunt just about growls at him.

Elias flinches, raking a nervous hand through his brown hair.

At least he's smart enough to shut his mouth.

"I was wondering why it was taking *my* baby sister"—the possessiveness in Imogen's statement is pathetic—"and Eileen so much time in the bathroom." She crosses her arms over her chest. "Now I know."

After a bitchy backstabbing move, Aunt Eileen forbade my stepsister to call her aunt. Both her and her soon-to-be husband are excommunicado. Imogen shifts her predatory gaze to me, her contemptuous expression matching mine. She jerks her head, sending a curtain of natural dark blonde hair behind her back. Then, she shoves her nose up as though I'm beneath her.

She's about to spout shit from between those red-painted lips.

"You *had* to make an entrance," she says in a huff. "The next three days are about *me*." She stabs a finger at her chest, before turning the weapon in my direction. "*Not* you."

What broom got stuck up her ass?

I cock a trembling eyebrow, my eye already twitching in rage. I ready myself to rip her a new one, but my great aunt cuts in.

"No one here is a child and no one here has limited mental capacity." Aunt Eileen snaps at Imogen. "Stop reminding us it's *your day,* or *your weekend,* or *your wedding*. We bloody well know." She huffs, exasperated. "That's why we're all here... *including* Shay."

"For your information, Shay wasn't trying to steal the spotlight from you," Briar comes to my defense. "Aunt Eileen and I decided to come out and meet her after she texted us to announce her arrival. If you thought we were going to the bathroom, that's on you."

"Who's this?" Elias asks, jerking his chin at the man standing next to me.

"He's Shay's incredible boyfriend," Aunt Eileen says.

Playing it up for our disgruntled audience, I loop an arm around my fake boyfriend's muscular arm. "Zane Keller, I'd like to introduce you to my stepsister, Imogen Manning, and her soon-to-be-husband, Elias Fitzsimmons."

"Congratulations on your big day." Zane thrusts a hand in Imogen's direction.

Even in her super high-heeled boots, she has to look way up to meet Zane's gaze. Alan is six feet tall. To Imogen's chagrin, she took after her mom who's only five feet tall. To her despair, she was never able to become a model and steal my thunder.

Imogen extends a hand, shaking Zane's, eyelashes batting a mile a minute.

"You're Shay's boyfriend?" Disbelief colors her voice.

"I know, I'm a lucky guy," Zane says.

"Hey, man." Elias extends a hand. "Pleased to meet you."

Zane lets go of Imogen's hand and takes Elias's in a firm grip.

My ex-boyfriend winces and grimaces between clenched teeth. "Christ."

Zane lets go of his hand. "Congratulations on your big day." It didn't hit me the first time around, but now it does. He didn't say *pleased to meet you* to either Imogen or Elias. As if I needed another reason to like him more.

Aunt Eileen is right, the man is *perfect*.

"Thanks," Elias says. "That's a hell of a handshake. What do you do for a living? Are you a wrestler or something? You sure have the punishing grip and the height for it. Seriously, you're the size of a freaking sequoia." He cracks up at his own stupid joke.

Elias's cackling is a high-pitched series of short gigglelike sounds. Like a hyena.

Aunt Eileen rolls her eyes hard.

Briar looks at him like he's a moron—which he is.

I blink at him, unable to believe I dated this imbecile.

The amount of ignorant testosterone emanating from this man is staggering.

"Don't be ridiculous, Elias!" Imogen admonishes her idiot of a fiancé, her tone biting. "He's not a wrestler. He's not sporting that trashy fake tan look." She zooms in on me. That arrogant chin lifts again. "You had me fooled for a minute there, Shay. Well played," she says with a boastful grin before a maniac chortle spills from her.

My eyes bounce from Zane's, to my sister's, to Aunt Eileen's.

From their expressions, I'm not the only one who's stumped.

I frown my confusion. "What do you mean?"

Imogen smirks.

She's savoring the moment.

She-devil.

I adopt a bored tone. "Are you going to say what's on your mind, or do we have to wait until Easter?"

"Yesterday, when I spoke to Dad, he said you were still single. I wasn't interested in knowing about your personal life, I wanted to know if you were going to be a no-show at my wedding. But you know how he is. He has a soft spot for you—God knows why, you're not his flesh and blood—so he went on and on and on about you." *She's begging for it.* "In any case, one day you're single, and now you show up with this guy?" She points a manicured finger at Zane. "He's an actor... unless he's an escort. Two professions that are readily available in New York." My hand is twitching to slap her across the face. "What's the rate of a *professional companion* these days, anyway?" My stepsister's lips set in a self-righteous line that makes her look like the evil witch she is.

Elias cackles. "Good one, babe."

Yep, he's pussy whipped.

As much as I despise these two, I must admit, they deserve each other.

Zane responds before I have a chance to put my ex in his place and dispel my stepsister's erroneous conclusion.

"If I were charging for my services, it would be an exorbitant price—"

"Because you're one of the top performers? Ladies can't get enough of you?" Imogen ridicules him. "Magic Mike for hire!"

"I'm not sure who Magic Mike is," Zane says, "but good for him for getting top dollars for his services as an escort. Let me set you straight, Imogen." He sticks his hands in his pockets, monopolizing everyone's attention. "As the CFO and co-owner of a family-owned *multibillion-dollar* company"—*Wait. He's a multibillionaire?*—"and when I say multibillion dollars, I'm talking in the high teens," Zane's tone is smug, bordering on arrogance. It's a side of him I have yet to discover. *Go, Zane!* "I'd need a pretty darn good reason to be in Boston—there's no lack of wheeling and dealing in New York, and since *'tis the season* and all, there's no shortage of VIP functions to attend." Zane pulls me into his embrace and places a kiss on the top of my head. "My incredible girlfriend *is* a pretty darn good reason."

Imogen opens her mouth to say something, then shuts it. Then opens it again. Then shuts it. She does that a few times, her incredulous gaze bouncing from mine to my *multibillionaire* fake boyfriend.

Mic drop!

Chapter 16

Zane

Although she's not my type, there's no denying Imogen is a beautiful woman. That said, the petite girl's sour attitude is repugnant.

It's unlike me to use my wealth as a calling card, but Shay's pint-size asinine stepsister asked for it. Her comment was demeaning. Not only to Shay, but also me. Who the hell does she think she is, coming off judging people without knowing them?

Shay alluded to bad blood between the two of them—which is understandable in light of what her stepsister did to her—but there seems to be more, especially from Imogen's side.

This woman has so much baggage, it could weigh down the heaviest aircraft ever built.

She's still eyeing us with an expression I can't decipher. It's been like that since we sat down to enjoy dinner. The woman is vibrating with discontentment. I don't get it. She got the guy. She got knocked up. She's getting a fairytale winter wedding. What more does she want?

Other than Imogen giving us the evil eye, the evening is pleasant enough. After quick greetings to the two dozen guests the couple invited, Shay, Briar, Aunt Eileen, and I are huddled on the opposite side to the couple on the long ass makeshift table the pub pieced together to accommodate us all. Briar was right. The food is surprisingly remarkable. Over a generous helping of warm sticky toffee pudding and vanilla ice cream, Shay and Briar catch up, while Aunt Eileen has me gasping for air with her hilarious stories.

She wiggles a finger, calling me close.

I lean into her.

"Are you a multibillionaire?" She whispers the question in my ear.

I pull away from her. "I usually don't lead with that, but yes, I am. My family and I have worked hard to get to this point. It wasn't an overnight success, but it was worth it. You'd never know we started from humble beginnings."

"You don't take it for granted." Notice it's not a question.

"Never."

She glances at me sideways and nods, seemingly satisfied with my answer.

"Your parents did an incredible job with you, lad." Her voice is playful, but the sentiment is sincere.

"Thanks." I turn the tables on her. "Taking the cheating out of the equation, what's behind your animosity towards Imogen?"

"That obvious?"

"You can see the tension between the two of you from Madagascar."

"I—"

A man's booming voice coming from the speakers interrupts her.

"Can you feel it, boys and girls? The countdown begins.

Our first karaoke participant will be on stage in fifteen minutes."

Pub patrons clap and cheer.

Aunt Eileen resumes her story. "I assume Shay told you about the heart-wrenching events that led me to become next of kin when my big sister and her husband died?"

"She did."

"I moved in with Katie to help when Briar was born twenty years ago," she says. "Briar is a twin. Her sister died soon after being born due to a heart malformation. Katie was an emotional wreck. On one hand, she was celebrating a newborn. On the other, she was mourning another baby. On top of that, she had to take care of Shay and deal with Imogen—who were young. As time went by and Briar became more independent, I hinted at moving out and finding a place of my own. Katie and Alan refused, stating it was ridiculous for me to live alone when I could live among family. I stayed. I had different temp jobs here and there until I landed in a good company. I was the assistant to the executive assistant of the CEO of a small medical tech start up. For the first five years of operation, instead of giving out big Christmas bonuses, the CEO gave us token ones, plus shares to a pending IPO. Alan balked at my boss's antics, stating the CEO was being a cheapskate, working employees hard, with promises of big money that may be nothing more than a pipe dream. Then, the company went public, making me—and many others—multimillionaires."

My eyes widen in surprise. "Really?"

She nods.

"Like many employees, I wasn't really sure what to do with my new status, so I kept working. I was way too young for retirement. I still am, which is why I now work with Alan and Katie at Alan's medical practice."

"I get that."

"After years of refusing to call me *Aunt* Eileen or showing me an ounce of respect, Imogen was syrupy sweet—"

"She found out you were a rich woman and changed her tune."

"The thing is, I didn't know how that happened since I kept the news quiet. Katie and Alan knew, but they kept the information to themselves—"

"Imogen overheard them talk?"

The corner of her lips curves up in a sneer. "It's far more devious than that." Her eyes swing to the opposite side of the table, before landing on mine. "Briar caught Imogen snooping through my papers—"

"Holy shit!"

"Bless Briar for her quick thinking. When she caught the little serpent red-handed, she pulled out her phone and recorded Imogen leafing through my files. The little bitch had the audacity to take photos with her phone."

"That's incredibly perfidious."

"That's Imogen for you," Aunt Eileen says.

"Let me guess. She lied through her teeth and denied the whole thing."

"Imogen was—still is—so arrogant, she didn't attempt to deny it when we called a family meeting and confronted her. She let it slip she had also been snooping through Katie's things."

"What a betrayal of confidence," I say.

Aunt Eileen nods in approval. "Despite the blatant disrespect, Katie had always been supportive of her stepdaughter. That was the straw that broke the camel's back. Katie gave Alan an ultimatum. That's how Imogen moved to New York to live with her cousin, then the mother who left her behind after the divorce to pursue an international political career at the US

Embassy in Belgian before becoming a news anchor in New York."

"Unbelievable—"

The loud music interrupts me mid-sentence and a man's voice echoes in the speakers. "It's showtime, boys and girls!"

"Let's watch the train wreck. I mean, the show," Aunt Eileen says.

I chuckle.

We turn our attention to the stage.

The MC steps on stage. The medium-height man is wearing a green Christmas sweater, bedecked with green garlands and red balls. Tacky doesn't even begin to describe how butt ugly the eyesore is as he kicks off the karaoke part of the evening. The first participant all but pirouettes her way to the stage, eager to showcase her vocal abilities.

Thirty minutes later, and my ears are bleeding.

The guy on stage is belching the last chorus to the 80s classic *Last Christmas* by Wham, and I thank God it's almost over.

Shay and I exchange a glance.

She's suffering as much as I am.

"Thank you for that performance!" the MC shouts. "Give it up for Jorge everyone!"

Claps and cheers erupt, reverberating around the pub.

The MC steps down from the stage and makes his way through the crowd until he reaches our table.

"Our next karaoke hopeful has a special request," the MC says, coming to stand next to Imogen. "Since the beautiful blonde selected our pub as part of her pre-wedding celebration, we're only too happy to oblige. But before we grant her wish, let's give it up for the soon-to-be bride and groom everybody!"

Pub patrons show their support by clapping and cheering.

Elias and Imogen stand up and wave to the crowd like

they're royalty. When the clapping subsides, Elias takes a seat, but Imogen stays on her feet. The MC hands her the mic.

She flings her long hair behind her and shakes and shimmies her shoulders before speaking. "It means so much to me that so many of my family and friends came to Boston to celebrate my big day," she says, placing a hand against her chest.

The crowd applauds.

She moves away from the table and heads in our direction. "But nothing warms my heart as much as having my stepsister here."

Shay squirms in her seat.

My attention snaps back to Imogen.

"She's a big deal—a former model turned makeup guru. I'm so, so proud of her."

Imogen's overly saccharin smile is so disingenuous, it gives me a toothache.

What the hell is this woman up to?

"It would be the best wedding gift ever to my honey and me if my stepsister would consider entertaining us tonight." Imogen sticks the mic in Shay's face.

My fake girlfriend stares at it like it's a stick of dynamite.

I pin her stepsister with a hard glare.

"Who wants to hear my lovely stepsister sing?" Imogen's question fans the crowd's excitement.

I just met her, so I shouldn't dislike her this much. She truly has a gift to be so detestable.

Several seconds tick by as Shay stares at the microphone, frozen.

"What the bloody hell are you doing, Imogen?" Aunt Eileen asks.

The evil stepsister doesn't even grant her a glance.

"Stop it!" Briar snaps at her half-sister.

Imogen ignores her, returning her focus to Shay who looks

more like a frightened little lamb and less like the bombshell who blew me away at first sight.

"Come on, big shot, you're so good at taking center stage. Let's see it!"

She's goading Shay.

Witch.

I shoot daggers at her.

She smirks at me.

She thinks she's going to humiliate Shay? Not on my watch.

I reach out for the offensive object.

Imogen tries to pull her hand away, but I'm faster. I snatch the microphone out of her hand with force.

Bitch.

"Hey!" Her protest lands on deaf ears. "Not you. Her—"

I stand up, towering over her, forcing her to take several steps back.

"You want her to sing? It's going to be a duet." I speak into the mic so everyone hears.

Her eyes narrow into slivers, radiating with pure hatred.

She opens her mouth, no doubt to object, but Aunt Eileen springs to her feet, chanting. "Duet! Duet! Duet!" She waves her arms around, coaxing everyone in the pub.

Briar follows her lead, standing up and chanting.

That creates a chain reaction.

The party sitting at our long table rise to their feet like a human wave and join my fake girlfriend's great aunt and sister in their crusade.

The crowd jumps on the bandwagon.

Only Elias remains seated. I'm not sure if it's in solidarity to his fiancée or because he's an idiot.

Soon, people are clapping and stomping their feet, voicing their opinion.

This is democracy at its best.

There are no shades of gray. The pub is team Shay and Zane.

Fucking perfect.

I can't stand to look at Imogen any longer, but I give her one last contemptuous glare before averting my eyes. "Do we have to stick to Christmas songs?" I ask the MC.

He leans into me and covers his mic. "Bonus points if you don't."

"You've reached your limit?" I keep my voice low.

"There are only a handful of Christmas songs. So, 'tis the season to go *loco* from hearing the same ones."

I chuckle.

I throw a song at him.

"I don't even have to check," he says. "We have that one."

"We're in business!" I look down at Shay and extend a hand.

She glances up at me, but doesn't take my hand.

"We're in this together."

"I— I can't sing in front of a crowd."

"This is a duet, so you won't be alone on stage."

She shrugs in response.

It's not a no, but it's not a yes.

"You can do this, Shay."

She stares at my extended hand, hesitant.

"If you don't take this fine man's hand, I will," a black woman sitting at the table next to us says.

Shay laughs and places her hand in mine.

"Come on, love, let's rock this house."

The crowd goes mental.

I steer her to the stage. As we're about to climb the steps, she pulls against my hand, forcing me to stop.

"I might face plant. I'm not comfortable in front of an audience."

What?

"I'm sorry gang, I need to confer with my duet partner for a second," I say into the microphone.

Myriad sounds of approval slip from the crowd.

I move the microphone away from my mouth so no one hears what I'm about to say, and return my attention to Shay. I lean into her, catching the signature scent of her perfume. "Weren't you a professional model? There are photos of you in lingerie walking the catwalk online."

Damn right I Googled you.

"Yes. But that was different."

"How so?"

"When you're walking the catwalk, your job is to look straight ahead and strut your stuff. You don't have to connect with the audience or meet a single person's eyes." She lowers her eyes for a beat. "It's not about you. You're a walking clothes rack. In this instance, it's about *me*—Imogen made sure of it with that devious shit she just pulled—and I have to connect with an audience that's going to judge my shortcomings."

Think fast.

"For the song I selected, the guy is the lead vocal," I say. "The female sings the bridge. There are few lyrics and they are repetitive. I'll flag when it's your turn to sing. Follow the prompts. When it's my turn to sing, keep your eyes on me. Connect with me," I gesture two fingers from her eyes to mine. "That way, it's the two of us against the world."

"I'm warning you in advance, I sound like a strangled cat when I sing," she says, worry audible in her voice.

I brush my fingers along her chin. "This is karaoke, baby. You're allowed to sound like a strangled cat and still get a standing ovation!"

She flashes me a genuine smile.

"We're doing this?"

"Okay."

Not the most enthusiastic response.

"I'm going to need more than that."

"Hell, yeah!"

"Now you're talking!"

We hop on stage and take our position to applause from the crowd.

I nod at Shay.

She responds in kind to let me know she's ready.

Then, I nod at the MC.

The music blasts through the speakers.

When the lyrics flash on the screen, I rap the opening.

Shay's blue eyes widen in surprise, threatening to take over her beautiful face. Her jaw drops open for a beat before she manages to recover and mouths her question. "You rap?"

I wink at her.

The rap part is only a few lyrics. The change comes quick.

Since Shay is still staring at me as if she's witnessing the Virgin Mary's apparition, I point an animated finger at the screen.

Your turn is coming soon.

She shakes her head, blinks a few times, and shifts her gaze to the screen.

Her voice is shaky and faint when she delivers the first lyric.

I stand behind her, so we're both facing the crowd, and snake an arm around her waist, pulling her close to me. My cock jumps in my pants when her round ass presses against my erection.

Focus.

"Louder," I say in her ear. "Sing it like you mean it."

She nods.

She delivers the rest of the lyrics with more bravado.

I give her a thumbs up.

She beams.

This woman is perfect in every way, but she can't sing to save her life. That little imperfection makes her that much more attractive.

She twirls in front of me, and my nostril catch the floral notes of her perfume and the scent of her shampoo.

Potent.

I flash back to the heady scent of her arousal drifting in the air of the hotel suite as she rubbed her pussy all over my greedy tongue, riding my fingers, as she chased her orgasm.

Goddammit.

Those breathy little moans followed by her hot as fuck climax, and the way her beautiful face twisted in pleasure, chanting my name. I'm unlikely to forget that scene anytime soon.

Jesus Christ, she looked good riding my tongue.

The saucy episode is safely stored in my spank bank. Well after we put an end to our fake relationship, it will remain at the top of the list of my go-to dirty visuals.

It's only when she points a finger at me that I snap out of my hedonistic haze.

When it's my turn, I tap into the recesses of my mind and belt out the lyrics to the song without even glancing at the screen. I know *"Dilemma"*—Nelly's old school smash hit, featuring Kelly Rowland—by heart.

For a nerd, rap music was a liberation. I could be badass within the walls of my bedroom. And nothing beats old school rap.

I let go of the sexy woman I'm holding to showcase my best hip hop move.

The crowd eats it up, showing me their appreciation in a boisterous way.

"Oh, my God!" Shay says in the mic. "I'm blown away!"

I point at her.

She shakes out of her stupor.

This time, her delivery is a lot more self-assured.

She even adds a saucy little hip shimmy move.

My cock approves.

It's honorable to take care of my fake girlfriend, but now I'm so fucking horny, I'm a lyric away from getting blue balls.

The black dress she was wearing earlier was stunning on her, but the navy one she's wearing now could stop traffic.

There is no way I can make it one more day without fucking her.

I want her too damn much.

She does this little sassy dance, her eyes pouring into mine.

She's coming out of her shell.

I clench my chest as if she just shot an arrow straight to my heart and the crowd cheers.

She throws her head back and laughs.

When she recovers, she blows me a kiss.

I catch it, bring my hand to my lips and kiss it.

She laughs again.

The crowd ooohs and aaahs.

We go back and forth.

It takes a few verses before Shay steps into her role as karaoke queen.

She's so in character, she doesn't even realize she's facing the crowd, singing to them, not bothered in the least she's off note.

My eyes land on Imogen.

She's still standing where we left her. Her arms are crossed over her chest, her jaw clenched so tight, I fear her teeth will shatter into pieces.

Damn right, bitch.

In contrast, Elias, is bobbing his head to the sound of the music.

What an oddly paired couple!

I face Shay, and we dance it out and sing our way to the last note.

The crowd goes nuts, applauding, cheering, whistling, and hollering.

It's wild.

"That was crazy fun!" Shay jumps into my arms.

I catch her and kiss her lips.

It was intended as a celebratory kiss, but it turns passionate.

The whistling reaches a fever pitch.

Okay, too much PDA.

I unlock my lips with hers.

She places the back of her hand against her forehead, her rosy cheeks a dead giveaway to her flustered state.

"That sure was impressive showmanship," the MC says, stepping onto the stage.

"Really?" Shay asks.

"I'm not pulling your leg. It was."

Shay jumps up and down in excitement.

"Encore! Encore! Encore!" The crowd makes its demand loud and clear.

"Are you two up for another song?" the MC asks.

I refer to my fake girlfriend.

"Yes!"

"Which song?" the MC asks.

"Since I picked the first one, I'll let my girl select the second one."

Shay's brows pull together, her lips puckering. She taps on her chin a few times. "I don't know."

"Why don't I help?" the DJ asks.

"Okay," Shay says. "But nothing too hard."

"Fair enough." The DJ nods. "Since you dazzled us with that performance and that little hip shimmy suggests you can shake your *thang*, what about Abba's *Dancing Queen*? It's a crowd favorite."

"Yes! The *Mamma Mia!* musical is one of my all-time favorites." Shay turns to look at me. "Do you know that song?"

"I've heard it, but I don't know it by heart. I'll follow the prompts."

"You get to join her during the bridge," the DJ says.

"I can handle that."

Shay lifts her hand in the air. "Let's do this!"

I high five her.

The MC brings the mic to his lips. "Music!"

The opening notes blare through the speakers. Before the first musical note even drops, Shay is already shaking her shoulders to the beat.

As soon as the first of the lyrics flies across the screen, she goes for it, not even glancing up for cues. Her big blue eyes are fixed on me.

Temptress.

She belts out the first set of lyrics with supreme confidence.

I clap my hands over my head, coaxing the audience.

They follow along.

A quick glance in Imogen's direction lets me know that she's still fuming.

That's right, Medusa.

Don't mess with what's mine.

Whoa!

Where the hell did that come from?

Shay points a teasing finger at me, preventing me from psycho-analyzing that far-fetched thought.

I grab the baton and run with it.

Following along with the lyrics, I deliver a show—hitting

high notes and dancing.

When it's Shay's turn again, she turns the volume way up with exaggerated hip undulations that are as sexy as fuck.

Be still my beating heart.

The timid redhead that sang the first lyrics of the previous song in a meek voice is now belting out this 70s classic like a songstress born to be on stage. She's still off key, but she doesn't give a damn.

Bravo!

When it comes to my turn again, instead of pointing at me, she sashays towards me, her step matching the rhythmic beat of the song.

My eyes are glued to those damn high heel boots that would look fucking good dangling over my shoulders, with her naked.

She reaches out and pokes a manicured finger at my chest. Everything about the move screams, *Tag, you're it.*

Her touch sends an electric current rushing through my body.

I grab her hand and bring it to my lips before dropping a soft kiss against it.

She pulls her hand away and waves her finger in a *no* gesture.

Oh, love, I always get what I want... and all I want is you.

I'm not a selfish lover—far from it—but giving without receiving isn't in my repertoire. We have to rectify this grave injustice before I lose my fucking mind.

My desire for this woman is off the Richter scale—well beyond the boundaries of our arrangement.

What is it about you, Shay O'Hara...?

A part of me knows I'm putting myself in a precarious situation, but another part of me, doesn't give a flying fuck.

I'm dying to suck on her heavy tits until I run out of air,

then I'm going to flip her on all fours, fist her hair, and fuck her until my cock falls off.

Shy of a natural disaster—or the apocalypse—I intend on being balls deep inside this woman as soon as humanly possible. Since there seems to be no love lost between Shay and her stepsister, I'm sure it won't be hard to convince her to cut the evening short.

With the crowd cheering us on, we go back and forth until we reach the last note.

The pub erupts in loud cheers, claps and whistles.

Like earlier, Shay jumps in my arms, her excitement as effervescent as a premium champagne.

This time, when I crush my lips against hers, I ignore the crowd. It's just the two of us, locking lips in a passionate kiss.

Fuck too much PDA.

"Oh, my God, I lucked out!" Shay says, as we step off the stage. "You're the best partner a girl could wish for."

"Anything for you, love." I wink.

She pulls against my hand, stopping me mid-stride. "Thank you. Without you, I would've made a fool of myself. I'm pretty sure Imogen must be pissed off her evil plan backfired."

"Frankly, love, I don't give a damn... nor should you."

"Is that your take on "*Gone With the Wind*"?"

I nod.

"You're right," Shay says. "She can shove her bitterness where the sun don't shine."

"That's the attitude!"

I drag her to our side of the table where Aunt Eileen and Briar are still clapping like fan girls.

"That was brilliant!" Aunt Eileen cheers.

Briar claps. "The way Zane came in to save the day like a knight in shining armor was priceless."

"Girl, not only is your man fine like wine, but he can rap, dance, sing, and the way he stepped in between you and that witch... that was all kinds of swoony." The black woman who was sitting at the adjacent table, and who is now standing, fans herself. "He's a keeper."

"Yes, he is," Shay says on the heel of a laugh.

Her answer shouldn't mean anything because this is all pretend, but for an inexplainable reason, the time limit we imposed on this relationship, irks me.

Two waitresses—a blonde and a brunette—carrying trays, topped with champagne flutes break our little powwow.

I cock a brow. "Compliments of the management for our back-to-back performance?"

"No, sir, the bride-to-be ordered champagne for the table," the blonde says.

I turn around and sure enough, everyone at our table is already enjoying a glass of rosé. Imogen is the exception. She's sipping from a straw plunged in a fruity looking drink in a highball glass. No doubt it's a virgin beverage since she's pregnant.

Is she admitting defeat?

I expected her to be a sore loser.

In a slow calculated manner, she lowers her glass.

At second glance, I notice her lips are stretched in a smile that doesn't reach her eyes.

That smile is as fake as plastic.

Okay, maybe this peace offering comes with some latent bitterness.

I turn around as the waitress hands Shay her drink.

The blonde waitress hands Aunt Eileen and Briar a flute each before handing me the last one.

We thank her.

Shay lifts her glass. "Here's to rocking the house!"

"I can drink to that." I wink.

We clink our glasses.

Aunt Eileen, Briar, and I take a long sip of the champagne.

Shay finishes half her champagne in one gulp.

She's still riding high from that performance.

"Slow down, slugger—"

Her eyes bulge out of her skull.

Her fingers loosen from around the stem of the glass, sending it shattering to the ground, before both hands go flying to her neck, clenching with force.

"Shay, what's going on?" I ask, concerned.

She can't talk.

She points at my flute.

My eyes drop to the glass.

"Strawberries." Her voice is as rough as sandpaper.

I frown.

"Strawberries."

I frown harder.

Is there such a thing as strawberry champagne?

My eyes bounce from the flute I'm holding to her eyes.

She looks terrified.

What the hell is going on?

Aunt Eileen flinches. "Good God, she's having an allergic reaction!"

"What?" I ask.

"Shay is allergic to strawberries," Aunt Eileen says. "She's having an anaphylactic episode."

I bring the champagne flute I'm still holding to my nose and sniff.

Not a hint of strawberry.

I'm confused.

"Where's her handbag?" Aunt Eileen searches around.

Briar snatches it from Shay's seat. "Got it!"

Shay's beautiful face is so red, it rivals the color of the fruit she's allergic to. It's a struggle for her to breathe. I'm useless, but her sister and her great aunt have a handle on things. Thank God.

"Hold this." Aunt Eileen hands me her glass of champagne.

I grab it from her and take a quick sniff.

This smells like champagne to me.

Now, I'm perplexed.

Unless the scent of strawberry is airborne, how the hell did it get into Shay's system?

I drop both glasses on the table and pull out my phone to dial 911.

"Don't bother," Aunt Eileen says. "She'll have recovered by the time the ambulance gets here," she says matter-of-factly.

I narrow my eyes at her. "How do you know?"

"An EpiPen equals 911, which is why she never goes anywhere without one." Aunt Eileen barks out an order at me. "Hold her!"

I tuck my phone into my back pocket and grab onto Shay, sliding my arms underneath her armpits, so her back presses against my chest.

She's like dead weight in my arms.

Her eyes are still open, but instead of their usual blue, they're foggy. It's as if she can't see me.

Holy fuck.

Stunned, I watch as Briar rummages through Shay's handbag and pulls out a tube.

With quick hands, Aunt Eileen inches up the skirt to Shay's dress, exposing her hosiery-covered leg. "Now!"

Briar removes the EpiPen's cap and in one decisive movement, she presses the orange part against her sister's thigh.

Dear God.

Chapter 17

Shay

Where am I?

And why is it so hot?

I try to open my eyes, but it's like my eyelids are glued together.

Why does my mouth taste like copper?

I attempt to open my eyes again with little success.

I groan in frustration.

"Nice and easy, love." That deep masculine voice is unmistakably Zane.

My eyes ease open, my head turning in the direction of his voice.

To my surprise, he's lying next to me, on top of the covers, fully clothed.

He caresses my arm. "Hey."

"Hey." *Fuck, my throat hurts*. "I'm parched."

He reaches for a bottle of water on the nightstand, cracks it open, and hands it to me.

"Thank you."

I drink half the bottle in one gulp and hand it back to him.

As he takes the bottle from me, I notice the time on the digital clock.

Six a.m.

God, it's early.

He returns his attention to me, his hazel green eyes boring into mine.

Self-conscious, I comb my fingers through my crazy morning hair.

Pointless.

"Was it as good for you as it was for me?" I joke, hoping to veer his attention away from my messy state.

"It's not what you think."

Figures.

From cupping his cock yesterday, it's clear, this guy is packing some serious heat. I would've remembered.

"Is there something wrong with your bed or were you itching for a sleepover?"

I'm on a roll.

"I promised your family I'd look after you. Sleeping in my bed wasn't a consideration. I wanted to be close by," he says without a hint of humor.

An unsettling wave of worry courses through me at the anguished tone of his voice.

"Why would you make that kind of promise to my family?"

Without waiting for his answer, I sit up.

That's when it hits me.

I glance down at my body.

"How did I get into my nightgown?" My worried eyes bounce to Zane's.

He levels me with a serious expression I can't discern. "Your mom, Aunt Eileen, and Briar took care of you when we got back to the hotel last night."

"Huh?"

"At around three o'clock in the morning, I sent them home, and promised them I'd take care of you."

"Huh?" It's too early in the morning for me to think.

It's his turn to sit up. He changes position, so we're now facing each other. I take in his ruffled hair, tired eyes, and stubbled chin. My eyes travel the length of his body to his bare feet. They're well-groomed and huge.

Perfect from head to toe.

He runs a hand through his messy morning hair. "You had an allergic reaction last night."

I squint my eyes at him, as I try to recall what I ate last night. "There were strawberries in the sticky toffee pudding?!"

"There were none," he says. "I personally checked with the pub's manager, who double checked with the kitchen staff."

I'm baffled.

I hold up my hands in the shape of a T. "Time out," I say. "Unless I'm allergic to the scent of strawberries, how did I develop an allergic reaction when the fruit that doesn't like me wasn't even in the food I consumed?"

"After the performance, a couple waiters approached us with rosé—"

"As in champagne?"

"Yes—"

"I'm not allergic to rosé."

"*You* weren't served rosé—"

"But you said—"

"*The rest* of us were served rosé." *I still don't get it.* "You were served champagne laced with strawberry liquor."

"What?" My eyes bulge out of my skull.

He nods.

"But I would've tasted it."

"You were riding so high after our second performance. When you were served the glass of what you thought was rosé, you guzzled half of it in a blink of an eye. Your body reacted before your senses did."

"Why was I served a drink I would never order?"

Since my mind is a little fuzzy, Zane gives me the play-by-play.

I rub two fingers along my forehead, struggling to digest this unbelievable story.

"As I was holding onto you so your sister could administer the first shot of adrenaline, I happened to look up. There are a lot of advantages of being the size of a sequoia tree—"

"Elias is an asshole and an idiot for saying shit like that."

"I'm not gonna argue. For a doctor, your ex isn't the sharpest tool in the shed. That said, there's no disputing I tower over a room. That's how I was able to put two and two together."

I frown. "What do you mean?"

"Over the crowd of agitated patrons, I caught a glimpse of the two waitresses who served our drinks—"

"Why would they want to hurt me?"

Zane lifts a hand. "Wait for it."

I nod.

"They were both in a state of panic, hands gesturing frantically, lips moving a mile a minute. My mind was reeling too fast and I was too far away to make out what they were saying, but one thing was certain, they were losing their shit on Imogen's ass—"

"What does my stepsister have to do with this?"

"It'll all make sense in a minute," he says. "Aunt Eileen and Briar were incredible. They went into action with the coordinated swiftness of a team of well-trained emergency personnel. One shot of adrenaline later, and you were doing better. I thought we were going to have to get you to the ER, but Aunt Eileen knew what she was doing."

"Desserts and cocktails can turn into traitors in a blink of an eye."

"I can imagine. I suppose Imogen knows you're allergic to strawberries?"

"Yes."

"Figures."

Where's he going with this?

"Once you stabilized, we filed into a taxi and made it back to the hotel. By the time we arrived, your worried mom and stepdad were waiting for us in the lobby. Briar had texted them. Your stepdad checked you over to make sure you were okay. He even had a doctor friend on standby just in case. Aunt Eileen ordered tea and bottled water from room service. For a while you were fine, but then, you bolted to the bathroom and started vomiting." I can't believe this story. It's like I blanked out part of the night. "Your mom and great aunt took care of giving you a shower and dressing you in a nightgown. Then, I carried you to bed. They stayed with you while your stepdad and I returned to the pub."

Huh?

"I needed answers," he says. "If it weren't for my height, I would've missed it—"

"Missed what?"

"When we got to the pub, the waitresses were still there. They were red-faced and teary-eyed. They stayed behind to inform the manager of what had happened. They were freaked out and scared. They were excited by the prospect of a huge tip, so they didn't question the special request. They had no clue they had conspired to hurt you... and potentially kill you."

The hard stare in his eyes causes me to shiver.

"Imogen paid the waitresses one hundred dollars each for them to serve *me* the champagne laced with strawberry liquor."

The ground shifts beneath my feet.

"Something got screwed up along the way—"

"Imogen was trying to kill me?"

"She didn't expect her devious plan would go awry. You ended up with the drink that was supposed to be mine. That little scenario wasn't part of her contingency list."

I stare at him, dumbfounded.

"Did you confront her?"

He nods. "Your stepdad was furious. The guy was seeing red. Not that I blame him. I was barely containing my rage. Granted, we didn't have all the facts, but your stepsister was coming across like a mental case. Like a coward, Imogen retreated to Elias's home, instead of your mom's and stepdad's. Alan tracked her down, showing up at the Fitzsimmons's at around eleven, while family members were caroling, drunk on spiked eggnog and God knows what else. Alan just about dragged your stepsister by the hair, demanding an explanation. She was tightlipped for a long while, her arms crossed over her chest, unwilling to fess up. Pigheaded fool. Exasperated, Alan threatened not to walk her down the aisle on Saturday. That was her breaking point. In between crocodile tears, Imogen confessed—"

"That she was trying to kill me?"

Rage spikes through me like a burst of flames expelling from the windows of a burning building.

"She was trying to snuff your flame," he says.

"She's the one who threw me to the wolves when she stuck that microphone in my face and demanded I take the stage. She knew what she was doing."

"I agree. She concocted a plan to humiliate you. She wasn't counting on you having an ally."

Thank God for this wonderful man.

"And for that she tried to kill me?"

"The thing is, when you operate from bitterness, envy, and

jealousy, you do stupid shit that can potentially be life-threatening—"

"She's a real-life Maleficent!" I bark.

"She was banking on us kissing. She figured you'd end up with a minor allergy—red blotches, itchiness... maybe a little discomfort. Like she holds a medical degree." The sarcasm is thick in his voice. "All that because she wanted to make sure you wouldn't be able to go back on stage."

My jaw drops, and I stammer, mouth opening and closing, like a goby fish for several seconds.

Zane continues. "There was something sinister about the way she was smirking at me just before I grabbed my flute of champagne. The sly uptake of Imogen's lips, bordering on gloating should've been a clue."

That fucking bitch.

Chapter 18

Shay

There are a couple perks to Imogen's failed murder attempt. One, I was able to bypass the wedding rehearsal and the wedding rehearsal dinner last night. Two, Zane Keller was my nurse from dawn to dusk.

Ma and Alan stopped by the hotel early afternoon yesterday to check up on me. Even though I was doing much better, they suggested I stay in bed.

I didn't argue.

Furthermore, Alan relieved me of my duties as the jilted stepsister who showed up despite it all, stating if I wanted to return to New York and forgo the wedding, he'd understand.

Briar and Aunt Eileen accompanied them to make sure I was okay. Although my great aunt tried to wiggle her way out of last night's pre-wedding events, Ma wouldn't hear of it. Unwilling to concede that easily, my great aunt used me as a scapegoat, reminding everyone it would be unwise for me to stay alone, given my condition. I had to let her down gently. That job was covered by a capable hunk.

So, here we are on the day of my stepsister and my ex-boyfriend's wedding.

I was less than enthusiastic to show up for this wedding in the first place, but wild horses couldn't keep me away today. Not after what happened on Thursday.

Throughout the wedding ceremony at the church, Imogen kept looking over her shoulder, fear shining bright in her eyes.

I wasn't sure if it was because she was afraid I'd retaliate or if she was expecting me to object to the wedding.

I barely managed to swallow the urge to throttle my stepsister for her stupidity, but kept my anger in check. Making a scene would reflect poorly on me, even if she had it coming. As for Elias Fitzsimmons. Good riddance. *You can have him, bitch.* Even during the wedding recessional, Imogen's eyes kept darting my way as she trailed down the aisle, hanging from the arm of her new husband. I had to dig into the archives of my days as a model to keep a stoic expression on my face. Aunt Eileen congratulated me on my resting bitch face. That said, I managed to smile, albeit unenthusiastically, for the wedding photos.

The wedding reception is taking place at the swanky and ultrachic Dorchester Room, located inside Storrow Manor—a historical mansion converted into a premier wedding venue. Four hours later and Mr. and Mrs. Fitzsimmons's wedding reception is still going strong.

The reception hall is decked out. White poinsettias decorate every corner of the spacious ballroom, while white calla lilies top the tables.

Since the snow is falling today, the fairytale winter wonderland theme is on point. It's enough snow to add a magical flair, without putting a serious wrench in today's festivities. In other words, Mother Nature cooperated.

Imogen had to put her stamp on the elegant décor. The

hard-to-miss ice sculpture and the over-the-top cake are the height of tackiness.

While Zane and Alan enjoy a cigar and fine whiskey in the smoking lounge with a bunch of other men, I'm hitting the dessert table for the second time.

My body convulses at the sight of tuxedo strawberries.

I steer away from the dangerous dessert, preferring the safety of mini cupcakes.

Briar comes and stands next to me.

"I don't care if that"—she crooks her thumb over her shoulder—"was inspired by an A-list celebrity wedding, Imogen's wedding cake is bordering on gaudy." My sister grabs a dessert plate and follows my lead, piling it with an assortment of scrumptious cupcakes. "The damn thing is ridiculous, if you ask me."

"Aye." I nod. "It's a wee bit much, lass." I channel Aunt Eileen when she leans into her Irish brogue. "For cryin' out loud, the bloody thing is so huge, I bet someone with binoculars can see the tower of flour, sugar, and frosting from Russia."

Briar dissolves in laughter.

My stepsister's cake is taller than she is. The stupid thing is as tall as my fake boyfriend.

Mrs. Fitzsimmons selected a seven-tier wedding cake. *Seven*. I was so dumbfounded, I personally counted them—featuring a twirling cascade of yellow and white flowers and hundreds—if not thousands—of shimmery pearls. The thing is so enormous, it required six kitchen staff to carry it out for the cake cutting.

I keep taking jabs at Imogen. "She needed some height to balance the freakin' carriage. Maybe in this fairytale, Cinderella grabs a wee bit of cake before she runs away from her prince charming."

Briar loses it.

In between laughing fits, my sister struggles to place her plate on the table before she drops it.

I have no idea how I manage to keep a straight face.

I'm on a roll.

"I know it's a long-honored custom for married couples to freeze the top layer of the wedding cake so they can enjoy it on their first anniversary for good luck––although in this case, you'd need a bloody industrial freezer for it to fit. Anyhoo, I digress. The important question here is, will Mr. and Mrs. Fitzsimmons be carving out chunks of the frosty carriage so they can prepare celebratory one-year anniversary martinis?"

That does it.

Briar is laughing so hard, she's crying.

I drop all pretense and join her.

She wipes tears from underneath her eyes, "I bet, my mascara is running and I look like a hot mess, but that was hilarious," she says, still laughing.

I do a little curtsy.

"Not bad, right?" I wink. "Seriously," I chance a glance at the ice carriage, "I get how an ice sculpture would fit nicely with the wedding theme and the season, but an unbelievably detailed sculpture of a carriage and its passengers is pretentious."

I'm not kidding and I'm not being facetious.

There's an actual big ass ice sculpture in the ballroom. It was brought in on a large pallet by a forklift before the cake cutting. The artist was pulling it, and his crew was flanking it to ensure it didn't topple.

Everyone was oohing, aahing, and clapping.

I was so flabbergasted, I could only blink in disbelief.

Briar, Ma, Alan, Aunt Eileen, and Zane, were equally stunned.

Imogen was beaming with pride, as if she were the one who had spent countless hours shaving ice.

"At least it's not a 'him and her' life-size ice sculpture," Briar says. "That would've been even worse."

"I'm sure it must've crossed Imogen's mind."

"The tragic thing is, I'm sure you're right. So pathetic." Briar shakes her head. "At least Dad didn't have to fork out money for that... thing."

"Thank God for small favors. It must have cost an arm and a leg, which is ridiculous when you consider it'll revert back to water by tomorrow."

Briar rolls her eyes. "Ashes to ashes, dust to dust."

We shake our heads.

One of Elias's cousins is married to an ice sculptor. The guy went from struggling artist to in-demand ice sculptor when he redirected his talent after watching a video clip of a Swedish ice sculpture competition online. Instead of working with metal, now, he works with ice. The wedding gift—a special request from the bride—paid off for the guy. He's already received several bookings from guests, and the mansion wants to talk business.

Briar picks up her plate and stuffs a mini cupcake into her mouth.

I follow her lead.

"The only thing that trumps the cake *and* ice sculpture is your stunning dress," she says, swallowing. "I just came from the bathroom and you wouldn't believe how many women stopped me—on the way there and on the way back—to comment on how beautiful my sister looks... and they weren't talking about the bride."

I beam at her.

If I had a dollar for every time a woman commented on my dress, I'd be as rich as Aunt Eileen. Other than Imogen's mom, who asked if my dress didn't come in less statement-making colors, everyone else seems dazzled. I ignored her and left her standing there, hanging from the arm of her third husband.

Like mother like daughter...

"I liked Zane from the moment I met him, but after this coup"—Briar waves a finger up and down the length of my body—"I love, love, love the guy."

My fake boyfriend decided to take Ma's word at face value.

After my parents left, Zane called Curves Envy Fashion's creative director, a guy by the name of Stephen King, and asked him to send a few dresses in my size on a rush delivery. They arrived early this morning. To my shock, they were all red. I'd never dream of upstaging a bride on her wedding day, but sometimes, you have to fight fire with fire. Since my stepsister was willing to kill me to dim my light, it's only fair I shine bright on her big day. All three sleeveless dresses are stunning. In the end, I selected the one that left Zane's jaw dropped. It has a deep V-neckline that showcases the girls in such a tempting way—sexy, but tasteful. The contrast of the fitted bodice and the lavishly flounced, twirl-ready skirt makes the dress. The design is straight off the cat walk.

"I like him, too." I brush invisible lint from her sapphire-blue dress. "He was so attentive yesterday. No matter how many times I told him he didn't need to spend the day fussing over me, he refused to listen. He declared he wouldn't leave my side for as long as I was stuck in the hotel room."

"He's good stock," Briar says.

"That. He. Is."

"Dad is team Zane after the way he ventured into the night like a knight in shining armor, seeking the truth, unwilling to rest until the villain was apprehended."

I cock an eyebrow. "That was a little Shakespearean."

"I can't help it. Zane's actions were heroic." She leans into me. "Everything considered, he went above and beyond the call of duty."

"He did."

Zane and I met six days ago. I didn't expect he'd have to chase a villainess in the middle of the night on my account, and I didn't expect him to keep such a vigilant eye on me today.

"The way Zane demanded the pastry chef come out and tell him to his face there were no traces of strawberries hidden in any of the desserts..." Briar taps a hand against her chest. "Ma is still swooning and her heart is still going pitter-patter over such fierce protectiveness. So is mine."

"I must admit, I didn't expect that much."

The second they rolled out the dessert table a few hours ago, Zane transformed into my own personal food taster before taking it up a notch and requesting the chef puts his mind—and mine—at ease. That's why there are little cards in front of a few desserts, flagging the ones I need to stay away from.

"I bet the two of you would make beautiful babies!" my sister blurts out. "I can see it now," she says with a grand hand gesture. "Adorable little munchkins that will grow up to be tall with blue or green eyes, and dark auburn hair like *moi*—their auntie." She flings her long locks behind her back, revealing her bare shoulders.

I have this sudden strange urge to create lots of tiny people with said blue or green eyes, dimples, and wavy auburn hair—unless, they end up with dark blond hair like their dad—

What is wrong with me?

Damn you, Briar, for putting that image in my head.

"First, you're starting to sound like Ma. Second, you're high, unless you're drunk from drinking the Kool-Aid. Third, there will be no babies..." I scan around to make sure no one's privy to our conversation. "Like Cinderella, I have to keep my eyes on the clock." *Don't you forget it.* "Tick tock. Tick tock," I tap two fingers against the bezel of my Cartier Ballon Bleu watch.

"Who says it has to end tomorrow?" Briar speaks in the same coded language as me.

"This was a favor," I say, matching her hush-hush tone. "I'm so not in Zane's league. I figured he was rich. I didn't know he was billionaire-rich. The guy lives in New York City. There are tons of options."

My sister does a double take. "And you're not a *great* option?"

"Rich and powerful men like Zane have their pick of women. The Big Apple is like a sumptuous buffet for men in that tax bracket. Not to mention, his parents' example of a turbulent relationship left a bad taste in his mouth." I peer over my shoulder before meeting her gaze. "This is all smoke and mirrors... we don't know each other."

"You live in the same city. It's easy for you to *get* to know each other."

"He agreed to three days. I have no right to expect more."

"The chemistry between you is hotter than a heatwave, Shay. And I'm not the only one who thinks so. How many people have viewed *and* commented on your stellar karaoke performances?"

"Thanks to you, too many."

She responds with a *not sorry* grin.

Brat.

My sneaky sister filmed my fifteen minutes of fame. She then took it upon herself to forward the clip to my assistant, who shared it on all my social media platforms. Guess who went viral?

She ignores my repartee. "The public has spoken. Millions of people think you two are perfect together."

I keep my voice low when I respond. "Yeah, well, other than you, no one knows it's pretend."

I swallow down the lump that seems to form at the thought of the expiration date on our fake relationship.

Something dangerous twists inside me.

Feelings?!

No, no, no.

I have no business feeling anything other than gratitude for Zane.

Briar considers me for a long beat. "If you're going to stick your head in the sand and ignore what's unfolding between the two of you, I hope you at least intend on having slutty wedding sex with the perfect match you're unwilling to acknowledge." She hooks a closed fist to her hip and shakes her head. "That man is *waaayyyy* too fine to pass up." *I've been told.* "I was too chicken to go through with the escort option as a date for the wedding—and even if I did, he wouldn't be Zane Keller caliber. You lucked out, Shay. You'd be a fool to let this end without getting *some benefits* out of it... if you know what I mean."

My comeback dies on my lips when an ecstatic Aunt Eileen comes rushing towards us, in a whirlwind of emerald-green silk. The maxi dress she selected for the occasion looks arresting on her.

"It's a fine wedding, lassies." She's all teeth.

Has she been drinking the Kool-Aid as well?

"Why are you smiling from ear to ear, Aunt Eileen?" Briar asks.

"Selfies rock!" she says. "I'm a convert!"

I frown. "You are?" She nods, her lips pursed. "Since when?"

A small smile teases at her lips. "As of a half an hour ago."

I shoot her a dubious side-gaze.

Aunt Eileen thinks selfies are the epitome of grandiose narcissism, followed only by selfie-posting frequency. I'm sure I don't have to tell you Imogen is the queen of selfies, which only makes my great aunt steadfast in her decision not to jump on the bandwagon.

Now, she's a convert?!

"What brought on the change of heart?" Briar asks our great aunt.

She smoothes down her perfectly coiffed blonde hair, styled in a low chignon, before playing around with a stunning gold earring. "I was taking a tour of the chic facilities when I wandered off to the other side of the building—there are three other weddings taking place, by the way." I'm not sure where she's going with this. "I was on the mezzanine, looking down at the magnificent interior garden encased in a glass cube. The white orchids hanging from the glass ceiling and the snow falling against the skylight... it was magical. I started snapping photos. For fun, I decided to take my first selfie to see what the fuss was all about. I did a double take when a flash of blonde hair and white lace appeared on my screen from the floor below. I took cover so I could peek without being noticed." *Okay, lady spy, get to the point.* "The woman in question had her fingers interlaced with a man's fingers in an intimate way..." Her eyes bounce from mine to my sister's. "So we're clear, it wasn't *her* man... it wasn't *her* husband." *What's up with the cryptic speech?* "Then, the two slipped into a room or a closet. I couldn't tell from my vantage point. In any case, when said bride came out from her hiding spot, she was looking disheveled. The same for the man... not *her* man... not *her* husband."

"Your story is complicated, Aunt Eileen," Briar says.

I gesture with my hand. "Get to the point before the ice sculpture melts."

My great aunt pulls out her phone and swipes through her photos. She hands me the device. My sister huddles closer.

"What?!" I clasp a hand over my mouth as hundreds of eyes glance our way.

"Maybe it's one of the other brides." Briar doesn't sound convinced. At least she isn't screeching in horror like I did. "You said there are three other weddings taking place in the venue."

I piggyback on her logic because holy shit, I can't believe my eyes. "That must be it."

Since Aunt Eileen has the latest iPhone, I can't blame an old generation camera for a blurry photo. Either that or these photos are putting the theory of doppelgängers to the test.

Aunt Eileen's devious smile, widens. "There are four brides in the mansion, celebrating their big day. I know because the interior garden is a popular place for photos." She lifts a hand and counts with her fingers. "There's a beautiful tall, black woman with short black hair, wearing a champagne-colored dress." She lifts another finger. "There's also a stunning Asian woman—I'm guessing Japanese from the traditional kimono she's wearing." A third finger pokes the air. "A brunette rocking a pixie cut, bubblegum-pink lipstick and blue shoes, looks radiant, *and...*" After a dramatic pause, a fourth finger appears. "The fourth bride is a dark blonde with long hair—with attitude as toxic as battery acid—wearing head to toe white. I'm sure I don't have to fill in the blanks since it's pretty obvious who I'm talking about."

"Dear God!" Briar says.

I gasp. "Unbelievable."

"A picture is worth a thousand words..." Aunt Eileen says. "God, I love selfies!" Her smile is diabolical.

Chapter 19

Shay

I'm still rooted in shock when a strong hand snakes around my waist, pulling me close to a wall of muscles.

"Ladies." Zane acknowledges my sister—who's still sporting a freaked-out expression on her face—and Aunt Eileen who still looks like the cat who ate the canary.

"Hello, handsome." Aunt Eileen does a little finger wave.

"May I steal my girlfriend for a dance?"

"Take the lass for a twirl!" Aunt Eileen says. "She looks like she needs something to shake her up." She punctuates her comment with a little shoulder shimmy.

"Will you do me the honors, love?" Zane asks me.

I nod.

Placing a hand to the middle of my back, he guides me to the dance floor where couples are already shaking their thing. As we make our way to the epicenter of the action, he asks, "What was that about? That conversation looked intense."

"Err..." I'm still processing the disturbing meaning of the scenes Aunt Eileen captured on photo.

Alan, who's cutting a rug on the dance floor with Ma, waves at us.

I use that distraction to avoid answering Zane's question.

Ma waves with both hands, still moving to the beat of the bumping tempo blaring through the speakers, the heavy bass vibrating through my body.

They're having a ball.

If they only knew...

Guilt hits me like a freight train.

I wave, meekly.

They're all smiles.

Their giddiness will be short-lived.

"Are you okay?" Zane asks me, jarring me from my thoughts.

"Yes." *This isn't your problem, Shay.* "Yes, I am."

Concern knits his eyebrows together. "Did Imogen go around spewing some of her venom?"

I shake my head.

"You're not trying to protect her because it's her wedding day, right?"

I shake my head again. "She had other things on her mind than to be the bane of my existence," I say.

"Good. She better steer far away from you."

The fierce protectiveness in his tone does something to me.

Tick tock.

Tick tock.

When we find a clear spot on the dance floor, we make it our own. He grabs me by the hand, twirls me around, before pulling me into his embrace.

His scent fills my lungs. It's a combination of expensive cologne and masculinity. I don't even mind the lingering scent of the cigar smoke clinging to his suit. I have the sudden urge to bury my face into his neck and inhale every note of the intoxicating concoction.

Even in my five-inch heels, his tall frame towers over mine.

He looks down at me. "I know I'm starting to sound like a broken record, but you look breathtaking in that dress."

I glance up into his hazel green eyes, a smile flirting against my lips, the train wreck I witnessed on photo, long forgotten. "Thank you. It's not hard to look good in Curves Envy Fashion couture."

"You're too humble, love. You look fucking good. Own it."

I wrinkle my nose.

He arches a brow.

"Okay, if you insist—"

"I insist."

"I look fucking good."

"Now we're talking!"

"If we're exchanging compliments, you put all other men to shame in your impeccably cut suit," I say, smoothing down the wool fabric.

Tiny little lines appear next to his eyes when he smiles. *Le sigh.* "When you're my height, bespoke isn't an option."

"It doesn't mean you have to look this good."

"Flattery will get you everything, love."

I hope so.

Granted I haven't had the pleasure of seeing him naked, but from the way his broad shoulders stretch across his jacket, I can already tell, this man is sculpted like the marble statues of Greek or Roman gods. Yesterday, he sported a scruff when he doubled as my male nurse. Today, he's clean-shaven. The man radiates cover model looks.

Seriously, his drop-dead gorgeousness is unnerving.

He makes the groom and the wedding party look like

awkward teenagers who borrowed their father's suit to play dress up.

Even by New York standards, Zane Keller stands head and shoulders above the rest.

The song changes to a mellower one.

Ooohhh, I love this song.

I love it even more now that I'm dancing with Zane.

A wave of sadness washes over me at the thought that from now on, I'll associate this song with this moment. This perfect and short-lived moment.

For a few more minutes, we sway to the sensual tempo.

Zane's hand travels down my lower back. It's still PG, but not by much.

Then, he presses me closer to his body.

My eyes widen in surprise.

Oh...

The bulge between his legs is unmistakable.

"Everything about what Imogen did to you on Thursday night infuriates me," Zane says. "But nothing pissed me off more than spending the night in bed with you without being able to satiate my unreasonable desire for you." My eyes flick to his, stunned by his admission. "Don't get me wrong. I'm not complaining about watching over you. I volunteered for the job, but I would've much preferred to be in bed with you for another reason..." He says that last part with a low raspy voice.

My heart is hammering against my chest.

His eyes bore into mine for several beats.

He breaks the silence. "I could be a good boy and wait until we get back to the hotel." He tilts his head side to side a few times, seemingly pondering on his options. "God knows when this evening will end, and then we have to account for the hour-long limo drive with your family—"

"What if you decided *not* to be a good boy?" The question comes flying out of my mouth without my permission.

A wolfish grin stretches his lips. "In that case, I'd enlist your help to take care of my *very big* problem."

I play along. "It would only be fair since you're doing me a solid."

He cocks a brow. "You have such a great business mind. I've done a lot of things at weddings, but I've never snuck out to seek relief... if you know what I mean."

"I know *exactly* what you mean."

"What about you?"

"I've never helped anyone seek relief before at a wedding." I gaze up at him from under my lashes, pulling my lower lip between my teeth.

He nods a few times. "It's a first for both of us?"

"It is."

"Two virgins."

"I'm sure you haven't been a virgin in a couple decades."

"I was a nerd. Until my twenties, I didn't have much game."

His answer surprises me.

"My bad."

He reaches for my face. "What do you say we skip this dance and find a quiet hideaway just for the two of us?" Zane's voice sends a chill of excitement running up my spine and goose bumps along my exposed skin.

We continue to move against each other to the music, his formidable erection digging into my stomach, his hands gripping possessively at my waist.

I swear it feels like the temperature in this room is cranked so high, the ice sculpture won't make it.

Good God.

Briar's words come crashing into me.

She's wise beyond her years.

Slutty wedding sex wasn't on the agenda, but now, it tops the list of priorities.

The longing in Zane's eyes is a palpable force in the room. So much so, I'm certain everyone senses it. The filthy desire reflecting in his irises leaves me speechless. He looks at me like I'm a woman about to be devoured. No one's ever looked at me that way.

My skin sizzles.

My pussy flutters with anticipation.

He leans into me, our lips flirting, our ragged breathing brushing each other's face.

"Are you gonna give me an answer?" he asks against my lips.

"Lead the way, big boy."

Chapter 20

Zane

I interlace my fingers with Shay's, determined to pull her off the dance floor so I can have her all to myself, but her stepfather chooses that moment to lift his head.

Our gaze meets.

He jerks his chin at me.

I respond in kind.

It's a bit awkward when you're about to defile a man's stepdaughter, but I'm done waiting. I'm so wound up, not even a natural catastrophe would prevent me from being balls deep inside this woman's pussy.

I guide Shay through the doors and down a long corridor, as we head to a hideaway I spotted earlier near the smoking lounge.

Good on Shay for keeping up with my long strides.

Impatience courses through me too much to slow down my cadence.

My step doesn't falter until we reach our destination.

"Where are you taking me?" Shay asks.

Her chest rises and falls rapidly, her nervous energy palpable.

"Wait here," I command.

I try the doorknob.

Bingo! It's still unlocked.

I open the door and disappear inside, scouring the room to make sure the coast is clear.

Bullseye.

I join her in the corridor. "I found the perfect spot for a little naughty fun."

"You still haven't answered my question."

"Elias's dad mentioned there was a library set-up like the original one that was in the mansion before the renovation. Other than the bookshelves lined with first editions, everything is new. Talented decorators aged the décor, so it's like being transported in time. Someone in the wedding party was curious, so we all made our way there after puffing on a cigar. Nowadays, the library is mostly booked for highbrow bachelor parties and business functions. Lucky for us, it's empty *and* the door is unlocked."

Her big blue eyes light up. "Oh... you're sneaky." Her expression changes. "I'm not sure if I should be flattered or insulted," she says.

"In what sense?"

"You had already scouted a hideaway before I even agreed to anything inappropriate."

"You have it all wrong, love," I say. "I was *hopeful*. That said, I've been known to be persuasive when I put my mind to it." I wink.

She shakes her head.

"Let's go inside before we get caught."

"You're right. We're sitting ducks out here."

I let her in first.

I follow after her, close the door, and lock it.

I switch on a few table lamps, providing a glimpse of the old-world décor.

When I turn to face her, she's sporting that confused expression again.

"What's wrong?" I ask.

"What if someone else in the wedding party has the same idea as you and decides to make this their naughty den?"

I set her mind at ease. "The door is locked, so they're going to have to find another place to play dirty."

She works her lower lip.

"Nervous?"

"Nervous energy," she says. "I've never been this turned on in my life."

Fuck.

With an animalistic growl, I close the distance between us in one long stride, already shrugging the suit jacket off. I toss it on a sofa on my way to her.

I cup her face in my hands as my lips softly brush against hers, tasting and teasing her. I pull her bottom lip into my mouth and she moans, granting me full access. That's all the invitation I need. My tongue slides between her lips, sweeping inside her mouth.

"Goddamnit, Shay."

"Oh, Zane."

I bite her lower lip before plunging my tongue into her mouth again. I take my time, making up for lost time. I had to curtail my desire for her yesterday as she recovered, but today, all bets are off. I'm getting my fill of this woman if it's the last thing I do.

I deepen the kiss.

She's clawing at my shirt, fumbling with the buttons with eager hands.

Then, everything stops.

She pulls away from me. "You're messing up my life."

I frown my confusion at her accusation.

"You're setting the bar too high." Her tone is scolding, but the delivery is breathy.

I can't help my smile. "It's a good thing."

She doesn't respond.

Something passes between us. Something I can't explain, but it's there. I can see it in the way she stares at me, she feels it too.

This pretend relationship is feeling real by the second. Too real, even.

She shakes her head. "Never mind."

I don't press. It's best that way.

By midday tomorrow, we'll go our separate ways.

Back to the program.

"I want you in front of that window."

"Wh—what?"

"You heard me."

"We're..." She gestures a finger between us. "You're..." She blinks. "Seriously?"

"I don't believe I stuttered, love."

"Isn't that a little out there?" she asks. "Pun intended."

"Vanilla sex isn't in my repertoire."

She opens her mouth, then closes it. She does that a few times before settling on an answer. "Of course, it isn't."

"Is that a problem?"

"No," she shakes her head.

"Good."

"I'm not sure I can keep up."

"I reckon you can."

She nods a few times, but she's still rooted in place.

"I gave you an order, Shay, I expect you to obey."

Her eyes widen so much, they take over her gorgeous face.

Given what I know about her ex, I'm not surprised she reacts this way.

We stare at each other for a long beat before she gives me what I want.

With a hesitant step, she trails towards the window.

She places the tips of her fingers against the glass, gets on her toes, and peeks outside. She looks left, then right. Then, she glances over her shoulder, beckoning me with her heated gaze.

She's ready to play.

I stalk towards her, my lengthening cock an impediment to my stride.

"As gorgeous as this dress is on you, it's now an annoyance."

I inch down the zipper, the sound a precursor to what's to come.

Yesterday, her wild red hair was flowing freely over her shoulders. Today, she's sporting a chic twist. As much as I want to fist her hair while I fuck her from behind, I can't bring myself to mess up her sophisticated hairdo.

When the zipper reaches her waist, I'm rewarded with a gift—smooth, silky alabaster skin.

Unable to resist, I lean forward and drop a string of kisses along her back.

She gasps and shivers.

She reaches back and rakes her fingers through my hair, holding my head, as if begging for more.

I oblige.

Each teasing kiss causes my eager cock to jerk.

I slide the dress down her body until it's pooling at her feet.

Fire races through my veins.

"Between the stay-ups and the garter belt, your choice of hosiery threatens to give me a fucking heart attack."

"I wore the stay-ups because of how you reacted on Thursday night."

Tease.

"You think you have me pegged?"

"No," she shakes her head. "There's no way I can get to know everything about an enigmatic man like you in less than a week." She smiles. "Your reaction was so... animalistic. Caveman-ish, even. Had it been any other man, I would've been turned off, but instead, I was flattered and turned on beyond belief. You made me feel beautiful."

I lower my lips close to her ear, and whisper my praise. "You *are* beautiful."

Even though her eyes are fixed on the nocturnal sky, I can see the wheels in her head churning from her reflection in the window.

"Maybe that was a wrong choice of words. You make me feel desired."

Her admission hangs in the air between us for several long breaths.

I could tell her all night long how beautiful she is, instead, I choose to show her.

I lower myself to her feet. "Step out of the dress."

I snatch it off the wooden floor, travel the short distance to the black leather sofa, and place her red dress there with care.

When I turn around, I freeze.

The city lights cast a halo around her curvy body, accentuating every perfect part of her. I've had my fill of dirty dreams of that ass, but by God, the sight upon me far exceeds any of my dirty, filthy fantasies.

Her luscious ass is a work of art.

My gaze burns over her skin, and my nostrils flare as I prowl back towards her, admiring her.

"Is the lingerie ours?" I ask.

She shakes her head. "I didn't expect the gift, so I didn't pack red lingerie. I only had a selection of navy and black underwear. In full disclosure, I have a limited supply of Sexy Curves Lingerie."

"We'll have to rectify that as soon as possible."

"You've already been generous enough, Zane."

"Can't a guy spoil his fake girlfriend?"

"Well... when you put it like that, how can I refuse?"

"You can't refuse. Just like you can't refuse me."

I unclasp her black bra.

Her arms are already in position, outstretched at her side.

Eager little thing.

I remove it easily and toss it over my head.

From this vantage point, I get an eyeful of her gorgeous breasts. Her nipples are erect, waiting to be toyed with.

With a gentle hand, I press against her back.

"What are you doing?"

"Trust me."

She goes with the flow.

"*Baby, it's cold outside.*" I sing. "And I want your nipples nice and hard for me."

She gets it.

She arches back, rubbing her ass against me as she bends forward until her nipples touch against the window.

"That feels so good..."

"I bet it does."

When she straightens, her nipples are as hard as bullets.

Fucking perfect.

I brush the back of my fingers up her tummy and trail the underside of her breasts, stroking back-and-forth in a languorous movement. "I've been waiting since Monday to get my hands on these."

Her body shivers under my touch.

She gasps.

Shay's large tits fit perfectly in the palms of my hands. I relish their shape and weight, teasing the nipples between two fingers.

Needing more, I grope her breasts and knead them at a languorous pace, her perky nipples scratching against my palms.

I press my erection against her back.

Her breath catches in her throat.

I let out a low guttural sound.

Alleviating the pressure of my heavy balls against her warm body feels so fucking good.

"You like the way I play with your tits?"

She nods.

"Answer me."

"Your kiss. Your touch. I want it all. No—" She shakes her head. "I *need* it all."

I shouldn't love hearing her say that this much.

I focus on the here and now.

I flick, tease, and toy with her nipples until they turn an arousing shade of deep red. Her whole chest is flush with color.

The pleading moans that drop from her lips harden my already impossibly hard cock.

My lips touch her earlobe. "I bet I could make you come just by playing with your nipples."

Her head drops back against my chest, her pretty blue eyes staring up at me.

I'm unprepared for what she does next. She reaches behind and grabs my ass, pulling me closer to her. She wiggles against my erection, jacking up my arousal.

It takes everything in me not to lose my shit like an inept teenager in my suit pants.

Tease.

I pinch her nipples hard in retaliation.

She lets out a piercing shriek of surprise.

"That's what happens when you play with fire, love. You get *rewarded*."

She lets out a long sigh.

I pull away from her.

Her head whips around, her eyes radiating with confusion.

"We have to get rid of your panties and I have to get undressed before I can fuck you," I answer her unspoken question.

I clasp my fingers around the waistband of her panties and lower them to the floor, crouching down with every inch as her beautiful ass is revealed and I'm on my knees.

She steps out of them without being asked.

I bring the lacy fabric to my nose and inhale her heady scent.

"You want me, love." My voice is as rough as gravel. Her response turns into a groan when I slide a finger between her pussy lips, skating around her slickness. Sliding my dripping digit between my lips, I suck it clean of her sweet juices. "You're so fucking ready for me."

I take a bite out of her luscious ass.

She yelps.

I stand to my full height, tucking her panties into the pocket of my pants.

She readies herself to turn around, but I stop her. "Did I tell you to move?"

"Um..."

She's like a fish out of water.

"You don't move until I tell you to move. Understood?"

She nods.

"Eyes up front."

She obeys and I can't help smiling at her reflection in the window.

I discard my clothing at breakneck speed. When I push my boxer briefs down my legs, my hard cock snaps against my stomach.

Fuck, I want this woman more than my next breath.

I reach for my pants and search for a condom in my wallet.

I take in every inch of her as I prowl towards her.

She's still staring at the gardens.

I cup her soft tummy with my palm, my teeth grazing at her earlobe.

"You're such a good girl. So obedient."

"It isn't fair I can't see you naked."

She gets high marks for not looking over her shoulder.

"Consider this an amuse-bouche," I say. "When we get back to the hotel, we'll make up for yesterday. Fair warning, don't expect to sleep much."

"I've been told."

Sassy little thing.

Slap!

"Ouch!"

"*Now*, you've been told."

"No one's ever spanked me before," she says, her tone hoity.

"I'm okay being your first."

She shakes her head.

"Notice you haven't asked me to stop or never do it again."

"That's because I haven't decided if I like it or not."

"Trust me, you like it. If you didn't, you would've objected the first time I spanked your luscious ass."

She doesn't have a retort.

"Are you on the pill?" I ask.

"I am, but—"

"We'll use protection."

"That's a good idea," she says, a tinge of shyness coloring her words.

I position myself behind her, grip my cock with one hand and guide it between her legs. I angle my body and slide my naked cock between her pussy lips, coating my raging erection with her juices.

"Fuuuuck!"

"Oh, oh, oh!"

I do it again.

And again.

And again.

I'm a breath away from going against my own rule and sliding balls deep into her inviting pussy without any barrier between us.

This is craziness.

I've never had an urge to take a woman bareback before.

Shay put a spell on me.

I mentally chastise myself because I'm losing sight of the boundaries of our arrangement.

Don't be an idiot, Keller.

Even though she's on the pill, taking a chance would be the height of stupidity. This relationship has a time limit. A baby is forever.

I bring the condom wrapper to her lips. "Tear it open."

She does as she's told.

With quick hands, I sheathe my cock.

"Hands on the window," I command.

She stretches her neck out and peers down.

"What if someone sees me?" she asks. "I'm kind of memorable with my red hair."

"Four hours into the wedding ceremony and most everybody is three sheets to the wind." I trail kisses along her shoulder. "If by any wild chance, someone *thinks* they saw you getting your brains fucked out, blame it on their beer goggles."

She laughs. "Okay."

Given the secluded location of the manor, passersby wouldn't intrude on our naughty time. That said, even though it's a cold winter night, I'm sure some brave guests from the four wedding parties are out there. Since the smoking room is reserved for cigar smokers, you have to bundle up if you want to light up a cigarette. Additionally, the large balcony stretching in front of us acts as a shield. You'd have to have laser eyes to catch the action. But let's face it, this is all about the forbidden thrill of potentially getting caught.

"Spread your legs for me."

Hands against the glass, she spreads her legs.

I slip a finger between her hot lips, finding her dripping even more. "Until we leave Boston, I own this pussy. Got that?"

"Yes." The word comes out without hesitation.

I growl as I push two fingers knuckle-deep inside her. I finger-fuck her, eliciting moans of pleasure that only remind me of how desperate my cock is. I fist the fucker and slide it inside her pussy an inch at a time. I take it nice and slow to give her plenty of time to adjust to my size.

She groans as I move in and out of her. "You're even bigger than I ever imagined."

"I'm a big guy all over."

"Dear God, there's no way I can give you a blow job without choking."

"Challenge accepted."

"I don't think I can live up to your expectations."

"I believe in you," I say. "I already know I wouldn't last long. The sight of you on your knees would make me shoot my load down your throat in a minute flat." My delivery comes out sounding staccato since I don't stop fucking her sweet pussy.

"Well, when you put it like that, I might give it my best shot."

"Atta girl."

I tighten my hands around her waist as I pull out of her and enter her in one deep push, a loud groan escaping both our mouths.

She's drenched, her juices dripping out of her pussy.

The thought of making her come as hard as she did a few days ago, fuels me.

I fuck her with more determination.

"Zane."

My name on her lips is like an aphrodisiac.

My thrusts are deep and quick, as urgency slams into me like a tidal wave.

Bang.

Bang.

Bang.

"For someone who was concerned she might get caught doing lewd things good girls would never be caught doing, you're eager to let everyone know we're up here. Keep banging against the window, and we'll have an audience."

"It's so, so good!" She wails her response.

Damn right.

I continue pumping in and out of her like a piston, the heat burning through my rampant cock.

Rocking her hips into my thrusts, Shay matches my cadence, slamming her round ass against my body. The way she's angled allows me to fuck her deeper.

"Fuck me good!" She hisses the words between clenched teeth.

With pleasure.

My cadence is frantic.

Her hands squeeze into fists.

"Don't you dare bang on that window."

"I won't. I promise." Her breath is labored.

Beads of sweat drip from my hairline down to my jaw.

I swear, I'm going to have a heart attack.

If I die fucking this woman's pussy, so be it.

Biting my lower lip, I double my efforts.

"Fuck, I can't imagine what it would be like to sink my cock into your ass."

She takes in a sharp breath.

"Relax. It's all fantasy, love. I'd only take your ass if we were both on the same page."

She nods.

She didn't say no.

Damn.

Changing the tempo, I slow my movements, guiding the length of my cock out of her pussy before I ram it back in, soliciting a shuddering moan from Shay that has my cock twitching and my hands flying to her tits.

Fuck! This woman's pussy is my drug.

She tilts her head back and our eyes meet.

I should demand she obeys my command, but I can't.

Fucking her while squeezing her tits and peering into the ocean blue of her eyes, heightens everything.

"Going without sex for over a year was worth—" She doesn't finish her sentence. She averts her gaze.

"Look at me."

Timid eyes meet mine.

"Finish that sentence."

"You were worth waiting for," she says. Her voice is so low, if we weren't fused together, I wouldn't have heard them.

"Right back at ya."

Her eyes widen in shock. "You've been celibate for over a year?"

"Not that long, but it's been a while. I haven't been with anyone since my cousin's wedding six months ago."

"Oh, wow."

"I guess I was waiting for you."

Her lips part in a timid smile.

Her eyes are burning into mine, full of intensity and desire.

I can't hold back anymore.

I slide my cock out a little and kiss her neck while I fuck her.

That triggers another drawn-out moan from her.

The combination of the hedonistic sound of skin against skin slapping, her beautiful ass jiggling with each thrust, her glorious tits in my hands, and the heady scent of sex permeating between us, revs my engine.

I dig my fingers a little more into the soft flesh of her tits, conscious, I might leave bruises. Secretly, I wouldn't mind leaving my mark on her.

We cry out together.

I'm so deep inside her, it's unlikely I'll find my way out.

I'm okay with that.

My heavy breathing mixed with hers fills the space.

We're lucky everyone else in this building is preoccupied, because we're not even making an effort to be quiet.

"Your pussy is so fucking good, Shay," I grunt, letting go of her tits and repositioning my hands, pressing them over hers on the window. I swing my hips back and bury myself to the hilt in one single thrust. I power into her, showing her no mercy.

"Oh God, Zane!" she wails.

I interlace my fingers with hers, driving into her faster.

"I'm close."

I let go of her hands, ready to take care of her clit.

The second one of her hands is free, it shoots down to her pussy.

"Jesus Christ."

The sight of my sexy-as-fuck fake girlfriend touching herself while I fuck her from behind is one that will be seared in my brain forever. Something about her allowing me to see her unraveled and unabashed makes this hotter than sin.

This, right here, just topped my spank bank.

I drive us both to the finish line by slowing my cadence enough to give her time to chase her orgasm.

Her fingers fly over her clit, and her juices are drowning my needy cock.

It's a trickle at first, but it soon turns into a fucking river.

When Shay comes, it's with a scream everyone in the manor must hear.

Goddammit.

My legs shake underneath me as I quicken my pace, moving in and out of her with more velocity as I chase my own climax.

I hold her tight and sink my teeth into the flesh at the base of her neck to muffle my animalistic growl, as I spill my release inside her pussy. My orgasm torpedoes through me. It's so powerful, I swear I see stars.

I have no idea how long we stay in this position. I'm too busy coaxing my heartrate to return to normal.

Sex has never been this mind-blowing.

Chapter 21

Shay

Since Zane Keller draws core-shaking orgasms out of me, cleaning up once we were done fooling around was... an experience. We went through two boxes of Kleenex. I love spending time with my family, but when my fake boyfriend hinted at skipping the rest of the reception, no way was I going to refuse.

When we got back to the hotel, I was expecting we'd take a shower together, but Zane had something else in mind. He insisted we take separate showers. I was a bit confused, but I didn't argue. The mischievous glee in his eyes suggested I should do as I'm told. When I stepped out of the bathroom, a large black box with a big red bow was waiting for me on the bed. I was just about to demand an explanation, insulted because I hadn't bought him a Christmas gift when he had, but the accompanying note set me straight. The items inside the box further drove the point.

This gift lands me on Santa's naughty list.

As I admire my reflection in the mirror, I'm still as dumbfounded and awestruck as I was when I first slipped into this daring combo. As a former runway model, I'm used to strutting around wearing not much. As a plus size woman, I've never put it all out there like this. Then again, I've never been with a guy who dared to push me out of my comfort zone.

There's a knock at the door separating our rooms.

Zane doesn't wait for me to answer. He walks in.

Dear God.

I blink a few times, my brain unable to form a cohesive sentence.

He speaks before I have time to get over the shock of seeing him wearing nothing but a white towel draped around his waist. "Holy fucking Christ. You look good enough to eat, love."

I lower my gaze as I dance from one foot to the other. "I feel kind of sexy."

"You *are* fucking sexy." He all but shouts.

Message received.

"I knew your body would look tempting as sin in this combo, but seeing it with my own two eyes far exceeds the fantasy."

I blush so hard, I'm sure my pale skin matches the flaming red color of the lingerie he selected for me.

"There's a reason I didn't give you this with the Divine Curves Couture dress you wore to the wedding." His voice drops an octave, smooth like a fine cognac. "There's no way I could've survived, knowing you were wearing that cock-hardening number under your dress." A wolfish grin stretches his lips as his eyes rake up and down my body. "I get to enjoy this all to myself."

"Ditto."

I return the favor, my gaze traveling across his broad shoulders, lickable chest, ripped abs, and well-defined arms.

My mouth waters, eager to run my tongue all over his impressive six-pack.

His body is fit, without being bulky—another notch to add to his belt.

Zane is gorgeous in a suit, but half naked like this, he's a sight for sore eyes.

I drink him in greedily.

Unable to help myself, my gaze drops to his feet.

Impeccable.

"You like what you see, love?"

I roll my eyes in a theatrical manner. "Do you have to ask?"

He winks. "One should never assume."

After our earlier tryst, there was too much going on for me to properly appreciate this man's Adonis body. Now, I can take my time.

"Give me a twirl."

I oblige.

He whistles.

"The back is something else."

Everything about this lingerie combination is daring, but he's right, the back is the showstopper.

Zane selected a plunging V-neck babydoll set. The chemise features sheer lace cups and satin trim spaghetti straps. There's zero support for the girls and the sheer fabric barely covers my nipples. I suspect that's the whole point.

This was designed with seduction in mind.

The super cute open back that showcases my ass is nothing more than an overt invitation. To complement the saucy top, he selected a thong. I don't do granny panties, but it's been a long time since I wore anything this sexy— No, this transcends sexiness. This is pure eroticism.

He closes the gap between us.

Like an inspector, he walks in a circle around me, his hazel green eyes taking me in before he stops in front of me. He towers over me, emanating power and dominance, his manly scent washing over me. He reaches out for my face, stroking my cheek with the backs of his fingers. "I needed to admire your gorgeousness a second time, up close and personal."

I smile, the compliment causing my cheeks to flush.

"How did you figure out my size?" I ask.

He reaches out and runs his fingers through my hair. He hasn't stopped touching my long strands since I pulled them out of the twist. "The same way I figured out the size for the dress."

"You checked the label on the dress I was wearing Thursday night?"

He shakes his head. "Different designers. Different sizes. Briar and I exchanged numbers before she left the hotel in the wee hours of Friday morning. So, before calling our creative director, I texted Briar first for your sizes. I guessed your size for the lingerie. It was a bit too personal of a question."

He went to that much effort for me?

Oh.

My.

God.

I can't help my smile. "You're full of tricks."

"I told you before. I'm not easily dissuaded when I have my sights set on something." Waves of intoxicating eroticism waft off him.

Touching a finger to the base of my throat, he traces it down my chest, between my cleavage, all the way to my belly-button. My nipples pucker against the sheer lace, the fabric rasping against my hard peaks. He closes his hand over my breast, feeling the weight, flicking his thumb over my erect nipple, which is as hard as a bullet tip.

My pussy throbs at his touch.

In one quick movement, he unwraps the towel from around his waist with his other hand, letting it drop to the floor.

My mouth waters at the sight.

He's so yummy looking, I have the compelling need to perform a soprano aria *a la* Puccini's *'O Mio Babbino Caro'* in salute of his impressive cock. Since I can't carry a tune to save my life, it says a lot.

I wasn't allowed to see him hard and ready earlier. It irked me, but I went along with it. Even though it was clear, when he thrusted into me, he was a big guy, seeing his erection pointing north is so darn hot. Knowing I do that to him is even hotter.

He takes my hand and guides me to his suite. His room is larger than mine—his is the master room and mine is the kids' room. Instead of heading towards the bed, he leads me to the living room area where a round, oversize ottoman takes center stage. Only the moonlight illuminates the room, bathing it in a sensual aura.

Anticipation floods through me.

"I want you to ride me."

My wide eyes peer up at him. "Me on top?"

He shoots me a playful glance. "Yeah... like a dirty cowgirl on top." He sits down and taps the ottoman. "This surface is better than the bed."

"I see."

My arousal heightens. The bed or the sofa would've been so predictable. Leave it to Zane for taking it up several notches.

He pulls me onto his lap, so I'm straddling him.

I lower myself until my covered pussy lands on his naked cock.

"You're so wet."

"When I'm around you, I'm turned on like a light switch. You keep pushing the envelope and keep me guessing. Not knowing what to expect is so... hot."

"That's the way it's supposed to be."

With his eyes boring into mine, he slides his fingers underneath the fabric of the chemise and tugs at my nipple a few times before I'm uncovering my breasts, eager for more.

I groan at the sensation.

My other breast receives the same treatment, forcing out another pained sound from me.

"Fuck, your tits are magnificent." The deep timbre of his voice travels to my clit.

His eyes bounce from mine to my exposed breasts.

The way he's staring at them feels indecent, but the lust veiling his eyes when they meet mine soothes my insecurities.

I don't have time to overthink it.

He lowers his head, grabbing my breast and pushing it inside his mouth while groping the other possessively.

My pussy throbs against his erection in response and I can't help grinding a little, rocking back and forth, pressing my needy clit against his cock.

He pulls away from me, allowing my breast to drop out of his mouth.

"My fake girlfriend is so impatient." He doesn't hide the amusement in his voice. "You came only a short while ago, but you want more. You're so greedy."

"It's all your fault."

"I'll take the blame."

His mouth is on me again.

He licks my swollen nipples like a starved man, teasing, flicking, toying. With each stroke of his tongue, he takes me higher and higher.

I rock my hips a little faster, pressing a little more against him.

Had I known dry humping could be this hot, I would've tried it more often. Then again, my pussy is dripping so much, I'm not sure if we can call it dry humping.

My breath catches in my throat when he bites my nipple

and my body hums with excitement.

I let out a series of inaudible prayers as I pick up my pace, gyrating on his lap.

I need more.

I reach between my thighs and pull the thong to the side.

There's nothing between us.

It's just my needy clit and his hard cock.

"Fuck, love." Zane grunts against my breasts. "That's it, chase your orgasm. Come all over my cock."

I lose all inhibition.

"Jesus!"

Placing my hands on his shoulders for support, I tilt my head back and ride him like my life depends on it, the tips of my long hair caress his thighs.

I'm no longer aware of what he's doing to my breasts.

The need to come is all-encompassing.

Thump.

Thump.

Thump.

My heartbeat is so fast and so loud, I'm sure he can hear it.

"Mother of God!"

Zane presses my breasts together. When he slides both nipples in his mouth and bites against them, I shoot off like a rocket.

"Oh, Zane!"

I literally stop breathing as my climax hits me hard.

Since adding benefits to our arrangement, all my orgasms have been explosive, but this one... there are no words.

"Good girl," he says in a gravelly voice.

I didn't even realize I'd closed my eyes. When I open them, a cocky grin greets me.

I can't even scold him.

He has superpowers and he knows it.

"I'm ready for round two, if you are," he says.

It hits me.

I'm such a greedy bitch.

I came, but he's still hard as a steel rod.

"I am," I say.

He produces a packet between us. I lean forward and capture the wrapper between my teeth. He pulls against it, ripping it open.

"Get up for a minute."

I do as I'm told.

"Don't even think of covering up," he says. "I want your tits hanging out."

It's like he read my mind.

I nod.

"Good."

With the moonlight illuminating the room, I can watch as he sheathes up. He lifts his gaze, catching me staring. I don't avert my gaze. I can't. The way Zane sheathes his long cock is so fucking hot. I've been with a handful of men and none of them turn the simple exercise of sliding on a condom into an erotic show.

He taps his lap. "Hop back on."

I'm about to remove my thong when he stops me.

"What are you doing?"

I point at my panties. "If I don't remove these, how is this going to work?"

"The panties stay on. You'll slide them to the side so I can fuck you."

I don't know if I can keep up with this man's dirty streak.

I hold onto his shoulders as I lower my body until my pussy is a few inches from his erect cock.

"This time, you have all the control." He winks.

"I don't believe that lie for a second."

"You have all the control, *to start*."

"I knew there was a catch," I say. "You don't come across like the kind of man who relinquishes control easily."

"Good assessment. I don't. The alpha in me makes it impossible."

I consider him for a beat.

"I shouldn't admit to this, but I like the way you take charge. I love the idea of surrendering." I hesitate. "It's a welcome change to be with a man who..."

"Go on."

"You know *exactly* what you want, and dare I say, you know *exactly* what I need—better than I do."

A slow smile spreads across his gorgeous lips. "That's what I like the most about you, Shay. You're a beautiful, strong, confident woman, but at the same time, you're willing to bend to my will. That's a fucking sexy combination."

I bite my lower lip, a little taken aback by his confession.

Slap!

I yelp when his palm makes contact with my ass. "What was that about?"

"My cock is waiting."

"Demanding alpha." I grumble my feeble protest under my breath.

"Cry me a river when you're coming all over me."

That's all the motivation I need.

I clamp one hand to the back of his neck, and slide the other between my legs. As per his command, I pull my thong to the side before lowering myself fully. I impale his huge cock inch by inch, moaning as pleasure washes over me.

"Jesus Christ."

His grunts drive me crazy.

His hand slides underneath my ass, allowing me to swallow him whole.

For a few long beats, neither of us moves.

"We're so close." I break the silence. "For some reason, this position feels even more intimate than you lying on top of me."

"I don't do the missionary position."

"Why am I not surprised?"

"Less talking! More fucking!"

He grips my hips and moves me up and down the length of his cock.

I take over.

He slides a finger between my lips and rubs my clit in a circular motion.

My head lolls back and I let out a long exhale.

This is pure bliss.

He stops.

I stare at him, my eyebrows knitted in confusion.

"You want me to continue playing with your hard little clit?"

I nod.

"Use your words."

"Yes."

"Yes, what?"

"I want you to keep playing with me."

"You want me to keep playing with your earlobe?"

"My clit." Impatience colors my voice.

"Don't get testy with me. Tell me what you want. And I want you to put it in a sentence."

"Zane, please, play with my clit."

"That's more like it."

He gives me what I want.

He rubs his thumb over my clit in sinful slow circles, sending me higher and higher with each revolution. He leans forward and captures a nipple between his lips and sucks on it greedily.

His groans and grunts only add to the hedonistic moment.

When he bites against my nipple, I swear, I see stars.

"Yes, Zane, yes! Please don't stop."

He does it again, biting a little harder this time.

"Jesus Christ!"

He grabs a handful of my ass and squeezes tight.

It's coming at me from all directions, heightening my senses.

I bounce up and down his cock with more determination.

He thrusts his hips up to meet me, slamming into me each time, and causing a ripple effect of pure pleasure to course through my body.

He lets my breast fall from between his lips and his eyes bore into mine. "Holy shit, Shay, your pussy was made for my cock."

"My pussy belongs to you." *I want to belong to you so bad.*

"You got that right."

Something—I want to say a flash of vulnerability—flickers in his eyes, but I'm sure I'm wrong.

I'm seeing things.

My mind is playing tricks on me.

That must be it.

I push the unsettling thought away because it's messing me up.

The forceful way he fists my hair and tugs at it makes it impossible not to be in the moment.

I resume my mission, bouncing off his balls, chasing my orgasm.

The weight of my arms presses heavily against his shoulders as I bounce up and down on his cock. I ride him with a confidence I've never experienced before in bed with a man. Zane is like an adrenaline shot to my ego.

"It's good?" he asks.

"It's fucking good."

He threads his fingers through my hair before fisting it forcefully. "Damn right it is."

Those words shouldn't mean much, but right now, they mean the world to me.

"Being your fake boyfriend *with benefits* is a heck of a lot better than fisting my cock, fantasizing of fucking you."

He cups my face in one hand and pulls me into a slow, passionate, and blazing kiss. My comeback dies on his lips. Every nerve ending lights up like sparklers as I continue to ride him.

This man...

Sex with past boyfriends has never reached this pinnacle. Sex with Zane is an all-compassing experience. I know without a doubt, from here on in, I'll compare every other man to him. He elevates my standards, but that also means he increases my chances of being thoroughly disappointed with future lovers.

A delightful sensation builds at my core, pulling my thoughts back to the moment, and my pussy clenches around his cock in strong staccato pulses.

God, yes.

"That's it, love. Milk my big fat cock. Force me to shoot my load deep inside your pussy."

I'm too close to respond or keep bouncing off his balls.

With trembling legs, I lower myself so I'm sitting on top of him.

He places a steady hand against my back. "Hold on for the ride."

I tilt my head back and grind against him in a circular motion, rubbing my needy clit against his pelvis.

"Fuck! The way your fine ass is moving on top of me is so fucking hot." Through a smutty haze, I barely make out his words. "Take what you need from me, dirty girl."

I change my rhythm, the urge to come overwhelming.

Instead of gyrating my hips in circles, I rock back-and-forth.

It's like I'm possessed.

"Christ, Shay!"

He places his fingers against my clit.

Without an ounce of shame, I grind against them.

I'm there. I'm there.

"You're gonna come hard for me?" he asks.

"Yes—yes, I will."

"Good girl. Show me how much you appreciate my cock."

His words push me off the cliff.

My body goes rigid.

"Oh, God, Zane!" I shout at the top of my lungs, not caring if I'm loud.

I keep chanting his name over and over again like a woman in a trance.

It feels as if all the blood in my body whooshes to my clit in one fell swoop. I tilt my head back, close my eyes and I explode, giving myself body and soul to a sublime orgasm, gushing all over him. I still don't understand how he's able to make my body come this hard, but I don't question it. I ride with it, unwilling to be embarrassed.

I could surrender to this man every single day of my life, for the rest of my life.

He grips my hips more forcefully, demanding more of my spent body.

Zane doesn't show me any mercy as he fucks my dripping pussy.

He's unrestrained. Wild, even.

With each pump, he grunts louder, more feral.

Fuck.

His feverish tempo is dizzying.

The sensation of my juices trickling down his cock and thighs is beyond lewd and naughty.

The temperature in the room is hotter than a sauna. The moonlight allows me to catch a glimpse of the string of sweat beads glistening against his skin. I suspect, it's the same for me.

To my shock, my clit pulses again.

The familiar tingling sensation is unmistakable.

Holy. Hell.

This man is a gift from God.

"Zane, Dear God— I'm— I'm—" I struggle through my admission. "I'm coming?!"

From my pained cry, you'd think I was suffering. Nothing could be further from the truth. This is one hundred percent unadulterated pleasure.

"Don't you dare hold back on me, Shay. Give it to me!"

Blindsided, a second orgasm robs me of everything.

I close my eyes and clench my pussy hard around his pistoning cock.

"Christ!" Zane's voice comes out sounding hoarse.

Before I know it, I'm coming again, as my formidable lover roars my name.

From the loud—suffering sounding—groans, I'm guessing his climax is as powerful as mine.

Still panting and struggling to catch his breath, he pulls my head closer to his. The closeness causes my sensitive nipples to scratch at his chest coated with a sheen of sweat. The delicious tingling sensation heightens the potency of our tongues dancing together.

For a few beats, we breathe in and out, before our lips meet in another blazing kiss.

This temporary boyfriend arrangement was meant for me to save face.

I was never supposed to become an addict...

Chapter 22

Zane

I'm flopped on my side, my bent elbow resting on the bed, holding my head as I admire a sleeping angel. Her long red hair splays across the white pillowcase. From the rise and fall of her body, she's still in a deep sleep. It's only six-thirty a.m., but my needy cock woke me up. As much as I'm dying to wake her up so I can fuck her again, I don't. I'm taking too much pleasure watching her sleep. I'm not a 'come and run' guy, but I don't do sleepovers. Never have. And I promised myself, I never would. I'm not a barbarian, I'll linger for the obligatory postcoital conversation. I make it a point never to fall asleep. It doesn't matter how exhausted I am. My body knows better.

Then, came Shay O'Hara.

In my defense, Shay and I are trapped in a hotel. Well, that's what I tell myself. The truth of the matter is, I wanted her in my bed. After I made her come two more times last night, she tried to slip away to her room. I wouldn't have it. For the first time in my life, the urge to sleep with a woman nestled in my arms, trumped the warnings in my head.

A sleepover leads to expectations.

A relationship leads to marriage.

Marriage is fucked up.

It's like all of that went out the window last night. Shay kept curling away from me on the far side of the bed. Every time she robbed me of her warmth, I'd reach out and drag her body against mine, wrapping a possessive arm around her waist, and burying my face in her cascade of hair. The feel of her round ass pressing against my cock—which stood on alert most of the night, eager to pleasure her at a moment's notice—was both Nirvana and torture.

Flashing back to last night, I smile at myself.

The lingerie I selected for her is part of our boudoir collection. I'll have to thank my baby brother. He's the brains behind the collection. Originally, it was designed for plus size women who wanted to capture sexy pregnancy shots. From the moment the line launched, our clients went nuts. We had to double down efforts to design some of the most demanded pieces to fit plus size women who weren't expecting, but were looking to ramp up the sexy factor in their relationship. That's how Tempting Curves was born.

I knew what I wanted to see on Shay's luscious body.

It looked so fucking good on her, she had to keep it on. Having her hold the thong to the side while I fucked her, was part of the naughtiness.

My eyes shift to the large window.

The snow is coming down, but not enough to keep us grounded. The pilot texted me to confirm.

This is our last day together. I should be relieved, not restless.

She stirs.

I trail a soft finger along her bare arms.

She flops over to face me.

Her wild hair is a glorious mess.

I'm about to reach out to curl my fingers through her mane, but she lifts an arm at the same time, stopping me.

She hides a lazy yawn behind her hand before stretching like a cat.

I watch her with rapt attention.

This moment seems so much more intimate than anything we shared last night.

"You're awake?" she asks, rubbing the sleep from her eyes.

I tuck a strand of hair behind her ear. "I am, love."

"Morning."

Her husky voice hardens my cock.

"Morning."

"Your deep groggy bedroom voice is sexy. I on the other hand, sound like a strangled cat."

I chuckle.

"It's because the roosters are still sleeping. My body has no business waking up this early."

"I reckon your body woke up early because it didn't get enough last night."

"Excuse me, mister, but it got plenty last night. *It* most likely won't be able to recover for a week. *It* is exhausted. *It* should be sleeping. There is such a thing as too much of a good thing."

"You believe that lie?" I don't give her a chance to answer. I grab her hand under the sheet, and place it over my erection.

"It seems your cock only has one setting—hard as rock."

I reach out and run the backs of my fingers against her hard nipple. "Around you, it does."

She responds with a beaming smile.

"Last night was..." I hold her gaze. "Let's just say, you lived up to all my fantasies... and then some."

"You're not just saying that?" Her insecurities come out loud and clear.

"Our relationship might be fake to the world, but I've told you already, when it's just the two of us, I'd never bullshit you."

The first part of my statement leaves a bitter taste in my mouth.

She worries her bottom lip. "It's a night I'll never forget."

"I'll make sure to give you a parting gift to make this day a day you will never forget." I lay it on thick.

"I'm all for gifts."

"Good," I say.

My hand runs down her stomach and brushes between her legs.

She pulls her lower lip between her teeth.

"This is why your body woke up early. I barely touched you and you're already wet. Your body needs me."

She stares at me through lidded eyes.

"Your pussy is dripping, love. I bet you were dreaming about me doing filthy things to you."

"I plead the fifth," she says in a weak voice.

I dip one finger inside her.

She gasps.

Her heady scent hits me and my mouth waters.

I slide another finger in.

She cries out and throws her head back, arching her body.

"Do you still plead the fifth?"

"No"—she shakes her head—"You win."

"No, love, *you* win... every single time I make you come your head off."

"Yes, please!"

I love how her body reacts to me.

I roll my hips against her, letting her feel my arousal, and she moans at the sensation.

I clasp a hand behind her head, bring her face close to mine and I kiss her hard, darting my tongue into her mouth.

Another hip roll has her meowling like a kitten.

"Let's try something different," I say before pulling the sheet off our bodies and climbing on top of her.

"What did you have in mind?" she asks.

"Spread your legs for me," I order.

She does as she's told.

I lean forward and place a kiss in the inside of her knee.

"Hey, that tickles."

I chuckle.

I place a hand against the mattress and reach between our bodies to adjust my cock.

"What about a condom?" The request comes tumbling out of her mouth.

I set her straight. "I'm not going to fuck you, I'm going to play with you."

Her eyebrows knit in confusion.

It'll all make sense in a second.

When I rub my naked cock up and down the length of her slick pussy, her eyes widen in understanding.

She wiggles underneath me. "Dear God."

"Stay still."

"How am I supposed to do that when you're torturing me?"

"If you settle down, torture will turn to something mind-blowing for both of us."

That does it.

"Good girl."

With my eyes locked onto hers, I move my hips back and forth. My cadence is slow at first, allowing us to savor every ripple of pleasure.

She lets out a pained exhale before digging her long nails into my ass, forcing an animalistic growl out of me.

Jesus.

Maybe I'm biting off more than I can chew. It seemed like a

good idea at first, but now, I fear it might give me a fucking heart attack. The sensation of her hard clit rubbing against my cock makes me see stars.

"Yes, oh yes," she begs. "Faster." She grabs my ass and squeezes tight.

I respond with a loud, throaty groan.

For a few long seconds, I'm lost, relishing every stroke.

She slides a hand between us and cups my balls.

I don't see it coming.

"Goddammit."

I pick up the pace, thrusting faster and faster.

She bucks her hips, adding more pressure against my cock.

Holy shit.

It seems I'll meet my maker two days before Christmas.

My pre-cum mixes with her juices in the most sinful way.

The slick heat feels like motherfucking heaven.

Each thrust of my hips builds momentum and elicits more and more delirious moans from her. The sweet sound travels to my balls.

She glides a fingertip up my shaft.

I steady myself to allow it.

Her fingers find my tip.

Fuck.

She keeps her hand there, and every time the head of my cock touches her fingers, it's like a shot of drugs, straight to my brain. That fleeting touch jacks up our naughty play.

This is so fucking hot.

"No other man will make you feel this good, Shay. Only me."

Words are coming out of my mouth without my consent.

This new experience has rendered me stupid. Insane, even.

"No one else will." She lets out a long moan. "Only you, Zane."

Her words hit me straight in the chest. But then, she takes it up a notch.

Her eyes are glued to mine when she says, "No other man will ever make me feel as sexy or cherish my body like you do."

I grunt between clenched teeth. "Damn fucking right."

My cadence is relentless.

My determination to ruin it for all other men fuels me.

The familiar internal spasm that precedes an explosion and a tug at my balls quicken my breath.

I'm about to shoot off like a fucking rocket.

There isn't much left to me.

"I'm coming!"

Thank God.

"Zane!" She shouts my name so loud, I'm sure people in the lobby heard her.

The frantic sound of my name on her lips and the way she's gyrating underneath me causes me to lose my bearings. Her climatic cries send me off the cliff.

"Oh fuck, Shay!" My voice booms in the room.

A torpedo-like orgasm barrels through me.

Shay grips my hips, holding me close to her.

"Let go." My demand comes out in a strangled voice. "Now!"

She obeys.

I barely have time to readjust myself as I shoot my load all over her stomach. It's a fucking big load. Trickles of warm cum trail between her legs. The sight is so arousing, it's enough to pull another orgasm for me.

My trembling legs can't support me.

I angle my body and drop next to her, my heavy weight causing the mattress to dip.

Christ.

Only ragged breathing echoes in the room.

When I come down from the adrenaline rush, I cup her face in my hand and place a gentle kiss on her temple. She places a hand over mine, holding it there.

"If this fake relationship was any longer, I don't think I could survive it," she says in a low voice.

"Why don't we put that theory to the test?"

Once again, my mouth runs away from me.

Her head turns on the pillow, her gaze snaps up to mine. She runs a hand through her tousled hair, her eyes as wide as saucers.

"What do you mean?"

I stroke damp strands away from her face.

I stare at her.

There's a chaotic chorus going on in my head—and my heart.

What the fuck is going on with me?

"Zane?"

I stomp all over my internal turmoil and speak. "This is going to sound crazy."

"Try me."

"I'm heading to the Hamptons to spend Christmas Eve and Christmas with my brother and my cousins. You'll be staying here in Boston to celebrate with your family." I run the pad of my thumb along the bottom of her lip. "Things don't have to end between us."

A curtain of lashes flutters. "Are you saying what I think you're saying?"

"New York is a big city," I say. "What if the reason we happened to meet on Monday—and sit next to each other at the bar—transcends us pretending we're a couple? Other than Briar who was in the know, I'd say we were successful at fooling everybody. Maybe we were so in character, we fooled ourselves." Her breath hitches. "We owe it to ourselves to explore if there's more between us than a convenient fake relationship with benefits."

My words spill out of me of their own accord, my thoughts running away from me. I struggle to understand where the hell this is all coming from, but at the same time, I don't want to take it back.

This woman has me twisted.

She doesn't answer.

Dawn hasn't given to daylight yet, so I can't make out the myriad emotions swimming in her big blue eyes.

I reach for her hand and grab it into mine. "Talk to me," I coax.

"I didn't even want to entertain the idea, because this is crazy and this kind of stuff only happens in movies. You just don't meet a gorgeous stranger who agrees to be your perfect fake boyfriend and for things to click. I've felt this unreasonable pull towards you from the moment we met. Given my over-the-top and unorthodox proposal, I thought it was foolish to hope for more—"

"It's not."

"Really?"

"We can turn this fake relationship into a real one." I snap my fingers. "Just like that!"

She's staring at me with bewildered eyes again.

My fingers wind their way into her hair, stroking. "I laid my cards on the table, Shay. Now it's your turn."

Chapter 23

Zane: I haven't seen you in six hours and the first text I get from you is you scolding me?

Shay: Sorry, but it's all your fault.

Zane: You're blaming me again?

Shay: This was a fake relationship. How dare you buy me a gift? What the fuck?

Zane: Someone needs to arrest me for such an offense.

Shay: I'm serious. I didn't get you anything.

Zane: This isn't tit for tat.

Shay: You bought me a **very** expensive gift. If you were going to stomp all over our arrangement, at least you could've done it with something a lot more low-key. And you could've given me a heads-up. I feel like a cheapskate.

Zane: First, this is no longer a fake relationship. Second, why would I buy my girlfriend something low-key? Third, read what I said earlier, this isn't tit for tat.

Shay: Until a few hours ago, we were **still** involved in a **fake** relationship for a wedding.

Zane: Newsflash. Things have evolved.

Shay: When the hell did you have time to buy me this gift?

Zane: Friday.

Shay: When on Friday? You spent the whole day on lockdown with me. We had a blood oath—as long as I was confined to a hotel room, you remained by my side.

Zane: I didn't break our blood oath.

Shay: Then how do you explain the gift?

Zane: I texted my cousin Gabriel because his wife has a serious jewelry collection, courtesy of her loving husband. He hooked me up with a contact at a high-end jewelry store in New York and they patched me through to their Boston store. The local rep and I texted back and forth until he showed me something that had your name written all over it. Briar confirmed I had nailed it, and she also supplied me with your parents' address, allowing me to put my devious plan into action.

Shay: You blindsided me.

Zane: I did. Since we weren't going to spend Christmas together, I wanted to get you a little something.

Shay: **Little?** <woman facepalming emoji> Stunning, two-tone gold, topaz and diamond earrings are more than a little something, and you know it. They're Pomellato, for crying out loud. They must've cost a fortune.

Zane: The color reminded me of your eyes, so I had to buy them. You're going to stop traffic when you wear them. I'll be proud to have you hanging from my arm.

Shay: You're incorrigible, Keller.

Zane. Sue me. Do you like them at least?

Shay: Do you even have to ask?

Zane: Since I'm emceeing a charity event in New York and you're in Boston, I have to ask because I'm not psychic.

Shay: I love, love, love them. They're absolutely stunning. They're officially my most cherished belonging.

Zane: You're just saying that.

Shay: I wish I could've shown my appreciation in person.

Zane: Are you talking dirty to me, love?

Shay: Nah. I can't measure up to your **formidable** skills. <laughing out loud emoji> I'm just saying, you robbed me of the chance to say thank you in person by **gifting and running**

Zane: You can make it up to me when we see each other on the twenty-seventh.

Shay: I intend on doing just that.

Zane: There you go talking dirty again.

Shay: You're rubbing off on me.

Zane: I'd much prefer if you were rubbing off on me… but I had prior commitments. Alas, that's how the cookie crumbles.

Shay: That was hilarious.

Zane: I have to cut this short. I just got the five-minute warning. The intermission is almost over. I'm going to have to step on stage soon and part rich people from their money for a good cause.

Shay: Go get 'em, slugger! It was great hearing from you.

Zane: Is that your way of saying you miss me already?

Shay: I could be coy about it, but why bother? I totally miss you.

Zane: Right back at ya, love. In fact, I'm not sure I'll be able to sleep tonight without being wrapped around your warm body.

Shay: I know I won't be able to sleep.

Zane: Why don't I video call you later when I get back to my place so you can rub one off, while I do the same… that way, we'll both sleep soundly….

Shay: <stunned emoji>

Chapter 24

Shay

Landing Zane Keller as a boyfriend two days before Christmas is like winning a first-place prize. Scratch that. It's like winning the freaking gold medal.

Santa delivered big time this year.

#BestChristmasGiftEver!

...With a hand stroking one of my new earrings.

Keeley fell off her chair when we had a video chat earlier and I filled her in on the avalanche of new and exciting developments in my life. I told her all about my tall, handsome, hazel-green-eyed, dark blond-haired—a la Chris Hemsworth back in the day—and generous boyfriend. Her piercing blue eyes popped out of their sockets when I flashed my bejeweled gift at the screen. She's thrilled for me. So am I. A week ago, I was a singleton. Now, I'm dating my fake boyfriend *for real*. You can't get more Hallmark than that. Except my movie of the week involves a lot of dirty, filthy sex with a formidable lover.

I reread my boyfriend's last line, blinking at the bluntness.

There was no pussyfooting on his part. He laid it out there.

My God, I love this man's dirty mind.

My cheeks flush.

He brings out the bad girl in me.

Sex with Zane is more adventurous, raw, hedonistic, and playful than it had ever been with previous boyfriends. I'm not much of a one-night stand girl, but the three I had, were nothing to write home about. The naughty encounters with my new boyfriend could fill the pages of a best-selling steamy romance book. I can't get enough of his alpha dominant streak.

A man who knows how to take charge. Thank you, God.

And then, there's his caring and fiercely protective side that makes me all kinds of gooey inside. The CFO and co-owner of Curves Envy Fashion was my male nurse for a whole day. My vain heart is quick to remind me he's seen me at my most vulnerable, and dare I say unattractive—me hunched over a toilet bowl, barfing. I'm sure that must've been a pretty sight. Still, he chose me as his *real* girlfriend.

I'm giddy as I drop my phone on the coffee table. After doing a happy dance in my head, I pick-up my plate, and keep eating as if I'm not hot and bothered.

Yum!

The perfect bite pulls my mind out of the gutter.

I look up.

Two pairs of eyes staring at me.

My sister is sporting a shit-eating grin that matches my great aunt's.

"What?" I ask around the bite.

I excused myself when my phone vibrated, and they were fine with it. Now, they're giving me attitude. What gives?

"Smooth." Briar snorts. "But not smooth enough. You keep forgetting, you don't have a good poker face, sis."

I shoot daggers at her.

"That wasn't your executive assistant. That was *your man*."

She's onto me.

"Fine. That was Zane."

"I knew it!" She does a little dance on her seat, a smug look on her face. "Dr. Elias Fitzsimmons is a snail compared to a whale like Zane Keller."

I choke on a bite of baguette and camembert cheese at the grotesque comparison.

If Briar's evil grin doesn't grow wider.

She soldiers on. "There's no way you guys were faking it. The chemistry between you two was flaming hot. And let's not forget the nickname he has for you, *love*." She still can't get over it.

Aunt Eileen chimes in. "To be fair, I called it first when I adopted Zane as our own the moment I met him. The karaoke drama confirmed what I already knew. He's good people."

"He is..." my voice trails, warmth spreading throughout my body, thinking of the tall, handsome stranger who came to my rescue and ended up becoming the man I didn't even know I was looking for. The man I needed.

Aunt Eileen adjusts her glasses by lifting them with the back of her hand and keeps eating, seemingly satisfied I agree with her.

"Glad you unstuck your head from your butt," Briar says.

My lips curl up in a snarl.

She sticks her tongue out at me like a three-year-old.

It's the three of us.

After that unexpected and mind-blowing declaration, I didn't want Zane to go. To extend our time together, I hopped in the limo and accompanied him to the airport. The driver dropped me off at Alan and Ma's house and I've been hanging out with my sister and great aunt all afternoon. When I got here, Aunt Eileen and Briar were in full Christmas Eve dinner preparation mode, picking up where Ma left off.

Once I change into something comfortable, I ran down to

the kitchen so they could put me to work. Between chopping, sautéing, stuffing, marinating, whipping up yummy desserts, and three dishwasher loads, we spent hours in the kitchen keeping our hands busy while chatting up a storm. Needless to say, wine was involved—enough to elevate the mood, but not enough for us to be sloppy in the kitchen, or worse, burn down the house.

As Aunt Eileen was slipping the three pecan pies into the freezer, the doorbell rang. A delivery man was standing at the door, holding an eye-catching gift bag. After I lost my shit all over my gift—my elation matched by my sister's and my great aunt's—it was time to chill out.

Now, we're lounging in the living room.

It's good to be home.

Briar is sitting, legs tucked underneath her on an over-sized armchair. Aunt Eileen's legs are stretched out on the two-seater sofa situated across from the three-seater I'm sitting on. We're enjoying an evening in, nibbling on a fancy charcuterie board arrangement—courtesy of my little sister—washing it all down with a beautiful red from Finger Lakes, New York, while listening to Christmas music.

I've never met a charcuterie board I didn't love.

This one is no exception.

Briar aced it.

Ma and Alan are at the Fitzsimmons's house for an intimate post-wedding gathering—immediate family only.

I passed.

I've had enough of Imogen to last me a lifetime. Two days spent in her presence exceeds my limit for bullshit for the next decade. Elias's parents know I had a bad allergic reaction on Thursday night, but they don't know their envious and twisted daughter-in-law tried to shut me up by causing my tongue to swell.

Aunt Eileen refused to go. She also had her quota. Ma didn't push.

As for Briar, I'm still not sure how the little brat weaseled her way out of participating, since Imogen is her half-sister and she falls in the immediate family category. I'm guessing Ma is defeated. Maybe she realizes now, no matter what she does and regardless of how much water she puts into her wine in her attempt to unite her family, it's in vain. It's like Alan and the rest of the family can't rub off on Imogen no matter how hard we try.

Considering the prolonged absence of Imogen's mom in her life, it puts the theory to the test—the apple doesn't fall far from the tree. Imogen will always be Imogen—a selfish woman who takes after her prima donna mom. It's like my stepsister doesn't share any DNA with her father. They're polar opposites.

Whatever.

Not that I intended on keeping my new relationship status a secret, because I was still walking on sunshine and I couldn't wait to shout my elation from the rooftops, but the arrival of my *little* gift, let the cat out of the bag. Briar and Aunt Eileen were ecstatic—they were literately jumping up and down. My sister was so beside herself, she texted Ma, who called to express her elation. Alan also voiced his approval. He's team Zane all the way.

Family, you gotta love 'em.

Zane's charm is irresistible to fake girlfriends, hopeful Irish moms, critical baby sisters, and great aunts with a scarily-accurate bullshit detector. Aunt Eileen now knows Zane started off as a fake boyfriend. Mom and Alan don't know yet.

"Excuse mc for proceeding with caution," I say in my defense. "It's not like I've had great luck with men."

"I told you before, lass, it's a matter of finding *the one*," Aunt Eileen says. "All the ones before him are a warm-up." Her voice softens. "And all the other ones after him will never measure up." A tinge of sadness colors her words. Even though she doesn't mention him by name, Briar and I know, she's talking about her deceased husband—the love of her life. Over the years, she's dated here and there, but it never amounted to much. He was her first and only true love. She talks big about Tinder and all, but she gave up on finding love again a long time ago.

"I have Briar to thank," I say, looking at my sister.

She flings her auburn hair behind her back, away from her face. Without makeup, Briar's face is dotted with freckles, a mirror of my own constellation. We sport our Irish roots loud and proud. "I love it when people give me credit for things I'm not even aware of, but what do you mean?"

"You planted the seed in my head with the whole absurd idea of hiring an escort to accompany you at the wedding. It was percolating in the back of my head, because fueled by liquid courage, I blurted out the most outrageous proposal to a stranger. Not only did he accept, but he turned out to be the most wonderful man."

Briar's smile is huge. She leans forward and taps her fork against the rim of her wine glass that's set on the coffee table. "Hear, hear! Forget about me being an auntie, I demand your firstborn." Her smile intensifies by several wattage.

"Puh-lease." I roll my eyes hard. "I'm sure Zane would object—"

Shit.

My stupid mouth.

"Busted!" Briar pushes the air with her fist. "You've been thinking of tiny, adorable little Shays and Zanes running around New York."

"Grow up!" I scold her to hide my guilt.

She snickers.

"The irony." Aunt Eileen shrugs. "You end up finding a remarkable man that stands ten feet tall on the weekend your cheating boyfriend's marrying your backstabbing, cheater stepsister. Priceless."

"Speaking of said backstabbing, cheater stepsister... I still can't believe those selfies, Aunt Eileen."

Briar nods. "Neither can I."

Aunt Eileen harrumphs. "Why are you surprised? It's not like it's the first time Imogen went after a man who's already taken."

"True," I say, "but Elias and I weren't married—"

"It's still cheating!"

I don't have a comeback. She's right.

"I wonder how long that's been going on..." My words trail.

"Same here," Briar says.

Aunt Eileen tsks and shakes her head, as if she's engaged in a conversation with herself.

Briar and I stare at her expectantly.

When she still doesn't speak, my sister and I glance at each other, her perplexed gaze, matching mine.

I coax her. "Why don't you come out and say it?"

"I'm going on pure instinct here"—Aunt Eileen shifts in her seat—"but I'm willing to bet a lot of money that when Imogen's baby pops out, it won't only be the sex that's a surprise..."

"I still don't get why she'd still go through with the wedding," Briar says.

"Time and time again, Imogen has shown she's self-centered," Aunt Eileen says. "It's all about her. Consequences be damned."

I can't believe Imogen would go that far.

On the day of her wedding, Aunt Eileen caught Imogen sneaking around with the best man, aka Elias's best friend, Calvin Fernandes. Elias and Calvin are both doctors. His best friend, who also lives in New York, specializes in family medicine. They've been friends forever. When I was dating my ex, you had to be blind not to see the strong bond between him and his best friend. Calvin's Venezuelan-born wife was at the karaoke bar and wedding. I didn't pick up on anything suspicious going on between Calvin and Imogen at the karaoke bar, but then again, I'm sure cheaters have their deceitful act down pat.

This scandalous tidbit will shake Elias's world with as much force as a category nine earthquake. If those photos are anything to go by—and trust me, they're incriminating—my stepsister's baby reveal will be epic... in capital letters. Imogen is good at talking her way out of any situation, but unless we all of a sudden become colorblind, she'll have a hard time pulling the wool over everyone's eyes.

I swear to God, my stepsister must have a magic pussy—or ass—to get men to do stupid shit like this.

Something uneasy rolls through me. It's an uncomfortable thought, one I can't quiet. "I should keep my mouth shut, but the decent person in me feels compelled to warn Elias. He has a right to know."

Briar sneers. "Pshaw!"

I frown. "He does."

She shoots me a challenging glance. "Like *you* had the right to know *he* was cheating on you with *your stepsister* behind your back for months before you caught them in the act?"

Chapter 25

Zane

On the twenty-third of December of every year, the members of the VIP Den—the private members only executive mastermind group located on the forty-first-floor of the Bymark Hotel, Max, my cousins, my brother and I are part of—hold a black-tie gala to raise funds for a charity. The charity changes every year, so does the MC. This year, I was selected as the master of ceremony. As much as I wanted to stay in Boston with Shay, shy of an emergency or a catastrophe, I never back down from a prior engagement. It's not in my genetic makeup. Not to mention, this is an honor.

Several silent auctions later, and we surpassed our goal by a significant margin. The two-thousand-dollar per plate admission fee, also helped. The charity of our choice will receive a massive injection of cash on Christmas Eve. There's no better gift for the men and women who work tirelessly to ease the burden of people who are less fortunate.

Once I was relieved of my duties for the night, I was able to join my family. Max's brothers and their wives are MIA. They're celebrating Christmas in Brazil, along with their parents. My mom is also in Brazil. So is my dad. No, they're not back together, but after so many years of marriage—interspersed with divorces—my Brazilian family still welcomes Dad with open arms. Tonight, it's Max, Candace, and Xavier. My baby brother is flying solo tonight since his girl had a prior function with her alumni.

We just finished dessert.

Candace is enjoying a third glass of wine, while my brother, my cousin and I are enjoying fine cognac.

Max drops his glass on the table. "You weren't forthcoming about how things shaped up in Boston. I didn't want to get into it before you stepped on stage, but I'm dying to know. What it's like to moonlight as a fake boyfriend?"

That's the beauty of owning two company jets. You decide on the takeoff time. I landed in New York an hour later than scheduled because I couldn't find it in me in to tear myself away from Shay.

I ready myself to answer Max's question, but my brother precedes me.

"It must've been smooth sailing because I didn't receive an SOS text from him," Xavier says.

Everyone around the table chuckles.

I sent Xavier and Max a text message to let them know I had arrived, but I didn't give them a play-by-play of events after that.

"Shay was delightful," I launch in story mode. "So was her family. Her great aunt—who almost everyone calls, Aunt Eileen—is a feisty character. I like her frank talk. Someone's feelings will get hurt, but that's none of her concern. There's only one outlier... Shay's stepsister. I swear, the woman has more issues than the longest running magazine in history."

"Remind you of anyone?" Xavier asks. "Ember had some scary pathology issues."

I scowl at the mention of a woman I'd love nothing more than to forget. Ember Dankworth—the two-week fling that should've never exceeded a few heated trysts will forever more be my biggest mistake.

"It's not the same." *After the champagne and strawberry liquor incident, I have to wonder.* "Ember was unreasonably jealous. Shay's stepsister seems to be fueled by deep-seeded insecurities."

"Drama is drama. End of story," Xavier says. "You don't need that in your life, and from the sounds of it, Shay is the opposite of drama."

"Right on the nose, little brother."

I give them the highlights of the wedding. I even tell them about taking things further with Shay. I hold back on the saucy details of our time in Boston.

"And you don't think Shay's stepsister is right up there with Ember?" My brother asks, his hazel brown eyes widening in horror at the mention of the unfortunate incident that took place at a karaoke bar. "Her malicious actions could've landed Shay in the hospital."

Max pipes in. "I agree. She's a nut case. What is it with psycho women?"

There are plenty of deranged men out there," Candy says. "Trust me, I spent enough time in the New York dating pool to know."

"Good thing I rescued you." Max teases her.

Candy laughs.

"Shay might want to consider getting a restraining order against her stepsister," Xavier says with the upmost seriousness. "It worked wonders for you... and me. Ember got the message and she hasn't been harassing you in months."

I never thought I'd ever have to go this far to get someone to stay the fuck away from me, but Ember only responds to extreme measures. I haven't heard a peep from her since she was served.

My little brother is no stranger to drama.

As a former professional European soccer player, he's used to delusional women. A few months ago, he dealt with an overzealous celebrity turned influencer who was unwilling to take no for an answer. She *showed* him her displeasure in a spectacular and grotesque way. It was so outrageous, the incident landed on the *'TOP 10 CELEB SCANDALS EVERYONE WILL TALK ABOUT FOR YEARS TO COME'* list.

"In all fairness—and I'm not trying to justify Imogen's callous actions—she wasn't intentional about it. Ember was."

"Good for you for not allowing Stalker Ember or our parents' revolving door of a relationship deter you from jumping in with both feet with Shay," Xavier says.

"Ember, our parents' three divorces, and my commitment phobia... it was all playing in the back of my mind." I rake my hand through my hair. "At times, I was dealing with a riot of emotions inside... many I couldn't even explain—"

"What about her made you change your mind?" Candy asks. "After all, a leopard doesn't change its spots that easily... especially when said leopard is a filthy rich executive living in the Big Apple."

I ponder on her question for a beat. "Shay was like this strong magnet I was pulled towards—like a planet orbiting around the sun. When I stopped questioning it, there was only one way to go. I traded in my *fake* boyfriend jersey for a *real* boyfriend one."

Xavier grins. "Nice sports analogy."

I return his wide smile. "Not bad."

"All this is lip service."

My head whips in his direction. "What do you mean?"

His lips curl up in a knowing smile, like a man who knows all the answers when everyone around him is oblivious.

"Are you going to say what's on your mind?"

An audible chuckle rumbles from his chest.

"Quit breaking my balls and spill it."

He points an insistent finger at the floor. "Shay is your forty-first-floor naughty hookup. No wonder you had to claim her."

Until now, it didn't even cross my mind.

Since seducing Candy, Max measures every woman who's ever joined the Keller clan by one deciding factor.

My brother chuckles. "I refuse to believe it, but maybe Max is onto something."

"I'm more than a tall, dark, and handsome billionaire." Max's mocking tone doesn't go unnoticed. "Think about it, Zane. Even before you knew Ember was a head case, you steered far away from the Bymark Hotel. You didn't even go there with her for a cocktail. A day after meeting Shay, you made her yours... even at the risk of getting caught." A slow grin stretches his lips. "Well played."

Chapter 26

Zane

Zane: Merry Christmas!

Briar: OMG. I can't believe you're wishing me a Merry Christmas. Totally unexpected. Merry Christmas to you and yours!

Zane: I had to reach out. You're my partner in crime. Without you, I wouldn't have been able to pull off the dress and earring heist.

Briar: LOL. You make it sound like we're Bonnie and Clyde.

Zane: In many ways we are. Is it snowing in Boston?

Briar: It is. How's Christmas in the Hamptons? Posh? All caviar and champagne?

Zane: It's pretty down to earth.

Briar: As a billionaire, do you even know what down to earth means?

Zane: I wasn't born with a silver spoon in my mouth, so, yes, I know what down to earth means. I even know what not having enough means.

Briar: My bad. Sorry for being presumptuous.

Zane: Don't sweat it. Is your sister up?

Briar: <confused face emoji> Why don't you text her?

Zane: I don't want to wake her up if she's still sleeping.

Briar: She isn't. She just finished shooting and uploading two Christmas Day makeup tutorials. Now, she's prancing around like a pretty peacock in an ugly Christmas sweater with her gorgeous earrings dangling from her earlobes. Good job, BTW, on the Christmas gift. It's stunning!

Zane: You helped.

Briar: You selected them. I just gave you the thumbs-up. You have excellent taste. My sister lucked out.

Zane: Thanks for the compliment.

Briar: I know your brother is taken, but maybe you have a college buddy you might hook me up with or a business associate? I'd even consider a neighbor. And I'm totally okay with older men. You have eleven years on my sister and it works. I'm down with the whole December-May relationship thing.

Zane: The whole December-May relationship thing only applies when the guy is in his fifties or sixties.

Briar: Oh. I'm okay with older, but not old enough for the guy to be my grandfather.

Zane: You're hilarious.

Briar: I'm on a mission. Stop distracting me.

Zane: Sorry.

Briar: You have to help me. My sister won at the lottery. I want to be that lucky.

Zane: I assume you're referring to Elias?

Briar: <rolling eyes emoji> God, no. I wouldn't want that guy if he was the last man on earth. I'm talking about you.

Zane: I'm flattered. As for your request, I'll keep my ears to the ground.

Briar: Promise?

Zane: Promise.

Briar: Because of you, my standards are much higher.

Zane: No pressure.

Briar: None whatsoever <winking face emoji>

Zane: Is the rest of the family up?

Briar: You have an inquisitive mind on a Christmas morning, Mr. Keller. If you must know, the O'Hara-Manning household has been up for a few hours. We already exchanged gifts and now we're preparing brunch. We skipped breakfast since we're still stuffed from Christmas Eve dinner. Too much good food, booze, and desserts.

Zane: Is your sister close by?

Briar: I'm no relationship expert, but I suggest you talk to her **directly** if you want this relationship to go anywhere.

Zane: Smart ass. Just answer the question.

Briar: She's here with me in the kitchen along with Ma and Aunt Eileen. Dad is in the living room, binge-watching a medical drama series on our ginormous big screen TV.

Zane: So, everyone's chilling?

Briar: Pretty much.

Zane: Someone is ringing your doorbell.

Briar: <laughing my head off emoji> And you can see that all the way from the Hamptons?

Chapter 27

Zane

I refused to accompany Ember to her older sister's big 3-0 birthday when I was seeing her. It was our second week, and I was already growing weary of our relationship. Setting false expectations would've been a losing game. Not that it mattered, because she's fifty shades of psycho.

It took less than a day and a half away from Shay, my girlfriend being a no show for our video sex session on the night of the charity gala—because she fell asleep on the sofa—too many glasses of expensive cognac, and a kick in the butt from Max to order the pilot to get ready for takeoff. I wasn't fully present yesterday on Christmas Eve in the Hamptons, my thoughts consumed by a certain curvy redhead.

Two-and-a-half-hours of flight later and I'm back in the City of Champions.

I left Boston less than forty-eight hours ago, and I swear it's at least twenty degrees colder and there seems to be a foot of extra snow covering the ground. On this sunny Christmas Day, other than a few people wearing begrudged expressions as they walk their dog in this icy weather, I'm the only crazy soul out here without a dog, braving the cold. Even dressed to affront a Siberia-like winter, my balls are still freezing. Same goes for my toes. And my nose.

I paced around the block for a while, suitcase in hand, pretending to be fascinated by rows upon rows of houses decked out in full Christmas mode, as I tried to convince myself I hadn't lost my ever-loving mind for my impetuous decision.

I had to make a decision.

Put up or turn around, and get back on the jet. Not only is it too fucking cold to stay out here and grow roots, but the neighbors would start to grow weary of a tall stranger, dressed head to toe in black, roaming aimlessly through their neighborhood.

Contacting Shay straight away, would've ruined the surprise. Briar was my decoy. As expected, she fell for my act, hook, line, and sinker.

The second I received her last response, I rang the bell.

Pulling up the collar of my cashmere coat, I take a step back from the door and wait.

Sure enough, a pretty face peeks through the white curtains. Green eyes, as big as saucers, stare at me in disbelief. When Briar gets over the shock, she waves with the same enthusiasm as a kid waving at Santa during the Christmas Parade.

"Oh my God." I can only read her lips, but from her baffled expression, I assume she's shouting.

She looks away for a beat, and the next thing I know, Katie, Aunt Eileen, and my girl come over to look out the window. Now, four pairs of bewildered eyes stare at me—though, Shay takes the cake. Her blue eyes bug out of her gorgeous face and her mouth hangs open. Then, as if rehearsed, the women start waving frantically with both hands.

I suppress a chuckle and respond with a small wave.

The front door of the decked out house swings open, and Alan steps out with his arms open wide. He's wearing a navy-blue robe over pyjama pants, an ugly red Christmas sweater peeking through, and unlaced expensive-looking boots with big white sports socks—he's the opposite of the elegant man in a suit I met for the first time on Thursday night.

"Is this a Christmas miracle or is it Shay's fake boyfriend?" Alan says, his jovial laugh echoing in the frosty air.

"Not sure about the former, but for the latter, you're dead wrong. I'm Shay's *real* boyfriend."

The lines around Alan's eyes crinkle with his smile. "Glad to hear it. I liked you since day one." He takes me into a bro hug, patting me a few times on the back.

Standing six feet tall, Alan isn't short. In fact, he's the same height as my baby brother. That said, I'm so tall, his head reaches my chin.

After a few short seconds of manly display of affection, he breaks our embrace.

"No wonder you had to come back so soon. Once you go *Bawstin,* you can't go back." He's still grinning from ear to ear.

I correct him. "*Bawstin* is nice and all, but I'm here for the girl."

He levels me with a stare that's equal parts triumph and pride.

"I hope you know you've set the bar high—unattainable, even. Briar's breaking my... *you know what...* so I might introduce her to men in my circle of *your* caliber. She's looking for a Zane Keller clone." He shakes his head. "Now, my baby girl expects me to moonlight as a freakin' matchmaker. All because of you," he pokes a playful finger at my chest.

"We're in this together," I say. "She's twisting my arm as well."

Alan laughs.

"You haven't checked into a hotel yet?" he points at the overnight bag sitting at my feet.

It goes against my grain to arrive at someone's house on Christmas Day without arms weighed down with gifts, but since this was a last-minute decision, it is what it is. Sure, I could've found a store open in New York, but since cheap gifts aren't part of my vocabulary, I refrained. I had to quell the overachiever and perfectionist in me, and go with the flow. While I'm here, I'm sure I'll find some ways to make up for showing up empty-handed.

"I haven't found a hotel yet." I didn't bother looking. I wanted to be with Shay too damn much. "I came straight from the airport."

"Must've cost you a pretty penny to fly—first class, I assume—today."

My lips curve in a sly smile. "That's where having two company private jets come in handy."

His jaw drops, his dark blue eyes the size of dinner plates.

There's still a lot he doesn't know about me.

The front door swings open again.

Four excited women, who dressed in a haphazard disarray, file out of the house.

Thanks to their unbuttoned coats, I catch a glimpse of more ugly sweaters.

There's a theme going on at the O'Hara-Manning house.

As Katie heads towards her husband, arms outstretched, her hands gripping a gray scarf, Shay comes running towards me, squealing along the way. The tutorial is over because she isn't wearing a speck of makeup. She's fresh faced and rosy cheeked. She's a glorious sight. I catch a glimpse of her earrings, pride swelling my chest.

She slams her body against mine.

I catch her in a hug.

The curve of her body beneath my hands feels right.

This is why I couldn't help the urge to be here with her.

I bury my nose in her mane, inhaling the unique scent I've missed so damn much. Her hair smells like cinnamon and sugar underneath my lips. I pull her to me and hold her close, the need for Shay burning inside my chest, unbothered by the overt PDA.

"OhmyGod. What are you doing here?" she asks. That comes out muffled because her face is smashed against my chest.

I drop a soft kiss on the top of her head.

"I wanted to spend Christmas Day with you, love."

For a breathless beat, my words hang in the icy air between us.

She pulls away, big blue eyes staring at me in wonder.

I brush a lock of red hair behind her ear.

"Seriously?" The word comes out faint, her breath shaky.

"After three days spent with you, going cold turkey was cruel. I needed to be with you."

Katie, Briar, and Aunt Eileen let a chorus out of oohs and aahs.

"You showed up here to be with me?!"

She's unconvinced.

My gaze sweeps across her face, amused by the surprise I read in her eyes. "I have a lot of super powers. Teleportation isn't one of them. That's where the private jet comes in."

She tilts her head back and roars in laughter.

Everyone joins in.

Shay's eyes glimmer under the sunny winter sky. She reaches up to lace her gloved fingers behind my neck. "Smart ass."

"You had it coming." I wink.

"Where are you staying?" Katie asks when her laughter subsides.

My attention swings to her, but I don't have time to answer.

"Oh, yeah, which hotel are you staying at?" Shay asks.

"He hasn't found one yet," Alan says. The glittering amusement in his dark blue eyes doesn't go unnoticed.

"Can you even find a last-minute hotel room on Christmas Day?" Briar asks.

Aunt Eileen chimes in. "And if you do, it's going to be at an offensively exorbitant price. I know the world is your oyster and all, but why waste good money?"

"I'm sure I can find a—"

"Nonsense!" Katie frowns. "It would be uncivilized for you to spend Christmas in a hotel." Her tone is indignant. "Not to mention, Aunt Eileen is right. Why waste good money?" She places her hands over her heart. "You came all the way here from the Hamptons to be with my baby, so that's what you'll do." Her face contorts and her lower lip quivers. For a minute, I'm certain she's going to cry.

"Katie—"

She shakes her head. "Don't Katie me, young man." She scolds me in a motherly tone. "You're part of the family now, Zane. You're staying with us." She slides her arms around her husband's torso. He's all bundled up in the scarf she handed him. The couple lock eyes. There's a discernible silent conversation between them.

I glance down at my girl.

Shay meets my gaze, and with her pink cheeks, beaming smile, and the joy in her blue eyes, she's breathtaking.

"My sweetie knows best," Alan says, pulling my attention away from my girlfriend. "Happy wife, happy life," his voice is conspiratorial.

Katie gets on the tip of her toes to peck a kiss on her husband's cheek before swinging her attention to me.

My gaze drifts from her to Alan, both of them looking at me with fierce determination.

"It's settled!" She claps. "And I won't take no for an answer."

Chapter 28

Shay

I couldn't shake out of the stupor of seeing my new boyfriend for a solid two hours after he showed up at our door. Heck, I'm still bewildered.

Zane is here!

His unexpected arrival made a perfect day a million times better. I should say, a *billion* times better.

I've had ex-boyfriends do thoughtful things for me, but no one has ever done anything as over-the-top as Zane. Granted he has more money than most and he has a couple private planes at his disposal. Still, he could've settled for a video call. Nope, he went all the way.

Talk about grand gesture.

Not that I needed more reasons to like this man more than I already do, but he had to up the ante. No wonder Briar says Zane ruined it for all other men for her.

Christmas Day brunch is animated in our household. This year, it was jubilant. My family is in love with my fake boyfriend. Elias was a hard sell from the beginning. Even though he's in the same profession as my stepfather, their first few encounters were awkward. Now, Alan is forced to tolerate him because he's his son-in-law... well, until Imogen pops out her baby...

On the flipside, Zane won my family over the first time they met him—no hard sale required. By flying to Boston to spend Christmas with us earned him some serious brownie points. Since everything is so new between us, I didn't have time to inform my stepfather and Ma about my new boyfriend's billionaire status. Throughout the meal, Alan couldn't stop circling back to Zane's private jet. After all, he's a wealthy doctor with wealthy doctor friends, but none of them are billionaires. We live in an upscale neighborhood in Boston, but I'll be honest, there's a tinge of pressure when you welcome someone obscenely rich into your home. Zane fit right in. From the outside looking in, you'd never know this was our first Christmas together. Ma was so elated, she pulled me into the kitchen after dessert, gave me an earful.

"He's perfect for you. Seriously, Shay-bear, you're good for each other. And height on a man is sooooo sexy, but when coupled with Adonis looks, intelligence, wit, and a caring heart, he's a winner. The fact he has a little money doesn't hurt, although money doesn't buy happiness and you should never judge a man based on the size of his wallet. And an older man is good. Very good. Daddy was eight years older and Alan is seven years older. Zane is eleven years older than you. That's a good age difference. Any more would've been creepy, like he was robbing the cradle. God, that height. My grandbabies are going to be sooooo beautiful. They're going to be bilingual. Hola! Trilingual, if Aunt Eileen teaches them Irish, which she totally will since you and Briar speak it. Oh, my God! That would make Aunt Eileen a young great-great aunt. Can you imagine?"

She didn't even take a breath.

And yes, she drooled over Zane's height twice.

It was like verbal diarrhea on steroids.

Talk about putting the cart before the horse.

I just rolled my eyes.

She was on such a high, I didn't correct her on the *Hola! and Buenos días!* part, flagging it should be *Olá! and Bom dia!* instead. Yes, I spent too much time quizzing Google on Portuguese words— I digress. We're talking about Ma's misplaced eagerness here, not my desire to understand the Brazilian culture of my boyfriend's heritage. It would've been equally pointless to remind Ma my relationship with Zane was brand new. Forget about babies being at the bottom of the list. They're not even on the list. I didn't touch on that last point because it was a land mine. And I doubt Aunt Eileen is ready for great-great aunthood.

"I apologize for the lack of subtlety my family displayed," I say, returning to the living room, carrying a tray.

We have the house all to ourselves.

To be a good sport, Zane didn't argue when Alan brought him one of his ugly Christmas sweaters to wear. Although the darn thing is too tight—my stepdad isn't as buff as my boyfriend—he manages to look as sexy as sin. He traded his designer jeans for a pair of hunter green sweatpants. Even casual, he still oozes of power.

How does he do it?

"I couldn't believe my ears when your mom said she'd call the landline, let it ring twice, hang up, call again, and let it ring twice again as a warning," Zane says.

I drop the tray on the coffee table.

"I love how Briar rolled her eyes hard," I say. "At least I'm not the only one who thought that was a bit much."

Zane chuckles.

"It would've been easier—and less embarrassing—for Ma to say, *We're stepping out for a bit to give you two some alone time.*" I shake my head. "That whole production was unnecessary."

It would be unthinkable for my Irish Catholic family not to go to church on Christmas Eve to thank God for the year's blessings. In keeping with tradition, we went to midnight mass after a copious dinner. You can imagine my surprise when Ma declared the whole family was going to attend the evening sermon. We never go to church on Christmas Day. We're usually too stuffed to move. She further surprised me when she insisted Zane and I *stay* back to enjoy the quiet house.

Instead of the Morse code-like warning to announce their impending return, she might as well have said, *I'll ring twice to make sure you kids are done fooling around or See you in an hour and a half.* I get where she's coming from—and I appreciate her—but that was uncomfortable.

First, we're not teenagers. Second, fooling around under your parents' roof is kind of weird. Hence, why Zane is staying in the guestroom at opposite ends of my childhood bedroom. All that to say, Ma went out of her way for nothin'. I'm elated to see him. Things don't have to get hot and heavy every time we're in the same room.

I grab a cup from the tray and hand it to Zane.

"Thanks," he says.

I sit next to him.

I grab my cup and lift it. "*Sláinte agus Nollaig Shona Duit!*"

"That sounded Irish to me."

I translate. "Cheers and Merry Christmas!"

He clinks his cup with mine. "Cheers and Merry Christmas, love!"

We both take a careful sip of the piping hot beverage.

Zane's wide eyes meet mine. "This is delicious."

"It's a specialty of mine," I say, not even hiding my pride.

Our brunch was a lip-smacking feast. Each year rivals the

previous one. There's a reason we end up spending the day in yoga pants or, in Alan's case, old sweatpants. That said, there's always room for hot cocoa... especially mine. There's hot cocoa, and there's Shay's Boozy Delight. We're talking about decadence in a cup—hot cocoa loaded with whipped cream—the real stuff—dotted with mini marshmallows, spiked with a generous amount of Baileys Espresso liqueur, and drizzled with a little melted milk chocolate. It's a tradition at our house.

For a few long minutes, our focus is solely on the drink. It's amazing that this early in our relationship we can sit in a comfortable silence.

"I love your family, but I have to side with your mom," Zane says, placing his cup on the coffee table. "Since this is our first Christmas together, some alone time isn't a bad thing."

"I agree."

His heated stare blazes through me at warp speed. To curtail the inappropriate thoughts assailing me, I take a long sip of my drink. In my attempt to calm down my lady parts, I drink a little too fast and end up with a whipped cream mustache.

Crap.

I place my cup on the coffee table. I'm about to grab a napkin from the tray, when Zane stops me. "Let me," he says.

I'm unprepared for what he does next.

He clasps a firm hand behind my head, pulls my face close to his, and licks off my milky mustache.

I moan.

He then swipes his tongue over my upper lip. He does the same to my lower lip before capturing it between his teeth. "Mmm..." His humming rumbles through me.

I slide my hand over his muscular thighs until I cup his cock.

His tongue snakes between my lips, meeting mine.

The passionate kiss grows hotter, deeper, all-encompassing.

Our chemistry is off the charts.

God, the man can kiss.

He hauls me into his lap, moving me like I weigh nothing. I squeal in delight and surprise.

His cock underneath me is hard, thick, and erect.

I still can't get over how he reacts to me.

An urgent pulse throbs between my legs, adrenaline pulses through my veins at an infernal speed.

His hand drifts beneath my sweater, his fingers caressing my skin until they sneak under my bra.

"Fuck, I missed your tits."

He flicks my nipples hard, and I gasp.

He growls and does it again.

I brace myself for the sharp sensation I relish so much, but he plays dirty. He twists my nipples so hard, I fold over.

Sadist.

I'm about to protest, but he precedes me.

"Staying down here is too risky," he says, flashing me a seductive look. "We should go upstairs."

"Err..."

"It wouldn't be a good idea for your family to return from church and catch us in the act." His gaze caresses my face and my lips. I swallow hard. "I haven't fucked you in two days. Things *will* get out of hand."

Hearing him say that sends shivers of delight up my spine.

The silence between us is crackling with a hedonist vibe so strong, my clit tingles.

My stomach flutters with nervousness at the thought of doing something this risqué, even though my pussy is clenching in eagerness, my panties slick with my juices.

Zane brushes a loose strand of hair to the side, kissing along my neck, biting my skin.

I purr with pleasure.

"Your mom gave us *carte blanche*," he soldiers on. "We might as well take full advantage of it..."

"You're a bad influence on me." My argument is weak at best.

"I know." His mouth comes down hard on mine.

Okay, I could be convinced to misbehave.

"Let's call this my Christmas gift." He puts his bargaining chip on the table.

Sneaky boyfriend.

I throw his words back at him. "I thought there is no such thing as tit for tat."

"I stand by my words. This"—he waves a finger between us—"is all about your *tits*." He flashes me a panty-melting smile, a wicked spark in his eyes.

Am I willing to cross that line?

"I can't believe I'm going to let you coerce me into crossing the line in my childhood home—"

"Which is why I suggest we keep it contained to your *childhood bedroom*." His smile is wolfish.

"You have an answer for everything?"

He shakes his head. "I still can't explain my unreasonable attraction to you. And for once in my life, I'm not itching for an answer."

His words tug at my heart.

His lust-filled gaze is my demise.

There's no denying our burning desire for each other.

It's hot enough in the living room to melt all the snow covering Boston.

Zane decides for both of us. He stands up with me in his arms. He carries me to the stairs, bridal-style. I wrap my arms around his neck and rest my head against his strong, hard chest, clinging onto him like a koala bear.

We reach the third floor.

He isn't even breathing heavy.

The man has so much stamina.

"You can drop me to my feet now."

"I'm not ready to let go of you yet."

"Okay!" My voice is giddy.

He strides down the corridor

With a rapid step, he reaches my bedroom. Once inside, he drops me to my feet, closes the door, and switches on the two nightstand lamps. The room is bathed in a seductive glow.

He turns around and faces me. "Strip."

I guess it's too late to second-guess this outrageous idea.

"I gave you an order, Shay. Why are you still dressed?"

His uncompromising tone snaps me back to reality.

I obey.

I pull the ugly sweater over my head and toss it, so it lands on the chair in the corner.

When I look down at my body, I freak out at the sight.

My eyes bounce to his. "I wasn't expecting you," I say. "Had you given me a heads-up, I would've worn sexier underwear than this plain Jane set." I gesture at my breasts.

He approaches me.

With gentle hands, he strokes my hair. He fists the back of my head, forcing my attention to him. His action is unsettling, and yet, so fucking hot. He leans into me until our lips flirt. His eyelashes are so close to mine, it wouldn't take much for them to get meshed together. "The only thing that makes me harder than seeing you in sexy lingerie, is seeing you naked."

He kisses me hard.

I'm so startled, I forget to breathe.

He pulls away. "Now, stop wasting time and get naked."

He doesn't have to tell me twice.

I strip out of my yoga pants and sensible panties in a flash, leaving both in a pile of mess at my feet.

His dark eyes rake the length of my body, taking in every inch of me.

He's unabashed and deliberate.

Instead of growing nervous under his inspection, I feel sexy and empowered.

"It isn't fair if I'm the only one who's naked."

"You want me naked, love?"

"How else am I going to suck you off?"

I guess I grew a pair of balls.

"I admire your eagerness." I pick up on the mocking tone in his voice.

Challenge accepted.

"You always take care of me. It's only fair I reciprocate."

He considers me for a long beat.

"You want me to fuck your face?"

Whoa.

"I still have my training wheels on with you. You're a big guy. If you fuck my face, I'll choke."

"You're right, I *am* a big guy"—he cups his cock and squeezes hard—"but I know you can take it. I know your greedy little mouth can make me come so hard, I'll forget my name."

Holy. Cow.

A tidal wave of pleasure floods my body at his naughty suggestion.

I thought I was wet before, but now, I'm drenched.

"But first, I need your nipples in my mouth."

I'm too drunk on his words to respond.

His mouth trails to my breasts. He licks his way across one nipple until he reaches the other, eliciting little moans from me. He pokes out his tongue, flicking my nipple in languorous strokes and I sink into the sensation.

Yes.

He tortures me like that for a few blissful seconds.

Until Zane, I had no idea my nipples were this sensitive.

I might have to bring up sucking him off more often if this is my reward.

His lips latch on to one nipple, suckling and tweaking, his eyes lifting to mine, shining bright with devilish malice.

When he grazes my tight peak with his teeth, I let out a desperate cry.

A chuckle rumbles out of him as he squeezes my breasts and submits my other nipple to the same pleasurable torture.

I gasp for air.

He growls.

"I'm fucking addicted to your tits."

"I'm fucking addicted to your mouth."

"Damn, love," he says in rasps, and sucks my nipple between his teeth.

I writhe beneath him, but he shows me no mercy.

His hands are rough and demanding, as he doubles his effort, his delicious torment threatening to make me lose my mind.

I swear I'm about to combust.

A familiar tingling builds at my core.

This can't possibly be happening.

With another lap of his tongue, he takes me closer to the edge.

I bring my legs together and start undulating my hips in a circle, seeking relief.

Oh, God. Oh, God. Oh, God.

I clench my pussy hard, chasing after my pending climax.

Then he bites against my nipple, sucks so damn hard, and I'm done.

"Zane!"

I arch my body forward as a strong orgasm courses through me.

Zane holds onto my trembling body as I dissolve into his arms, lost to the sensation.

This climax is so strong, I swear, my body soars to new heights.

Holy shit.

When we were on the forty-first floor of the Bymark hotel, he alluded to nipple play. I thought it was all talk. Now, I know better. The right lover can make you see God.

"One down!"

It's only when he speaks, I realize I had my eyes closed. Since I'm still panting hard, blood pounding in my ears, I'm surprised I can hear him. When I pop my eyes open, his gorgeous face fills my vision. He studies me with an intensity that's unnerving.

"You survived."

"Barely."

"But you're still with me. That's all that counts," he says. "Let me get undressed. I need to make you come again."

I should tell him I need a respite after that mind-blowing orgasm, but I don't.

He's transformed me into a nymphomaniac.

In a blink of an eye, he stands in front of me naked. His erect cock is pointing north, hiding his happy trail.

I take my time appreciating his six-pack, his mouthwatering V-muscles, and strong thighs before allowing my eyes to travel up his body. When I meet his gaze, a smile plays on his lips and cockiness is etched in his handsome face, as if he's asking if I like what I see.

"You're looking at me like a woman who's desperate for my cock." He grabs me by the hand. "Let's do something about it." He's already pulling me to the bed. He sits on the mattress. "You'll be on top—"

"Like we did at the hotel," I say, my heart palpitating,

flashing back to the saucy memories. "Sitting on top of you with our eyes locked was so fucking sexy."

"That's not what I had in mind," he says in a husky rasp. "I want you to sit on my face."

I blink.

He continues, oblivious to my internal turmoil.

"You do me. And I do you," he says. "A sixty-nine allows you to fulfill your fantasy of sucking my cock while you ride my tongue—allowing me to have my mouth on your sweet pussy."

I hesitate.

That's not how I had envisioned it. Not by a long shot.

I was thinking more along the lines of me on my knees as I give him a blow job.

Granted, Elias was never that adventurous, but... sitting on a man's face?! That's pushing the envelope way out of my comfort zone.

I stare at Zane's extended hand for a long beat before meeting his expectant gaze.

He arches an eyebrow. "You didn't hear me?"

"I heard you."

"What are you waiting for?"

I pull my lower lip between my teeth. "I haven't—" I shake my head. "It's just—" I let out a sigh of frustration.

"Yes?"

Old insecurities creep up.

I inhale a fortifying breath. "I'm much more comfortable with my body now than I ever was, but—"

"But what?"

"If I sit on your face, I might... suffocate you. I'm not a small girl. I have a lot of curves."

I wrap my arms around myself, feeling self-conscious and vulnerable.

He stands up.

He brushes away a few strands of dark blond hair flirting with his eyelashes, reaches for me, unwinds my arms, and pulls me into his embrace, his hard cock pressing into my belly.

"That's the point, love. I *want* your luscious ass to suffocate me while you chase after your orgasm, riding my tongue like a dirty, filthy slut. *My* dirty, filthy slut with plenty of sexy curves. I worship every single inch of you... *especially* the ones that *aren't* that small." His dirty talking is enough to have me changing my mind, but he layers on the goodness. "I've been stiff as a board since I left Boston and no matter how many times I jerked off, nothing compares to being inside your pussy." His words make me melt inside. "On top of that, you missed our video sex session." He pauses. "You think I would've fueled up my jet on Christmas Day for a skinny-mini who doesn't have what it takes to make me hard? Unlikely."

I didn't see that coming.

I crack up.

His words dissipate my worries as fast as the beaming rays of the sun melts snow.

"Well... when you put it like that..." I glance up at him from under my lashes.

"I worship your body, so I never want to hear that kind of talk ever again." He warns me in a gentle scolding tone.

"Never again."

"Good. Now, are you gonna smother my face with your sweet pussy?"

"You need to assume the position first—"

Slap!

I yelp.

"*I* give the orders."

"Yes, sir," I say, rubbing the sore spot.

Still holding my hand, he sits on the bed.

He situates his tall frame to the middle of my queen size bed.

The king size bed we shared at the Mandarin Oriental hotel barely contained his six-feet-six frame. My queen size bed looks like it belongs in a doll house.

Big shot New York City CFO—and dominant alpha—lying in my girlie purple and white bedroom with his feet dangling from my bed, eager to corrupt me. What a comical scene.

"Don't worry about my long legs. That'll be the last of your concern when you come all over my face," he says as if reading my thoughts. "Come," he calls me over, "you're wasting precious time." His unwavering voice is daring me to challenge his command.

I don't.

I'd be a fool not to give him what he wants.

I climb on the bed and assume the position.

I glance over my shoulder.

The naughty sight is indescribable.

I'm on my hands and knees, with my pussy hovering over Zane's mouth.

He clamps his hands on my hips, lowers my body towards his waiting tongue, and parts my ass cheeks.

This is intimate.

He parts my pussy lips with his tongue before teasing my clit.

The first lick is mind-blowing.

I moan with pleasure.

"Fuck, I missed your pussy."

He continues licking me in slow, languorous strokes that has my body burning up.

"Weren't you dying to suck my cock, love? What happened to your eagerness?"

"For now, it takes backseat to watching you lick my pussy."

Slap!

Ouch!

"That's not the agreement we have," he says. "My cock needs TLC."

With a cocked brow, I move my attention to his monster erection. I wrap my fist around it. Already, pre-cum leaks from his tip.

I lower my head, the desire to taste him is overwhelming.

I poke out my tongue and lick his tip.

His tangy taste assaults my taste buds.

I moan.

He licks me in rhythmic strokes, toying with my clit and driving me out of my mind. The sweet pain sends shivers down my spine and jacks up my hungry mouth.

Fueled by a brazenness I don't recognize, I wrap my lips around his enormous cock. In this position, I control how much of him I swallow.

I can take more of him without choking than I thought.

I take a few seconds to adjust to his impressive size before sliding my mouth up and down his cock.

I'm awkward at first, but soon, I find my rhythm, matching the tempo of his licks.

He groans, his hands gripping my hips in a way that tells me he'll leave his mark on me. Instead of being off-putting, the thought arouses me even more.

Fuck.

Wrapping my hand around the base of his cock, I slide it up and down, keeping up with his tongue strokes. I pull back, so only the tip of his cock is still lodged between my lips. I hollow out my lips and lick at the head with earnest.

He grunts, the vibration tingling my pussy lips.

He thrusts his hips upwards, demanding more.

I gasp and I swallow over the protruding head that grazes my throat, causing my gag reflex to kick in.

He rewards me by pulling my hard clit between his lips, sucking it with avarice.

"Mmmm..." I hum.

He echoes my moan.

I pull away, letting his cock slide out of my mouth.

I gently cup his balls and run my tongue up and down his shaft.

He responds by slapping my ass before groping it.

Fuck, that's hot.

Like a greedy girl, I'm about to do it again, but he plunges two long fingers inside my pussy. His mouth and fingers take me to a place I never thought existed.

My eyes roll to the back of my head.

He pushes the envelope further, when he slides the fingers that were inside my pussy to an untouched part of my body.

My breath hitches.

It's pure panic at first, but as his digits slide inside me, I let go of the tension and enjoy the pleasure.

Good God.

What happens next defies rational thought.

It's like I'm a woman possessed.

I rock back-and-forth over his tongue and fingers, barely managing to keep his cock in my mouth.

His fingers. His mouth. The lewd sound of his hedonistic slurps. It all takes me higher and higher, my climax so, so close.

My cadence is frantic.

I'm like a wild mustang, unleashed and untamed.

It's a pity I had to wait this long to find out how good a man's tongue could feel against my clit.

With one quick movement, he changes tactics.

"Your clit is pulsing against my tongue and it's making my cock rock hard. I'm dying to shoot my cum inside your mouth."

I whimper.

I'm too far gone to string a sentence together.

He yanks his fingers from me, sending sparks to my clit and causing me to yelp.

"Good girl," he says and grips my hips, holding me in place, forcing me to take what he has to give. Zane's masterful tongue flicks at my clit in quick fluttering motions.

It's dizzying.

Oh my God.

There's no holding back as I shatter into a million blissful pieces.

I scream out his name as I grip his head with my thighs, a toe-curling climax ripping through me with the force of a cyclone.

Zane takes over the reins, not that I was ever in control.

He jerks his hips up and down, fucking my mouth in the most unrelenting way.

I take it.

Although I'm spent, I want him to come. I want him to mark my mouth.

One, two, three thrusts, and Zane explodes in my mouth, roaring like an animal.

Holy motherlode of cum.

It's like drinking water from a firehose.

It's a struggle to swallow the geyser shooting down my throat. There's so much of him, his warm release drips all over the place. His cock and balls are covered with the proof of his climax.

Wow. Just wow.

For a few long beats, I'm a dead weight, unable to move.

I'm certain I've transcended into another world.

Zane strokes my ass in soothing circles.

"Come here, love." His voice is gruff.

I flip around and crawl on all fours, letting my sweaty body slump into his open arms.

He pulls my hair back and crushes my lips.

It takes everything in me not to purr like a contented kitten.

The taste of my arousal on his lips catches me off guard.

Then it hits me, he must taste his climax on my lips.

That's so hot.

Closing my eyes, I snuggle against his muscular body. The heat of his body seeps through me, and I relish the closeness.

His hand slides up and down the bare plane of my back.

That feels so good.

With a slow hand, I stroke his chest.

This man is everything to me.

We lie in my bed in a comfortable silence, our breathing echoing in the quiet room. We stay like this for several heartbeats.

The landline rings somewhere in the house.

Two rings and the call ends.

Since I'm lost in a salacious haze and still floating, it doesn't register at first.

The phone rings again.

It's the same MO as before—two rings and the call ends.

What the—

Ma's Morse code signal.

My eyes pop open, panic beating at my chest.

"Oh, shit! They're on their way!"

Chapter 29

Shay

Ma wasn't the one who caused me to have a heart attack with that complicated Morse code. My little sister—little devil—is the one who rang the warning bell. She figured there was no way in hell I wasn't going to show Zane my appreciation for the unexpected and delightful visit.

Damn, I hate she knows me that well.

Things got hot and heavy while my family was at church.

The three flights of stairs to my bedroom saved our asses. That was plenty of time for Zane and I to get dressed, tidy up the bed, crack open the windows a smidge, and pretend I was filling my boyfriend in on entertaining stories of my childhood.

Right.

For the rest of the evening, we behaved.

Since he was at arm's length, I could steal a glance and drool all over him to my heart's content. When I snuggled close to him while we watched movies, no one raised an eyebrow.

I stayed three extra days in Boston with my family, but Zane got on his fancy jet and flew back to New York mid-day on the twenty-sixth. That was a ridiculously expensive twenty-four-hour trip, which makes our time together that much more special. I wanted him to stay longer, but my billionaire boyfriend couldn't. He had a string of functions with his extended family. We had a lengthy—and filthy—video chat session when he got back to his place to make up for the night I fell asleep on the sofa, but it wasn't the same. And I'm not only talking about the sex.

Now that I'm back in New York, I get to see my boyfriend and hang out with my best friend.

After spending most of the day catching up on social media, responding to private messages and emails, and shooting three video makeup tutorials for New Year's Eve parties, I met up with Keeley for a post-Christmas gift exchange dinner.

There was a lot of gal gab.

I gave her a lengthy scene-by-scene replay of my eventful Christmas Day. Keeley's blue eyes bugged out of her skull when I told her about misbehaving with my boyfriend in my childhood bedroom and the call that prevented us from getting caught. She got a good chuckle out of the Morse code warning alarm.

I also shared the full story of Imogen's attempt on my life because she's a jealous bitch. And when I told her about Aunt Eileen's selfies, Keeley's jaw dropped.

It's all speculation so far, but since we're talking about my stepsister, where there's smoke, there's usually fire.

Keeley had a lot to fill me in on as well. After years of crushing over her older brother's best friend, things might be looking up for her.

YAY!

There was so much to share, since we sat down at the restaurant, we couldn't shut up. We met for a quick breakfast on the day I left for Boston, but since then, we've been texting and calling. Nothing beats sitting face to face with your BFF.

Two hours into the evening and we were in full relax mode, enjoying an exuberant and lively girls' night out, when my past came crashing into our fun time. I answered a call, even though I didn't recognize the number. Big mistake.

Elias has a new phone number.

Sneaky bastard.

I blocked his number and Imogen's as I was bolting out of his house after catching them having sex. He and his wife are also back in New York. Since this is the holiday season, they decided to push their honeymoon to the second week of January.

He called because he wanted to talk.

I have nothing to say to my ex, and I was about to hang up in his face, when he alluded to an overdue apology *sans* Imogen.

I was curious.

Keely protested, but I agreed to meet the cheating asshole anyway.

If he's willing to grovel, I'm more than happy to listen.

Since Zane was supposed to pick me up at the restaurant, I fired off a text to let him know to meet me at my place, avoiding the real reason for the last-minute change. After exchanging air kisses with my best friend, I hopped into a taxi, and headed home.

Despite my busy day, I managed to tidy up my place and get some groceries. My fridge is full. I even have some yummy desserts and a freezer packed with my favorite ice cream flavors.

Aunt Eileen even made sure I brought back a couple of pecan pies since my boyfriend ate three quarters of a pie by himself. The only thing I didn't have time to grab is wine. I figured Zane and I could grab a few bottles when he picked me up. Since the plans changed, I asked the cabbie to drop me off at a liquor store not far from my place. After purchasing a good bottle of white, I trail back to my brownstone.

While I was selecting the perfect wine to pair with the dessert I intend on serving tonight, Elias texted me *three* times to let me know he was waiting for me in front of my place.

How dare he be impatient?

He's lucky I agreed to see him. He can wait. If not, he can go back to his wife. He's on my turf. I'll get there when I get there.

Like every neighborhood in all five New York boroughs, Brooklyn Heights is all decked out for the holidays. Since I don't make it a habit to walk at night, I'm able to appreciate all the dazzling decorations. Colorful lights twinkle around me.

My neighbors don't kid around.

None of these houses come close to the O'Hara-Manning fairyland of twinkling lights. Aunt Eileen oversees the decorations for the most wonderful time of the year. You'll be pressed to find one spot in our house that isn't decorated with some festive trinket. It takes her a whole week to take down the Christmas decorations, but bless her for going all the way.

The temperature in New York isn't as frigid as it was in Boston, so I don't complain about the cold night air that makes me shiver. I turn the corner to my street and I'm halted in place as I run straight into a human wall.

"Shit!" I squeal, tightening my hold around the wine bottle so it doesn't end up crashing to the ground, forming boozy icicles at my feet.

Strong hands clamp around my shoulders.

Panic steals my breath.

During the week between Christmas and New Year's, a lot of my neighbors tend to travel, so the streets are more deserted than usual. This is a safe neighborhood and we rarely have any issues. That said, you can't put a border on crime in a mega city.

Who knows? Maybe this is a prime week for criminals to break into unoccupied homes or practice easy muggings.

"Careful, Shay *mon chéri*," a voice I recognize says.

My initial panic gives way to annoyance.

It's supposed to be, *ma chérie* since I'm a woman.

Idiot!

I stare at my ex, fury burning in my eyes. "Elias, I hated that nickname when we were together, I despise it now," I say, my tone admonishing. "Keep it to Shay."

Pissed off, I pull away from his grip.

He ignores my warning. "What's the nickname your sequoia tree has for you?" He pretends to think. "Oh yeah, *love*. So fucking pretentious." His speech is slower than usual.

"Are you drunk?"

"I've been drinking." He slurs his words. "I have good reason."

"In other words, you're drunk."

"Whatever." He brushes it off with a sweep of a hand.

"I hope you didn't drive?"

"Taxi."

He might be an idiot, but at least he's not a danger to fellow Manhattanites.

"Where's your wife?" I couldn't help myself.

"At her mother's place, scheming on ways to destroy a poor sucker's life."

I'm not sure what he means by that, but I let it slide.

"Isn't it early in your marriage not to get along with your mother-in-law?" I shouldn't go down that road, but I'm taking way too much pleasure here. According to Briar, Imogen's mom barely tolerates Elias.

"Not sure she likes me much, but she likes my profession a lot." He punctuates his statement by jabbing his gloved finger in the air. "Her little girl married a doctor. The fact I come from a family of doctors raises me above the level of undesirable husband." He sneers.

Okay... that sound is a bit manic and the scorned expression on his face is derisive.

"Big fucking whoop-de-doo." He swirls that same finger over his head. "My mother-in-law is all about appearances."

Just like your wife.

Elias's momzilla-in-law's jaw dropped when she set her eyes on the sparkling three-carat diamond ring designed to show off that he selected for Imogen—it's an in-your-face design shaped like a blooming rose with a bling center stone. Only then, did she give her blessing.

"You've only been married for four days. Give her a chance. She'll come around." No sooner than the words leave my lips that I realize he may never have the chance.

"It's kinda cold to be having a conversation outside," Elias says. "Why don't we go back to your place?"

"No." I shake my head. "It would be inappropriate."

"It wouldn't—"

"You're married."

"It's nighttime, it's fucking freezing, and I've been pacing in the cold, waiting for you."

"Elias"—there's an edge to my voice—"I thought you were going to sit in your car, with me standing at your window while you extended your apologies. I was never planning on inviting you up."

"Fine." His tone is sour. "In that case, let's go to a bar nearby? It'll be cozier."

He takes a step forward.

I lift a hand up to stop him.

"This"—I wave a gloved finger between us—"isn't a social call. Given your deceitfulness, I didn't have to give you the time of day. Consider yourself lucky I did. Talk or taxi it out of here."

He considers me for a long beat.

With each passing second, I become more irate.

"Good night, Elias—"

I make to pass by him, but his question stops me in my tracks.

"Did you know?"

I wait for him to elaborate, but he doesn't.

For the love of God. "Did I know what?"

"You've never been a good actress, so cut the crap!"

That sets me off.

"You scared me shitless because I wasn't expecting you when I turned a corner. You show up drunk. You're slurring your words. You're speaking in incomprehensible codes. And now, you're insulting me. This conversation is officially over—"

"Let me spell it out for you, Shay—"

"It's about fucking time."

"Did you know your cunt of a stepsister was sleeping with my best friend?"

This is the last thing I expected him to bring up.

Aunt Eileen, what have you done?

Did Briar spill the beans?

My mind reels.

To buy myself time, I skirt his question. "This meeting isn't about you apologizing for being a dick. You wanted to meet me under false pretenses." I spit out in his face. "Your question suggests Imogen and I are on speaking terms." I sneer. "We're not."

That was a tour de force.

"Maybe I should've listened to you about Imogen." I should feel vindicated, but I feel for Elias. "For years, I've been trying to get my cousin to stop smoking. It turns out his nicotine addiction might've saved me from a lifetime sentence."

Since I'm unsure where he's going with this, I say nothing.

He lets out a derisive snort. "To keep warm while Big Dick was out for a smoke, he started walking around the manor—"

"What's the point of this flashback?"

"What my cousin saw matters! So, let me finish."

I let out an exasperated breath.

Keep running your mouth, dude.

"Big Dick was freezing his balls off, but he needed his fix." At six-two, Richard Fitzsimmons is much taller than the rest of Elias's family. He also has the shoulder width of a linebacker, hence the nickname. "He took one last puff, flung the butt somewhere in the snow, and re-entered the building. To his surprise, he found himself near the internal gardens. It was a crowded area with a lot of people taking photos. As he was about to make his way to our ballroom, he noticed *my* bride, holding hands in an intimate way with *my* best friend, heading towards a hideaway. There was no mistaking the bride because none of the other three brides who got married that day was a petite, Caucasian blonde." He narrows his eyes. "See where I'm going with this?"

Dread twists my stomach.

Shit.

"I was hoping you'd tell me so I don't have to figure it out on my own." I manage my delivery without wavering my gaze from his.

The side of his lip curls. "Big Dick picked up quick on what was going on. He took cover and waited. He said it was a good twenty minutes before Imogen and Calvin re-emerged from a room or a closet—Big Dick wasn't certain. Not that it matters. All that matters is what my cousin observed. My new wife and my best friend looked disheveled. The peck on the lips sealed the deal. There was no tongue action, but there's no fucking reason for those two people to kiss in the first place!" I flinch at the intonation in his voice. "Since there was still a kerfuffle of activity around the garden, Imogen and Calvin didn't notice Big Dick lurking or snapping photos." His eyes holding mine.

This is an awkward situation to be in.

I'm relieved Aunt Eileen or Briar weren't the ones who tipped him off.

Elias keeps talking. "I had dinner with my cousin earlier this evening. He wasn't sure how to broach the delicate subject... he needed a couple days to process it all. Not that I blame him. How do you pull the rug from underneath a guy's feet? A family member, no less." The question is rhetorical because he doesn't wait for my answer. "I thought my cousin was bullshitting me at first. After all, my wife loves me. *We're* in love. That's why we got fucking married!" He pinches his lips together. "Then, Big Dick showed me proof." He launches into another tirade. "I couldn't believe my eyes, but a photo doesn't lie... unless it's Photoshopped. In a fit of rage, I went back to my house and confronted my fucking cunt of a wife."

He grinds his jaw together, his nostrils flaring. It's a little too dark for me to see his eyes, but the energy shifts around us, causing me to shiver—and not in a good way.

He's unhinged.

"Imogen *thinks* the baby is mine, but she's not one hundred percent certain. Can you imagine the surprise when that bundle of joy pops into the world?" He shakes his head, grunting something incoherent.

I choose my words, careful not to set him off. "It's unfortunate you're going through this... a few days after getting married."

"You don't sound surprised."

Crap.

"No outcry of indignation. No, *I told you so, Elias*. No, *you reap what you sow*. No, *once a cheater always a cheater*. No, *how could she do that?* You're reacting with the same indifference as if I'd told you we received one too many Kitchen Aid mixers in orange as wedding gifts."

He takes a menacing step towards me, causing me to take one back, my back hitting a brick wall. His face is mere inches from mine. Even outside, his breath reeks of alcohol. This close, the turmoil swimming in his eyes is impossible to miss.

"You knew." He grits the accusation between clenched teeth.

My eyes blink at a rapid pace.

He clamps a hand around my jaw in response.

"Answer me!"

"Let go!" I spit out in his face.

He growls. "I fucking asked you a question, Shay."

"You're hurting me."

"Did you know Imogen and Calvin were sleeping together behind my back?"

I've never seen Elias in this state.

I would've sworn on a stack of Bibles he'd never hurt a woman. Now, I'm not so sure. There's an underlying hint of a threatening predator I never picked up on before. Maybe it's the alcohol talking. Maybe it's the asshole in him. My body reacts irrationally at the demented undertone in his voice.

Instead of being a coward, a fierce lioness roars. "My stepsister uses sex to overlord her power on the men who are too weak and too stupid to know she's playing them like a violin." Unable to keep the venom from my voice, I lash out full force. "I warned you Imogen destroys everything she touches." Even though it's a challenge to speak with the way he's gripping my jaw, I'm intent on ripping him a new one. "Her pussy—or ass—was so good, you were willing to piss on everything we shared. Now, you show up at my door, demanding answers about a woman who's proven time and time again she'll do anything as long as it benefits her. Fuck off!"

"So, you fucking knew!"

"Go to hell!"

"Big Dick caught Aunt Eileen on the mezzanine, phone in hand, grinning like a loon." *Okay, I didn't see that coming.* "That woman hates me. There's no way she wouldn't brag about my misfortune."

"Leave my great aunt out of this. Imogen is the bad apple, rotten to the core."

"See! You fucking knew!" He accuses me again.

The man is deranged.

I narrow my eyes at him. "You need to up your meds or get on new ones!"

"Is this revenge? Are you taking sick pleasure in knowing your stepsister backstabbed me like she backstabbed you?"

"Don't act like you weren't part of said backstabbing! You had no problem sticking your fucking dick in her slutty pussy." I'm so incensed, spit goes flying from my mouth into his face.

He doesn't bother wiping it away. He's too steadfast in his victim role. "Sure, I fucked her. I'm just a man. She kept throwing herself at me, coming by my office in revealing tops, without a bra or panties, promising the sky's the limit. Unlike you, Imogen was willing to satisfy every one of my fantasies." *And now, she's willing to satisfy Calvin's.* "You didn't want to be my domme and you didn't want to go to a kinky club. That's a vanilla sex mindset. You're so narrow minded, you refused to let me fuck your ass. Heck, you even refused the idea of wearing a strap-on dildo to fuck my ass and squirt fake spunk in my hole. I wanted to spice up our sex life, but nooooo, you wanted to stick to boring, predictable sex. Yawn."

"So, it's my fault you cheated on me?" My words ring out and they're laced with a heavy dose of sarcasm. "I'm responsible for you sticking your dick into Imogen's greedy pussy?"

"If you had been willing to be more open-minded—"

"You arrogant asshole!"

"Is that what your sequoia tree is offering you? Safe, vanilla sex? He looks like the uptight type who would like sex as starched as his shirt."

His low blows at my boyfriend irritate the fuck out of me.

"Let go of me, Elias! I'm not going to ask again." My voice heavy with a new wave of boiling rage.

He tightens his grip.

The absurdity of this situation flares something in me.

"Take your fucking hands off me, or I'm going to hurt your balls until you start howling like an excited hyena. How's that for fucking BDSM?"

He snorts. "Even if we're the same height, I'm still stronger. You're just *fat*." The mockery is condescending. "Beauty by *fat* Shay. Ha!" My head seethes. The insult stings like a slap in the face. Acid burns my throat. Towards the end of our relationship—when he was fucking Imogen—he'd drop comments about my weight, but never this demeaning. "I'm not letting go of you until *I* decide."

My heart races out of control.

"You're a piece of shit!" I slam the palm of my hand against his chest hard.

He jerks a little, but his body doesn't move.

He smirks. "Told you, you ain't going nowhere."

Under the light above our heads, my gaze reflects into two small black holes.

Those are the eyes of evil.

Worry is a hand choking me.

This isn't a rational person.

I'm in over my head.

"Help! Someone, help me!"

Elias's eyes widen in shock.

The idiot didn't see that coming.

"Shut up, Shay!"

"Help!" I yell at the top of my lungs.

That does it.

He lets go of me and takes a step back.

There's movement behind him, and the next thing I know, my ex goes flying in the air, shrieking in fright as if he's dropping from an airplane without a parachute.

Chapter 30

Zane

Although it's only been three days since I left Boston, I couldn't resist seeing Shay tonight. When I got back to New York on the twenty-sixth, I spent the evening hopping between three family functions. On the twenty-seventh, Max, Xavier and I met with a bunch of members from the VIP Den who we have a great connection with. We met at one of the guy's ultra-luxury three-level penthouse located in one of the many skyscrapers on 57th Street, aka Billionaires' Row. The building isn't too far from ours. I won't lie. That was one hell of an apartment—three floors perched in the Manhattan sky. One hundred million dollars buys you a lot. That said, it doesn't buy you a vantage view of Central Park. Our building does. Timing was on our side when Max received an early invitation to purchase a unit in a fully renovated building. He snatched up the penthouse. Gabriel, Lucas, Xavier, and I scooped up a unit each. On top of that, we pitched in to buy two other units as investment properties we can rent to wealthy people. All in all, that evening was about rich men hanging out, drinking expensive booze, eating great food, and shooting the shit. Until

Christmas Day, I was the only single guy of the bunch. What a difference a fake relationship makes.

Yesterday, my cousin Luisa and her husband invited us to their new house for dinner. As expected, her Irish American brothers-in-law drank us under the table. It took half the day for my liver to recover. I blame it on too many tumblers of Macallan 25 Year Old. But damn, was it worth it.

One thing I learned at Imogen and Elias's wedding is that not every Irish American—or plain old Irish—is able to swim to the bottom of the barrel and back. That wedding was far more contained than Luisa's post-Christmas dinner. My cousin's wedding was some crazy shit. I'm surprised no one got seriously hurt.

Thank God, tonight was more subdued.

Low-key is good if I'm to survive New Year's Eve. Max always throws a lavish catered party in his penthouse. My brother, his girl, and I spent the evening at Max and Candy's place. We enjoyed a spectacular dinner and I filled them in on my impetuous trip to Boston. Max listened to my tale with a smug, knowing look on his face. He hasn't even met my girl yet, already, he's team Shay. All because of the naughtiness on the forty-first floor.

Un-fucking-believable.

Even though my girlfriend texted me with a change of plans, I decided to cut my time with my family short. I was eager to kiss her luscious lips again. That, and because Max and Candy started complaining about not feeling well. When Candy started sneezing, I made my exit. Knock on wood I'm healthy as a horse. Instead of risking catching whatever my cousin and his fiancée are coming down with, I'd rather sit in front of Shay's house and wait patiently for her to show her beautiful face.

Living in the same building as your brother and cousins has

its privileges. I drop by my place to pick up the assortment of Brazilian desserts I bought for Shay earlier today, but kept them in my refrigerator to avoid snarky comments from my cousin and my brother. I also got her a few bottles of vintage wine, but left those on the backseat of my car. With the box of desserts in hand, I head to the garage, hop behind the wheel of my Mercedes-Benz S-Class Coupe, and head to her neighborhood. The week between Christmas and New Year's is a respite for us New Yorkers who stay in the city. The flow of heavy and unbearable traffic dwindles to something a lot more manageable. That's why at nine p.m. on a Friday night, I'm able to zoom through the city in record time. That also explains why I'm able to find parking not too far from Shay's Brooklyn Heights brownstone. Normally in a neighborhood like this, I'd have to either circle around for a while or park on another street.

I'm about to exit my vehicle, when my phone rings.

I pick up without hesitation.

"Hey, Mom."

"*Meu filho.*"

"What's up?"

"I hang up the phone with your brother. After the dinner at Luisa, I want to make sure I didn't lose my sons. Keller men are *hard-in-the-head-mules*, and you take all the challenges. You remember Luisa's wedding?"

I roll my eyes. "Of course I remember. I was there. I reckon, Xavier was more piss drunk than I was."

"Not the same anymore."

"What do you mean?"

"He has good woman now to take care of him if he is sick."

Even after years in the US, Bárbara Barros Keller, aka Bebe, can't shake off her Brazilian accent, and she still speaks with broken English.

"I'm a big boy."

"So, you don't have good woman to take care of you now?" There's a challenge in her voice.

I hesitate. "Where are you going with this?"

"Xavier is at Max's house in the sky." Penthouse isn't colorful enough for her. "They are both there with their good women. You are not there." *You already know that.* I can't make sense of this conversation. "I ask your brother where you are. Your brother tell me you go meet *good woman.*" *Now I get it.* "Why you don't tell *sua mãe* you have good woman in your life, Zane? Everybody know, but I not know."

I rub my hand over my face.

I can't believe my brother would throw me under the bus like this.

"First, I didn't announce it—"

"Candy say there is viral video of you with good woman." *Great, one more person who's part of this conspiracy.* "The whole planet know. Your mother not know."

"Mom, the relationship is new—"

"Ah..." One word that holds so many unspoken ones.

"Ah, what?"

"You never say *relationship.* You say *fling.* Even with the crazy Ember woman. This good woman different."

I let out a loud sigh.

"Yes, Mom, this good woman is different."

She blurts out something in Portuguese.

Cheers and claps erupt from the background.

"Please tell me you didn't announce this to the rest of the family."

"My oldest son has *relationship.* I tell the world." Her laugh is light and bright when it fills the line.

"Mom—"

"What is her name? I meet her when? Candy say she is

beautiful model. A lot of models they come from Brazil. *Mulheres brasileiras*—the most beautiful women. If you have beautiful good woman, I will have beautiful *netos*—"

"She's a former model. She's now a beauty vlogger with her own line of makeup—"

"What it means vlogger?"

"She does beauty and makeup videos."

"That means she's *muito linda garota*—that means more beautiful *netos*."

Grandbabies? What the fuck?

"Yes, Shay is a beautiful woman, but I just started seeing her, so—"

"Oh, I love her name."

She makes yet another announcement in Portuguese to the rest of the family.

This conversation is getting out of hand.

I shake my head.

"Like I was saying, Mom, I just started seeing Shay. Let's not start talking about grandbabies yet."

"Okay. Okay," she says, a small pout in her voice. "I will not put the horse in the cart."

"You mean, you won't put the cart before the horse."

"Whatever. The American expression too complicated."

In the background I hear one of my aunts ask when I'm going to come down and visit with my new girlfriend.

I pinch the bridge of my nose.

There's no such thing as a secret in my family.

"Tell *a família*, we're not there yet—"

"You bring Shay with you to Brazil when you come in January to work."

"Mom, Shay has a business to run."

There's a beat of silence on the other end.

"I know, I know. *Muito. Muito rápido*."

"Yes, Mom. Too much. Too fast."

"*A família* is happy for you," she says. Good luck winning an argument with her. "Everybody want to see the model, beauty vlogger girlfriend. Now they will Google Shay. I will see the viral video of you two."

Dear God.

"Mom, I have to go. Shay is waiting for me."

"You go. It's not good to make good woman wait. You say hello to Shay from Bebe. You tell her I make her good Brazilian dinner when I am back in New York. I can't wait to meet her."

The eagerness in her voice suggests she would be willing to beg a family member to drive her to the airport, buy a last-minute ticket, and make it back to New York by tomorrow morning to speed things up.

"Oh!"

What now? "I'm listening."

"*Seu pai* is having dinner at Tio Cristiano and Tia Patricia's house. I call him—"

"Please don't call Dad. I'll tell him myself."

"Ohhhh. It is *relationship*. You only tell us about Ember when she become crazy and you have to go to the court. Shay *is* the one."

I need to end this call. Now!

I lie my way out of this conversation. "Mom, I'm right outside Shay's house, and she's waving at me."

"Go, go, go." I have no doubt the words are accompanied by a waving hand gesture. "*Eu te amo, meu xuxu.*" She punctuates her endearment with a loud smack of a kiss.

"Love you too, Mom."

I end the call.

I'm sure she's going to spend the rest of the evening Googling the shit out of Shay and picking out baby names.

I'm going to have to prepare my girlfriend CIA-style for that first meeting—

Whoa.

I never thought the day would come where I'd consider introducing a woman to my family.

I shake my head, jerking out of my stupor.

I tuck the phone in the inside pocket of my coat, slip my gloves on, and get out of my car. As I engage the lock, shouting echoes nearby. Minding my own business, I shrug it off as a lovers' spat.

The faster I get inside Shay's home, the less likely my balls will turn to ice cubes.

Clouds of steam from my breath float in the frigid night air. I adjust my black cashmere hat on my head, pull up the collar of my cashmere coat to ward off the late December cold, and set off to Shay's brownstone.

I hum a song.

I smile.

That iconic oldies tune will forevermore be linked to the first time Shay and I met at the Evangelista Lounge.

That was only twelve days ago.

Unbelievable.

I check both ways on the road, cross the street, and charge ahead, already counting the seconds until I see her beautiful face.

More loud voices.

What the hell?

I crane my neck to see down the street, but a thought distracts me.

Shit. I forgot the pastries and the wine.

The conversation with Mom threw me off.

I halt my step.

I'm about to turn on my heel, but freeze in place, my blood turning to ice as chilling words reach my ear.

"Let go of me, Elias! I'm not going to ask again. Take your fucking hands off me..."

Elias? Shay's Elias?

The rest of the sentence gets lost in the wind.

With a rushed step, I charge forward.

A woman accompanied by two children, and another woman walking two tiny dogs, hustle in the direction of the loud voices.

"Help! Someone, help me!"

Goddammit. It's Shay!

What the fuck?

When I spot a flash of red hair spilling from a gray hat with a pompom, I double my speed. Passing the group of people in front of me, I hasten my pace.

"Shut up, Shay!" Elias shouts.

"Help!" Shay yells at the top of her lungs.

My feet eat the snowy street, my mind races through myriad possibilities, settling on one—destroy the motherfucker.

I close the distance between me and my girlfriend's assailant in a few long strides and grab Elias by the collar of his coat with strong hands. Anger boosts my adrenaline and instead of yanking him back, I lift the asshole off his feet, and throw him in a snowbank. He shrieks like the pussy he is as he flies through the air.

He stares up at me with a dumbfounded expression on his face.

For a few seconds, he seems lost, looking around in a daze. Then, his beady eyes laser in on me.

"What the fuck, man?"

"I should be asking you the same question, motherfucker."

"Shay and I were talking. Fuck off!"

I place one booted foot on his stomach and lean in, so he feels my weight. "What did you say?"

"Get off me, you fucking sequoia tree. You're hurting me."

I lean in, shifting more of my weight to his disadvantage.

He makes a choking sound.

My eyes meet Shay's. "You okay?"

My heart is thundering in my chest.

Even in the cold, I'm sweating.

She responds with a jerky nod.

"You sure?"

"I am now."

As I swing my gaze away from her terrified face, I notice a crowd of people huddled around us. Some have their phones out, but I don't have time to worry about that right now.

I return my focus to the sack of shit at my feet.

I roll my neck, easing the muscles in my shoulders.

I've been dying to rearrange his face since the day I met him.

Tonight, I get my wish.

"You know... a sequoia tree is heavy... heavy enough to crush every fucking bone inside you." I make my point by adding more pressure on his body.

"Stop! Please! Stop!"

"Why the fuck did you have your dirty hands on my girlfriend?"

"We—we were talking." Elias stammers his response.

"Liar!"

"I—I wanted to make sure I had her attention."

I humored the idiot. "Why's that?"

He turns his head to the side, avoiding my gaze.

"I asked you a question, dipshit!"

He doesn't answer.

He doesn't look at me.

He closes his eyes.

What a fucking loser.

Shay comes and stands next to me, looping an arm with mine. We're both shaking, I suspect not for the same reason. "The rug was pulled from under his feet."

"What the hell does that mean, Shay?" My annoyance is misdirected at her, but I can't help it.

When she stares up at me, a barbarian fury takes over. I'm about to set off like a fucking volcano. "He left fucking bruises on your face," I bark. "I'm going to make the asshole wish he was never born—"

"Don't!" Shay firms her grip around my arm.

She's protecting him?

What the fuck?

"Give me one damn good reason—"

The screeching tires of a police car parking right in front of us cut me off midsentence.

Fuck.

Chapter 31

Zane

I was certain tonight was going to be a low-key night. It turns out, I was dead wrong.

"I can't believe I waited twenty-six years to discover how delicious passion fruit is," Shay says.

We're sitting in her kitchen, enjoying the desserts I brought.

We started with the *pudim de leite condensado*. After savoring the condensed milk flan, we've moved onto the second dessert.

I've polished off my first two glasses of wine in one gulp and I'm already on my third one. It's in poor form to drink a three-hundred-dollar bottle of wine this fast, but after this eventful night, I sure as hell need it.

"There are a lot of Brazilian desserts I love, but the *mousse de maracuja* tops the list."

"I can see why. Who knew passion fruit mousse was this lip-smacking good. I don't care what anybody says, I'm having this tomorrow morning for breakfast!"

I nod, my mood still murderous.

Every time I look at her beautiful face marred by the dark spots running along her jaw line, I want to bolt out of here, hunt down Elias, and make good on my promise. That said, if I go after him, I'll get arrested for sure this time.

One of Shay's neighbors called 911. When the police arrived, the officers ordered me to move away from Elias. Then, they forced me down on my knees with my hands behind my head. As much as I wanted to protest and shout my indignation, I didn't. I was the giant using the full advantage of my weight and height, lording over a peon lying on his back, begging for mercy. In a few succinct sentences, Shay dispelled any confusion. Even though my girl isn't going to press charges against her scumbag ex, the officers took Elias away for disorderly conduct. The older woman who called the police caught all the action on her phone. So did a few of the people witnessing what had gone down.

I screw up my face.

Abusive fucker.

I wish I'd had time to deck him in the face. Cameras or no cameras. He deserved to lose his teeth.

A waving hand snaps me back to the moment.

My gaze bounces up to Shay's.

She's staring up at me, concern evident in her blue eyes.

She drops her spoon on the saucer and places a comforting hand over mine. "It's over." I should be the one easing her torment. Not the other way around. Even if Elias didn't strike her, he left his mark on her. "I'm fine, Zane. The bruises will heal. As a beauty vlogger, I can make them disappear with makeup—" Her expression changes. "God, that's the kind of thing a battered woman would say."

My jaw tightens so hard, I'm certain my teeth will turn to dust from the excessive pressure.

Elias roughed her up in the past?

"He put his hands on you before?" I don't even recognize my own voice.

"No."

"You're sure?"

"He's never done anything like that before."

I regard her for a long beat.

She wouldn't lie about something like that, would she?

"I swear to you. I wouldn't stand for it," she says to appease me. "Aunt Eileen has been looking for a good reason to castrate him. Trust me, her knifes are as sharp as swords and she wouldn't have missed her chance had the opportunity landed in her lap."

I'm confident her great aunt would've rid the asshole of his family jewels.

I nod.

She continues. "I was making a point. I can use makeup to conceal the bruises just like that." She snaps her fingers.

My nostrils flare and my brows dip even more in response. They've remained wrinkled and my jaw tight since the incident. Despite Shay's attempt at humor, I'm thirsty for blood.

I consider the last swallow of white wine in my glass.

After little deliberation, I polish it off.

The wine barely eases my anger, but going for a fourth glass in such a short space of time would be pushing it. Getting drunk when you're seriously considering strangling another human being—although a lowlife scumbag, but still, another human being—could lead down a treacherous road.

"It should've never happened in the first place. You shouldn't have bruises to cover, Shay," I manage in a barely contained voice.

She lets out a heavy sigh. "Not that I condone how Elias reacted to the news—since I'm the victim—but days after his marriage, he discovered, it was all a big fat lie. As it stands, he'll end up losing a woman he claims to love, a best friend he's had since he was a kid, and potentially, his unborn child. I wouldn't want to be in his shoes."

I frown my confusion. "I understand Imogen is a cunt and Elias might want a divorce, but that doesn't excuse him from stepping up to the plate when it comes to his child. That kid shouldn't have to pay for having two stupid parents."

"That's not what I mean," she says. "The baby might be Calvin's."

What the fuck?

My bewilderment must be evident, because she keeps talking.

"Calvin Fernandes was born in Suriname. He came to the US when he was three years old. His dark complexion, curly black hair, and dark brown eyes are a contrast to Elias's who's one hundred percent Irish American. My ex shares his parents' and older brother's pale complexion, light brown hair, and hazel brown eyes. We both have to lather on copious coats of sunscreen protection on a beach vacation. That, or wear a full wetsuit so we don't end up looking like lobsters," she says. "Calvin isn't a saint in this story. It takes two people to cheat. He's married *and* he has a four-year-old son." My jaw drops. "The queen shit-stirrer, aka Imogen, is Irish American on Alan's side. Her mom is from North Dakota with a strong Scandinavian heritage—"

"Holy shit! Everything makes sense now."

Shay nods. "Imogen won't be able to pretend Elias is the father, if in fact, he isn't the sperm donor, which won't be hard to tell... even without a DNA test—"

"Not only was your stepsister having an affair with a married man, but they weren't even using condoms?"

"They weren't."

Talk about the height of stupidity.

"If the baby isn't Elias's, Imogen won't be able to hide her cheating ways. Her new husband has to wait *seven* more months to find out how deep this deception runs. God knows how he'll react then."

Holy fuck.

Chapter 32

Shay

I arrive at Overindulge, located in the Lower East Side, at a quarter past twelve to find Keeley already seated at a table for two near the faux-fireplace at the back of the cozy eatery. A delightful aroma of sugar, vanilla, java, and myriad other comforting smells tingle my nostrils and tickle my belly.

My eyes scan the space.

There isn't an empty table, but contrary to usual, there isn't a line running around the block. I navigate through the restaurant to join my friend, dropping *I'm sorry* here and there as I wiggle my way through the tiny eatery to our table.

Keeley is already on her feet, arms wide open. It's as if we didn't see each other last night.

God, I love this woman.

After hugs and cheek to cheek kisses, she sits down.

I remove my baby blue hat and tuck it inside my tote bag. I peel off the winter layers and hook my grey winter coat on the wall near our table.

I rub my hands together to warm up as I sit down.

This table is the most coveted in the eatery. Its location

allows for a little breathing room, so you don't feel like you're sitting on top of the table next to you.

I meet Keeley's gaze. "Great minds think alike..." I pull on my long braid."

"I couldn't be bothered." She tugs on her long, black braid. "You could say the same about our outfits. We're both sporting sweaters and yoga pants." There's a twinkle in her blue eyes. "Is your head-to-toe baby blue combo from your *boyfriend's* collection?"

I laugh. "Yes. It's Curves Envy Fashion, circa last winter."

"You're a great ambassador for the brand."

"Thanks."

"That I'm-a-lucky-bitch expression on your face gives me a clue as to why you're late."

I cringe. "Sorry about that."

"Pffh! Puh-lease," she says with a sweep of a hand, "your sexy as fuck boyfriend stayed over. Of course, you're late." She ends her sentence with an exaggerated wink.

I'm about to burst your bubble.

Zane dropped me off before heading back to his place. I can't wait for my best friend to meet him, but today isn't the day. There's so much Keeley and I need to talk about. I don't want the first time they meet to be connected to Elias and Imogen in any way, shape, or form. Those two have been scavengers in my life for long enough.

"Nothing happened between us—last night or this morning."

She flinches. "Don't tell me the honeymoon is already over?" The concern in her voice is audible.

"No." I reach out and place a hand on top of hers. "It's nothing like that."

"Phew." She brushes the back of her free hand across her

forehead. "I would've been devastated. So, what was the hold up about if you two weren't getting freaky with it?"

"Among the many things that transpired this morning, I struggled to get my makeup just right—"

"I appreciate the effort, but you didn't have to get all dolled up to eat with me. I'm just your best friend."

"It has nothing to do with vanity, and as much as I love you, it has nothing to do with you. It's..." I shake my head, hoping to dislodge the memory of a flashback from last night. "Let's just say, it's a situation I never thought I'd ever find myself in."

She frowns. "I don't like the sound of that. What's going on?"

"Let's eat first."

She shoots me a suspicious side gaze.

"I'm not sweeping this under the rug, Keeley. I'll tell you everything. I promise. I'm hungry."

"We'll eat first, as long as you don't break your promise."

"I won't." I reach for the menu.

"I already decided what I'm having," she says. "I'm in the mood for the maple bourbon pecan pancakes."

I peruse the menu.

"Ooohhh!" My eyes light up, my mood jacking up by several notches. "The pancakes with *dulche de leche* whipped cream have my name written all over them."

A waitress approaches our table.

Right on time.

We place our orders.

When the waitress returns with our lattes, I say a silent prayer.

As we sip on our double espresso lattes served in bowls, like the French, my best friend and I chat about her long-standing crush for her older brother's best friend transitioning from fantasy to reality.I don't hold back on my elation.

Go, Keeley!

By the time our food is served, I'm all caught up on her love life.

The food is way too good to ruin the experience by talking about last night's drama, so I'm grateful we're too consumed by our yummy pancakes.

"Thank God this restaurant isn't around the corner from my brownstone," I say, polishing off the last bite. "I'd be in serious trouble."

"Same!" Keeley leans back against her chair. "Now that our bellies are full, are you going to tell me what's going on?"

I crumple my napkin and drop it on my empty plate. "Remember what I told you about Aunt Eileen and the wedding selfie?"

Her eyes bug out of her skull. "Please tell me Aunt Eileen didn't instigate anything. No one in their right mind should touch that with a ten-foot pole. When the shit hits the fan, it's going to be ugly."

"Well... the shit hit the fan last night. And yes, it was ugly."

I give Keeley the scene-by-scene.

"The fucker calling you fat was a cheap shot." Steam is coming from her ears. "You were a big girl when he met you. How dare he use body shaming to make up for his shortcomings?" She crosses her arms over her chest. "What a pathetic loser."

"Anger, alcohol, disappointment, and shock prompted the insult, but that doesn't justify it."

She huffs. "Damn right it doesn't."

I tell her the rest of the story.

Keeley squints at me. "That's fucked up."

"Yes, it is." I nod. "But there's more."

Her jaw drops.

"Part of the reason I'm late," I say, "is because Richard

dragged Elias's sorry ass back to my place this morning to apologize."

"And you let them in your house?"

"Zane was there, so I knew nothing would get out of hand. That said, Richard's tone was decisive. He didn't want Elias to get off easy."

"Did you get a *real* apology this time?"

I nod. "Richard apologized for telling Elias he spotted Aunt Eileen on the mezzanine. He never suspected his cousin would come after me for answers—"

"Good for Richard for manning up, but did your idiot ex grow balls?"

"I got a sincere apology. He even apologized for calling me fat. Since I had left that part out of the story, Zane lunged at him, ready to send him back to his maker. Elias cowered behind Richard, using his cousin as a human shield. That only flared Zane's anger. I had to beg my boyfriend not to knock Richard out of the way so he could bash Elias's face. It was a scene straight out of a reality TV show."

Disbelief is painted all over Keeley's face.

"I never thought I would say this, but in many ways, your stepsister did you a favor. Elias is spineless."

"I couldn't have said it better. Richard picked him up from the police station last night and drove him to his place. He then called Elias's parents and told them everything."

Keeley's eyes are as wide as dinner plates. "They dropped all that money on a wedding that was a sham."

I nod. "They're livid. And offended. It's not only the money. It's also the humiliation. There were two hundred people at that wedding."

"What a cluster fuck." Keeley shakes her head. "I'm impressed by Richard's courage. That must've been a hard conversation."

"Nowhere near as hard as the conversation I had with Ma and Alan after Richard and Elias left my place."

Keeley's eyes widen. "You didn't tell them last night?"

"Ma and Alan had a dinner with friends that ended late. Not to mention, I was a bit shaken and needed time to process it all." I shred my napkin to pieces. "Then, I called my sister and Aunt Eileen."

"Aunt Eileen must be sharpening her knives as we speak."

"I asked her not to kill him."

"That bad?"

I nod.

"Poor Alan," Keeley says. "He's such a good man. How the hell did he end up with a daughter like that? How did he take the news?" I'm about to respond, but she keeps talking. "Not that anyone can blame him if he blew a gasket. After all, his queen bitch of a daughter's favorite pastime is to fuck up other people's lives."

"He didn't have a reaction. He just stared at me on the screen with a blank look on his face. On the polar opposite end of the spectrum, Mom was beside herself—not as bad as Aunt Eileen's reaction, but she wasn't impassive like her husband."

"Alan didn't yell? He wasn't upset? He didn't threaten to get on the next plane to New York and hunt his daughter down? He didn't promise to order a hit on Elias's head?"

"None of the above."

Keeley's head jerks back.

"His face was made of stone... and that worries me." I bite my lower lip.

"It is a lot to process."

"I texted Briar right before entering the restaurant to find out if he might've had a post-news meltdown, but no, nothing. It's business as usual. Maybe he'll have a delayed reaction."

She snaps her fingers and point at me. "I'm sure that's it."

I let out an audible sigh. "And then there's the third reason why I was late."

"There's more?"

I pull out my phone from inside the crossbody bag still strapped across my waist. I search through my photos and turn the device so my best friend can see my screen.

"Elias did that to you?!"

"Yes." I nod.

Her blue eyes turn dark and menacing. Fury blazes in them.

"Even though I decided not to press charges, Zane insisted we take photos," I say. "He has copies on his phone." I turn my head from side to side. "With a pound of makeup, you can't see them much, but the black and blue bruises are there as proof of how my ex's life has derailed. Elias did this to me, but Imogen fanned the flame—"

"Like she always does."

Chapter 33

Shay

My doorbell rings.

He's here!

I check my reflection one last time in the mirror.

Since everything is still so new between Zane and me, I still get butterflies around him.

I give myself a little twirl.

I'm not ashamed to admit I want to look good for him.

Mission accomplished.

The doorbell rings again.

"Coming!" I yell from upstairs, knowing full well it's unlikely he'll be able to hear me.

With a spring in my step, I exit my bedroom and balance on my black patent leather peep toe high heels as I descend the stairs. I didn't bother with hosiery because I wanted to showcase my toes painted in red.

I'm so excited to see him, I do a little jog all the way to the door. I spot his reflection through the stained-glass window. That was one of the major selling features to this house. I bought the brownstone two years ago. It had recently been remodeled, so I didn't have much to do. I paid a lot more than if I was willing to purchase a fix-me-up like Keeley, but I'm not the home-reno type.

When I open the door, Zane is standing there, looking all kinds of handsome.

Even in winter gear, there's no hiding his imposing figure.

His long black cashmere coat only accentuates his tall form.

Good God, he's handsome.

Some sort of innate need to produce little humans with him sets off at the sight of him. Zane is the kind of man who would rock a suit all week, come home before the kids' bedtime for some play time, and then fuck my brains out in our bedroom.

Enough with the crazy dreams, Shay.

"Hey, you!"

His response takes my breath away.

He takes my head in his hands, and presses his lips to mine. My skyscraper heels give me an advantage, although, he still towers over me. *Just like I like it.* My body buzzes with excitement. The kiss is pure Zane—hot and urgent. It's so intense, I feel it in every cell of my body. I slide my hands up his arms and loop them around his neck, hoping he'll deepen the kiss. He grants my unspoken wish. It's a lip-lock frenzy so passionate, it could melt snow. The low moans he makes as he unleashes his fervor makes me vibrate with need. A few more tongue strokes, and I swear I'll climax.

Though the cold winter air blows in, my skin prickles with heat.

Scratch that.

I'm ablaze.

I push on his chest, concerned I'm about to combust. I pull away from him and take a step back, already missing the warmth of his body seeping through mine.

"You're right," he says in a low, raspy voice, "we should go inside so the neighbors don't end up calling the police again."

I was more concerned about my ability to remain standing on my shaky legs, but offering my neighbors a peep show might be divulging too much.

He gives me a onceover. "You look fucking amazing, love." His gaze drops to my feet. "Those cock-hardening heels are as sexy as fuck." The low rumble in his voice makes my knees buckle.

It's not a Curves Envy Fashion couture, but I suspect he already knows that.

"Thank you. It's just a little black dress," I say from beneath my eyelashes with a touch of coquettishness.

"Tsk, tsk, tsk." He wags a disapproving finger in the air. "It's a weapon of seduction on your heavenly body." Heat rushes up my neck and floods my cheeks. "I hope my birthday gift includes you out of that gorgeous dress, stripped naked, sitting on my face with your luscious pussy smearing your sweet juices all over my tongue."

Well, there goes a perfectly good pair of panties.

I fan myself at the deluge of dirty talking.

Zane's lips quirk.

The bastard knows the effect he has on me.

I spent three hours getting ready and it's already paying dividends.

"It's only seven o'clock. Your birthday isn't for another five hours."

"Don't skirt the issue, woman."

"You'll find out soon enough what I have in store for your birthday gift." I have no idea how I manage to say that with a straight face.

"If it doesn't include you naked and your luscious curves on display for my pleasure, I'm out of here," he makes to leave, but I grab hold of his arm.

"Whoa! Cool your engines, dirty executive."

Without Zane Keller in my life and his unabashed adoration of every imperfect part of me, Elias's insult would've been a much bigger blow.

"So, I get to ring in the New Year *and* my birthday with you riding my cock or my tongue? Better yet, both."

His words sear along my nerve endings, lighting them up like sparklers.

God, I'm in trouble.

"You're incorrigible and too impatient for your own good."

He leans close and tugs at a strand of my hair spilling over my shoulders. "I'm waiting for an answer, love."

With a feigned exasperated huff, I concede. "Let's just say, you won't be disappointed."

He considers me for a beat. His stare is direct. Intense. "Good enough."

I shake my head.

Secretly I'm tickled pink. I still can't get over his desire for me.

"Are you going to come in now?"

"Let me run back to my car. I brought a few things—"

"I told you to bring your sexy self and nothing else."

"I know, love, but since Max had to cancel his New Year's Eve party at the last minute, the caterers still delivered his order because it was ready. As usual, Max ordered a lavish display of food for a party of twelve. As a result, his fridge and freezer are stuffed. Which means, my brother and I ended up with the surplus. And there's a lot. I grabbed a little of everything, so you can taste it all."

I place my hands over my heart. "There's nothing worse than being sick over the holidays."

"The only thing worse, is being sick over the holidays when it's your birthday. Thankfully, God spared me."

"I feel for your cousin and your brother, but at least they're not spending New Year's Eve alone," I say.

"No, they have company in their misery. It's a good thing because they're in no condition to leave their apartments. It's a *TV* and chill evening for them... and a lot of cough syrup, tea, and Kleenexes."

"No bubbly at the stroke of midnight. Gosh, that's rough."

"They've been suffering all day, but later this afternoon, all four took a nosedive," he says. "They're coughing, hacking, sniffling, and sneezing. The whole kit and caboodle. At this rate, it's unlikely they'll make it to midnight. They'll crash well before then. Like I said, knock on wood, I didn't catch whatever nasty virus that's put a dent on their New Year's celebrations."

"Happy *healthy* birthday to you!"

"Thank you, love." He drops a quick kiss on my lips. "Give me a minute and I'll go grab everything."

"Okay!"

When Zane announced this morning the New Year's party at his cousin's penthouse was a no go, that didn't mean we should ignore his birthday. Without hesitation, I invited him to my place. I adore my brownstone and it's a good size. I'm sure it's nowhere near Zane's massive apartment with a view overlooking Central Park—I haven't seen it yet, but I've been told—but since it's his birthday, I insisted he comes to my turf. I don't want him to lift a finger tonight. I have everything covered.

He's back in a flash, his hands weighed down with bags.

"Holy shit! you weren't kidding when you said there was a lot of food."

"I have another trip to make."

My eyes widen in shock.

He runs out to his car and returns with more bags.

I'm dumbfounded.

Max Keller doesn't believe in half measures.

He closes the door, locks it, and we make our way to my kitchen.

When we place all the bags on my kitchen island, they overtake the surface.

My fists resting at my waist. "I won't need to do grocery shopping until spring."

"And you'll be feasting on the best. The caterer Max uses is one of the top ones in the city." *Why would a billionaire settle for anything less?* "This isn't meant to overstep whatever smells so good," he says, sniffing around. "We can keep everything for tomorrow."

"I like that idea. I have a feast prepared for tonight—including lip-smacking desserts—but tomorrow and the day after, I'm not going to be in the mood to cook."

"Deal!"

No one will ever confuse me for a top chef. There are so many food options within an arm's reach, I never made the effort to perfect my cooking skills. That said, I can manage the basics. A morning video chat with Aunt Eileen and I was bursting with confidence. I was also armed with a yummy menu.

"You know where the coat closet is. While you get rid of your coat, I'll pour some of the red I opened earlier to let it aerate in the decanter."

"This evening is sounding better by the second." He winks and then he's gone.

I grab the decanter, and pour the dry red cabernet franc from a New York State winery into glasses.

I pull out the containers from the bags Zane brought and

head to the fridge. It takes me a few trips to put everything away. When I'm done, I stare at my full fridge.

Unbelievable.

I pull out the platter of appetizers I prepared and place it on the counter.

I beam with pride.

When Zane re-emerges in the kitchen, I do a double take.

Holy hotness.

He's breathtaking.

He looks irresistible in black pants and a burgundy cashmere sweater that accentuates the green in his hazel green eyes. Although the echo of his heels on the wooden floor was a precursor, my eyes drop to his feet. He swapped his winter boots for a pair of elegant looking black shoes. Although a little on the casual side, I'm sure his outfit cost more than the property taxes on this brownstone.

He struts towards me like a predator, snakes an arm around my waist before crushing his lips against mine. Without his coat on, his expensive cologne permeates. The musky scent of his maleness—his potent masculinity—causes my body to react. All this male pheromone is making me dizzy. His mere presence causes all my cells to hum.

Down, girl.

"Thank you for tonight," he says, breaking the kiss.

"It's my pleasure."

It's unlikely we would've been able to get on the list of any New Year's Eve party or reserve a table at a restaurant at the last minute, but I'm glad we're staying in.

An indulgent smile curves his lips. "If I have to be a good boy and wait until later to eat you out, what's on the menu?"

After a satisfying meal, we're kicking back in the dining room, enjoying a second bottle of red wine—another winner from New York State. The rich food absorbed the alcohol, so I'm not even feeling a buzz. That's a good thing because I need to be stable on my feet for the second part of this evening. Given Zane is taller than I am and he's a guy, I'm sure he's not even feeling the wine. That's also a good thing, because what I have in store for him is an activity that might cause him to fall asleep if he's a little too drunk.

"At the risk of repeating myself, that was amazing, Shay," Zane says before sliding the last spoonful of dessert in his mouth.

"You're not just saying that?"

Zane shakes his head. "I had doubles of everything. And I inhaled the pudding."

When he asked for a second ramekin of the dessert, I was giddy.

I'm not going to lie. I was so nervous.

Although Aunt Eileen selected a menu I could execute with ease, I was afraid I'd screw things up. Instead of sending me on a wild goose chase around the city for ingredients I never use, she considered what I already had in my pantry, fridge, and freezer. I ended up with a delicious menu that surpassed my expectations, but it meant nothing if I wasn't able to impress Zane.

We started with marinaded garlicky shrimp, which I served with a baguette. For the main course, I prepared juicy roast chicken thighs with lots of garlic, roasted carrots with an addictive creamy dressing and a whole roasted cauliflower with whipped goat cheese. I also served extra-buttery mashed potatoes as another side dish. The chocolate, Nutella, and hazelnut pudding was a little tricky. I screwed up the first batch, but aced the second one.

Zane sets his wine glass down. He's sitting at the head of the table, and I'm to his right, near the kitchen. He shifts in his chair and our knees touch. Warmth spreads through me, gathering between my legs.

Our eyes meet and hold.

God, the smouldering look in his eyes...

The fine lines starting to show only make him sexier. More rugged. More manly. More intoxicating.

"All that to say, thank you for a great birthday." A smile eases across his sexy lips. "You spoiled me, love."

"It was just dinner."

He shakes his head. "I beg to differ. It was an incredible dinner prepared just for me. That makes it special."

"I'm glad you liked it," I say.

He leans forward and strokes a finger along the swell of my breast. "Can't wait to see what else I get for my birthday."

My flesh prickles under his touch.

"Patience."

"Don't I get a hint?" His finger slides underneath my bra, finding my erect nipple.

I gasp.

Damn him for playing dirty.

"And kill the surprise?" I barely manage to control the tremolo in my voice.

"It seems you're determined to make me suffer."

"Good things come to those who wait."

He pulls his hand away from my breast, and checks his expensive designer watch before meeting my gaze.

"It's ten o'clock. We have two hours to kill before I get you naked—which is my ultimate birthday gift, by the way. How do you suggest we spend that time?" His voice is thick and seductive, and I pretend it doesn't affect me in the least.

He's flipping the question on its head.

"You're tenacious."

"Not that I want to talk about your asshole ex, but because of his stupidity, I didn't get my fill of you a couple nights ago. Since Max, Xavier, and their fiancées are sick like dogs, we decided it was best if I didn't come over last night to make sure I wouldn't catch whatever they have. Translation, I haven't seen you naked in six days. That's a crying shame right there."

I laugh, and laugh, and laugh.

When I regain my composure, I reach out and place my hand on top of his. "You do wonders for a girl's ego."

He taps the tip of my nose. "And I've told you, I do nothing. I praise what's already there."

His eyes bore into mine.

Something passes between us.

My God, this man would be so easy to love—

Whoa!

What kind of ridiculous and far-fetched thought is that?

Love?

We met two weeks ago today.

Enough of this silliness, Shay.

"Where did you go just there?" he asks.

I shake out of my stupidity.

"I know how we can spend the next couple of hours..."

"Now, we're talking!"

"Why don't I go upstairs and get ready?" It's best to keep things on track.

He arches an eyebrow. "You need to get ready?"

"Yes."

"This sounds like a production."

"In many ways, it is. I was thinking I'd lavish you with all my attention..." My tone is suggestive.

He flashes me a seductive smile. "Don't let me stop you."

I grab my cloth napkin from my lap and place it on the table.

With my eyes still locked with his, I get out of my chair.

I head to the console, grab my phone from the speaker dock, and select another playlist.

A sultry vibe seeps from the surround sound speakers.

Biting my lower lip, I look over my shoulder.

"If the music is a precursor of things to come, I approve," Zane says.

"You have no idea."

He gives me a wolfish look that has my panties sizzling.

"Get to it, woman." His voice is as smoky as a fine cognac.

Aware I have a rapt audience, I sashay out of the dining area with an exaggerated swing of the hips.

Zane whistles and woofs.

I'm tempted to giggle, but keep it together.

Now that I found my lady balls, I need to remain in character.

With a hurried step, I climb up the oakwood staircase with ornate banister to my bedroom.

I kick off my heels, change in a flash, and tie my hair back with an elastic band, twisting my locks in a messy, low bun. Once I'm in costume, I head to one of the two guestrooms. I open the door and scan the space.

I'm ready.

I stroll to the top of the stairs. "Zane, you can come up now!"

"I have to travel for my birthday gift?" His voice resonates throughout the house.

"Don't worry, you won't have to leave state lines."

He chuckles.

The chair scrapes against the floor.

He's willing to play.

That was an easy sell.

The heels of his expensive shoes echo throughout the house, clanking against the wood as he strides towards the staircase.

He looks up. "Holy shit, Shay!" His eyes widen in surprise.

Butterflies take flight in my tummy.

"I like what you're wearing. I like it a lot." His eyes eat me up and down, stopping at my bare legs. "Are you naked underneath the robe?"

And... action!

"Good evening, sir. My name is Shay and I'll be your masseuse for tonight."

"Does the massage include a happy ending?"

"This is a reputable establishment, sir." It's a challenge to keep a straight face.

"I apologize. What's your name again?"

"Shay."

"Pretty name for a pretty girl. My mouth sometimes runs away from me. It's because I'm so taken aback by your incredible beauty. Of all the masseuses in this joint, I end up with you." He flashes me a wide smile. "Have I mentioned I have a thing for tall and voluptuous redheads?" He gropes his cock and squeezes it hard. "They turn me on."

"Sir!"

"I'm sorry." That cocky grin says he's not sorry one bit.

"I have another appointment after you, may I suggest we get started."

"Right."

He jogs up the stairs.

"Oof. You're even more stunning close up."

His praise means everything.

"I'm flattered, sir. However, I'd rather we keep it professional. I have a boyfriend."

"Really?"

"Yes."

"So, I'm out of luck?"

I bite the inside of my cheek to avoid laughing.

"You are."

"Is it serious between you and this guy?"

Is that a genuine question or is it part of our game?

We're dating, but is it serious?

It is for me.

He shakes his head as if his torment matches mine.

"The good ones are always taken." He pouts in mock disappointment. He's back in the game. "Lucky bastard."

"*I'm* the lucky one."

"If you ever break up with him..."

"Sir, you don't even know me. How can you be that taken by me?"

He gives me a onceover.

He works his jaw for a few beats before answering. "I know enough."

If the timbre of a man's voice could make you come, I just did.

"If you'll follow me," I say, my tone overly formal.

"I'm right behind you, love."

"This is a bizarre coincidence, but please refrain from calling me love. That nickname is reserved for my boyfriend. My name is Shay."

"I'm sorry. I overstepped my boundaries. I blame it on being under your bewitching spell."

I lift my chin. "I'm going to let that slide, but it's the last time."

"I promise to be a good boy." His wicked grin is epic.

Liar.

"You're in the Azur room." I turn around. "This way." With a hand wave, I instruct him to follow me.

"I might get thrown out of this fine establishment and your boyfriend might hunt me down and beat the shit out of me for saying this, but holy Jesus, your luscious ass underneath that robe and the way the silk caresses said fine ass every time you take a step is cock-hardening."

My step falters.

"You know what, I'll leave you a big fat tip for that slip of the tongue... unless you'd like me to slip my tongue between your pussy lips instead. I bet you'd be all wet, slick, and sweet. Imagine me sucking on your hard clit. I bet I can make you come—"

I whirl around. "Sir, which part of I have a boyfriend do you not understand?"

He hangs his head low. "I've never been attracted to a woman at first sight before. I apologize for my appalling behavior."

"That was your last chance."

"From now on, I will keep my dirty, filthy, lewd, and downright bawdy thoughts to myself."

I'm so turned on, I don't know what to do with myself.

I knew I was no match for him, but I didn't expect him to derail me this early in the evening.

I head towards the guestroom and open the door.

He approaches, a cocky smile still stretching his lips.

I shake my head.

"There's a towel behind the door. Please change. When you're ready, please lie face down on the massage table, underneath the towel—"

"Time out," he says forming a T with his hands. "The massage table wasn't there yesterday."

Although there's a queen size bed in the room, there was enough space for the massage table.

"It wasn't. I rented it this morning. This is New York. You can get anything delivered… even on New Year's Eve."

He nods. "So, I get a little role-playing for my birthday?"

Too fast, too soon.

Crap. This is a bad idea.

Cosmo, did you steer me wrong?

Suggestion number one of the '*10 Spontaneous and Sexy Ways to Turn Up the Volume in Your Relationship*' was supposed to be a winner. Not a bust.

"Where did you go just now?"

My eyes snap up to his.

I give him a one-shoulder shrug. "What do you get a guy who has everything and who can buy anything?"

He places a hand on my shoulder, tilting my chin back with the other. "That wasn't a criticism, love. The idea is as sexy as fuck." A little thrill runs through me and I beam with joy. "And you're right, I have everything. Contrary to your sucker of a client, I have you as my girlfriend." He winks.

I stop breathing for a second.

Heart, calm the hell down.

He leans towards me and drops a soft kiss against my lips.

"Sorry if I took you out of character."

Flirty devil.

Get it together, Shay.

"I'll give you five minutes to change and I'll knock on the door to make sure you're ready," I say, slipping back into character. "I'll go through a basic list of questions—your medical history. Then, we can get started with your massage."

"Sounds good to me," he says, amusement shining bright in his eyes. "One more question."

"Yes."

"Do I strip down to my boxer briefs, or do you want me naked?"

I throw the ball in his court. "It's up to you."

"Then you're getting me naked."

I try not to show my delight. "As you wish, sir."

He slips into the room and I wait outside.

He lets me know he's ready by knocking three times against the door.

I didn't expect that.

Eager much?

I open the door and enter the room.

I light up the many candles I had set up to add a little ambience. Since I have surround sound throughout the house, the sultry music plays in the background.

I walk up to a tray on the dresser and grab a night mask.

"This makes for a much more enjoyable experience," I say, handing it to him.

"I'm all about mystery," he grabs it from me and slips it on. He makes sure it's snug. "I'm ready when you are!"

"How do you like your massage, sir? Soft or rough?" I ask, heading to the tray to grab some scented oil.

"Normally, I'd say the latter, because I like it rough, but I'm going to go with soft because I want the feel of your hands to linger all over my body. Dammit. I did it again. Let me try that again." He cocks a brow. "Soft, please."

"As you wish."

Careful not to make a sound, I remove the turquoise silk robe and drop it on the bed.

I tippytoe back to the dresser.

"You're still in the room?" Zane asks.

"Yes, sir. I'm selecting a massage oil." He doesn't need to know I'm naked. Not yet, anyway.

"Got it," he says. "No fruity scent."

"No chances of that happening."

"We're on the same wavelength."

"We are." I'm pretty proud of myself.

I grab a bottle and head towards a little table I set up near the massage table. I pour oil in my palm and rub my hands together to warm it. Although lavender is my favorite scent, I select a musky scent. It's more masculine.

He groans when I rub his shoulders.

"That's where I hold all my pressure. You're so intuitive, Shay."

Bless him for playing along.

"A few vigorous strokes and you should be back to normal, sir."

"Vigorous strokes..." He doesn't have to finish that sentence for me to know his mind is in the gutter. Again.

Putting into practice everything I learned from my crash course—aka several YouTube videos—I keep rubbing his shoulders, using my weight to add enough pressure.

This man's body is truly a work of art.

My hands glide along the surface of his muscular back, from his shoulder blades down to the upper part of his fine ass. I massage said fine ass over the towel.

He lets out a rumbling sound of contentment.

That only fuels me.

I change my tempo, the touch of my fingers becoming more and more sensual.

"Fuck, yeah."

I lean forward so my hard nipples scratch his arm as I bring my lips to his earlobe. "How's the pressure, sir?"

Zane flips over in a sitting position.

I yelp as I jump back.

He yanks the mask off his face and tosses it to the side.

His wide eyes take in my naked body.

Is it my imagination or did he grow by a couple of inches since Boston?

"Jesus," he sucks in a breath. "You're so goddamn beautiful."

He stares at my naked body with wild eyes and flared nostrils, muscular chest heaving, his jaw clenched.

He lifts off the massage table and with one stride, he's standing in front of me.

As his gaze eats me up, my eyes are fixed on his massive erection pointing north.

The way he wants me makes me feel so fucking sexy.

"Don't expect me to have any self-restraint when you're exposing yourself," my eyes lift to meet his. "You're begging for it, love. You could've kept the robe on, but no, you *want* me to fuck you." A thrill runs through me. Pure adrenaline races through my veins, causing my wild heartbeat to go ballistic. "Consider yourself fucked."

I don't have time to respond.

He lifts me off my feet, places both hands beneath my ass, and walks us both to a wall.

I gasp when my back hits the hard surface.

"Since I wasn't privy to your wicked intentions, the condoms are downstairs. I can go get them—"

"I'm on the pill and I'm clean." The words rush out of my mouth.

"Same here. Minus the pill part."

"My ex-boyfriends used condoms."

"Are you saying what I think you are?"

I nod. "If we're both clean..."

He lets out an animalistic a growl. "Fuck, Shay, you're killing me."

"We don't have to if you don't want to—"

"Damn right I wanna fuck you bareback. I've never wanted that with any other woman before in my life."

My heart skips a beat.

"You sure about this?"

"I place my oily hands on his cheeks and bring his face closer to mine. I drop a soft kiss against his lips and say, "I'm one hundred percent certain. I want to feel you come inside me."

"Oh, baby."

He angles his body and enters me in one thrust.

Dear God.

He pounds me with his huge cock, slamming me against the wall. He's so hard there's no way I won't be bruised tomorrow. I'm okay with that. His hungry cock plunges inside me so ferociously I have to wrap my arms tighter around his neck and yank myself as close as I can get. It's a bit of a struggle because my slippery hands make it challenging to get a good grip, but I manage. If I don't hold on for this ride, I may not make it to the finish line.

I'm amazed he's fucking me standing up. It's a long-time fantasy of mine. Until Zane Keller, no other boyfriend had the stamina to make it happen.

He clutches my ass and pulls me closer.

My clit brushes against his pelvis.

Goddammit.

My eyes roll to the back of my head at the contact.

Pure bliss.

His cadence is so intense—punishing, even—I forget how to breathe.

"Your pussy is so tight. So sweet," he says and slams me deep.

"God, I love your big cock."

He hammers me harder in response.

He's so forceful and so deep, it's as if he wants to nail me to the wall.

With my legs spread open, he holds all the power. I'm helpless. I can only hold on tight and take it.

Each thrust causes friction against my clit. I clench around his cock to heighten the intoxicating sensation.

He pulls his head back until our gazes lock. "I'm warning you right now, I'm never fucking you with a condom ever again. Your pussy feels too good around my cock."

"I'm okay with that."

"Fuck, Shay, I'm close. Tell me you're close."

"I am."

"Thank the fuck God." His breathing is as labored as mine. "You're gonna come hard for me?"

"Yes, I will."

"I'm about to christen your pussy with my cum. Show me you appreciate it."

I'm holding on by a thread.

"I better hear my name on your lips when you come or else I'm going to redden your ass before I fuck it."

The threat should frighten me, not turn me on.

"Jesus..." I tilt my head back. "I'm so close."

"Milk my cock, you filthy girl."

He pounds me again and again and again.

I make a sound I'm sure I've never made before at the onslaught of his sexual fury.

Each thrust sends my breasts bouncing and the friction of my nipples against his chest only amplifies the volcano threatening to explode inside me.

"Zane."

"I want you to scream my goddamn name when your juices come gushing from your greedy pussy. *Not* whisper it."

"O—okay."

"Good."

Not that he was taking it easy on me, but he doubles his efforts.

He presses my body against the wall and digs his fingers in my skin before spreading my ass cheeks, forcing me to open wider for him.

I didn't even know I was this flexible.

"I—I." *Dear God.*

I grind down on his magnificent cock, taking everything I can from him.

The contractions in my core are uncontrollable and my pussy pulses like crazy under the consuming sexual charge.

Shit. Shit. Shit.

"I'm coming! Oh, my God. Oh, Zane!"

It's as if my climatic cry triggers something inside him.

His response comes out in a hiss. "Fuck, yeah, love, come hard for me,"

And I do.

I close my eyes and lose myself to pleasure.

I come, and I come, and I come as my wonderful lover turns my world upside down and my pussy inside out with his formidable cock.

"Fuck baby, you came hard for me. Good girl." His voice is thick with desire.

I can only answer with a sob.

"I'm going to shoot my load deep inside your tight pussy and mark you as mine."

Zane slams into me, plunging his cock so deep, it's as if our bodies have always been intertwined like this.

"Christ!" He sounds like he's teetering on a thin ledge of self-control.

A wave of victory courses through me at the idea a dominant man like Zane is about to lose control between my legs.

He thrusts once, twice, three times.

The last thrust is so powerful, I choke on an exhale. With a violent jerk that pins me to the wall, Zane climaxes.

My clit tingles, and my mind struggles to understand what's happening.

Against the soundtrack of my own delirious cries, I clench his cock hard and come apart, screaming out his name. My second orgasm is sudden and violent. An explosion of pleasure, layering on top of another one I'm still high from robs me of everything.

"Mine." Zane growls the possessive word in the crook of my neck.

I'm high from hearing that possessive word.

Then, he empties himself inside me, spilling a river of cum inside my welcoming pussy.

Good God.

Zane's heavy breathing reverberates against the walls, echoing over the soft music playing in the background.

I'm not faring much better.

When my legs start trembling, he drops me to my feet before wrapping me in his strong arms.

We remain entangled like this for several beats, wrapped in a haze of post-climatic exhaustion, the smell of sex in the air. His warmth wraps around me comfortably like my favorite blanket on a cold winter night.

He breaks the silence. "I love how your body responds to me." *Me too* "Your pussy swallowed every inch of my cock." *And what a hell of a cock it is.* "You didn't even complain once." *Hell, no.* "And I wasn't gentle." *You were a beast. I'm sure I won't be able to walk tomorrow.* "You took everything I had to give you." *Because you turned me into a greedy little vixen, I wouldn't have it any other way.*

I brush a strand of sweaty, messy dark blond hair that's

falling into his eyes before bringing my hand to touch his cheek. "I—" My breath comes in pants as I try to find words to express this mind-blowing experience. It's a struggle to speak, let alone think. It's like my orgasm robbed my brain cells of oxygen. "I—" I try again with the same result. "We—" I coax myself to line up my thoughts so I can at least string a coherent sentence together. "Holy shit."

Well, that was an epic fail.

"I feel the same way, love." His voice comes out low and ragged. "I'm not about to forget this birthday anytime soon," he says. "That was a hell of a gift."

There's no point in trying to speak.

I can only pant.

"You're a keeper, Shay O'Hara."

You're the best thing that's ever happened to me... and I'm falling for you.

The jarring thought is unsettling.

I don't understand the tsunami of feelings coursing through me.

Partly because I'm wondering if it's not because Zane is the best lover I've ever had, and maybe I'm confusing amazing sex with more. And partly it's because I don't want to set myself up for disappointment. We've been dating for six days. *Six days.* You can't even call that a relationship. We haven't even had a fight yet.

Chapter 34

Shay

Three weeks later

No, no, no.

I'm pacing grooves into the floor of my bathroom, my mind reeling.

I'm pulled out of my thoughts when there's an urgent knock on the door.

I freeze, my gaze shifting to the door.

"Shay," my best friend calls from the other side, "what's the verdict?"

I don't answer.

I can't.

I can't even breathe anymore.

I'm too stunned.

Scratch that.

I'm mortified.

My freak-out state is, in part, because of the stick I'm holding and the fact I'm a breath away from a total mental breakdown.

"Shay, do I have to bust this door down to get an answer?"

My bewildered eyes shift from the door to the two pink, double lines staring at me from the stick I'm holding. They're still there, still taunting me. Haunting me.

How is this even possible?

"Shay, for the love of God, give me an answer." The concern in Keeley's voice is audible.

On shaky legs, I walk to the door.

Taking a deep breath, I try to calm down and not give into hysteria.

I inhale through my nose and out through my trembling lips.

Keep it together, Shay.

I'm not one to cry at the drop of a hat, but I want to bawl my eyes out.

Stupid hormones.

I attempt to collect myself before I open the door. When I do, eager eyes meet mine.

"So?" my best friend asks.

I attempt a smile—to convince myself, more than her, I can handle this—but I fail.

"You got the same result?"

No doubt my despondent expression speaks volumes.

I nod. "It's official, I can't blame the Vietnamese restaurant we ate at a few days ago. It's not food poisoning. I'm pregnant." I produce the evidence between us.

Why couldn't it have been food poisoning?

Keeley blinks.

She blinks again.

And again. This time, her eyelashes are fluttering at a rapid rate, shock radiating from her blue eyes.

Her gaze drops to the stick I'm holding before bouncing to mine. "You're pregnant?" That comes out in a slow drawl.

Long gone is her hopeful expression.

I nod and toss the offending object in the bin where it lands next to the other one.

Out of sight, out of mind... for now.

There's a part of me that wants to claim the two tests are faulty, but I'd be delaying the inevitable.

"Holy shit!"

"I couldn't have said it better." I purse my lips.

"It's true what they say. The pill isn't one hundred percent effective. It's not like you were on medication or antibiotics. Unlike his brother and cousin, Zane never caught the flu."

"No, he didn't." I shake my head. "He was as healthy as a horse."

"So, it wasn't food poisoning after eating at that Mexican restaurant?"

"Nope. My sudden bout of vomiting wasn't caused by bad chicken or cheese."

"Shoot. You're pregnant."

At least I'm not the only one who's in disbelief.

"I'm that girl who gets knocked up not even a month into a relationship. Zane agreed to be my fake boyfriend. Not my baby daddy."

"Unlike Imogen, at least you know who the father is."

I glower at her. "Don't put me in the same category as that homewrecker."

She cringes. "Sorry. Bad choice of words."

My expression softens.

"Are you going to call or video call to tell Zane?"

I shake my head.

"Why not?"

"Keeley, the man left six days ago on an important business trip—"

"This is important."

I sigh. "It is, but since the baby isn't going anywhere, I can wait." I have time to shatter his world. "This isn't the kind of news I should drop when the man is on the other side of the planet."

"You're right. So, you have to wait another week and a half before he's back in New York?"

I respond with a one shoulder shrug.

"Okay. Okay." She nods. "It's not like you have to wait a month."

I rub my hands over my face. "He's going to be furious."

Keeley pries my hands away from my face. "You don't know that."

"This is so cliché, it's pathetic. How do you bag a billionaire?" I point at my tummy. "I'm sure men like Zane think a pregnancy is entrapment. Like I'm looking for an ATM machine that'll spew out a wheelbarrow worth of money every single month for the next eighteen years."

"There isn't a golddigger bone in your body. Zane knows that."

"Keeley, the only thing he'll care about is the fact he has a child on the way and I can drag him to court to suck out as much as I can from him—"

"Which you would never do because that's not the kind of person you are." Her tone is razor sharp. "You're an independent woman. And successful, to boot—"

"Which is a good thing, because I might end up raising this child by myself."

"Why would you say that?"

"We just started dating. It's a far cry from raising a child together."

Keeley places her hands on my shoulders. "I don't think he's that kind of asshole, but if he does a three-sixty and turns into a dipshit, you know you're not alone. I'm here, and so is your family."

Panic washes over me.

My eyes widen as realization sets in.

"Oh, God. My family." Tears burn my eyes. "They're going to freak out. Sure, Mom was joking about grandbabies over the holidays, but I'm pretty certain this isn't what she had in mind."

"Shay, you need to calm down!"

I flinch.

"Sorry," she says. "I didn't mean to be short with you, but you're blowing things out of proportion. You're not alone in this world. You're doing well financially for yourself. If you have to move back to Boston to be close to family, you could rent your place out. You're not confined to New York City with your profession. You could shoot videos anywhere in the world. And last, but not least, you haven't even given Zane a chance to man up—" Keeley stops midsentence.

"What is it?"

"The karaoke night."

I'm confused. "What about it?"

"Does the adrenaline from an EpiPen negate the effect of the pill?"

I blink.

"Err… I have no idea."

"What about vomiting?"

I flinch, jolted by the question.

Shit.

"You emptied your stomach the night Evil Imogen paid off two waitresses to lace Zane's champagne with strawberry liquor in the hopes you two would lock lips. Isn't that how that three-time gold medalist Alpine skier got pregnant and couldn't participate in the last Olympics of her career? She had a bad case of food poisoning and spent half the night barfing."

Even when she isn't trying, my stepsister screws up my life.

Chapter 35

Shay

"…When you're lost, you may be tempted to roll your eyes when someone tells you, *when one door closes, another one opens*, but I assure you, from my personal experience, it's true." I scan the room from the podium where I'm standing, staring at the smiling faces. "When I stepped off the catwalk, I never thought I'd become an influential beauty vlogger and I never imagined I'd have the honor to speak to a crowd of wonderful, strong, kickass women—real survivors. As a parting note, I can only say, it's possible. It might not be easy and you might want to give up, but don't. Thank you so much for inviting me to hang out with you," I say. "You ladies," I open my arms, "are the true inspirations. Go out there and show them what you're made of!"

A room full of women rise to their feet and start clapping.

Public speaking is right up there with singing in front of a crowd, but I couldn't say no when the event coordinator for Bottomless Closet invited me to be their keynote speaker for their *Inspiration Friday Lunch* which takes place on the third Friday of the month.

The event is held at a New York hotel generous enough to waive the fees for the use of one of their dining rooms. Today, it's held at a five-star hotel in SoHo. For over two decades, the organization has helped empower New York City women in need—mostly mothers on public assistance—with clothing, interview skills, and the confidence to enter the workforce and achieve success.

Along with being a speaker today, I also donated a shit ton of my makeup. I may not know what poverty is, but I know what it is like to start over. The executive director was surprised when I showed up this morning with a check for a generous donation. This isn't my first charitable donation, but after finding out I was pregnant last night, I was compelled to give more. I might end up being a single mom, but I have the means to support my child. The women this organization supports, don't.

I'm going to be a single mother...

To avoid blurting out news that should be discussed in person, I've avoided Zane's attempts at a video chat all last night. He blew up my phone with text messages, but I ignored those as well.

I speak over the loud cheers with a little head bow. "Thank you, ladies."

That only fuels the crowd.

Emotions take over me.

I was hoping to inspire. I didn't expect a standing ovation.

It takes a few long minutes before the claps and cheers die down. When they do, I step off the podium.

Two tall, curvy women dressed to the nines are standing at the bottom of the stairs, smiling wide. From the expensive looking frocks, designer heels and handbags, and the perfectly applied makeup, I'm willing to bet my brownstone, they're not part of the group the organization helps. I turn on my megawatt smile because donors are the lifeblood of this organization. No doubt these stunning looking women fall into that category.

I'm not sure why they look familiar.

"You talk *so, so* beautiful," the blonde says in a heavy accent.

"Thank you," I say.

"I feel here," the brunette says, placing a hand against her heart.

Her accent is as heavy as the other woman, but I'm not sure if I can place where they're from.

"I'm touched," I say.

We three talk?" the blonde asks.

"Sure!"

We take a step away from the stairs, so as not to block traffic.

"I Bruna Alvares," the brunette says.

"Pleased to meet you."

She points at the blonde. "This Benita Alvares."

"It's a pleasure, Benita."

"Pleasure for me," she says.

"We are sister twins," Bruna says.

"We are the supermodel sisters," the blonde says. "The most famous plus size models in the world."

Now I know why their faces look so familiar. I'm sure I've seen them grace the pages of *Sassy* magazine. Unless I've seen them on the Curves Envy Fashion website, modeling their clothing.

"It's a pleasure to meet you ladies. Thank you for coming out today."

"You too model like me and Bruna," Benita says in response.

"Yes—"

"But you not supermodel like me and Bruna," the blonde says.

"I never reached that pinnacle."

"What that mean?" Benita asks.

"It means I was never a big model like you." I point at them.

"Ah!" Benita beams. "But you model in Europe. We model in Europe, too."

"Well, that's my past life. These days—"

"We do the selfie!" Bruna has already whipped out her phone. "The model big girls together."

"Selfie!" Her sister cozies up to my side, and I'm flanked by two grinning supermodels.

A few *hundred* clicks later, and we're done.

Okay. That was a bit much.

I was merely smiling at the camera, but those two women were posing.

I pick up where I left off. "Like I was saying, my modeling days are behind me. Now, I'm in front of the camera for another reason... as a beauty vlogger."

"We know," Bruna says. "We watch your videos long, long time," she says with a hand gesture. "We like to watch the makeup with the big girls because we big girls. And you beautiful like we beautiful. Red hair very *seksi*."

"I'm flattered." *I think.*

The way she said that sounds a little conceited, but I guess it's the sentiment that counts.

Bruna chimes in. "We see also the video with Zane."

"The one go viral." Benita clarifies for her sister. "Everybody see it."

I can't believe the reach of that video. "That video is like the gift that keeps on giving."

Benita's perfectly shaped eyebrows dip into a frown "What that mean?"

"It's an expression."

"Okay. What that mean?"

"All that to say, I'm still shocked by the popularity of that video."

Benita puckers her full lips. "Yes, popular. Zane is in video."

"You know Zane?" I hedge the question with caution.

Both women beam.

"We from Brazil." Benita puts an end to my guessing game. "The mother for Zane also from Brazil. His family know my family. We all from same place in Porto Seguro. Neighborhood the same."

I nod. "I see."

Benita continues. "So, we know Zane long, long time. When he not so *seksi*."

I frown, surprised by her disparaging comment. I open my mouth to defend my boyfriend, but her twin sister jumps in.

"When Zane was boy, he spend all the time with the books," Bruna says.

Benita chimes in. "No time with the football. No time with the girls. Not good." She punctuates her sentence with a *tsk*.

"Now, Zane all man... *seksi* man—"

"Very *seksi* man," Benita says, interrupting Bruna.

I try to make heads and tails of that sentence. Other than the part where they find my boyfriend sexy, it all sounds a little German to me. I'm not sure how I feel about them drooling all over Zane like that.

"On the video, Zane kiss you on mouth like man kiss woman. You girlfriend?" Benita asks. Her tone is brisk. Accusatory, even.

The question is not only invasive, it's creepy.

From the sound of it, these women didn't come out today for the cause or to hear me speak.

Was she Zane's ex-girlfriend? Was Bruna?

Are they freaking stalking me?

Like all my other speaking engagements, my assistant posted the event on the website. I've never had issues with crazies before.

Hmmm... we might have to put a stop to that.

As I'm trying to get out of this bizarre conversation, the event coordinator saunters up, a warm smile stretching her lips.

"Shay, some of the women would love to take selfies with you," the petite black woman says. "You inspired them so much."

"I'd love to do selfies with them." I latch onto this lifeline. "I might need to run to the bathroom first."

"Not a problem," she says. "I'll go tell them."

With that, she's gone.

I turn to the Brazilian twins. "It was a pleasure to meet you, but I have to go."

I scurry off without giving them a chance to respond.

"We talk more about Zane after you back." Benita throws her parting words over my shoulder.

It's official. They're nut jobs.

I hurry to the bathroom the organizer suggest I use because it isn't as busy. Sure enough, it's empty when I get there.

I take care of business, exit the stall, head to the sink, and wash my hands.

As I give myself a onceover, the door opens.

A blonde, wearing an elegant long-sleeved black dress, enters the bathroom.

I let out a sigh of relief that it isn't Bruna or Benita.

This blonde is closer to Imogen's height than mine. Translation, she isn't the most famous plus size supermodel in the world.

Eye roll.

A second glance lets me know the woman still staring at me isn't a natural blonde.

Her makeup is a bit heavy handed for the day.

Shame.

I bet without all that gunk on, she's still beautiful.

She strides over in her black high-heeled boots and drops her handbag on top of the counter. She pretends to rummage through her designer handbag, but from her reflection in the mirror, her eyes are on me.

"You're a natural on stage," she says.

"Thank you. Were you in the audience?"

"Yes. I noticed the event on your website and I was compelled to meet you in person."

"I'm flattered."

She attempts to pull her lips up in a smile, but it seems to freeze partway, and ends up looking more like a grimace.

"You have a lot of videos," she says out of the blue.

"It's a professional hazard when you're a beauty vlogger." I smile.

She doesn't.

"The viral video of you and Zane Keller was... interesting."

My shoulders snap back. Something about the way she said that combined with that strange conversation with the stalker twins has me on edge.

She confirms my suspicions. "That was quite the passionate kiss."

The air feels icy cold between us.

This is turning out to be Zane Keller's ex-girlfriends' convention, instead of *Friday Ladies Who Lunch.*

It's official. I'm no longer posting future events I'll be speaking at on my website.

I don't need to be harassed like this.

And, how many women has Zane been with?

Enough of this talking in the mirror crap.

I turn to face her.

She does the same.

Since I'm much taller than she is, she has to tilt her head back to look me in the eyes.

Towering over her is a wicked thrill.

"Are you *one* of Zane's ex-girlfriends?" I ask her point blank. "There are a few of you out today."

Her blue eyes narrow. "Who else is here?" Her gaze searches the bathroom as if Bruna and Benita might be hiding in one of the stalls.

"It doesn't matter." I'm about to speak, but her name tag catches my attention.

Ember Dankworth.

"Listen, Ember. Whatever you and Zane shared in the past, I don't care." It's a lie. I do care. Especially now.

Her lips twist into a scowl. "Oh, Shay, you're so missing the big picture here." Her tone is patronizing. It takes everything in me not to bitch slap her. "You may not care about the past I shared with Zane, but I'm sure you'll care a great deal about what we'll share in *the future*."

That was cryptic.

"What do you mean?"

"Zane and I were taking a little break. *I'm* his long-time love." She points at her chest before turning her manicured finger towards me. "*You* were merely a distraction."

My laugh is caustic. "Keep telling yourself that. *We're* dating." I barrel on, committed to drive my point. "He's *my* boyfriend." *Until he finds out I'm pregnant.* "Deal with it."

She rolls her eyes in an exaggerated way. "It's never going to work between the two of you."

My blood is boiling. "Why's that?"

"He belongs to *me*."

Zane has a thing for women who are unstable in the head.

Not sure how I fit into this mess of past lovers, but I need to deal with this short bitch.

Hands at my waist, I glower down at her. "Usually when people break up, it's for a reason. It means they weren't supposed to be together."

For the first time since she entered the bathroom, Ember flashes me her teeth. But it's not a warm and fuzzy smile. It's the type of smirk a movie villainess flashes before wreaking havoc on innocent people's lives. I've seen that smirk many times before. It's one of Imogen's favorites. "When Zane finds out I'm *pregnant*, he'll come back to me."

I'm stunned into silence.

My eyes drop to her flat stomach.

"I'm not showing yet," she says as if reading my mind. "Unlike you," her gaze roams up and down my body, disdain shining bright in her blue eyes, "I'm a tiny little thing, so I'll be showing in no time."

I don't have time to dwell on the insult, too troubled by the slap of reality.

Zane is having a child with this woman?

No, no, no.

This can't be happening.

This has to be a prank.

Ember reaches into her handbag and pulls out something from it.

"He told me he was out of town, so I haven't told him yet." *Zane spoke to her?* The news is like an arrow straight to my heart. "I want to see his face when I announce the joyful news. He'll be thrilled to find out we're having *twins*."

Tw—twins?

The gut-wrenching admission breaks my heart a little more.

And then the bitch adds salt to an open wound.

"Here's proof," she produces something between us.

Whatever she puts in my face is so close, I have to jerk my head back.

I blink a few times before my eyes can focus.

Waves of horrified shock surge through my body.

God, please, no.

I blink again.

"It's an ultrasound," she says. "Two hearts. Two babies. Two little Kellers."

Wh—wh—what?

She stares up at me, waiting for me to say something, but nothing comes out.

I should tell her I'm also pregnant, but I feel protective of my unborn child. I don't want this woman to know. She's a mental case. For the love of God, she tracked me down here. I don't want to get involved with her level of crazy.

"See, Shay O'Hara, you were a distraction. Zane and *I* are building a family together." She pats her tummy, and grins at me in a demonic way.

I feel sick to my stomach.

I'm still unable to speak and I'm still incapable of moving. I can only stare at the woman that pulled the rug from under my feet with her announcement.

Ember gets real close. Given how short she is and with my heels, the top of her head barely reaches my shoulder.

She pokes a finger in my face. "You stay away from *my* man."

My heart bangs against my chest.

Even though Ember is much shorter—and smaller—than me, I take a step back. Her crazy is staring at me and it's scaring the living day lights out of me.

Chapter 36

Shay

I needed to get the hell out of New York.

A pang of guilt still beats against my chest at the way I bolted out of the five-star SoHo hotel. After Ember dropped that bit of shocking news in my lap, I had to get away as fast as humanly possible. I refused to allow her to see my despair or my tears. I only allowed myself to give in to my sorrow once I was sitting in the back of a taxi. Instead of taking the selfies I promised, I made a beeline to the room that doubled as the green room, grabbed my handbag that was tucked away in a safe and I ran. I sent a heartfelt apology to the event coordinator, blaming my disappearance on a sudden bout of vomiting. It's a partial lie. I did vomit this morning, but thanks to saltines, I managed to calm my stomach.

Once the cabbie dropped me at my place, I climbed the steps up to my front door and raced inside and up the stairs to my bedroom. I pulled out a suitcase and in a frenzied hurry, I grabbed some clothes and stuffed it all inside, without bothering with my usual neat packing. I called a car service to take me to the airport. I had to wait a couple of hours, but I managed to get a flight on standby. When my world comes crashing around me, there's only one place I want to be—home.

I've been standing in front of the door, a little overwhelmed by what's going to happen once I announce I'm here. I grab my phone and use the camera app to check my face. I spent the two-hour flight from New York to Boston, crying. My heart was —still is—as mangled as a beer can being crushed under a heavy foot. The man sitting next to me was uncomfortable, but I couldn't find it in me to keep my shit together. Sadly, he was forced to share my despair. He was kind enough to flag the flight attendant for tissues. He even offered to pay for an alcoholic drink of my choice. That only made me cry harder. It was a reminder of my predicament. I couldn't even drink to pretend Ember Dankworth hadn't fucked up my whole existence.

Sigh.

Now that I'm in Boston, I'll be forced to relive the traumatic events from earlier. Even though I have a key, I never have to use it because someone picks me up at the airport. Since no one knew I was running away from the Big Apple, they're not expecting me.

I let out a shaky breath. I feel drained, as languid as if I were coming down with the flu.

Mustering all my courage, I ring the doorbell.

I don't have to wait long until I hear bolts being pulled and the door swings open to reveal my sister's shocked face.

"What are you doing here?"

I blink to keep the sudden influx of tears at bay, I plaster a small smile on my face.

I don't even have time to say hello. She jumps into my arms and gives me a bear hug.

"I didn't know you were coming." The glee of excitement in her voice is audible. "Oh my God, you were here a month ago. I didn't expect to see you so soon." She blurts all of that still hugging me.

She pulls away from me.

"EEEP!" She squeals and does a happy dance.

Her smile is so enormous, it takes over her beautiful face.

I try hard to respond to her smile, but I can't find it in me. In her jubilation, my sister hasn't picked up on it yet.

She waggles her eyebrows "Did you fly commercial or… did you arrive in style on board your boyfriend's private jet?"

I open my mouth to set her straight, but instead, I burst into tears.

"What's going on?" my sister asks.

I cry harder.

Briar takes me into her arms, swaying side to side in a comforting motion.

"Talk to me, Shay-bear—"

"Briar, who's at the door?" Aunt Eileen calls out from somewhere inside the house.

"It's Shay! And something's wrong."

Aunt Eileen appears at the door.

She takes one good look at me and her gray eyes widen in shock. "What's the matter?"

"I— I— I—" I hiccup. "I'm cursed." I wail like a toddler.

Aunt Eileen's brows furrow. "What do you mean, lass?"

"Za—Zane—" A sob rips from me.

My great aunt's pretty face softens with concern.

"What did he do to you?" Briar's eyes are blazing with fury. "I'll rip his balls off if he—"

"Whatever happened between Zane and Shay, should be discussed behind closed doors," Aunt Eileen snaps.

My body was convulsing so badly from the torrent of tears ripping through me, my sister had to remove my coat. She dragged me by the hand inside the house as Aunt Eileen rolled my suitcase. My sister sat me at the kitchen table, rushed to the bathroom for a wet washcloth, returned to me and cleaned my face with so much care and attention, it made me cry harder. Sensing I needed more than tea, Aunt Eileen poured *the good* whiskey in three tumblers. I didn't touch mine. That conversation is for later.

When Briar coaxed me to drink, I said I was too dehydrated from the flight and crying. Aunt Eileen was on her feet in a flash, rushing to the fridge to grab a bottle of Perrier.

Once I was no longer a blubbering mess, I ran upstairs to my bedroom to change. The second I walked into my room, memories of Zane and our saucy time together flooded me, deepening my sorrow. It's with herculean effort, I didn't crawl into bed, cover my head with my down duvet, and sleep for the next week. Maybe Aunt Eileen can read minds after all because she came up to check on me not even five minutes after I had left the kitchen.

After a quick trip to the bathroom to splash cold water on my face, I trail back to the kitchen, the weight of the world still on my shoulders.

"Sit, child," Aunt Eileen gestures to the chair I was sitting on.

I do as I'm told.

"It smells good in here." I was too troubled earlier to notice, but the scent of sugar and spices tickles my nostrils.

Aunt Eileen flashes me a warm smile. "A little something to lift your spirits, lass."

I place a hand over hers.

She does the same thing.

Our hands are layered on top of each other.

The contact brings me so much comfort.

"Thank you, Aunt Eileen," I say, making an effort to return her smile, even if it's a weak one.

"What do you think family is for?" she says.

"I called Ma and Dad to let them know you're here," Briar says, returning to the kitchen. She drops her phone on the counter and takes a seat next to me.

That's one of Ma's hard rules. No phones at the table. That includes Alan. Since he's a dermatologist, there are few life-or-death situations he ever has to deal with once he's home.

"Oh, yeah, I forgot they left for a medical conference this morning," I say.

"Ma says, and I quote, *You're an O'Hara and a Doherty. Chin up, lass, you're made of good stock. You'll survive this. You're stronger than you think.*" Briar relays in a pointed Irish accent. "She also said she and Dad will call you later."

"Okay."

"She wants to know what's going on. Since I don't have any intel, I couldn't fill her in."

I read between the lines of my sister's comment.

She's itching to know what drama I'm dealing with.

I have no doubt Aunt Eileen is as curious, but she's a lot more subtle in her approach.

So far, other than tears, I haven't shed any light on my sad, sad situation.

"Here you go, lass." Aunt Eileen approaches the table, holding a tray. "Seems like you're not into the whiskey." I shrug. "Not a problem. Strong, dark tea is soothing after a good cry," she says in an exaggerated Irish lilt. She places the teapot, cups and saucers on the table. She pulls out her cherished Wedgwood, Made in England and bought in England, during the Christmas holidays and when there's a crisis. She hooks her hands to her waist and looks at me. "We'll have a wee bit of food to start, followed by some sticky toffee pudding." She winks. "They're still in the oven."

That's when it hits me.

My eyes widen with excitement. "I don't remember the last time I ate."

She gives me that motherly look that says, *I know you better than you do, lass,* before scurrying off.

I didn't want to eat before my presentation because I don't trust my stomach these days. After meeting Ember, my appetite was gone. The mention of food combined with the mouth-watering aromas, and I'm famished.

Aunt Eileen is back.

This time, the tray is weighed down with an assortment of sandwiches cut into triangles.

"We'll start with high tea," Aunt Eileen says. "Later, we can have a proper dinner."

"Sounds good," I say at the same time is my sister says, "Even if you're having a shit day, Barry's will soothe your worries away."

The popular Irish tea Aunt Eileen prefers above all others *can't change my reality. I'm about to become Zane Keller's baby mama. Ma will have a shit fit, God knows how Alan will react, I'm pretty sure our great aunt won't think Zane is good people once she finds out he's about to have a family with two different women, and knowing you—*

"Jesus, Shay, you look like you're carrying the weight of the world on your shoulders."

Briar's words snap me back to the moment.

I offer her a weak smile.

"Are you going to tell us what's going on?"

"I will."

Aunt Eileen nudges Briar. "Give the lass some time."

My sister gives me a side-eyed glance full of skepticism.

She allows enough time for me to sip on my tea and nibble on two triangles before she interrogates me.

"Do you need me to reach out to the local Irish Mafia so we can put a hit on Zane Keller's head?"

I stare at her, horrified. I expected a question. I didn't know she was plotting to commit a felony.

She's not done with her diabolical scheming. "I'm sure they have ties with the New York family. Since we're at it, we might as well also put a hit on Elias Fitzsimmons. You know, a two for one special..."

My eyes pop out of my skull. "Have you lost your mind?"

She shrugs. "Men are shit!"

"True, but that's not enough of a good reason for us to end up in prison. Can you imagine me in orange prison wear with my hair color?"

"You can always shave it off—"

"Briar! Enough with this ridiculous mafia talk!" Aunt Eileen admonishes my sister. "Mafia romance *isn't* real life, lass."

My sister rolls her eyes hard.

Aunt Eileen shakes her head, tsking.

"Why don't you start from the beginning, Shay," my great aunt says.

I sigh, a great big heavy sigh that has me on the verge of bawling my eyes out again.

"You don't have to be alone carrying your burden, lass," Aunt Eileen says. "Whatever it is, we'll deal with it as a family."

I take a fortifying breath and spill my guts.

Since so much has happened in the last few days, I decide to ease my sister and my great aunt into it. I bypass my little condition for now. I fast forward and share the details of today's eventful day. I share the details of this morning's presentation, highlighting the strange meeting with the Alvares sisters. I'm honest about my suspicions. They were so territorial, I'm certain both of them dated Zane at different times. I end my tragic tale with the *pièce de résistance*—Zane has been in contact with his ex. My mic drop moment is epic when I tell them Ember is expecting twins.

For a long moment neither my sister nor my great aunt speaks.

They stare at me, dumbfounded.

Then, they stare at each other.

Their bewildered gaze is on me again.

"Are you shitting me?" Briar asks.

"I wouldn't be sitting here if I were."

Briar slams her hand on the table. "Bastard!"

I was hoping you'd be different.

My sister isn't done expressing her outrage. "And for the record, Ember is a whack job. That woman has the profile of a bunny boiler. You don't wanna mess with crazy bitches like that. Good for you for walking away. As for Zane, I'm so calling the Irish Mafia on his ass—"

"Forget about the bloody Irish Mafia," Aunt Eileen seethes through clenched teeth. "I'll take care of castrating the bastard myself."

"Oh, but there's more..." All eyes turn to me. "Ember isn't the only one who's pregnant."

Chapter 37

Zane

I should be more excited about being in Brazil.

The newly renovated offices are sweet. Contrary to New York, I'm not freezing my balls off every time I step outside. And I wake up to beaming, blinding sunshine as opposed to a gray sky. While the temperature hits another frigid low in the Big Apple, it's smoldering hot in Rio de Janeiro. On top of that, nothing beats waking up to fresh fruits picked straight from the source. Or the exceptional coffee.

A month ago, coming down to our Brazilian headquarters was a great break from the chaotic rush synonymous with living in Manhattan—especially during winter months. This time around, I'm itching to go back. I didn't expect to miss Shay this much. Sure, our nightly video chats can get pretty hot and raunchy, but it's not the same. Coming in the palm of my hand pales into comparison to spilling my cum inside her inviting pussy. And it's not only about the sex. I genuinely miss everything about Shay O'Hara... even the little things. Falling asleep with her in my arms gives me a feeling of bone-deep pleasure—an inexplicable contentment unlike anything I've ever experienced with a woman before. I don't fuck and dash, but I never stay the night. Slipping out of Shay's bed or ushering her to a town car or taxi after I've made her come so many times she forgets her own name, is unthinkable. I need her in my bed.

Mom has been back in New York for a few weeks, but she made sure to pass along the baton to the women in the family. Translation, my grandmother, aunts, and cousins have made it their mission to send me daily reminders of how they can't wait to meet my girl. I can't tell you the number of variations of *Shay é linda* they've texted me since I arrived in Brazil.

Yes, Shay is gorgeous.

Yes, I know.

Yes, we make a good-looking couple.

No, we are not having good-looking babies anytime soon.

The distance between Porto Seguro—where Mom is from—and Rio de Janeiro is my saving grace. The hour-and-a-half flight—or sixteen-hour car ride—prevents my Brazilian family from camping outside the HQ, waiting to bombard me with even more questions about my girlfriend and our future plans to procreate.

My uncle moved to Rio when he was a young man for a woman. The relationship didn't last, but he never returned to his hometown, choosing to settle his roots in the second largest city in the country. When Max inherited our uncle's business, he relocated the operations to a much safer part of the city when he bought out a clothing manufacturer that was going out of business. He also hired most of the workers since they were far more qualified than the ones working for my uncle. Smart moves on my cousin's part. In no time, we were able to go from being in the red to turning a hefty profit. In the past few years, sales have been skyrocketing. Since my little brother became COO and implemented some ingenuous marketing ideas, we can barely keep up. It's a good problem to have. That's also why I'm working late.

It's seven p.m., and I'm fully immersed in work when a text message flashes on my phone.

I ignore it.

I have an important all-day meeting first thing on Monday with my cousin Luana Monterroso, who manages our swimwear production in Brazil, and her team. I need to review these spreadsheets so I'm ready. This is Brazil. Working on the weekends is sacrilege. One more hour and I'll hit my favorite hangout.

Another message flashes, breaking my concentration.

My eyes dart to the device sitting on my desk.

I frown.

Two other messages follow.

What the hell?

My work long-forgotten, I snatch my phone from the desk, open my text app, and read the messages.

Briar: You're like every other man.

Briar: You're no better than Elias. And I consider him a peon and a lowlife. Shay cried all night because of you. Fuck, she's been crying since yesterday and your sorry ass is the culprit.

Briar: Stay the fuck away from my sister and my family.

Briar: And tell your baby mama to stop harassing and stalking Shay. My sister got the message loud and clear. She's having your twins. Congratulations and have a good life. Don't bother responding because I'm blocking your number. Asshole.

Dumbfounded, I reread the messages a second time.

What did I do to make Shay cry?

Who is having my twins?

What is Briar talking about?

Until Shay, I hadn't been with a woman in a long time, and other than my girlfriend, I wrap up.

And how dare Briar compare me to dipshit Elias? Has she lost her goddamn mind?

"None of this makes any sense."

Even though she warned me, I dial Briar's number.

It goes to voicemail.

I scowl, cursing under my breath.

I read the messages a third time. This time, starting from the last one. Maybe if I read them in reverse, I'll clue in on the hidden meaning behind these cryptic texts.

Nope. I'm still in the dark.

"What are you trying to tell me, Briar?"

My frustration is at an all-time high.

I stand up from behind the desk and move to the floor-to-ceiling window.

I try calling Shay.

It goes straight to voicemail.

"Fuck!"

Something happened and I need to know what. Right the fuck now.

I wear a hole in the marble floor as I pace back-and-forth across the office.

There's a knock at my door.

"Not now!" I bark in Portuguese.

"*Mas—*"

"*Eu disse, agora não, Luana!*" My tone brooks no comeback.

She lets out a huff. "*Entendi!*"

Heels clack against the marble floor.

She got the message.

I look out the window over the city.

I usually relish the spectacular view from our window.

Today, the horizon stretching in front of me is blurred.

I'm still clenching my phone with one hand. The other travels behind my neck, rubbing the tight muscles there.

As my mind spins, my phone rings.

It's not who I was hoping to speak to, but I'm sure this person can give me answers.

Chapter 38

Zane

I'm usually able to catch up on a lot of work on the flight to and from Brazil. Sometimes, it isn't about crossing off items on my to-do list. Sometimes it's about thinking, strategizing, and planning. This time, my mind was too restless and I was far too agitated for any of that. The flight from Rio de Janeiro to New York seemed interminable, but I willed myself to be patient. It's not like I had any other choice.

On the night Shay had an allergic reaction to the strawberry-flavored champagne, I exchanged my number with her family. At the time, it was for precautionary measures. I'm happy I did. I needed Briar's help for my girl's gift and I needed her as my decoy when I landed in Boston on Christmas Day unannounced. I never expected the phone number swaps to come back and bite me in the ass. Briar chewed me up and ripped me a new one, while leaving me in the dark. Aunt Eileen told me off, but at least she was forthcoming as to why she was contemplating calling a hit on me. I swear to God it was like someone had injected my veins with ice cold water when Aunt Eileen dropped Ember's name in her tirade.

My two-week fling was showing off her crazy. Again.

There was no convincing Aunt Eileen things weren't as they seemed—not that I blame her, I've been on the receiving end of Ember Dankworth's lunacy. The manipulative bitch can be convincing—so, after a while, I stop trying.

Since action speaks louder than words, I cut my business trip short. Thank God my cousin was still in the office. I hung up with Aunt Eileen at eight p.m. last night, gave Luana a quick rundown of my predicament, and texted the pilot. I was on the private jet within two hours of Aunt Eileen's verbal lynching. I barely slept on the plane, but that's okay because it gave me more time to *plot*.

Ember, the sneaky bitch, found a way around the restraining order against her. Instead of harassing me, her new favorite sport is harassing my girlfriend. From what Aunt Eileen shared, it's clear the only reason Ember knows about Shay is because of the viral video. Steam was billowing out of my ears. I was so enraged, I could've blown a gasket.

So here I am, back in New York, and ready for battle.

Saturday mid-morning is an ideal time to drive, but I don't trust myself. Not to mention, who knows what state I'll be in when all this is said and done.

Best to play it safe.

I landed in New York at eight a.m. this morning after ten hours of flight. My chauffeured car was waiting for me. I didn't even bother going to my place to shower and change. I'm too eager to deal with Ember.

After a few necessary pitstops, I arrive at my destination. I give my driver instructions, get out of the car, and head to the front door of an apartment building I never thought I'd set foot in again. In fact, I swore up and down on a stack of Bibles I never would... yet, here I am.

Desperate times call for desperate measures.

"Good morning, Rosalinda," I say, entering the building.

"Good morning, Mr. Keller," she says in a pronounced Hispanic accent. "Long time no see."

I approach Rosalinda's desk. "December was a blur and I was traveling." I flash the security guard a bright smile. "I got back in town an hour ago."

"I forget. Your other company is in Argentina?"

"No. Brazil. Rio de Janeiro, to be precise."

"Ah..." She nods a few times. "That's why I don't see you here for so many months."

"You got it."

"Good to see you again, Mr. Keller."

She knows my name because I had to hand her my driver's license to obtain a parking pass on the first night I stayed over at Ember's place. It was safer to park my expensive wheels in the visitors' underground designated area instead of leaving my Benz on the street. Since Ember was running late, Rosalinda and I chatted while I was waiting. I was careful to meet Ember at her place because I prefer to keep my sanctuary private. Thank God I did since she turned out to be a loon.

"Since you mentioned you work the graveyard shift from Sunday to Thursday while your kids stay with your mom so you can take them to school first thing in the morning, I thought I'd bring breakfast for the whole family. There's no school today." I stretch my arm out to check my Patek Philippe watch. "So, you get to enjoy a late breakfast together." I drop one of the bags I'm holding on the counter.

She grabs it and peeks inside. Wide dark brown eyes meet mine. "Muffins and scones from A Touch of Sugar?!"

"No? You don't like their goods?"

"I never buy there. I only go to the store one time when it opened and run back out. *¡Ay, caramba!* Five dollars for one scone? No." She shakes her head. "Everything so expensive...

Too much for single mom with three kids. You know how much boys eat?"

"I'm sure my parents can sympathize with you." I chuckle. "God knows I could eat a full refrigerator all by myself when I was growing up. My little brother also has quite the appetite."

"So, your parents know."

I nod. "They've walked in your shoes."

Her brown eyes lower to the bag for a beat before meeting my gaze. "Thank you, Mr. Keller."

"It's my pleasure," I say. "I got you two dozen of the muffins and the scones. I'm told they freeze well. Since I wasn't sure about allergies, I made sure the young girl who was helping me noted the ones with nuts."

You better believe I'm layering on the charm.

"Thank God. No allergies." She knocks on the faux-wooden desk.

"Good stuff."

She smiles up at me. "You are good. That is why Miss Dankworth she never want to let you go."

Of course, Ember is still pretending we're together.

There's so much I want to say, but I bite my tongue.

I wasn't sure how I was going to tackle that obstacle, but Ember's pathology gave me the green card I needed. If Rosalinda thinks Ember and I are still dating, I won't have to come up with a bullshit story why I'm here and why I need to go up to Psycho Ember's apartment.

"Speaking of which, I was hoping to go up to Ember's place and surprise her," I say, lifting my other hand to show the other bag of goodies. "She partied hard last night, so I'm here for the rescue. Carbs are the best cure for hangovers."

Ember believes in kicking off weekends with a bang. I doubt that's changed.

Rosalinda sighs. "The young and single in the Big Apple... I love my boys, but no more party for me."

I chuckle.

"Okay, I stop talking. Too much information from me. You go surprise your *mamacita*." She punctuates her sentence with an exaggerated wink.

"She'll be surprised all right." *Just not like how you imagine.* It's with herculean effort I manage to contain the anger boiling inside of me so it doesn't come pouring out with the same force as water gushing from a fireman's hose. Rosalinda has nothing to do with this clusterfuck of a mess.

She buzzes me in.

I thank my lucky stars.

I take the elevator to the fourteenth floor.

Thankfully, the few people riding the car with me are too consumed by their phones to pay me any attention. When the doors open, I head to Psycho Ember's suite in a series of long strides. Then it hits me. There's a kink in my plan.

Shit.

Going back downstairs and explaining myself to Rosalinda isn't an option.

I have few resources in my arsenal. I'm sure I'm going to annoy one of her neighbors, but so be it. Consequences be damned.

I knock.

No answer.

I knock again.

Same result.

Fuck!

I knock a third time with more urgency.

Still nothing.

She must've partied hard.

I'm about to knock a fourth time, when I hear the door chain being released and the door flies open.

My brows shoot high.

A guy with dark brown bed hair, scratching his balls over his boxers, peers up at me through one open eye. He reeks of alcohol and sex.

I take a step back to make sure I didn't knock on the wrong door.

I'm at the right place.

I fix my gaze onto the guy. "Who are you?"

His head jerks back. "Shouldn't I be asking you that question?"

Okay. Good comeback.

"Breakfast delivery!" I say, bringing the bag to eye level. "Freshly baked muffins and bagels." I sweeten the pot. "I made sure to include a large container of double-whipped cream cheese and an assortment of jam from Nantucket."

He narrows his hazel brown eyes at me. "When did Ember order breakfast? She's still sleeping."

"We offer such great service, we think ahead of our clients." I place a hand above his head on the door, and letting myself inside the apartment. Out of courtesy, I'd normally remove my snow-covered winter boots when entering someone's home, but Ember doesn't deserve that.

"Hey!" Ember's fuck buddy protests, but I don't give a fuck. "You can't walk in here like this."

"Ember promised me a big fat tip." It's a lie. "I'm here to collect."

"Seriously, dude. Wait at the door."

I spin around, leveling him with an icy glare.

With my eyes locked onto his, I take a threatening step towards him.

He winces and shuffles back.

If I had to guess, I'd say the guy is about five-eleven. In other words, he's no match. Unwilling to waste my breath, I resume my mission. I turn around and keep walking straight to Ember's bedroom. I halt my step long enough to drop the bag on the coffee table. The breakfast items were props. I needed something to get a foot through the door. Since Ember has expensive taste, I wanted to make sure the production was believable.

"I'm gonna call the police." Ember's fuck buddy shouts his warning over my shoulder.

I stop dead in my tracks and turn around.

I flash him a menacing grin before stretching my neck side to side, as if trying to get rid of a kink.

I didn't expect this obstacle.

If he keeps getting in my way, I'm going to have to swat him like a fly.

He brings his hands up to shield his face.

With the way I'm fuming, I'm sure I look like a boxer warming up, dead set on knocking out the opponent in the first round.

Pussy.

I didn't even raise my fists.

I narrow my eyes. "What's your name?"

"Err... Douglas."

Notice how he forgot I'm the intruder.

"Go on, Doug, call the police. Make. My. Fucking. Day."

He seems to reconsider his position.

I set off towards Ember's bedroom.

Before opening the door, I pull out my phone, power it up, tap on the recorder app, and press the red button. With my phone in hand, I burst through the door. I open it with such force, it hits the wall with a loud thud.

"What the fuck, Doug?" A man sits up in bed, his bewildered green eyes meeting mine.

What's going on here?

"Doug, why are you making so much noise?" Ember asks, a groggy voice from somewhere under the covers.

The woman could sleep through a nuclear explosion.

"It's not Doug," the dark blond guy who's in bed says.

"He said he was the delivery guy, but he doesn't dress the part." Doug supplies his commentary as he walks past me, one of the blueberry muffins I brought in hand, and climbs in bed with Ember and fuck buddy number two.

Nothing irritates me more than people who eat in bed.

At least he had the decency to grab a paper napkin.

"These are amazing, by the way."

The dark blond guy looks at him, his eyes filled with a hundred questions.

Fuck buddy number one takes another huge bite of the muffin and chews. "Can't wait to try one of the bagels. Never had Nantucket jam before."

Unbelievable.

"Muffin? Bagel? Nantucket jam? What delivery guy? Who are we talking about?" Ember fires off a series of questions, sitting up in bed. She brushes her messy, long blonde hair off her face before stretching like a cat, her eyes still closed. The black sheet that was covering her, slips, revealing her naked body.

There's no mistaking what's going on here.

"Me," I say.

Ember's eyes pop open.

Huge saucers stare at me.

"Fun night?" I ask, my eyes shifting from fuck buddy number one to fuck buddy number two.

"We hit it off with Ember at a party last night, so she invited us back to her place," fuck buddy number two says. "Doug and I... are partial to double stuffing."

Too much information.

"There's nothing like getting two of your holes fucked at the same time to kick off the weekend." I sneer.

Ember's face is as white as a sheet.

Fuck buddy number two looks me up and down. "You seem a little too uptight to understand."

I bet you'd understand if I punched you in the mouth and knocked all your teeth out.

"Let me get this straight," I say, lifting a hand up, "Ember, you had sex with two men at the same time last night. I'm confused—"

"Who the fuck are you, anyway? Her father?"

I ignore fuck buddy number two's outburst. "If you're already pregnant with my child, there's no danger of you getting pregnant again—and I hope for your sake you practiced safe sex—but don't you think that's a little debauched?" There's no hiding the sarcasm in my voice.

Fuck buddy number one and fuck buddy number two's heads snap in Ember's direction. If I wasn't about to erupt like a volcano, I'd find it comical.

"You're pregnant?" Doug asks.

"And he's the father?" The question comes from fuck buddy number two.

"About that—"

"Don't worry, we're going to get it all sorted out today, Ember," I say.

She furrows her eyebrows. "What do you mean?"

I respond to her question with one of my own. "How did you know I was in Brazil?"

"I might've called your office to inquire about your whereabouts," she says in a low voice.

I let out a wry laugh. "Figures, because I sure as hell haven't been in contact with you in months—not since I demanded you to stay the fuck away from me."

She doesn't respond.

"I'm sure you'd rather fuck these two all day, but you need to get dressed, Ember," I say. "We have a doctor's appointment to get to."

She does a face. "What are you talking about?"

"It seems you had an ultrasound and I wasn't there. I can't wait for you to show me the ultrasound you showed my girlfriend, but as the father who was robbed of an epic first, I'd love for us to re-create the whole experience. That way I won't feel like I missed out."

Who knew I was such a good actor?

My cousin Luisa's husband's aunt is a pediatrician. It'll never get to that point because Ember is lying through her fucking teeth, but the good doctor is on standby, willing to conduct the test at her clinic on a Saturday. She was as horrified as my cousin was of Ember's false claims.

"You're pregnant and you're fucking other men?" Doug keeps drilling Ember.

Glad to see he has morals.

"Why didn't you tell us last night?" fuck buddy number two spits out. Ember seems to shrink in size, but she doesn't answer. "Have some goddamn self-respect, woman. How can you fuck around when you're carrying another man's child?"

"Twins," I correct.

Fuck buddy number two's jaw drops.

Ember's face turns a deep shade of red.

Her tits are still hanging.

She's sitting on a bed, naked, flanked by two strangers who she fucked last night, trying to cover up a big fat lie.

She repulses me.

"Considering I always wrap up, I was surprised when word reached me that you were pregnant, but hey, condoms break." I shrug. "Like I said, I can't wait to see the ultrasound with *my own* two eyes." I clap a couple times against my thigh. "Hop to it, Ember! We don't want to keep the doctor waiting."

"I— I'm not..." She lets her words trail.

I lean in and place my fingers to my ear. "I'm listening."

She stares at me, one eyebrow cocked in insolence.

I don't condone violence against women, but right now, I want to push the lying, manipulative bitch out the window.

Fuck buddy number two elbows her. "You owe the guy an explanation."

With her lips pinched in annoyance, Ember elbows him back. For a few short seconds, it's a tug-of-war. "I'm not pregnant, you fucking idiot!" she barks at him.

The truth comes out.

"What did you say?" I ask. I want to make sure my phone is capturing all of this. So far, no one seems to clue in on the reason why I'm holding my phone.

Good.

Ember turns to face me. "I'm not pregnant," she says in a meek voice.

Don't go all shy on me now, bitch.

"I'm sorry, Ember"—I say her name like it's a weapon—"if you're going to fuck with people's lives, you better speak up!" My booming voice bounces off the walls.

Anger twists her features. She's all flustered and worked up. "I said, I'm not pregnant!" She throws her words at me as if I had tortured her until she came clean. "Satisfied?"

Seriously?

It takes everything in me not to lunge towards the bed and shake the hell out of her. The woman has no concept of how her actions impact others. Either that or she finds pleasure in other people's misery.

"What would've brought me satisfaction is if you had stayed away from my girlfriend," I say, pointing an agitated finger at her. "You already pulled that shit once and I got a restraining order against you." Her nostrils flare, and splotches of red spots appear, coloring the creamy skin of her chest. "How dare you approach my girlfriend!"

She sticks her chin in the air, crossing her arms over her bare chest—because yes, she's still naked—arrogance shining bright in her blue eyes. "There's no restraining order against Shay O'Hara. She was fair game," she says, smugly.

To think I used to find this woman gorgeous. Now, she's just demented.

"So, you decided to mess with her head?" I ask.

"Something like that." *Bitch.* "You shouldn't be with another woman. You should be with me. Only me."

Fuck buddy number one and fuck buddy number two shake their heads. From their expression, it's clear they're as incredulous as I am.

Welcome to my fucking nightmare, guys.

"We had a two-week fling." I flash two fingers. "I got a restraining order against your ass because you don't understand, *it's fucking over*. Now, you skirt the law to wreak havoc on my life and people that matter to me? You don't know who you're dealing with, Ember. I'm going to make sure you regret this latest little stunt."

No response.

I acted in haste, and since it's Saturday, I haven't spoken to my lawyer yet, so I tread with caution. That said, first thing Monday morning, I intend on stretching the limits of the law to make sure this woman stays the fuck away from me and everyone I know.

I can't stand to look at her and want nothing more than to distance myself from this psycho, but one mystery remains.

"If you're not pregnant, how did you get the ultrasound?" I ask.

Ember averts her gaze.

"Answer the fucking question!" I bark so loud, I'm sure Rosalinda heard me.

All three fuck buddies jump.

"They sell fake ones online," she says.

My head jerks back. "What the actual fuck?"

Fuck buddy number one grunts. "Are you fucking kidding, Ember?"

"What the fuck is wrong with you, woman?" fuck buddy number two asks.

"Where did you buy it?" I ask her.

"eBay."

Fuck buddy number two does a double take.

Fuck buddy number one's blueberry muffin freezes in mid-air.

I can't believe my ears. "You can buy fake ultrasounds on eBay?"

"Yes." The arrogance in her voice softens.

I glare at her.

If I thought Ember's face was red before, I was wrong. Her face is about to burst into flames.

Fuck buddy number one's eyebrows touch when he says, "That must've been some serious Photoshopping to make them look convincing."

"It costs a bit more to get your name scripted on them, but it was well worth it." A cyclone of rage stirring inside me threatens to explode. "Your girlfriend was fooled." Forget about psycho. This woman is certifiable. She should be in a straight jacket. "I hope my ruse was convincing enough for her to break things off with you."

I'm speechless.

"This party is over." Fuck buddy number two jumps out of bed. "Doug, we're out of here."

At least Doug was wearing boxer briefs. I didn't need to see fuck buddy number two's junk.

"Don't go, you guys!"

Fuck buddy number two sticks a finger in Ember's face. "You're a fucking nut case. No pussy—or ass—is worth that kind of trouble." He moves his attention to his friend. "Let's go. Now! I can't stand to breathe the same air as her."

Doug finishes the last bite of his muffin and says, still chewing, "Right behind you."

In no time, the two amigos gather their clothing.

"Have a nice life, bitch." Fuck buddy number two throws his parting words over his shoulder before making his exit, his friend in tow.

I end the recording and place my phone inside my coat pocket.

Ember and I remain in the bedroom.

For a few long seconds, we enter a Mexican standoff.

"You're pathetic, Ember."

She rolls her eyes in response.

"If I were you, I'd lawyer up," I say. "I'm going to make sure you feel the full weight of my wealth and my power. You want to play stupid games? eBay..." I shake my head, still unable to believe that's how she fooled Shay. "Fucking up people's lives entertains you? Guess what? The buck stops here." My nostrils flare. Ember stares up at me, and for the first time, I see real fear in her blue eyes. *Good.* The last time she pulled this shit, I didn't drive my point with enough conviction. This time, I will. "As for Shay, I'm not going to allow you to ruin things between us." My jaw working. "I don't care if I have to walk barefoot over burning coals. I'm determined to get back the woman I love."

Whoa.

Where the hell did that come from?

Chapter 39

Zane

Snatching the A Touch of Sugar bag off Ember's coffee table on my way out—the bitch doesn't deserve breakfast I paid for—I left her sorry ass behind. Doug and fuck buddy number two, whose name is Scott, were outside Ember's building when I busted out of there. They were waiting for their ride to arrive. Since it's frigidly cold, I suggested I give them a lift. It's not that I wanted to be a Good Samaritan, but I recorded some pretty personal things about them. Before I could broach the subject, Scott told me they would be willing to back up my story in front of a judge. That's when I came clean about the recording. They were a bit taken aback at first, but they didn't break my balls over it. Instead, they sympathized, telling me that given the circumstances, they would've done the same thing. Additionally, as successful young business owners, Doug and Scott had no problem with me recording their consent. I'm sure my lawyer will be relieved. When I arrived, I was a lone warrior. I didn't expect to end up with two allies.

I dropped the pair off at the Tribeca penthouse they share,

Doug too eager to accept the muffins and bagels. After we exchanged numbers, my driver dropped me off at my place. Since a face-to-face with my brother and my cousins would've eaten up too much precious time, I sent everyone a long text—including Mom and Dad, and my cousins Louisa and Luana. After a quick shower, I jumped into some clothes, packed an overnight bag, and head back down to the chauffeured car that was waiting for me.

Six hours after landing in Manhattan, I'm in Boston.

An hour ride later and I'm in the North End, aka Shay's neighborhood.

I check my Patek Philippe watch.

Three o'clock.

This time, I didn't use Briar as my decoy. I'm still persona non grata. Aunt Eileen was more accommodating. I didn't tell her everything, because there's so much to tell, but I told her enough to be back in her good books. As my ally, she suggested the family attend the Sunday mass instead of a late Saturday afternoon one, so they would be home when I arrived.

I take a deep breath and ring the doorbell.

The door opens.

From the indignation burning in Alan's eyes, I'm the last person he expected to see show up at his door.

"What the hell are you doing here?"

No warm greetings. What a departure from the last time I was here.

"I'm here to see Shay—"

"She wants nothing to do with you."

"With all due respect, sir, she's a grown woman. I'd like to hear it from her."

"This is my house"—he pounds a closed fist against his chest—"and you're not coming in." He crosses his arms and takes a defensive stance. Everything about him screams, *I dare you.*

I can stand here and argue until I'm blue in the face, but that would be a losing battle. Instead, I pull out my phone. A few taps later, and the recording from earlier plays.

I stare at him dead in the eyes and wait.

Alan's eyes widen so much, I fear they'll take over his face.

"Holy shit."

"Alan, who's at the door? And why are you arguing with them?" Katie appears. "It's you—"

Her gaze drops to my phone, and realization sets in.

Her blue eyes are the size of dinner plates when they meet mine. "Dear God!"

"What's going on?" Briar appears with Aunt Eileen by her side.

Briar fixes her laser beams on me. Soon, she's sporting the same astonished expression as her parents.

Aunt Eileen growls when she hears Ember divulge the truth. "That little witch. She's a no good, lying cunt—"

"Aunt Eileen!" Katie frowns. "Language!"

"She is!" Aunt Eileen stands firm in her resolve, even crossing her arms over her chest to drive her point.

"Sweetie, Aunt Eileen is right," Alan says. "What this woman did is appalling. Not only to Shay, but also to Zane. She's so despicable, she doesn't deserve to be called a bitch. She's a cunt."

Briar points to her dad. "What he said."

"Where did everyone go? I went to the bathroom and you guys—"

My eyes shift to the gorgeous redhead that poked her head through the small crowd gathered at the door.

"Hey, love."

Her expression goes from soft to hard in a New York

minute. "Zane, what are you doing here?" She doesn't give me a chance to respond. "Newsflash. By avoiding your calls, I was sending you a pretty clear message—stay the hell away."

I open my mouth to defend myself, but Briar precedes me.

"Ember is a lying cunt. She was never pregnant to start off with. She fucked with your head and you believed her. In other words, she got what she wanted—a rift the width of the Mississippi between Zane and you. In my opinion as a medical student, she needs to be institutionalized. Pronto!"

Shay stares up at me, baffled.

"There's a lot for us to talk about," I say.

Chapter 40

Shay

Z*ane is here!*

He flew back from Brazil overnight, stopped in Manhattan to squeeze the truth out of Ember, and then he hopped on his private jet to come after me. Without knowing the full story of what transpired between him and the evil bitch, I was already levitating.

All that for me.

I couldn't wait to hear the truth, but Aunt Eileen insisted that talking things out over a good cup of strong black tea was the only way to go. Since we were about to have mid afternoon tea, a few nibbles, and more sticky toffee pudding, the stage was set. To give us some privacy, Ma, Dad, Briar, and Aunt Eileen declared they were going to a nearby café.

"I could survive on this dessert alone," Zane says, polishing off the last bite of sticky toffee pudding served with a scoop of vanilla ice cream—the good stuff bought from a small local shop.

"Same! Although it's a British dessert—and not Irish—Aunt

Eileen aces the dense sponge cake made with chopped dates, topped with a sweet toffee sauce."

"Indeed."

Without bothering to ask, I pour more tea.

"Thank you," he says. He takes a sip.

"Two women you know came to my speech," I say from over the rim of my cup.

His brows furrow. "Who?"

"Bruna and Benita—"

"What did they say to you?" His expression is murderous.

"Do you have a history with one of them?"

He drops his cup on his saucer. "With both of them."

I stiffen.

What the fuck?

"Those women thrive on drama." He frowns. "I never dated either of them—I'm not that stupid—but I know first hand how they enjoy leaving a trail of destruction in their wake. What did they say to you?"

"They went on about their parents and your mom coming from the same area in Brazil. They recounted stories of you when you were younger. They demanded we take a selfie, which turned into a hundred." I sigh. "I don't know why, but I was uncomfortable around them, so when the opportunity arose for me to excuse myself, I took it. I got away from them as fast as I could."

"Smart move. You can't trust anything that comes out of their mouths. They have a nasty habit of bending the truth to manipulate people." Zane shakes his head. "Those two are so full of themselves. Yes, they are excellent at what they do, but their attitude..." He lets out a heavy sigh. "Enough about the Alvares twins."

Yes, enough about the most famous plus size models in the world and their over use of the word *seksi*.

After a few sips, he lays his cards on the table, "Since we're on the subject of women who make drama their calling card, are you ready for the truth about Ember?"

"As long as the truth is an expansion of what my sister divulged, yes, I'm ready."

He grabs his phone. "Hearing my words isn't as powerful as hearing it from the horse's mouth."

I furrow my eyebrows. "Did you have to torture her to get the truth out of her?"

"I came close, but I managed to spare her. I've been down this road with Ember before—"

"You have?"

He tells me about the last time Ember pulled the I'm pregnant card.

I shake my head. "She needs help."

"My lawyer will make sure she gets it." Sarcasm laces his words. "I didn't know what to expect, but I knew it might turn into *he said, she said*. Ember made such a scene at the Evangelista Lounge the last time, there were witnesses. And, she was caught on camera entering the lounge. She couldn't pretend she was never there. Furthermore, there was no mistaken identity since the photos captured her face. This time, everything was different. I was going on her turf. I expected it would be the two of us behind closed doors. This"—he points to his phone, sitting on the table—"is my insurance policy." Given the extraneous circumstances, Ma's strict no phone policy at the table doesn't apply.

I take a fortifying breath. "All right, let's hear it."

He presses the start button on the recording app.

I bring my cup to my lips, but it freezes halfway. "What in the actual fuck?"

Zane nods.

"The day after she shattered my world, she was getting

fucked by two men?" I'm irate. "While I was licking my wounds, she was getting double-stuffed? Seriously?"

"I gotta say, I didn't see that one coming."

"Unbelievable."

He sneers. "Oh, but there's so much more."

I keep listening.

The recording ends as the two men Ember was fucking leave her bedroom.

My mouth is still open, my eyelashes fluttering a mile a minute.

My incredulous gaze meets Zane's.

He offers a *I told you so* expression.

I don't even know where to begin, so I settle for, "Ember needs to find a new hobby other than sabotaging people's lives and stalking you and people who are close to you."

"Fool me once, shame on you. Fool me twice and you won't fool me again," Zane says. There's an edge to his voice. "First thing Monday morning, I'm going to sit with my lawyer to make sure Ember doesn't come within a hundred feet of you. You're going to have to be present, though. I don't want her anywhere near you."

I nod. "I don't want that woman in my orbit. She's poison."

"She's worse than a venomous snake."

"Well said."

"Now that we got that out of the way, where does that leave us?"

"I thought we were in a good place."

He takes my hands in his. "So did I."

Our gazes meet.

"So, we're back to where we were before I left for Rio?" he asks.

"Yes." The word comes out in a near whisper.

"Good." He reaches for my face and brushing a strand of hair behind my ear. "Very good."

The familiar touch sends a jolt of excitement through my body.

God, this man...

I've barely had time to wrap my head around the reality of being pregnant. Before Ember polluted my life, I thought I had another week and a half before telling Zane. After she conned me into believing her lie, I wasn't sure what I was going to do. I need to put my big girl panties on. He has a right to know, and since my family knows, it's not fair he's still in the dark.

I open my mouth to bear my soul, but hesitate, a tinge of worry twisting my stomach.

What if he doesn't want a child?

What if he walks away?

After all, this situation has so many shades of Psycho Ember.

Find your lady balls, Shay!

"Why do I feel you're hiding something from me?" Zane says.

Just tell him.

"I love you!"

Zane's eyes widen in shock.

What the hell?

My hormones must be fucking with my brain.

"That's not what I meant to say."

"You don't love me?" Zane asks.

I avert my gaze.

"Shay, I asked you a question."

I could lie, but the words are out there, so I take ownership of them. I should say, I try. "It's okay if you don't feel the same way I do, Zane." That was a copout.

"In a strange twist of fate," Zane says with a smile, "I ended up telling Ember I was in love with you before telling you."

My eyes widen. "Wh—what?"

He chuckles.

"My parting words to her were, *As for Shay, I'm not going to allow you to ruin things between us. I don't care if I have to walk barefoot over burning coals. I'm determined to get back the woman I love.*"

"You love me?"

He nods. "It's crazy, I know. We've only known each other for a little over a month, but I've never felt like this about any other woman in my life. In fact, I never thought I would. But yes, I love you, Shay."

I jump out of my seat and into his lap. "You love me?" I ask again.

"Yes! I love you!" His tone is solemn.

"I love you too, Zane."

He tips my head. "It's been too long since I last kissed you." That's the only warning I get before he crashes his lips against mine. My eyelashes flutter closed and I surrender to the possessiveness of his kiss with a sensual moan. My lips part in a soft sigh of satisfaction and longing. I welcome the soft sweep of his tongue inside my mouth, my whole body tingling with anticipation.

God, I've missed his mouth on me.

He breaks the kiss.

I let out a grunt of disapproval.

He buries his face in the side of my neck with an animalistic growl.

He cups my breast and squeezes hard.

I gasp, my chest heaving from the sweet assault.

"How long do you think we have before your family comes back?" he asks.

I want nothing more than for him to claim me, but there's still something we need to discuss. "About that—"

"You're right, maybe you should text Briar so she can be a decoy like last time. Now that I'm in your parents' good graces again, I wouldn't want them to walk in on us and become persona non grata," he chuckles.

"That's not what I was going to say."

"Fuck, baby, it's been a week and a half. Tell me you're not going to make me wait until we get on the jet to fuck you." *I wouldn't mind joining the mile high club.* "If I didn't think I'd insult your parents, I'd get a hotel room for us for tonight, but since your mom insists I stay in the guestroom..."

This man. "I don't think I'll ever get over how much you want me."

"Get over it," he says. "It's a fact. Accept it."

"There's something you need to know."

Pull the band-aid off, Shay.

He frowns. "What?" his tone is cautious.

My heart is beating hard like a drum.

"What is it, Shay?"

"I don't want you to think I'm trying to trap you—"

"What are you talking about?"

Giving myself a mental kick in the ass, I blurt out the words stuck in my throat. "I'm pregnant."

His whole body freezes.

His hazel green eyes stare at me, unblinking.

Oh, gosh. He put me in the same category as Psycho Ember?!

Then it hits me.

He doesn't know if I'm bluffing or not.

"I *am* pregnant. I haven't been to the doctor yet, but I took two pregnancy tests the day before the talk... the day Ember tracked me down—"

"Fuck!"

That's not the response I was hoping for.

Okay, now I'm worried.

Maybe I should've waited a few days.

I try to wiggle off his lap, but I don't go far. His strong arm circles my waist, keeping me against his muscular body.

"I don't mean fuck you're pregnant," he says.

I shoot him a side gaze.

He lets out a beath. "Now, I know why you ran away. You thought I was having twins with another woman at the same time as I was having a baby with you?"

I nod.

"What a clusterfuck of a mess that would've been. Three babies. Two baby mamas who hate each other."

I let out a boisterous laugh.

"It was a little too much drama for me," I say when I regain my composure.

He caresses my hair and drops a soft kiss against my forehead. "Thank God I'm having a baby with *the right* woman."

My head jerks back. "You're not upset?"

He shakes his head. "It's unexpected, but no, I'm not upset." His voice is so calm, so self-assured.

I search his eyes for any flicker that would contradict his words. There is none. Still, I press. "Really?"

"You're mine, Shay"—he places a hand over my tummy—"and this baby is also mine. End of story. I guess I should say, *beginning* of story. The beginning of *our* story as a family."

Elation, relief, bliss, and a symphony of other euphoric emotions crash into me all at once, and I dissolve in a puddle of tears as an explosion of joy goes off inside of me as I imagine our life ahead.

Epilogue

Zane

Three weeks later

Given the big news, I postponed my return trip to Brazil. Shay and I stayed a couple extra days in Boston. Her family is now my family. We returned to New York with Katie, Alan, Briar, and Aunt Eileen.

When you're used to flying on your own private jet, you take it for granted. Watching Shay and her family soak in the extravagance of such privilege was amusing. A private plane is over the top even for a wealthy doctor. Imagine having two? It's the height of luxury.

Briar had me fooled. The whole flight, she pretended it was no big deal. She was blasé about it. When we landed, I overheard her gushing over the phone to a friend about the mind-blowing luxury of flying on a private jet.

Shay's family stayed at her brownstone. I wanted to keep them a secret for as long as possible. Since I was alone in my large apartment, hiring the right people to set the stage was child's play.

Two days after returning to the Big Apple, I invited my cousins, my brother, Mom, and Dad over to my place for dinner. My family had already met Shay before I left for Rio de Janeiro. This was the first time meeting her family. I made sure they wouldn't spill the beans. I didn't even give Xavier a heads-up, and I tell my little brother everything. I wanted to surprise them all. Especially, Mom. She couldn't contain herself. She figured Shay and I were taking things to the next level since she was meeting her family. Even though champagne was flowing all evening, and my girl only drank Perrier, Mom didn't clue in.

When it was time to announce to my family that we were pregnant, we did it in style. Instead of telling them, it was a big production.

I dropped by my favorite Brazilian pastry shop and ordered a large *pavé*—a popular Brazilian layered dessert cake similar to tiramisu. On it, there was a large rectangular piece of white chocolate scripted with *Surpresa, estou grávida!* (Surprise, we're pregnant!) in chocolate sauce. I asked Mom to serve the dessert. She was recounting a funny story from when my brother and I were kids, and she wasn't paying attention. When she opened the lid to the box, she nearly had a heart attack. Dad had to hold her because she stumbled back several steps, still gripping the sharp knife in her trembling hand. Then, she let out a deafening screech before dissolving into tears for a solid fifteen minutes. When she got over the shock, she called the family in Brazil on a video chat. Everyone was elated.

Three days later, I returned to Rio de Janeiro. I bought Shay's family first-class tickets for their return to Boston. The week and a half away from my girl was cruel, but there was no way around it. Then, there was a five-day conference in Chicago. Followed by a couple of days in Dallas to catch the tail end of another conference. I was supposed to return to

Silicon Valley for a four-day trip, but I canceled it. I had to be in New York this week.

Today is our first ultrasound. On top of that, it's Valentine's Day. No way was I going to miss those two big events. To cut back on travel time, Shay stayed at my place. We still haven't figured things out, so for now we decided to bounce from her place to mine. Her studio is set up at her house, which means she can't stay at my place all the time.

My excitement was palpable the whole way to the doctor's office. Hell, I didn't even curse at the impatient driver who was zigzagging from one lane to the other. Even while we waited at the clinic, I could barely sit still. When we got called, I sprinted to the room, dragging my pregnant girlfriend behind me. The nurse checked Shay over. Once that was done, she asked Shay to strip from the waist down and sit on the table. My girl isn't showing yet, but I can't wait for that to happen so the world knows the woman I love is carrying our child.

When the nurse leaves the room, Shay wiggles her butt on the table, the paper crinkling underneath her.

She scrunches her nose. "Well, this is comfortable."

I'm sure it's not, but I keep that to myself.

"It's worth it, though." She flashes me a wide, beaming grin. "We get to see our little peanut. What a way to celebrate Valentine's Day."

"I can't wait to meet our *son*," I say. "And don't worry, love, you'll get a big fat Valentine's Day's present later today."

She rolls her eyes.

I chuckle.

It irks her when I tease her like that and I know it. So now, she's an easy target. Boy or girl. It doesn't matter to me, as long as the baby is healthy. After this peanut pops into the world, we're going to try for more. Baby number one is the beginning for us. We're aiming for three or four kids.

Shay looks down at her toes painted in a dark red nail polish, her legs dangling like an impatient kid. She lets out a suffering sigh before biting the inside of her cheek.

After a long moment of silence, she says, "I hope the baby is fine... healthy." Her gaze is still trained on her feet.

"Look at me."

She obeys my command.

Her blue eyes flash with worry.

I place a comforting hand on her clasped ones.

"I'm not a doctor, and I don't pretend to be one, but you can't worry like that, love," I say. "My Brazilian family is so religious"—I move my hands to her tummy—"they've been praying for this baby from the moment we made the announcement, and they'll keep praying for that child until the end of time."

My attempt to lighten the mood, fails.

She responds with a jerky nod. "Imogen wasn't my favorite person in the world, but I feel for her. Despite it all, I can't imagine what it's like to be in her shoes."

"I feel for her, too."

In a matter of weeks, Imogen's life turned into a soap opera. A part of me sympathizes with her, but at the end of the day, she made her bed... and now she has to lie in it.

Elias is filing for a speedy divorce and her soon-to-be ex-husband's parents are suing her for the cost of the wedding, every penny they spent on the pre-wedding festivities, and the cost of the hotel rooms to accommodate family members who flew in from out-of-town.

Calvin's wife is divorcing him, even though she's pregnant with their second child. What a shame for those poor kids. Calvin not only loses his wife, he also loses his best friend. That long-lasting friendship is now a thing of the past.

To add to the list of doozies, Imogen lost her father. Alan

isn't dead. He's very much alive. He's just not Imogen's *biological* father.

It took him forty-eight hours after Shay told Katie and Alan about the incident with Elias for him to react. He got on a plane and debarked in New York City, heading straight for Imogen's mom's place for answers.

In the heat of a virulent argument, where Alan accused his ex-wife of being single-handedly responsible for Imogen's fucked up disregard for people and the consequences of her actions, Deborah spat the truth in his face. She had an affair with her married boss who died in an accident in LA on the same day Alan returned to the United States from a year spent volunteering for the Health Volunteers Overseas at the Dermatology Institute Skin Health and Referral Center and two other hospitals in Nepal. Both Alan and Deborah had agreed she would stay in the US since she had landed an incredible new job opportunity. Kathmandu isn't for everybody, and Alan was only there temporarily.

Alan is in talks with his lawyers to sue his ex-wife for a wrongful paternity lawsuit. He's so pissed off at everything Imogen has done. Even with all that, he wasn't planning on cutting out Imogen from his life. After all, he was her father for twenty-eight years. Shay's *no longer* stepsister shut the door in his face, stating they've never had anything in common, so why keep up the charade since they don't even share DNA. She even spat in his face she'd be changing her last name from Elias's to her mom's once the divorce was final.

Defeated, Alan gave up.

Katie supports his decision. So does Briar. Aunt Eileen is baffled by everything that's transpired since the wedding. She's even more flummoxed—and mad as hell—by the way Imogen was quick to sever ties with a man she's known all her life as her father. So am I.

To top Imogen's distress, she had a miscarriage four days ago. Elias called Shay to let her know. He's shaken by the whole experience. So much so, he took a leave of absence from his practice. He's picking up the pieces of his life somewhere in the Swiss Alps for a month.

Swallowing hard, Shay says, "Until the baby gets here, you don't know. You could be fine one minute, the next, folded in half, in pain, bleeding."

I'm about to comfort her, when the door opens.

A short, mixed-race woman, with a bright smile, steps inside.

"Good morning, Mom and Dad," she says.

"Good morning, Dr. Daniels."

Shay decided it would be uncomfortable to select an ob-gyn who she would also see at family gatherings. My cousin Luisa's husband's aunt referred us to her best friend Olivia.

"How are we doing today?" she asks Shay.

"I'm good."

"And the baby?" the doctor asks.

"He or she is good," she says.

Dr. Daniels's gaze shifts to me. "How's Dad?"

"If Shay's okay and our *son* is okay"—I point to Shay's belly —"I have nothing to complain about."

"Oh, you're one of those dads."

I wink. "I'm messing with my girl's head. I'm good either way."

"Glad to hear it. Ready to get started?"

"I am!" Shay says.

"We'll start with the exam, and when I'm finished, the tech will be in for the ultrasound, and you two get to leave with a sonogram. How does that sound?"

"Sounds good," Shay says.

"Fine by me," I say.

"Lie down on the table and slide down until your bum touches the edge." Dr. Daniels motions with her hand. Shay does as she's told. The doctor covers her lower part with a white sheet before sitting on a stool. "Slide down a little more for me."

Shay complies.

Dr. Daniels disappears between Shay's spread legs, hidden under the sheet.

I don't know why, but I feel compelled to hold my girl's hand.

She responds with a warm smile.

The doctor goes about her business.

I feel useless.

The doctor is the expert and my girl is the courageous trooper who will deliver our baby.

She hisses, squeezing my hand tight.

I wince.

Jesus, I can't imagine how hard she'll squeeze my hand when the baby comes.

"Are you okay?" I ask.

"I'm okay," she says in a strangled voice.

"Almost done," the doctor says.

Shay bites her lip and closes her eyes.

She isn't okay.

Fuck.

It's on the tip of my tongue to ask the doctor if the baby is okay.

Dr. Daniels lifts her head. "All done!"

Shay lets out a sigh of relief.

"Everything looks great, Mom and Dad."

Thank you, God.

I wink at Shay. "Told you our peanut was a champion. Lots of people praying."

I'm rewarded with a tearful smile.

The doctor gets up and removes her surgical gloves. "The tech should be in to pick up the baton. Once you're done, make sure to book your next appointment before you leave."

Shay nods. "I will."

"Have a great day," Dr. Daniels says before leaving the room.

Not a minute goes by before the technician walks in.

A young, curvy brunette enters the room, dragging a rolling table, topped with a machine and a computer behind her.

"Good morning!"

"Good morning!" Shay and I parrot.

"First time parents?" she asks.

"Yes!" Shay says," at the same time as I say, "Isn't it obvious?"

"The worst is behind you for today," the technician says. "This is going to be painless."

Glad to hear this won't hurt Shay. I was worried there for a minute.

"Let's get this party started, Mom and Dad!"

She's full of energy this morning.

"It's too early to tell the sex," the technician says, "but we should be able to hear the heartbeat, measure your baby, and determine the due date."

"We'll be able to hear the heartbeat?" I ask her, my voice full of amazement.

"We sure will, Dad."

Shay tightens her grip on my hand.

I bring them to my lips and kiss them tenderly.

An indescribable feeling expands in my chest.

Our baby.

I take a few deep breaths to calm my nerves.

I'm elated and freaked out at the same time.

After covering a wand with what looks like a condom and then squirting a gel substance all over it, the technician goes to work. In no time, the screen fills with a grainy black and white image, shifting to a sepia-colored one. Everything is pretty blurry to me, but I make out a shape. It's nothing more than a blob.

Wow.

It's hard to believe that little dot is going to turn into a human. Then, the technician flips a switch, and the room is filled with a crazy thumping sound.

Holy shit!

Shay squeezes my hand. "Our baby's heartbeat!"

"Unbelievable—"

"Oh!" the technician says.

My head jerks back. "What is it?"

She frowns in response.

"Is everything okay with the baby?" The concern is audible in Shay's voice—it's the same one beating at my chest. I haven't met this little human yet, but I couldn't bear to lose our little peanut. I'm not sure Shay would—

I don't even want to think about it.

After what seems like an eternity, the technician swivels the computer so we can see what she sees.

She makes a few adjustments on the screen, points at it, and says, "I see *two* babies, so essentially we're listening to two heartbeats!"

Wh—wh—what?

Shay gasps.

I blink.

I blink again.

I blink a third time for good measure.

"Oh my God!" Shay squeals. "Really?"

I'm still incapable of finding my voice.

"Really," the technician says with a firm nod. "Happy Valentine's Day, Mom and Dad! You're having twins!"

Bonus Scene

Hudson

After giving my name to a hotel employee posted at the greeting desk, I enter the Seymour Lounge.

My buddies and fellow VIP Den members, Logan Ellison and his brother Walker, stand up to greet me.

After a few back slaps and handshakes, we take a seat on the modern wingback navy-blue armchairs.

A waiter rushes our way.

"What do you want to drink, Kincaid?" Logan asks.

I look up at the waiter. "An espresso martini—" I shake my head. "Nah, that's not gonna do it. I'll have a vodka Red Bull, please."

With a bow, the waiter rushes off.

"Hard day?" Walker asks.

I meet his gaze. "Hard week."

The waiter is back with my drink.

Two other waiters trail behind him, carrying trays of appetizers.

My nostrils tingle, the aroma awakening my appetite.

I'm already salivating.

The staff displays everything with a flourish.

We thank them, and the trio disappear as quickly as they appeared.

My gaze drops to the lip-smacking Mediterranean and grilled meat platters.

Damn.

"This looks delicious. Especially considering I didn't have time for lunch today."

"Same," Logan says.

"I barely managed to stuff a blueberry muffin down my throat at eleven this morning." Walker checks his statement gold watch. "It's eight p.m. now, which means I've been running on air and adrenaline all day."

"I've been on the same diet," I say.

Logan points to the feast. "Dig in."

He doesn't have to tell me twice.

"Don't mind if I do."

Logan and Walker pile a generous amount of appetizers on their plates.

The medley of flavors explodes in my mouth, and I have to suppress a moan.

For a few beats, we enjoy our food in silence.

The Ellisons have the Midas touch when it comes to hiring the best chefs in the city.

I wipe my mouth with a white cloth napkin before placing it on my empty plate. "Thank you. That hit the spot nicely."

Walker nods. "It did."

"The joy of carrying the world on your shoulders," I say. "Your days are so jampacked, you can't even manage to squeeze in the time for a meal. Today was a carbon copy of yesterday. Busy, busy, busy."

"I hear you," Logan says. "Thank God not every day is as

frantic as today's breakneck pace, or else I'd have to hang up my CEO hat."

"If you decided to take a step back, you'd still have your three siblings to hold the fort." *Not in my case. One of the downfalls of being an only child.*

"Have you considered..."—Walker levels me with a serious stare—"finding a new business partner?"

"No." I shake my head. "Never."

He holds up his hands in truce. "It was just a suggestion."

"I appreciate your concern, but I have trust issues. Been burned a few times."

"In that case, I understand your reticence," he says.

"I just have to make peace with the fact I'm the only captain. Thank God for my incredible crew."

"The payment processing industry you dominate is a world apart from the hospitality industry," Logan says. "Still, I'm in awe of you. I'm the CEO of this massive conglomerate of hotels, corporate rentals for professionals and executives, restaurants, lounges, and bars, but my siblings are my allies when it comes to big decisions. I have Walker"—he jerks his chin in his brother's direction—"Kayla, and Tristan to bounce ideas off. When things are murky, they help me see through the fog. And when the shit hits the fan, they're there to help me weather the storm. Same for my cousins spearheading operations in the different states and countries we have flagships in. You're steering your vessel alone."

I loosen my tie. "So often, I fear I'll suffer the same fate as the Titanic."

"I was paying you a compliment, Kincaid. You're taking it like an insult."

"I'm not."

"Sounds like it to me." Logan shifts his attention to his brother. "Am I wrong?"

"You're selling yourself short, Hudson," Walker says. "Your company is thriving. You're kicking ass and taking no prisoners."

"Ever since..." I expel a heavy breath. "Every day, I feel like it was a lucky day—a fluke—and the next day, I'll wake up, and the other shoe will drop." A lump forms in my throat, forcing me to loosen my tie even more.

"I understand where you're coming from," Logan says.

My eyebrows hit my forehead.

Logan narrows his eyes at me. "Don't look so surprise, Kincaid."

"It's not something I ever expected you to say. From the outside looking in, you're juggling all your balls with ease, whereas I'm juggling glass balls, praying they don't drop and shatter."

"Just because I'm not steering this vessel alone, doesn't mean the pressure isn't on. It's on. Every. Single. Day. Long-standing companies go belly up all the time. I thrive for success. Not to become a statistic—"

"Because when you become a statistic, hard-working people end up without a job," I say.

He nods.

"I'm known for being an uncompromising boss—"

"He is," Walker says.

"At least I'm not known for being a grumpy boss."

"Asshole!"

The Ellisons enter a Mexican standoff for a few long beats.

I clear my throat.

Logan swings his gaze my way. "I have zero tolerance for underperformers and even less for slackers. Don't get me started on this new epidemic mentality of quiet quitting. You want to do the bare minimum? No problem, but don't expect me to pay you. I have no problem telling them, *'You're fired!'*.

But letting good people go because of downsizing due to the fact we're not crushing it, that's unacceptable to me. True, there are circumstances you don't see coming, and therefore, you can't plan for. Albeit a natural catastrophe or for an unfathomable reason, the world would come to a standstill, my mission is to avoid having to downsize at any cost. That's what gets me up in the morning, fired up, and ready to go. Some might say I'm hardcore..." He shrugs. "Whatever. And yes, that responsibility can be overwhelming at times. Hitting—or surpassing—your goals year after year demands dedication, which would explain why I don't have a life outside of the family business."

"And it's not only the CEO who feels the heat," Walker says. "As the second in command, I feel the pressure as much as my big brother does."

I never thought they could relate. After all they have each other to lean on.

"My anxiety over making sure I don't fail the hundreds of employees depending on the money my company wires to their account every other week isn't stealing my breath like it used to when I was saddled with the crushing and heart-wrenching reality that I was going to have to manage the company on my own, but it's always at the back of my mind." *Niggling at me. Making me doubt I'm fit for the job.*

I never expected to be doing this by myself.

It wasn't supposed to be like this.

But then again, losing people I love is the story of my life.

Time to change the subject.

I scour the empty space. "You guys keep buying up hotels and renovating the ones you've acquired. This is an impressive renovation."

"The Seymour Lounge is our most ambitious renovation at the Bymark Hotel," Logan says.

"Only to be surpassed by the nearly completed renovated Banks Lounge," Walker says.

"Which 90s supermodels are associated with your latest renovations?"

"This lounge is named after Stephanie Seymour," Walker says, "and the other lounge is named after Tyra Banks."

"I'll have to Google them," I say. "I enjoyed being educated on the supermodels associated with the other lounges in the hotel."

"You're welcome," Logan says.

"Fucker."

He ignores my jab. "Our visions often clash when it comes to creative decisions, but when our sister wanted to leverage her adoration of 80s and 90s supermodels, we were on board after googling those beauties," Logan says.

"I bet."

"In my humble opinion, the models of our generation don't measure up," Walker says. "For the few who are gorgeous, they're replaceable. The 90s supermodels are irreplaceable. That breed of superhumans were the epitome of beauty, they all had a memorable personality that shone on photos and on the catwalk, and they weren't size double zero."

"You sound like you're their freaking casting agent," I say.

"Guilty as charged. I've spent too much time googling them, but can you blame me?"

"I was content gorging on slim beauties until a couple weeks ago."

"Who is the mythical creature who has the superpowers to make a pigheaded man like yourself change his tune?"

"You're lucky I consider you as a friend, or else I'd kick you out of my hotel, Kincaid."

"Avoiding the question, Ellison?"

"We hired a new station chef in one of the restaurants at

the hotel. She's smoking hot." He does a chef's kiss. "She's a brunette, so, not my usual MO. But damn, I'd break all my rules for her."

Walker's head whips in his brother's direction.

A blast of icy cold air, that has nothing to do with the A/C, engulfs the lounge.

"What?" Logan asks.

Walker's nostrils flare.

"Why are you looking at me like you want to gouge my eyes out, or worse, plunge a dagger into my chest?"

Walker's jaw ticks.

"Jesus, Walker, you look like you're about to blow a gasket. What the fuck is your problem?"

Slowly, the younger Ellison pulls his gaze away from his brother and settles his furious eyes on me.

Whatever is going on between you and your brother, don't take it out on me, buddy.

"As someone born and raised in Texas, I'm all for curves," I say. Give me a drop-dead gorgeous woman with slender tempting curves anytime of the day... or night.

Logan lifts his martini glass. "I'll drink to that!"

I do the same.

Logan and I take a swig of our drinks.

Walker remains mute behind a wall of silence.

Logan's eyes meet my own. "You're coming to the official opening of the Seymour Lounge next week?"

"Wouldn't miss it."

"Is your director of French communications going to be your plus one?"

"It will only be lil' ol' me."

"How come?" Logan asks. "I thought she was your wingman at events."

"She'll be in Paris, meeting new prospects," I say. "You guys will be here, your brother and your sister, the Kellers will be here as well. Bryce Van Der Linden and his brother-in-law Nikolaj will also be here. There are fewer chances I'll open my mouth and say something to someone who gets easily offended and ruffle their overly sensitive feathers." The Ellisons chuckle. "So, I'm coming alone like a big boy."

"I was looking forward to seeing your director of French communications again," Logan says. "Speaking of drop-dead gorgeous women, that beauty is all that and more. I fail to understand how you're able to work with her and not want to flip her over your desk and fuck her senseless every day. Unless you have her on one of your conference room tables, drilling into her as strings of sexy French words spill from her pouty lips."

Tell me how you really feel about her. "There are labor laws."

He gives me a non-committal shrug.

"I make it a point not to agree with my brother as often as I can, but Logan is right. That woman is sex on legs," Walker says. "But I understand your dilemma. Office romances are..."

"Ill-advised," I say.

"I was going to say tricky, requiring finesse, and paperwork spelling out it's consensual," Walker says.

"Have you ever been in that position?" I ask him.

"Nah. I'm the master of my balls. R words—romance and relationship—open the door to more drama than I have the capacity to handle."

"Love is a disease, and I'm as allergic to relationships as my brother is, but if it weren't for our friendship, I'd ask your director of French communications out."

I hold Logan's gaze. "She'd turn you down."

The corner of his lip curves up. "I'm very convincing when I put my mind to it."

"Trust me, she'd turn you down."

"You'll never be on the receiving end of—"

"She's a lesbian."

Logan's head jerks back.

That shut him up.

Walker's eyes widen. "No shit."

I nod. "She's always preferred women."

"I'm heartbroken," Logan says.

Did he just pout? "Do you even have a heart?"

"Don't quit your day job, Kincaid."

Walker points a finger at me. "Good one."

Logan pulls at the sleeve of his shirt peeking from underneath his navy blue checkered jacket. "It doesn't matter if I'd rock her world in bed—or against a wall, or on my desk, or in the back of a car, or on the terrace of one of the suites in the hotel, or somewhere we might get caught—I don't have the right equipment."

My eyebrows arch high.

No, he hasn't been obsessing over her. "Boasting your own praise again, Logan?"

"I'm not tooting my own horn. It's an irrefutable fact. All my past lovers will attest."

I shake my head.

Logan crosses a leg over the other. "If she won't be accompanying you, that opens the doors to possibilities for the evening. There will be a lot of gorgeous women present."

"This is the perfect moment for me to fess up for why I suggested we meet—"

"So, this wasn't about us spending quality time together?" The sarcasm is thick in Walker's voice.

"No, we won't be braiding each other's hair tonight or painting each other's nail in bubblegum pink."

"I'm crushed, Hudson." He's full of shit.

"You'll survive, Walker."

"Okay, so you didn't want to connect for a touchy-feely, bonding evening. What's on your mind?" Logan asks me.

"At the charity event we attended a couple weeks ago, you two—along with your brother—educated me on the art of executive dating." My eyes shifting from one brother to the other. "I'd like to know more."

Walker slides his attention to Logan. "Sounds like our friend is looking to hire an escort."

Logan nods before his eyes lock onto mine. "It's been a long time. You're finally ready to get your dick wet." He rubs his stubbled chin. "Which kinks are you looking to play out, Kincaid?"

"You can take the boy out of Texas, but you can't take the Southern out of the boy."

Logan tilts his head to the side. "Care to translate?"

"I don't kiss and tell."

"Even when you're paying for it?" Walker asks.

"Even when I'm paying for it."

No way am I revealing all the filthy things I intend to do to the woman I'll be matched with...

Bonus Secret Chapter

For a bonus secret chapter about Zane and Shay (the swoony proposal—two weeks after the first ultrasound), subscribe to my newsletter!

www.MyRomanceAddiction.com

Who's The Next Billionaire In This Illegally Hot Series?

Hudson Kincaid is a member of the VIP Den and he hangs out with Max, Xavier, and Zane.

The blue-eyed billionaire (born in Texas) struggles with social niceties. Since Hudson is as allergic to drama as much as he's allergic to pointless chitchat, he secures the services of a professional for an evening where he plans on closing an important deal.

When you hire your date, you know what to expect... unless nothing about her fits the mold of a New York City escort...

Binge-read now: A Very Wicked Arrangement

Psst... you can read a sneak peek of A Very Wicked Arrangement at the end of this book.

Reviews are like a box of chocolate. One morsel of chocolate isn't enough!

It only takes a few minutes to leave a review, which makes a huge difference for an indie author like myself.

Here's the link to leave a review for: A Very Fake Boyfriend

Scarlett's Book Banter!

Dear Sexy Reader,

Zane is so, so hot.

And I totally love curvy girl Shay!

Don't even get me started on Shay's Irish family. Love Aunt Eileen and Briar is totally adorable. I didn't expect her to have such a major role in the story.

Zane Keller is my first former nerd alpha. He was a great alpha to write.

My inspiration for Zane and Shay's plot

My inspiration for Zane and Shay's plot is a mashup of two popular chick flick/rom-com movies—*The Wedding Date* and *My Best Friend's Wedding*.

I loved *My Best Friend's Wedding* the first time around and I loved it when I watched the movie again before writing this book.

Critiques slammed *The Wedding Date*, but women loved the idea of two random people coming together for a specific goal and end up falling in love. All fake romance EVER.

Why did I set the story over the Christmas Holiday season?

There's so much magic and family drama during the month of December, and the drama is often ramped up between Christmas Eve and the 2nd of January. Having a wedding a few days before Christmas is hairraising for the bride and groom, their family, and their guests. Also, I love meddling families, and Shay and Zane's family played their roles to a T.

Inspiration from other books of mine for Zane's story...

I included a pretty amazing Christmas scene in **Billionaire Hotshot—Holt**, and of course, I had to include some of my favorite Christmas songs and my favorite Christmas movie of all times.

I loved writing the karaoke scene in **Billionaire Hotshot—Jace** so much, I had to include one in this book. Let's face it, there's nothing like a guy serenading a girl. Pure romance gold.

Well, enough of this banter or else it'll turn into a novella.

All that to say, I hope you enjoyed reading Zane and Shay's love story as much as I loved writing it.

Why did it take me this long to write the fake romance trope?

I love, love, love this trope!

I wrote Zane's book on the heel of another fake romance book. I invite you to read another fake relationship that's so hot, it leaves readers gobsmacked. Yeah, I kind of pushed the envelope on **Billionaire Phoenix's** romance.

Billionaire Mogul—Phoenix is an arranged marriage romance that sets a new bar for just how dominant a hero can be. Get ready for an explosive storm of naughty and lots (and lots) of sexy times (wink-wink).

***Você fala português?* Do you speak Portuguese?**

Well, I don't, but the fabulous young woman who helped with the Portuguese in Zane's story does.

A huge thank you to loyal reader Rebecca Eddy who enlisted the help of her "bonus granddaughter" to help me with Portuguese words/sentences.

Luisa Tremeschin Uezono came into Rebecca's life as an exchange student who lived with her grandson's mother. I'm grateful Rebecca claimed Luisa as a bonus grandbaby.

So, what's next?

Hudson and Angelica, aka the Texan billionaire living in New York and the virgin escort... two orphans who live in completely opposite world, who were fated to meet in the most unexpected way in a mega city.

Blurb

My predictable life is turned on its head when **my reckless identical twin sister** announces she borrowed an ungodly amount of money from a scary looking loan shark with an unpronounceable name. To make a payment (for which she's already late), she hustles a *'Pretty Woman'* gig.

The problem is she's dealing with a delicate feminine issue that involves an unpleasant fungus. So, I agree to do ***the ultimate twin swap***. The fact I'm still holding onto my **V card** makes me woefully inadequate for the job.

My twin's first client is a commanding CEO with a sexy Texan twang. The blue-eye demigod is all charm and swagger, oozing with the kind of confidence that goes straight to a girl's head.

One magical evening leads to a string of them.

New York is bursting at the seams with gorgeous models, sophisticated socialites, and kickass boss ladies, but the dreamy man I was never supposed to meet, chooses me—a curvy, nerdy book editor in disguise.

As an orphan, it's impossible not to fall hard for a man who wants to take care of me. A man who wants to make all my problems go away.

It's a Cinderella fairytale until the truth behind the wicked arrangement I made with my twin blows up in my face...

USA Today Bestselling Author Scarlett Avery brings you an intoxicating romance between a powerful billionaire who would move mountain and earth for the woman who captures his lonely heart and a book nerd who's only pretending to be *Pretty Woman*.

Pre-order now: A Very Wicked Arrangement

More sexy Keller men...

If you haven't read Zane's cousin Max's romance, you're totally missing out.

Max Keller is obsessed with women with plenty of curves.

Curvy girl Candy had pretty much given up on love.

One chance encounter changes everything when sexy billionaire

Max strikes up a conversation with her.

When the billionaire catches sight of Candy's luscious curves, all bets are off.

What happens when a coincidence turns into an illicit and smoldering encounter?

Billionaire Factor—Max is a passion-filled BBW romance with the right touch of naughty.

Max is part of the **Billionaire Factor** series.

The **Billionaire Factor** alphas kicked off my writing career (via **Billionaire Factor—Bryce**). From day one, I decided my billionaires would hold a PhD in dirty talking and they would be dominant AF.

P.S. Who loves reviews? I do! I do! Thanks a *billion* in advance!

P.P.S. I keep writing because of your hunger for my stories. Thank you for your fervor, love, and loyalty. I'm humbled and incredibly grateful. Without you, there's very little reason to keep coming up with new stories.

P.P.P.S. For access to an EXCLUSIVE Secret Chapter, go to the next page!

Get the Secret Chapter for A Very Fake Boyfriend!

Thank you for purchasing this romance!

I have an EXCLUSIVE Secret Chapter to share with you!

For the Secret Chapter, we travel two weeks into the future for Zane's swoony proposal to Shay.

Trust me, you're going to love the extra tidbits.

When you sign up on my list, you'll receive an email with further instructions!

Sign up TODAY!

www.MyRomanceAddiction.com

***If you've already signed up to my list from previous books, you can visit the same page to download the Secret Chapters and/or Storyboard for this romance. ***

Sneak Peak of A Very Wicked Arrangement

Chapter 1 | Angelica

Leaning against the kitchen counter, I shove a spoonful of ice cream into my mouth, cursing the universe.

The second the creaminess and ice-coldness of my dessert concoction hit my tongue, I can pretend to forget all about my shitty morning.

Without ice cream, there would only be darkness and chaos.

I can't remember who the wise soul is behind that quote, but I wholeheartedly agree.

I'm about to dig in for another spoonful when I hear keys at the door.

The sound of my sister's heels clicking against the wooden floor of the entrance resonate throughout the apartment, announcing her return.

"Ange!"

I don't bother answering my sister. The apartment we've lived in since we were five years old isn't very big. She'll find me soon enough.

Arya appears in the doorway, barefoot.

She squints her green eyes at me. "Ice cream at eleven-thirty in the morning on a Thursday?"

"Not just ice cream, but *boozy* ice cream." I scoop up said boozy ice cream and lift it at eye level. "Häagen-Dazs vanilla ice cream with a generous dose of Baileys."

"You splurged?!"

"The Irish cream liqueur is a Christmas gift from a client who appreciates my contribution to her writing. As for the ice cream, it was on sale. With the coupon I downloaded online, the pint came to only three bucks."

"Delicious and frugal. What a winning combo."

It's the only way we can afford dessert these days. Turbulent times and all. "Booze. Fat. Sugar. The ultimate soothing trio."

"In other words, you pulled out the heavy artillery."

"I had to. Since it's cocktail hour somewhere on the globe, boozy ice cream is perfectly acceptable."

"Rough morning?"

"A shitty morning that tops an even shittier week."

She approaches me and places a hand on my shoulder. "What happened?"

"I had a heated conversation with a client—"

"Don't tell me, the author who would rather die than cut back page after page of incessant internal dialogue?"

"Yes, that one."

"You fired her as a client?"

I shake my head. "*She* fired me as an editor. Apparently, I was dwarfing her creative genius by suggesting she cuts back on her characters' inner reflection, curtails her overuse of adverbs and unnecessary italicized words, and uses pussy instead of moist vaginal walls."

My sister rolls her eyes. "You don't need that kind of negativity in your life."

"Perhaps, but I need the money. Just in case you forgot, we're up to our eyeballs in debt."

"How can I forget? You keep reminding me."

I bite off a bitchy reply.

One fight per day is my quota.

I change the topic. "You were cagey as to why you had to get out of here so early this morning you aren't exactly a morning person."

My sister sighs.

"Is something wrong?"

"Well, the nighttime medical service called me last night to let me know my doctor had a cancellation. So, I set up three alarms to pull my ass out of bed to make it to his office for an eight o'clock appointment."

"You're sick?"

She shakes her head.

I expect her to elaborate, but she just looks at me in a way I can't quite decipher.

The delightful pleasure I was deriving from the boozy ice cream concoction is long gone, replaced by worry. I drop the bowl on the countertop.

"What's wrong?"

She averts her gaze.

I place a hand on her arm. "Talk to me, Arya."

Her green eyes meet my own.

"My va-jay-jay is sick." Her lips pull down in a frown. "I have bacterial vaginosis."

I take a step back, my eyebrows dipping low.

"It isn't contagious, Ange." She lets out a self-deprecating laugh. "It's an extreme form of yeast infection and it's annoying as hell."

"That's why you were complaining about your lady parts itching?"

"Yes. That, and the unpleasant fishy smell coming from down there." She screws up her nose and points at said sick va-jay-jay. "Despite the use of feminine spray. I figured it was time for a doctor's appointment."

I cringe.

"At least we know what the issue is now. It's not like you contracted gonorrhea. Even an extreme case of yeast infection is curable."

"So pragmatic."

"It's my job as the big sister."

"You beat me into this world by fifteen lousy minutes. You'd think that after twenty-two years, you'd stop reminding me," my identical twin says.

"Keep dreaming, Ary." I'm unlikely to stop reminding her of that any time soon. "I assume the doctor gave you some kind a prescription cream?"

"Yes."

"Shit. More expenses."

"I know. I'm sorry. It's not like I planned for this to happen."

I cross my arms over my chest in frustration.

She lets out a sigh. "Even when I try to make things right, the universe conspires against me."

"What are you talking about?"

"I was trying to find a better paying job than waitressing."

I'm swept away by a momentary wave of excitement at the idea of making a dent in our colossal debt. Even though three months ago she upgraded from being a barista at a coffee shop to waitressing in a trendy sports bar in SoHo, she still makes minimum wage. The super sexy outfit guarantees generous tips, but living in New York doesn't come cheap, even when you live in one of the boroughs. "Did you find one?"

"I did." Thank you, God! "But I might not be able to make

it. The doctor told me that, given the severity of my condition, it might be seven days before the infection clears up. In the meantime, he cautioned me to be careful. That's a problem with my new job. A big problem."

"Your condition should have no bearing on your new job. I'm sure whatever cream your doctor prescribed will help with the smell, if not eliminate it all together."

"It doesn't work like that in this type of job..."

Well, that was cryptic.

"What kind of job is it?"

She presses her lips in a thin line.

"You're not going to tell me?"

"You have to promise to keep an open mind."

"Wasn't that what you said when you introduced me to your ex... the one who sold us tickets to board the Titanic?"

"The Titanic sank and everyone dies, except for Rose. She lives on to tell the story."

I cock an eyebrow. "The last time I checked our bank account, we were doing slightly better than the people who drowned on that ship, simply because we're still breathing. Not because we have their wealth."

"See"—she points an accusatory finger at me—"this is why I'm hesitant to tell you about my new job."

"Just spit it out, Arya."

She takes a breath. "On my last day at the coffee shop, after pulling the evening shift, I bumped into one of my regular clients. She doesn't look much older than us, but there's something about her... she always looked like she had her shit together. I usually see her dressed down, but on that day, she looked like she had stepped off the catwalk during New York fashion week. That's when I found out she wasn't a trust fund baby, she wasn't married to a billionaire, she didn't have a sugar daddy, and she wasn't a creator of a wildly successful app—"

"I still don't get what this has to do with your new job."

"I'm getting to it!"

I wind the air at her, coaxing her to get to the point.

"She gave me her boss's number and promised to give him the heads up. Fast forward, it took me two months before getting an appointment with Todd. The interview lasted a grueling two hours, but in the end, I made the cut! I became one of his girls."

"I still don't follow."

"Todd is in the *hospitality* business."

"That's a fairly straightforward profession. There are loads of hotels in New York City. After all, it's tourist central year-round. Why did you have to beat around the bush?"

"Not *that* kind of hospitality."

"What other kind is there?"

"Todd caters to incredibly wealthy men who either prefer not to show up at a function alone or who prefer drama-free hookups where all parties are on the same page. He's sort of a... matchmaker."

"Huh?" I scrunch my nose. "That went way over my head."

"Todd (without a last name) is my booking agent. He runs Elite Encounters Escorts."

My head jerks back, shock washing over me.

I must have misheard her.

"Come again?"

"I'm one of Elite Encounters Escorts' new girls!" Her grin is epic.

"Escorts?! You—you're a prostitute?!" Our mother is turning in her grave.

"No, I'm a *high-end escort*."

"If you look like a duck, swim like a duck, and quack like a duck, then you're probably a duck. In your case, little sister, that means you're a prostitute."

"There is a world of difference between the two paths." She's being all philosophical about this? "And the money is *way, way* better. I'm set to meet my first client tomorrow night—"

"But your sick va-jay-jay cockblocked you?" I couldn't help it.

"Smart ass. Newbies don't get cock."

"Huh?"

"Todd has changed the way he does things. Nowadays, he prefers to ease his girls into it. Clients who are looking for naughty arrangements—aka sex—are paired with more seasoned escorts. Newbies are paired with clients looking for arm candy—"

"It's still an illicit arrangement—"

"There's no exchange of fluids." She arches a brow. "Big difference." I roll my eyes. "Clients looking for arm candy range from men who don't want to show up at an event alone, gay men who prefer to keep their sexual orientation private, exhibitionist couples looking for an audience in the privacy of their home, and men who can't get it up even with Viagra, but don't want their peers to know their dick is out of commission." I open my mouth to ask a question, but she keeps talking. "Those are easy assignments, since your only job is to look sexy as fuck. As for playing voyeur for an evening, it's no different from watching porn online." I should argue that last point, but there are bigger concerns.

"So let me get this straight, you'll be arm candy for a while until you graduate to being a fully-fledged escort?"

"Yes."

My dear twin sister. While I tend to walk the straight and narrow, she prefers to walk on the wild side. It baffles me how we were created at the same time, shared our mother's womb for nine months, and have identical DNA.

"And what happens when you have to actually fuck for money?" I ask.

"That won't be for another three months, but I'll make a heck of a lot more money than simply being arm candy."

Of course, she can't see the forest from the trees.

"But Arya... that's wrong."

"Desperate times call for desperate measures, sis."

"There must be other jobs in New York that pay more than waitressing and don't involve you selling your body."

"First"—she lifts a finger in the air—"unlike you, I don't have a college degree. "Two"—she lifts another finger—"I'm not being pressured into this. Three" —a third digit goes up—"Todd vets his clients with CIA-like diligence. He meets all of them in person. Most of his clients are referrals from other satisfied clients. You know how it is. Rich guys know other rich guys."

"No, I don't know how it is. And neither do you."

She tuts. "Stop worrying your pretty little head, Angelica. I'm going in with my eyes wide open—"

"Are you really?"

"I totally am!"

I pinch the bridge of my nose and exhale a loud breath laced with annoyance. "Have you even taken into consideration the risks?"

"The rewards trump the risks." Her retort is as quick as a whip. Consequences don't apply to Arya McQuinley. Typical. "When I have sex with random guys, I may or may not come—most times I don't. Of course, to avoid bruising the guy's ego, I'll fake it. The reality is, you don't always know what you're getting in bed. Sometimes it's toe-curling. Sometimes it's wham! Bam! Thank you, ma'am! Sometimes, you get an unpleasant parting gift..."—she points to her lady parts— "like an infection. With Todd's high-end clients, even if I have to fake it, I get a prize, aka *lots of dollas*. Not the case with a random dude."

This is exactly the kind of logic that gets her into trouble every single time. Still, I'm willing to play devil's advocate.

"Enough *dollas* not to feel like you're selling your soul? After all, you'll be spreading your legs and getting fucked by strange, dirty men." I purse my lips. "Sugarcoat it as much as you want, you're still a prostitute."

"Not that I'm class-shaming my counterparts, but the difference between a prostitute and a high-end escort is spreading open your legs for a hundred to two-hundred dollars a fuck versus *fifteen-hundred dollars* an hour, with a minimum of three hours booked."

Blink.

Blink.

Blink.

"A high-end escort gets paid one-thousand-five-hundred dollars an hour?"

"*Or more*, depending on the client's kinks."

"Jesus."

"The most in demand girls are booked up five days a week. Multiply that by four weeks."

My jaw drops as I compute the numbers in my head.

"Yup!" Arya pops the P. "They make more a month than most people earn in a year. And then there's another level." She gestures with a hand. "When a client wants to book you for a weekend, a week, *or* a month, it's like winning the Powerball."

Dear God.

"Being just arm candy doesn't mean you end up with chump change. The rate is seven hundred fifty dollars per hour." The staggering number is like getting splashed in the face with a bucket of ice-cold water. "*Cha-ching!*" She starts doing this ridiculous dance, her booty sticking out, her hands wiggling over her head, and shouting at the top of her lungs, "Show me the money!"

"Stop it!" I chastise her.

She puts an end to her circus. "You asked," she says with a one-shoulder shrug.

"A simple answer would've sufficed. You didn't need to put on a show."

"Count yourself lucky. You got a two for one special." She grins from ear to ear. "All that to say"—she soldiers on—"that kind of money solves *a lot* of problems—"

"But then you'll have other problems." One of us has to be the voice of reason, and of course, that job seems to always fall squarely on my shoulders.

"Name one."

I accept the challenge. "Well... you'll have to live with yourself after."

"Trust me, it won't keep me awake at night as I sleep on my pillow stuffed with *dolla bills*."

I give her my best resting bitch face.

"Ange, any problems that arise for me becoming a high-end escort can be easily solved by throwing money at it."

I shake my head.

"Working for Todd isn't like walking into McDonald's and ordering a Happy Meal. Do you know how many women apply and never get a call back? The competition is fierce for this kind of coveted position. And I'm one of the lucky few who got selected." She points at her chest. Not that I'm willing to admit this to her, but that kind of money would be a gamechanger. "But since life decided to be a bitch today, she threw a wrench into my plans." She points at her lady parts.

"If you're just going to be arm candy for the evening, why would your infection be an issue?"

"Todd has a few ironclad policies, and I quote, *If you feel a sniffle coming, contact me pronto, so I can find a replacement. If Aunt Flo comes knocking, same thing, unless it's one of the client's kinks. Any vaginal infections—mild or severe, stay the fuck home. Ditto for STDs. Our premium clients pay way too much to catch nasties."* Arya lets out a dramatic sigh. "For my first gig, Todd booked me with a prominent plastic surgeon for four hours—a charity fundraiser. *Four hours*, Ange. That's *three thousand dollars* for a few hours of *work*."

"Holy shit!"

"I know, right?" That is a lot of money. "It's way too easy-peasy to be called work." She pulls her lips down into that sad puppy face she uses when she wants to wrangle something from me. "But I have to kiss all that money goodbye. I can't violate one of my boss's cardinal rules on the first gig. That's the equivalent of kissing my career as an escort bye-bye before it even starts."

Her eyes bore into mine and the energy in the kitchen shifts.

The other shoe is about to drop... I feel it in every fiber of my being.

"I got a loan from someone."

"A loan from someone?"

"Yes."

"From who?" My tone conveys genuine trepidation.

"He only goes by Yevsei. His Russian last name is unpronounceable."

My hands go flying in the air before landing on my thighs in a loud thump. "Good grief, Arya, when does it end?"

"I'm doing something about it!" Her tone drips with as much impatience as mine.

"Why the fuck did you get involved with this Yevsei?"

"Ramsey—"

"Ramsey this. Ramsey that. And now Ramsey is nowhere

to be found because he skipped town after stealing every dime we had to our names."

"You asked for an explanation, and when I give one to you, you attack me. How was I supposed to know Ramsey was a bad apple?"

"He wasn't a bad apple, he was like a terminal cancer!"

We engage in a Mexican standoff, our nostrils flared, our eyes squinted.

Until Ramsey came into our lives, we never had these types of virulent fights.

I coax myself to suppress the rage bubbling inside me. "What's the deal with this Russian?"

"If I tell you, you have to promise not to lose your shit."

I doubt I'm capable of such restraint, but I'll humor her. "I'll keep my cool."

"Promise?"

"Just spit it out, already!"

"I topped off our investment with Ramsey."

"Why did you do you that, and more importantly, why am I only finding out about it now?"

"Ramsey said"—it takes everything in me not to roll my eyes—"we'd be guaranteed an eye-popping return if we invested a certain minimum. I knew you wouldn't go for it, so he hooked me up with Yevsei."

My gut churns.

"If Ramsey had told you to jump off a fucking cliff, you would've done it like a fool. You had that much blind faith in the guy."

"You came along in the end." The smug expression on her face irritates me to no end.

I glare at her.

She cocks an eyebrow, the smirk still tilting her lips.

"Yes, because you and that scumbag kept badgering me

about not missing out on an opportunity of a lifetime that would set us up for life before we celebrated our twenty-fifth birthday!"

"I just wanted a better life for us!" My sister yells her response.

"Yeah, well, now, our life is a fucking nightmare!" I yell right back.

"It won't be once I'm able to pay off Yevsei!"

"That still won't account for the money Ramsey stole from us!"

I'm certain people living in buildings two streets down can hear us shout.

"The police will find him." That blind optimism again.

Since there isn't anything I can do about Ramsey, I focus on the new clusterfuck of a mess she got herself into. "How much do you owe Yevsei?"

She averts her gaze.

"Arya!"

"A lot." I rub my hands over my face, praying to God to give me patience so I don't end up strangling my twin. "The thing is Yevsei is a scary looking motherfucker who walks around with beefy guys who wear scars on their faces and tattoos on their necks and knuckles."

Fear beats at my chest. Great. The friendly Russian monster has henchmen. "A loan shark who only goes by his first name and who walks around with tattooed goons sounds a bit Bratva, don't you think?"

She rolls her eyes. "This isn't a mafia romance novel. Yevsei is a legit businessman. He owns several dry cleaners and a few restaurants, so he gets a constant flow of cash sales—hence, the beefy security guards. The heavy flow of large cash amounts allows him to give out loans to people who need it."

"What kind of interest is he charging you?" I ask.

She averts her gaze.

"Arya, I asked you a question."

Her green eyes train on my face. "Fifteen percent—"

"Fifteen percent interest a month on a loan isn't bad—"

"Fifteen percent interest *a week*."

My insides plummet with dread. "Mother of God, that's sixty percent a month. That's outrageous!"

"It's a bit high, but beggars can't be choosers." Great logic. Not. "In any case, I'm late on my payments by two weeks, and now Yevsei is demanding I make a payment within the next forty-eight hours."

"Un-fucking-believable." I shake my head. "The hole just keeps getting deeper and deeper. And you don't even have a shovel to dig us out of this shit."

"But I *have* a shovel!" She says that like a toddler who went wee-wee on her own for the first time and now expects a lollipop. "Which is why I was crossing my fingers, toes, and hair, praying to become one of Todd's girls. Mission accomplished!" she says, flinging her long ponytail.

"I'm sinking deeper into this fucking nightmare, like I'm being sucked into the Bermuda triangle during a catastrophic hurricane," I say, picking up steam. "May I remind you, I never signed up for any of this."

"How was I supposed to know behind the handsome face, custom-made suits, Rolex watch, Italian shoes, and pricey sports cars, Ramsey was a piece of shit, scam artist?" I fold my lips between my teeth to avoid answering. It's called not falling for assholes. Again. "In my defense, I just wanted us to have a better life—"

"By gambling the little we had left from Dad's life insurance after his death?"

"Investments are all about timing, Ange." She lectures me like she's a Wall Street Wolf. "I figured getting in first would set us up for life." Well, it didn't. It ruined us. "I have it all under control." The famous last words that landed her ass, and mine by proxy, knee deep in shit. "Working for Todd is *our*"—she waves a finger between us—"ticket to freedom. One evening hanging from a rich dude's arm, and I'll have the money I need to make a payment on my debt with Yevsei."

"Except, you can't be arm candy to your first client."

An expression that should trigger fear in my heart and have me running for the hills veils her eyes. "No, but *you* can."

Sneak Peak of A Very Wicked Arrangement

Chapter 2 | Hudson

A knock at my door breaks my concentration.

My eyes lift from my computer screen. "Come in!"

The door opens and a head of long, blonde hair pokes into my office.

"Do you have a minute?" Marine asks.

I rest back against my seat. "I'll take any excuse not to have to pore over this spreadsheet."

She steps inside and sashays her way to my desk, looking as chic as she always does.

Men or women. Fashion is an Olympic sport in the Big Apple. That was a big adjustment for a poor kid from Summerville, Texas whose parents considered Target stores high-end, and therefore, out of reach. I've upped my game, but some people were born with an impeccable sense of style—like thirty-four-year-old, Toulouse born, Marine Renault. My director of French communications takes fashion seriously. Today she's decked out in a light-blue pant suit, a low-cut white blouse, and white sky-high heels. Her makeup is perfectly applied. Like always.

"*Bonjour*," she says, placing a cardboard tray on my desk.

"*Bonjour*." It's one of the rare French words I know.

"I stopped by Project Espresso on the way from my meeting," she says. "I thought I'd bring you a late morning pick me up. An extra hot, double espresso latte." She points to the tall cup. "I also popped by next door at Sugar Lane for a slice of sugar high. Lucky me. They had your favorite."

My gaze drops to the cup and brown paper bag.

Someone is buttering me up.

"What is it that you want from me?"

"What makes you think I want something?" She feigns innocence. "Is it a crime to bring your boss coffee and dessert?"

I make a show of stretching my arm before checking the time on my Cartier Ballon Bleu watch. "It's not even lunchtime yet. Don't you think it's a bit early for dessert?"

"*Mais non*." She shrugs. "Why be so restrictive?"

What game is she playing?

"We have a kickass coffee machine imported from Italy in the kitchen."

"Pods will never be the same as freshly brewed."

"There are many, more than acceptable coffee and pastry shops right at our door. You had to make a detour for these?"

Her expression is a pure annoyance. "I thought I would be able to ease you into what I have to tell you by bringing you your favorites."

I motion my hand in a circle. "Don't beat around the bush. You know I hate surprises."

With elegance and grace, she lowers herself into one of the guest chairs. Leaning back, she crosses one leg over the other, and brushes off fictitious lint from her pants.

"Come on, Marine, lay it on me."

She sighs. "Well, I know tomorrow night's launch party at

the Bymark Hotel is the opening we've been waiting for to land this LA prospect, but I can't be your date."

Shit.

"I thought we were on?"

"We were, but my girlfriend just informed me a reporter from New York Times Style Magazine will drop by at the art gallery for tomorrow night's exhibit." Impressive. "The reporter will be accompanied by a photographer and a camera crew for photos and videos for their website. I was planning on only staying an hour at the event before making my way to the gallery, but given the big news..." Her words trail. "We just started seeing each other, but things are going well. I want to be there the whole evening to support her."

"I get it. That's a big deal."

"It is." Pride shines bright in her eyes. "That's the only reason why I would ditch you at such short notice. I know how much you hate showing up at these functions alone."

Even after five years living in New York and my colossal wealth, I always feel out of place at these parties.

"I can find someone else to accompany you," Marine says. "There are a few female employees who don't have a significant other or kid to go home to."

"It wouldn't be the same dynamic with another employee. You and I have a good thing going on at these events. We play off each other." Until she met her girlfriend two months ago, Marine was a serial dater, so she was happy to accompany me to these shindigs. My grueling work schedule prevents me from having long-term relationships.

Marine's blue eyes widen. "Are you saying you're willing to do the impossible, Hudson Kincaid? You're willing to fly solo?"

I shake my head. "No way I'm showing up without a wingman. I need someone who can handle vapid conversations better than I can. My fuse is short, I'm blunt, my bullshit meter is set at zero, and I take pleasure in ruffling people's overly sensitive natures."

She laughs, clapping at the same time. "All this time, I thought it was my personality, but you were using me as a buffer so you wouldn't get kicked out of those chichi events, or worse, beat up someone who rubbed you up the wrong way."

"Pretty much."

She shakes her head and waves a motherly finger at me.

"That, and you're gorgeous, smart, you seem to never run out of conversation, and your debating skills are impressive."

"It's a byproduct of being French. We learn how to debate in kindergarten," she says. "About the event. If you don't intend on showing up alone— Wait." She lifts a hand up. "Are you seeing someone?"

"No, I'm still very much single. Since your girlfriend came into your life, I knew my days were numbered. So, I made sure to have a contingency plan."

She cocks her head. "Meaning?"

I snatch my Montblanc pen from my desk and tap it against my chin. "If I play my cards right, tomorrow night's event could be a turning point towards closing a huge account that's slipped through our fingers for far too long." I shake my head, disappointed by our past failed attempts at landing this prospect. "I know exactly how to find a last-minute date that has far better social graces than I do. Someone who, like you, knows how to charm the pants off any sucker."

I might only be twenty-eight, but it's not like I was born yesterday. I was well aware escort services existed, but until recently, I didn't know how many high-powered men preferred to avoid the hassle and unpredictable nature of taking a random date to an important event by hiring a professional. It's the best way to nix the drama factor. Sometimes sex is involved. But sometimes, it's strictly for arm candy purposes. Given Marine's relationship status, it's very likely I'll have to rely more and more on Elite Encounters Escorts' services. Good thing I became a member not long ago.

Right after my director of French communications left my office, I placed a call.

Many hours later, I'm catching up on emails, when my phone rings. I snatch it off my desk.

"Todd," I say, answering.

"Mr. Kincaid. How are you?"

"No complaints. And you?"

"Ditto," he says. "I'm sure you must hear this all the time, but your deep twang is damn sexy."

"Thank you?!"

"Don't worry, I can read the neon signs. You don't swing my way. That said, it needed to be said. Again." I don't have anything to add to that. "Back to business," he says with a heavy sigh. "We met a month ago. I rarely have clients wait that long to enquire about companionship with one of my girls."

I keep my answer brief. "Until today, I didn't need the companionship of one of your girls. However, things changed on my end."

"Change is my friend," he says. "Well, I'd like to officially welcome you to the club. I'm certain you'll be very happy with my girls."

"I have no doubt," I say. "I know my request is last-minute—"

"Please, Mr. Kincaid, we specialize in last-minute. Since you left it up to me to select a girl on your behalf—and may I say it's a huge honor that you place such trust in me—"

"You know your girls better than I do."

“I picked the perfect girl for your first date.” There’s pride in his tone. “She’s a tall, model thin, natural blonde with big amber eyes. She has a college degree in international studies. She speaks fluent Norwegian and knows basic French.”

“I’m sure she’s gorgeous.”

“All my girls are stunning beauties. I’m very picky. Very, very picky.” Good to know. “Should I send you her photo, just to be one-hundred percent sure she fits the bill?”

“I trust your judgement, but I’d love to see a photo.”

Binge-read now: A Very Wicked Arrangement

Very New York Billionaires

A Very Bossy Billionaire (Xavier)

A Very Fake Boyfriend (Zane)

A Very Wicked Arrangement (Hudson)

Xavier and Zane Keller are **Max Keller**'s cousins, and they kick off this smoking hot spin-off.

Max is part of the **Billionaire Factor** series.

Billionaire Factor—Bryce

Billionaire Factor—Nikolaj

Billionaire Wedding Factor—Nikolaj

Billionaire Factor—Max

Billionaire Factor—Easton

You'll find **all my books** and **reading order** on my site:
www.ScarlettAvery.com

I hope you enjoyed ***A Very Fake Boyfriend***! Can't get enough of Xavier and Adeline? Subscribe to my mailing list and you'll get instant access to an exclusive ***A Very Fake Boyfriend*** secret chapter and/or storyboard. Just use the QR code below.

Already subscribed? You would've received the link in the first email I sent you. If you can't find it, you can email us. If you've changed your email address, simply resubscribe.

About the Author

USA TODAY Bestselling Author Scarlett Avery unapologetically pens all-consuming love stories featuring sexy as sin billionaires who have the determination of a thousand warriors. These filthy rich heroes bow to no one. Only the women who steal their hearts can bring them down to their knees.

Scarlett's stories are intense and passionate, emotional and steamy, and leave you begging for more. In other words, they're the perfect blend of swoony and sinful. Once you start reading Scarlett's novels, there's no going back!

Fair warning...

You should always expect edge-of-your-seat twists.

Printed in Great Britain
by Amazon

22801231R00261